Dayaran Gidumal Shahani

The Life and Life-Work of Behramji M. Malabari

Being a biographical sketch, with selections from his writings and speeches on

infant marriage and enforced widowhood

Dayaran Gidumal Shahani

The Life and Life-Work of Behramji M. Malabari
Being a biographical sketch, with selections from his writings and speeches on infant marriage and enforced widowhood

ISBN/EAN: 9783337015558

Printed in Europe, USA, Canada, Australia, Japan

Cover: Foto ©Raphael Reischuk / pixelio.de

More available books at **www.hansebooks.com**

THE
LIFE AND LIFE-WORK

OF

BEHRAMJI M. MALABARI

(Being a Biographical Sketch, with Selections from
his Writings and Speeches on Infant Marriage
and Enforced Widowhood, and also his
"Rambles of a Pilgrim Reformer").

BY

DAYARAM GIDUMAL, LL.B.; C.S.

ACTING ASSISTANT JUDGE, AHMEDABAD.

O Father, touch the East, and light
The light that shone when Hope was born.
— Tennyson's *In Memoriam*.

Bombay:
PRINTED AT THE
EDUCATION SOCIETY'S PRESS, BYCULLA.

1888.

TO THE MEMORY

OF

RAM MOHAN ROY,

DAYANAND SARASVATI,

AND

KESHUB CHUNDER SEN,

THIS BOOK

IS

Reverently Dedicated.

PREFACE.

MEN of originality are apt to be misunderstood. While some consider Malabari sufficiently enthusiastic to be a "Western Reformer," there are others who, utterly ignorant of the almost ascetic life he leads, have dubbed him "a Luther of rose and lavender." It occurred to me that a plain unvarnished narrative of his career was likely to do good, and I therefore induced Malabari to permit me to publish what I knew about it.

I also thought that a selection from his writings and speeches on the Hindu Social Reform question would be welcome to all interested in it. It seemed an anomaly that while the opinions elicited by his writings should be before the public in two bulky volumes, the writings themselves should lie scattered in the files of the *Indian Spectator*. It was no part of my plan to publish all his writings on the subject, and this volume contains only what appeared to me to be worth preserving.

The net proceeds of this book, should there be any, will be set apart as a nucleus of a fund to be handed over to any Social Reform Association or Mission which the educated Hindus might organize. It is sad to see that, in spite of so much talk about social reform from within, during the past three years and a half, nothing has yet been done to create a machinery for carrying out such reform. The creation of such machinery means self-sacrifice, and self-sacrifice ought certainly to be the distinguishing characteristic of all really educated men. I trust they may still fulfil the just expectations of all our well-wishers, and found a National Association, equipped with even larger funds than the Countess of Dufferin's Association, and sustained by a genuine unselfish missionary spirit, without which there is no hope for India.

TABLE OF CONTENTS.

1884—continued.

1885.

1885—continued.

1886.

1886—*continued.*

1887.

1887—*continued.*

Chapter I.

BOYHOOD.

My boast is not that I deduce my birth
*   From loins enthroned, and rulers of the earth;*
But higher far my proud pretensions rise,
*   The son of parents pass'd into the skies.*—Cowper.

Howe'er it be, it seems to me,
*   'Tis only noble to be good.*
Kind hearts are more than coronets,
*   And simple faith than Norman blood.*—Tennyson.

CHAPTER I.—BOYHOOD (1853–1866).

A Bird's-eye View of Malabari's Early Life.

I think I had better begin with a bird's-eye view of Malabari's early life. The *Bombay Review* and the *Hindoo Patriot* published, in 1878, a short extract from the *Jam-i-Jamshed,* which, though there are a few inaccuracies in it, is useful for this purpose. Here it is :—

"The *Jam-i-Jamshed,* a respectable Parsee paper, gives a very interesting account of the early days of Mr. Behramji Merwanji Malabari, the well-known young poet and journalist. According to our contemporary, Mr. Malabari, whose original name is Mehta, was born at Baroda in 1853, whence in less than two years after his mother had to escape with him to Surat under domestic persecution. At five the boy was put to school, where he was remarkable for nothing but perpetual listlessness and mischief. Having thus made the school too hot tor himself, he was apprenticed to carpenters and other mechanics, who soon found him out to be a good-for-nothing pupil. His pranks and frolics are still remembered at Nanpoora in Surat. People also remember the sensation he made there by singing impromptu songs of a controversial nature, called *Khials* by natives. It is in this exhibition of poetical powers at the early age of eight or nine that we find the promise of his future literary successes. At nine he bethought himself to go to school again. For a year and a quarter he studied Gujarati, and was then admitted to the English school, where, though his progress was incredibly rapid, still he was not at all behindhand in recklessness and wandering about the town. Having been once caught in the act of some unusual mischief, the boy was ordered to be flogged. This mode of punishment he declined to undergo, having never done so before ; but though the Assistants interceded in his behalf, the new Head-Master was inexorable. The boy had at last to hold out his hand ; but after the very first stroke his features and his whole frame became convulsed. Further punishment was remitted, and the boy was refreshed with water. The first thing he did, however, on coming to, was to turn wildly on the master, and after rating him soundly bolt from school.

A

On his way home he resolved to complain to his mother of what he thought to be his barbarous usage at school ; but when he reached home he found the mother laid low by a fell malady. The poor fellow now forgot his own misery, and night and day he ministered to the comfort of his dying parent who did not, after all, survive. The boy's life here underwent a complete change. All the fun and frolic of youth and all love of mischief left him in one day. It is many years since he lost his mother ; but he has not yet done mourning her loss. In after-life he says, speaking of her untimely death :—" God punished me most severely for my disobedience to my master ; it is a punishment more bitter than death." The boy of twelve now made up his mind to prosecute his studies and also to earn his own living. He joined the Surat Mission School, and took in pupils of almost twenty. In less than three years he became very popular. The late Rev. Mr. Dixon, the Principal of the School, has written of his English progress as "wonderful," and of his conduct as "most exemplary." The same gentleman used to say " if any boy is destined to make a name in the world, it is he.". The Head-Master of the school writes : " He possesses great natural powers, and I cherish a very high opinion of him. I hope he will meet with success in the world." Before sixteen Mr. Malabari went to Bombay, where, for want of interest, he had to struggle for some time as teacher at a private school. At this time he had with him a volume of verse in Gujarati and English, which he did not shew to any one till he was eighteen. At last our worthy townsman, Mr. Sorabji Shapurji Bengali, happened to read them ; and he wrote to the author a warm and encouraging letter. Shortly after the verses were submitted to the worthy and learned Missionary, Mr. Taylor, who was so much pleased with them that he forthwith introduced the author to the late Dr. Wilson. Mr. Malabari published his verses, and made his name. He was introduced by Dr. Wilson to the leaders of the European and native communities. How much his English verses have been appreciated by Her Majesty the Queen-Empress and others, a particular friend has explained in these columns. Not only native but European writers are known to hanker after such honours as Mr. Malabari has attained. And though he has attained these honours at the tender age of 25-26, they have not in the least elated him. He is really a very quiet, retiring and good-natured man. He has not left off his simple habits. He is very studious and has a fair knowledge of several languages. He is not at all vain of his great talents, but anxious as any school-boy to learn, he goes about his business with his books under his arm. He has given up the pleasures of life, and is never seen to mix with the public on a holiday. Many people avail themselves of his interest, but his name is always held back. He spends the larger part of his well-earned income for the relief of the poor invalid and the student. For the last two or three years Mr. Malabari has been contributing to English journals and periodicals, and it is known to all that his writings are the admiration of the English reader. He explains by public and private writings the greatness, worth and bene-volence of the English, and what good they are capable of doing to this country. He corresponds with several great and influential men in England, and devotes much of his time to the welfare of others. Such a life is indeed worthy of imitation. Mr. Malabari's career teaches three things :—1st, a child should be left to learn *when* and *what* he likes ; 2nd, natural talent will rise from the very depth of obscurity ; 3rd, a good mother is a priceless blessing to the child."

Malabari's Father and Adoptive Father.

The name of Malabari's father was Dhanjibhai Mehta. He was a poor clerk in the service of the Gaekwar of Baroda, on a salary of Rs. 20. I know nothing more about him than that he was a mild, peace-loving man, with a somewhat feeble constitution and not overmuch force of character. Malabari lost him at the age of six or seven.

Malabari's adoptive father was Merwanji Nanabhai Malabari. He was a relation of Malabari's maternal grand-mother, had consigned two wives already to the Towers of Silence at Surat, was in 1856 about 50 years old, and in easy circumstances He had a large grocery shop and was an importer of sandalwood, sugar, scents and spices from the Malabar Coast—hence his surname Malabari. He had no issue and therefore thought fit to adopt the little child who has made his family name famous throughout India and favourably known even in Europe and America. Merwanji also married the boy's mother—a union she accepted from a sense of filial duty and which turned out very unhappy.

Merwanji is not highly spoken of. A few years after his adoption of little Behram, a serious misfortune fell upon him. A country vessel bringing an uninsured cargo for him from the Malabar Coast sank in the sea, and Merwanji was reduced to great straits. He had to cut down his business and take to humbler pursuits, practising for some time as a sort of Hakim.* This latter accomplishment he had been in the habit of exercising even in his palmy days, but now it became a source of a small income which was exceedingly welcome. His adopted son had often to do a great deal of pounding and pulverising for him in both the branches of his calling, the Hakim's and the grocer's, and at the age of twelve was able to bring him 10 or 12 rupees a month, besides keeping his accounts and assisting him generally. The first concern of the young man when he came to Bombay was to redeem the family house which had been mortgaged for Rs. 300 ; but the money was not forthcoming for a long time, and when it was, the house could not be redeemed, the mortgage having been foreclosed. The mortgagee seems to have borne a grudge to Merwanji's next-door neighbour, and as soon as he was master of the house had it pulled down

* Native doctor.

in order to make the neighbour's house shelterless. For the same reason he refused to sell the plot for any consideration, or to build on it. An eccentric man this! I do not know what provocation he had received. Let us hope it was not as bad as his retaliation.

Merwanji passed his latter days in peace. He died about six years ago.

MALABARI'S MOTHER.

Malabari owes a great deal more to his mother than either to Dhanjibhai or to Merwanji. For Bhikhibai was no ordinary woman. Rather undersized, like her son—with the same light brown complexion, but a rounded face and big almond-like eyes, she was a homely humble housewife, handy at all kinds of domestic work —an expert in cookery, a deft-fingered sempstress and a first-rate nurse. She had what her husband lacked—a strong will, a masterful mind, and an irrepressible energy. With these she combined a tenderness for the poor — she was one of them—and a large-heartedness not rare in her sex. She had truly "a tear for pity, and a hand open as day for melting charity." She was often to be seen in the sick-room of her neighbours, Hindu or Parsi, with little Behram toddling behind her, or holding on to the skirts of her simple sari. She knew many of those well-tried herbs which bring almost instant relief to ailing children; and her skill was seldom exerted in vain. She was freely consulted by the women in her street in their troubles. What was most admirable in her was her catholicity and impulsive unerring goodness. I know of no Hindu woman who would care

to tend, far less to suckle a gasping little waif lying in
a basket near her house, without first inquiring to what
caste it belonged. But Bhikhibai did such a thing one
day, though she had to brave a scandal, for the waif
turned out to be the street scavenger's child. It was
a very small infant, and so weak that one would be
almost afraid to handle it. But the good woman at
once yielded to her first impulse when she heard it
moaning piteously, and taking it up tenderly, put it to
her breast. It's mother came up shortly afterwards and
relieved our heroine of her charge. But Bhikhibai had
a bad time of it for several days with her Parsi neighbours.* Still few could help loving this utterly unselfish woman, and when she died she was sincerely
mourned by all who had known her. Her memory
remains embalmed in her son's poetic tributes of
affection.

FIRST LESSONS IN PRAYING AND WEAVING.

Little Behram was finally weaned some time after
he was sent to school. This may sound curious, but it
is a fact. He was the only solace of his mother, and she
loved him as only such a mother could love. The boy
was fond, too fond of his mother's milk—and he has too
much of it in him. He would cling to her breast even
after returning from school; and his school, I am afraid,
was not a particularly pleasant one. The school-master
was believed to have been a centenarian, for he had
taught not only old Merwanji but Merwanji's father

* This incident forms the subject of a poem in Malabari's *Indian
Muse in English Garb*. It is headed " Nature triumphant over
Caste. " The merit of the act is given to a Hindu widow.

also. His son was a greybeard, and it must have
been a sight to see this patriarchal family assembled at
their meals. Our " old Antiquity's ", name was Minochehrdaru. He sat in a small room with about twenty
little Parsi boys, among whom was our Behram. He
held a mighty long elastic bamboo cane in his hand,
which worked quite like an automaton, and could put a
girdle round the little flock in less than a second. It
is a venerable face, Minochehr's, but his eyes are 'awful'.
His limbs are rather stiff, and he cannot move about
freely ; so he has a comfortable seat which he seldom
leaves, especially as his wiry cane does everything for
him. It is his dainty Ariel in a way ; but he has,
unlike Prospero, not a library full of magical lore, but
a common, primitive, humdrum loom, and the boys have
to weave as well as to pray—our schoolmaster did not
teach out of the educational primer, but the Parsi prayer-
book. As soon as all the boys have mustered, after doing
some domestic drudgery in Minochehr's house, and
the threads have been ranged lengthwise—the veteran
centenarian is out with his monotonous sing-song, and
you hear twenty little throats repeating at the top
of their voice the sacred formula *Ashem Vohu,** the
master and his favourite disciples plying their shuttles
at the same time. The little ones do not know what
these mysterious words mean, or that scholars have
differed about their meaning. They only know that

---

* This celebrated formula has been variously translated. My friend
Mr. Navroji Dorabji Khandalovala has discussed the various
meanings and comes to the conclusion that the right translation is as
follows :—" Purity is the best good, a blessing it is, blessing to him
who (practises) purity for the sake of the Highest purity." (*Vide*
' Primitive Mazdayasnyan Teachings." p. 18.)

any mistake made in following their Dominic means a
taste of that tingling ubiquitous cane, and they have a
salutary dread of it. In this way Behram learned to
make pretty little wefts out of warp and woof and to
mumble the mystic words of " Ahuno Vairyo*" and
"Ashem Vohu" and such others. Before we take leave
of Minochehrdaru, we might as well read a little
sketch of this worthy by Malabari himself.

" White flowing beard, small chirping voice !
White white his all, but red his blinking eyes !
A man mysterious of the Magus tribe—
A close astrologer, and a splendid scribe—
A faithful oracle of dread Hormuzd's will—
A priest, a patriarch, and a man of skill.
A master weaver, and—to close details,
He weaved long webs and lord ! he weaved long
   tales.
Hard murd'rous words, that wisdom's lips defied,
Would thick portentous from his nozzle glide !
And here we stuck, tho' long and hard we tried ;
He curs'd, and can'd by turns, we humm'd and cried !
This could not last ; our mutual failings seen,
He left his preaching and we left our dean.†

---

* There is more conflict regarding the meaning of this formula
than that of " Ashem Vohu ". Mr. Khandalevala's translation is as
follows: As is the Will or (Law) of the Eternal Existence so (its)
Energy solely through the Harmony (Asha) of the perfect mind is
the producer (Dazda) of the manifestation of the Universe and
(is) to Ahura Mazda (the Living Wise one) the power which gives
sustenance to the revolving systems." The accomplished and genial
Bishop Meurin gives another rendering of this most ancient formula, and establishes a common origin between "Ahuno Vairyo"
and one of the oldest Christian prayers.

† *Indian Muse*, p. 82.

First Lessons in Gujarati.

Behram's next teacher was Narbheram, a nephew
of Jivanram Mehta who was then a well-known
astrologer and mathematician. Here is a picture by
Malabari of his little school which was quite a curiosity in its way.

I am not " the oldest man living." But it may surprise the
oldest man living to know something of my first school and earliest
schooldays. What a marvellous improvement is 1885 upon 1860 in
matters educational! And yet it would be scarcely fair to call
the change an *improvement* in all respects. Let the reader judge
for himself. My first school was just behind our house at
Nanpura, Surat, and Narbheram Mehtaji was my first teacher.
He was a Bhikhshuka Brahman—tall, majestic and taciturn, the
sort of man who inspires awe by his Shivalike habits. In his
nature, as in name, he was truly a Nirbhaeram—fearless and fear-
inspiring. He made a most efficient teacher. The school
was a commodious little shop, with the floor strewn over with
street dust and an elevated square for the master. On the
square squatted the master and on the floor squatted his flock, Hindu
and Parsi. There was no fee to be paid for the instruction—only
a handful of grain, a few flowers or some fruit now and then. There
were no tables nor benches, nor slates nor pencils, nor books nor
maps, not one single item of the literary paraphernalia of the modern
school-room. Each pupil had a wooden board, *pati*, which served
him for slate, and a pointed stick, *lekhana*, which he used as pencil.
He also carried with him a rag. With this piece of cloth he sifted
the dust over the board, and on that bed he traced figures and
numerals, wrote letters, petitions, &c. This task work was submitted
every noon to the master, who held a rod in his hand, with one end
pointed. Glancing over the dust work, he would now give a grunt
of satisfaction, and strike the board with the pointed end of his stick.
The figures of dust would at once disappear, and so would the lucky
pupil—for tiffin. If unluckily the task was badly done, Narbheram would apply the butt end of the rod to the pupil, instead of to
his board, often gently, sometimes heavily too. The pupil was

condemned for the day. There were worse methods, of course, the sharp and supple cane, the thong, the pebble under the knee, the stone across the shoulders, the twisting of the nose, the shaking by the neck or by a knot made with the delinquent's *topi*,* or *chotli*.† Worse still, sometimes the little urchin was swung across the beam, and at times stripped of his scanty dress. Oh the tortures of the mid-day ordeal! How my heart sank within me as I crawled up to the master's *gadi*!‡ Life or death——what is it to be? I died on an average two deaths a month. That was because I was too small to deserve attention, quite a beginner. Besides, was not Narbheram's uncle and patron, Jivanram the one-eyed, the famous mathematician, astrologer and match-maker, a particular friend of my foster-father's? But for all that, whenever Narbheram condescended to notice me, he did it heartily. I have not yet forgotten his heaviness of hand and ferocity of looks. What added to the misery of the situation was the inviolable silence on both sides. It was something like a struggle between the lion and the mouse, the one too proud to roar, the other too timid even to squeak.

But to return to the school-room. The written work was gone through in the forenoon. Everything was done on a versified system. The numerals were drawled out in versified form. The different processes——addition, subtraction, multiplication and division, were gone through in the same manner. Rigid accuracy was enforced throughout. The system of multiplication was elaborate to a degree. Integers and fractions were alike treated from the minutest to the most magnificent scale.

The boy was expected to say by rote the $\frac{1}{4}$, the $\frac{1}{2}$, the $\frac{3}{4}$, the $1\frac{1}{4}$, the $1\frac{1}{2}$, the $2\frac{1}{2}$, and $3\frac{1}{2}$ of any number up to 100. These were respectively called *paya, ardha, pauna, savaya, dohda, adhiya* and *utha*. A good deal of this system was gone through by the boys on their boards in the forenoon, and verbally in the afternoon. The dux of a group was now and then challenged by the dux of another group, the master arbitrating. $\frac{1}{4}$th of 95, $3\frac{1}{2}$ of 79, $\frac{3}{4}$ of 65 ?——the ques-

---

* Cap.

† Tuft of hair in the centre of the head.

‡ Cushion.

tions had to be answered no sooner than they were asked. And woe be to the poor wight who halted or made a slip. Like the fractions came the integers up to 100×100. Thus, *Pachi pachiram chha pachisa* ($25 \times 25 = 625$), and so on, from $1 \times 1 = 1$ up to $100 \times 100 = 10,000$. The process was a powerful aid to memory. I doubt if the ablest Professor of Mathematics or even the readiest Finance Minister of the day commands such an elastic and almost intuitive power of manipulating figures. We had quite an exhibition of mnemonic wonders every afternoon. I am not sure if this mode of acquiring knowledge is a permanent aid to memory. I myself happen to have a weak memory so far as the form of things is concerned, though the spirit is easy enough to catch and retain. I cannot recite from memory ten lines of even my favourite poets, but can reproduce the image of a whole poem in my own words. But, speaking generally, the discipline above referred to is found most useful in after-life. The Native system of accounts is immensely superior to the European system. In dealing with the heaviest and the most intricate figures the Native accountant has merely to sing a verse, and there the result is ready to hand!

We learnt the Alphabet also on the same plan. Every letter had a nickname and a familiar versified description. That is to say, the form of the letter was likened to some object of common use and thus impressed upon the mental vision. It was what I may call object lesson--kako kevelo, khakho khajelo, &c. Europeans are coming to that system, judging from recent publications of juvenile literature. There was a fair amount of literary instruction, too, imparted at Narbheram's school. Some verses from Ramayan and Mahabharat, done into simple Gujarati for the occasion, served as history as well as poetry. I excelled in this as also in letter-writing orally, so to say. What splendid letters I dictated to my seniors, myself ignorant of the art of writing! Letters from wife at Surat to husband at Mumbai Bunder, now gushing, now whining, now asking for remittance, now threatening to go to the parents' house. Letters from the principal of a firm at Cambay to his factotum at Karachi, advising the departure of the good ship Ruparel, laden with pearls and precious stones. Letters from father at Broach to his son at Delhi, with the love of the distracted mother and with basketfuls of advice as to how to live in "this remote and foreign country." I enjoyed these

studies exceedingly well, and was often presented with fruit or
flower and the cheering words———ja bacha aj tane chhutti chhe
(go, boy, you are free to-day.) But when it came to figures, I was
usually an "uncle of the camel," "born of blind parents," and other
things indescribable. I was bad at receiving the rod, also, so that
the flogging of a neighbour would send me directly into fever. Narbheram knew this, and was kind enough usually to send me out of
the room when a culprit had to be hauled up.

In asking for permission to retire boys had to hold up the thumb,
(for a drink of water) to raise the least finger, to bend down the
middle with the forefinger (for the other purposes) and so forth.

One day a refractory boy had to be brought to his senses.
Narbheram had tried all his punitive regulations on him. This
time, therefore, he made him kneel upon pebbles and placed a
heavy slab on his back, and over the stone he himself pretended to
sit. This was the last straw, and the boy gave such a shriek of
agony and fright that his male relatives, who knew he had to be
punished, came running into the school. But Narbheram was no
respecter of persons ; he took up his rod of office and kept the men
at a distance. The boy, in the meantime, was shrieking at the top
of his voice, and I was very nearly fainting. It may be mentioned
that the stone was by no means too heavy for the fellow, the agony
was all mine, his was merely the shrieking. But it brought his
mother and grand-mother to the scene : they lived next door to the
school. These dames were well known for their muscular development and the free use they made of it. They went up to Narbheram, gave him a good deal of Billingsgate and some clawing, and
released the boy. He was withdrawn that day. I too went home,
never to return to the school again. At night I was in high fever,
and shortly after in the clutches of Sitla-mata, the goddess of small-
pox. For weeks I was confined to bed, dreaming of the boy who
had been, as I felt, crushed to death. I was not expected to out-
live the shock, but was somehow brought round, as my poor mother
said, by daily prayers and sacrifices on her part, and by nightly
vigils before a small silver figure sprinkled with red ochre, the
Mata. For weeks together she had lived upon parched rice and

water once a day.* And this was her reward, she explained to our friends, in meek thankfulness, when they met at our house to do justice to the good things prepared in honour of my second birth. One of the first things I heard on recovery was the death of poor Narbheram Mehtaji, from cholera. I was informed of it in a whisper. It was hard to realize how a man like my dear old guru,† born to command and to conquer, could have succumbed to even such enemies as Cholera and Death. Narbheram had appeared to me to be a special dispensation from Providence to lick the youth of Nanpura into public usefulness. Strange that such a mighty one found one who was more than a match for him! My respect for the great man underwent a sudden diminution, but my love for him remains.‡

THE PARSI PANCHAYAT SCHOOL AT SURAT.

Having taken his first lessons in Gujarati, we next find our little man in the Parsi Panchayat School which gave religious as well as secular instruction. The religious education was in the hands of a Parsi priest—another Daru—who was about 45 years old and was, according to Malabari, "a very ungodly-looking man of God, and the terror of all city imps and street arabs."§ Surat house-wives called him by a Gujarati sobriquet which may be translated "urchin-herd," if such a compound is allowable. He certainly deserved the title. Here is a description of this terrible teacher :—

A zealous man he was, a man of parts,
With scanty science, but a host of arts.

---

* "I too had a very strong attack of small-pox, and my mother prayed and watched and sang for over a fortnight. She was a strong-minded woman, but yielded to superstition during my illness."
—*Private letter.*

† "Guide and philosopher," though not friend.

‡ *Indian Spectator,* January 3, 1986, p. 10-11.

§ *Indian Muse,* p. 82 *Note.*

With pointed paws his fierce mustache he'd twirl,
And at the culprits the direst vengeance hurl.
His jaws he'd rub, his grizzl'd beard peck,
Till rubb'd and peck'd, the whole appeard a wreck.
A wag by nature and a stoic sour,
' Tis hard to fix his equivocal pow'r.
Good cheer he lov'd, and oft a dainty dish
His wrath diverted, as we well could wish.
When thus begorg'd, joy, joy was all his work,
His air all blandness, and his face all smirk !
But woe betide the hour, if e'er his meal
Was late ; that would his hidden traits reveal.
His zeal rose higher, as his stomach fell ;
And hard his fervour on our skins would tell !
Sharp went the whizzing whip, fast flew the cane,
And he fairly caper'd in his wrath insane !
He chanted pray'rs, oh Lord ! in such gruff tones
'T would set on rack the hoar Zoroaster's bones !
....
He shriek'd and stagger'd on his zealous rage,
Till he looked an actor on a tragic stage !
And when our whines the neighbouring women
                                            drew,
The man of zeal at once persuasive grew !
Expounded doctrines, in a fervid breath,
Preach'd patience, virtue, truth, and tacit faith !
Thank God I'd then too small religious wit
To understand that canting hypocrite."*

* " *Indian Muse*," p. 83-84.

There was one characteristic of the man which
has not been well brought out in these lines. It was
this. Whenever he wanted to administer a flogging,
he used to order his class to pray vociferously in order
to drown the cries of his victim. The school contained
both boys and girls, and Malabari well remembers how
the ruffian used sometimes to seize a girl by her long
hair and whisk her violently about in the air, as if she
was a lifeless marionette, while the room was resound-
ing with invocations to Ahurmazd recited by her
school-fellows. Another favourite amusement of this
monster of a school-master was to roll up an erring
boy in a carpet-piece or put the poor wretch under his
capacious Jama,* and then strut about from one end
of the school-room to the other. His gesticulations on
such occasions used to send a shiver through the little
ones who witnessed his performances. Often, when
angry, he would dash off his turban, and glare so fero-
ciously with his bull eyes and contort his face into
such frightful grimaces, that some of the more nervous
children would swoon at the sight of these exhibitions. If
any boy was late this zealous priest was forthwith at his
door and walked off with him without notice, though
the boy might be just washing his face, or taking
a morsel of food from his mother. I have said he had
a capacious Jama. That sufficed not only for kidnap-
ping little boys but even for confining the diminutive
master who used to teach reading and arithmetic in the
last class. Behram and his class-mates, after having
their turn with the Daru, used to go upstairs to this

---

* The long robe worn by Parsi priests.

diminutive teacher. Once it so happened that they went up later than the appointed hour, as they had been detained by the Daru, and of course assigned this reason to their teacher. Shortly afterwards the Daru came up and the teacher addressing him rather roughly inquired why the boys had not been sent up at the usual time. The Daru's reply was a swift and sudden jerk which sent the inquirer flying into space, followed by another which sent him softly under the folds of the Daru's Jama, and thus enveloping the Liliputian knight of the three R's. he stood, with a Harlequin's grin, in the midst of the amazed children. Of course since that day little Chagan lost the respect of his boys while the Daru continued to be dreaded, if possible more than formerly. He had influential friends among the visitors and was moreover a priest, a silk mercer and a toddy-seller, and thus he always managed to escape scot-free. Such teachers were not very rare in those days, and may even now be met with in some indigenous schools in out of the way villages.

ANOTHER SCHOOL.

Having learnt a little Gujarati, Behram was sent to the Sir Jamsetji Anglo-Vernacular School at Surat. His first master was a Parsi getting the handsome pay of Rs. 4 a month; but he made up for this scanty allowance by employing his pupils to " hew wood and draw water " for his household, and even to shampoo his legs. He appears to have been a snob of the first water, although one would hardly expect snobbery from such a low-paid teacher. Behram was about a year under him.

The boy's next teacher was Mr. Dosabhai. He is still working as a teacher and on very friendly terms with his former pupil. Malabari also remembers Mr. Haldevram, a Brahman, who spoke excellent English, and Mr. Fakirbhai, a Bania, who was a first-rate arithmetician. This latter was deaf, was often deceived by his pupils, as he could not make out if the oral answers given to him were right or wrong. Mere motion of the lips sometimes sufficed for him—and the little ones used often to have a laugh at the expense of their worthy master.

Behram had a lift frcm the 2nd Standard class to the 4th. He wrote a pretty hand, and Mr. Curtis, the Educational Inspector, liked it so much that he sent the boy's copybook to all the schools in his Division as a model. But in the 4th Standard class the teacher was a martinet and a pharisee. His pupils had to fetch his tiffin and do other little menial services for him. He used often to come late, and then go to prayers. In short, he had no idea of his duty, and the boys consequently made but little progress under him.

*Life, " a light and lasting frolic "** marred by the presence of the school-master.*

I have purposely given no dates above, as exact dates are not ascertainable. But I take it that Malabari was born in 1853, went to school when six years old, was for two or three months with Minochehrdaru, about as many months with Narbheram, about a year and a quarter in the Gujarati school, then about a year with a carpenter to learn carpentering (his mother belonged

* *Indian Muse,* p. 81.

B

to a bhansali or house-building family)—and about two or three years in the Anglo-vernacular school. He lost his father when he was six and his mother when he was in the twelfth year. These facts taken together might lead to an inference that he could not have led a gipsy life for a long time, but the truth is that Behram, before the death of his mother, was quite a different being from what he became after his sad bereavement. Upto eight he liked nothing so well as fun and play. He was skilful in flying kites and in other boyish sports. When he was nine Merwanji lost his little fortune, and Behram and his mother had to look poverty in the face. But the spirit of the boy was no way damped, and he apparently did not see why a poor boy should not be merry on even nothing a day. He had a capital voice, that of "a lark and of a nightingale together" —and he could sing. The streets of Surat were in those days frequented by the *Khialis*, and the poor dear itinerant minstrels who ought to be (but are not) the pride of the country. The *Khialis* are now dead at Surat, and the minstrels are probably singing their last lays. But Malabari remembers both yet, and is not likely to forget them. These *Khialis*, his mother and the missionaries were the three potent forces which have made him what he is, and we may therefore pause for a minute or two to see what manner of men the *Khialis* and the street-singers were in those days.

The street-singer, fortunately, is not yet an extinct species, and may, therefore, be studied by anyone who does not deem it *infra.dig.* to talk with such a humble creature. He can sing you historical ballads

and religious myths, love tales and devotional songs.
His dress is generally ragged, and he has often, nay
almost always, to live from hand to mouth.   He
timidly approaches your door, strikes up a tune on his
one-stringed guitar, and then breaks out into a ditty of
Premanand or Dayaram, of Kabir or Tukaram, full of
lively or pathetic music or diving into aphoristic philosophy, speaking

> " To mortals of their little week ;
> Of their sorrows and delights ;
> Of their passions and their spites ;
> Of their glory and their shame ;
> What doth strengthen and what maim."

Sorrow knows not how to sit heavily on this humble "bard of passion and of mirth," who is content
with a largess of a pice or two, who cares not for the
smiles or frowns of fortune, and though in this world
appears to be hardly of it.

The Surat *Khiali* was of another breed. *Khial,*
which literally means 'thought' or ' fancy,' is one of the
varieties of what is called the *Desi* system of music, as
opposed to the *Margi*. A learned Hindu expert in
musical lore would call the *Margi* system 'classical'
and the Desi system 'romantic.' Mr. Balwant Trimbak
Sahasrabudhe, an undoubted authority on Hindu music,
writes :—"Desi with its numerous ramifications is the
system now obtaining in India.........The Desi system
first acquired importance from the Buddhist musicians,
and received fuller development from Mussalmans who
introduced *khial* from the Hindu Dhruvapada system."
In Gujarati *khial* is a particular kind of metre.

The Surat *khiali* was a poet-philosopher. There were two sects of these wonderful men—the Kalgiwalas and the Turrawalas, so called from the instrument of music used by them or the dress worn by the leaders. The Kalgiwalas were Sakti worshippers, in other words, they held the female energy to be superior to the male, and, therefore, the Hindu goddess Parvati superior to her husband Shiva. The Turrawalas, on the contrary, held Shiva superior to Parvati, and the male energy superior to the female. Curious as it may seem, though much of the poetry and thought of the *khialis* was Hindu, their creed was eclectic and knew no distinction of caste, race, or colour. Indeed, the tradition is that Alahbax, a Borah, who used to sew gunny-bags, was the leader of the Kalgiwalas at one stage of their career, while Bahadursing, a small gatekeeper at Line-no-rasto (Soldiers' Lines) at Surat was his rival. Bahadursing was, of course, a Turrawala and a disciple of Maharajgir who was a disciple of Tukangir, the founder of that system. In Malabari's days, the Kalgiwalas were in the ascendant, but as usual with Malabari in after-life, he attached himself to the weaker party. An opium-eating pupil of Bahadursing took kindly to him and taught him about 2,000 *Khials*, *Ghazals* and *Thumris*. Some of the Khials or controversial songs of Bahadursing and Alahbax, it is said, were almost Miltonic in their grandeur.

Socrates had his symposia, and the *Khialis* had theirs. Let us go to one of these, and see what takes place. Bahadursing and Alahbax are of course no more, but their disciples are alive, the initiated as well as the uninitiated. In a prominent part of the Bazar, a carpet is spread and the *Khialis* of one school seat themselves on it and commence their songs. It is a still evening or twilight gray, and the people have leisure to listen. A large crowd assembles, but the singing at first goes on smoothly enough. The leader of the singers, however, suddenly espies a *Khiali* of the other school, and without naming him, challenges him in an impromptu verse to answer a knotty question in history, science or metaphysics. After a few minutes there is a reply—and a rejoinder follows, and a sur-rejoinder, all in ex-tempore verse. The smaller fry take their part in the controversy, and soon descend from high and dry philosophy to vulgar satire and abuse. Our Behram is among the Turrawalas, and he is often trotted out on special occasions. Like the others he has his shoes in his hand, in order to display the better part of valour in case the stronger side should show their teeth—makes an impromptu attack on the Kalgiwalas, not philosophical but sarcastic, and then takes to his heels with the other young *Khialis*, followed by the enraged Kalgiwalas. And so the symposium ends. It must, however, be remembered that this picture does not belong to the palmy days of *Khials*.

The initiated *Khialis*, when they took care to exclude the uninitiated, used to have calmer sittings sometimes extending over a week or two together. My idea is that their difference mainly turned upon whether the Creator should be worshipped as our Father in heaven or as our Mother in heaven. The Vaishnavas imagined the relation of the human soul to the Eternal

Spirit to be that of wife and husband or lover and beloved, but unfortunately they embodied this conception in the loves of Krishna and the Gopis. Our *Khialis* drew on the mythological biography of Shiva and Parvati and their children, Ganesh and Okha, and thus like the Vaishnavas, found themselves in a vortex of materialistic legends. Every pure fresh current of religious thought has fared in India (as in other countries) like a pellucid stream descending from mountain heights to the plains below, and growing muddier and darker in its progress to the sea. The Ganges in the Himalayas is quite different from the Ganges at Hardwar, Benares, or Calcutta. The farther it goes from its lofty source, the more has it to mingle with the dirt and *débris* of the lowlands, and the more impure it becomes. Similarly, when a "towering phantasy" has given birth to a great religious truth, its dissemination would seem to keep pace with its corruption. The history of Latin Christianity, as well as of Buddhism, bears out this view; but the history of Hinduism, more than that of any other religion, affords its aptest and saddest illustrations. It ought, therefore, to surprise nobody that the latter-day *Khialis* often indulged in ribald and obscene songs unworthy of the founders of their schools—unworthy of philosophers as much as of poets—and that at times they ended their controversies with the unanswerable argument of fisticuffs.

Behram was not one of the initiated, and did not then understand the philosophy of his sect. But he appreciated their poetry, and could compose his own *khialis*. There are several good ones in the *Niti Vinod*.

They are on homely subjects—for the *Khialis* often descended from their altitudes to discuss the affairs of every-day life or the merits of their city or river or their places of pilgrimage. But we have had enough of *Khialis* now. Suffice it to say, that they exercised a more powerful influence on Behram than all his masters, excepting the Revd. Mr. Dixon.

JUVENILE PICNICS.

We have seen Behram at a *Khiali* symposium. We may now accompany him to a picnic. It is as strange as the symposium. He has a rival *improvisatore* among the Kalgiwalas, a Borah boy of the name of Adam. Though rivals, the two, unlike other rivals, are great friends. Both have good voices — Behram's was noted for its volume and its melody— and both have not much of pocket money. They can, however, afford a pice between them, and with this they have bought some parched rice and now proceed on a moonlight night to enjoy themselves on the bank of the Tapti. The parched grains are thrown on the sand, and the two friends are picking them up one by one and singing away for dear love. Behram has a rude flute or a *sarangi* and he varies his singing with instrumental music while his companion keeps time on a *thali* (a metal platter). Women turn up and take an unconscionably long time to fill their pitchers from the river, for they are filling their ears with the music of the two boys. Women in Gujarat have a song-literature of their own, and they are obliged to sing on certain occasions. Their songs are mostly *garbas*, and I have occasionally seen a mother with two or three water-vessels well balanced on her head hearing her little daughter repeat a *garba* taught on the previous night, as the two wend their way home from the Sabarmati. These *garbas* are well worth study. I would specially commend them to the attention of those who deny that there is any premature marriage among the Hindus or that such marriage is an evil. The *Garbas* and *Khials* of Gujarat are full of this subject. They mostly take the form of a lament by a widow who has lost her husband in her prime, or by a girl married in infancy to a greybeard, or by a grownup bride whose wedded lord is yet in his cradle. It was only the other day that I heard of a Visa Nagara Brahmin girl married at the age of a year and a half who is now a widow at two. Behram was fond of these *garbas* and *khials* and could sing them with an irresistible pathos, and I take it this was the best preparation for the future campaigner against social vices.

SWIMMING AND DRINKING AND WALKING.

Behram was an early riser, especially when he had to go to school in the morning. His house was very near the Tapti, and I am sorry to say he learned swimming and drinking almost at one and the same time. I have not kept back the fact that our hero before he lost his mother—for we are now talking of that period only—took part sometimes in obscene songs, and I am bound to state that once upon a time he tossed off no less than nine copper cups containing not under a half pound each of that seductive liquor called Surti Daru (*i.e.* Mhowra liquor)—though now he is as good as a teetotaler. His antidote and that of his companions—for he took care to sin in company—was generally a plentiful quantity of lemons—a plunge into the Tapti from the parapets—a swim across to Adajan on the opposite bank—a deep draught of toddy there (Adajan is famous for its toddy)—and a swim across again. Many of my readers perhaps do not know what a Parsi *jasan* or *ghambar* is. I am only concerned with the *jasan*, for Behram was more than partial to this "rouse before the morn"—though his means would not permit of his indulging in it except occasionally. Slices of pomegranate, pameloes, pine-apples and guavas in the first place, a piece of unleavened bread in the next, and last but not least the "all-softening, over-powering" Daru were the three courses of Behram's *jasan*, and after taking his antidote he did not seem to be much the worse for his dissipation. He would dry his clothes with his little fellow-sinners, and quietly walk to the school, as if nothing had happened. Behram also used to join walking matches and would tramp it to Nausari from Surat. Even now, he is a splendid walker and climber, doing 15 to 20 miles at a stretch and climbing the steepest ascents when in health.

RIDING ON THE SLY.

It goes without saying that Merwanji, and therefore Behram, had no horse, and yet the boy taught himself to ride. Here, too, it is necessary to make a confession. There was a timber-seller in Surat of the name of Abdul Kadur. He did not sell his timber himself, but employed agents. He kept also several ponies for hire, but did not give them out on hire himself. He was a religious man, busy with his God,

and while so busy, Behram and his friends used often
to take out the ponies for exercise and have a ride free
of charge. The good man never even once resented
these trespasses, but on the contrary often did a kindness to those who offended against him and his property.
" He was," Malabari tells me, " my boyhood's hero,"
and later on we shall see him quoting Abdul Kadur's
famous prescription against fever :—" Starve out thy
fever, my son, and make *her* sick of thee by constantly
moving about." Abdul Kadur was certainly a remarkable man. His business throve, though he did not
attend to it. It was his ancestral trade, and he kept
it up. But what right had he to the income ? It was
given by God, and to God's wards, the poor, it must go ;
and Abdul Kadur with such thoughts kept little of
his earnings to himself. But they were not his earnings
and there was no merit in giving them away. Hence
this strict bondsman of his conscience used to put on
a cooly's coarse garments every second night (in those
days steamers used to leave Surat for Bombay every
second night), earn a few pice by carrying loads in the har-
bour, buy a little oil and milk, with these return to his
Mosque, distribute the milk among the blind and
the maimed at the Mosque, give some drops of it to the
old dog there, and then lighting a little lamp with the
oil offer his meed of praise and prayer to Allah. No
wonder he excited the admiration of Behram.

The Little Knight of La Mancha.

" The child," it has been said, " is father of the
man," and it is instructive to see Behram in the morning
of his life interesting himself in the cause of the widow

and the child-bride. The following two instances related by Malabari speak for themselves ;—

It may amuse, but will scarcely surprise, the reader, to hear of me as a match-maker. I have had fair training in the match-making line, and have at times tried my hand at match-breaking, too. The first match that I helped, in a humble way, to render happy was in the case of Manchha. Manchha was a Hindu maiden of the milk-seller caste at Surat. She happened to have lost her boy-husband when only a child, and at about 20 she was married to a widower of her own caste. The remarriage was, of course, very strongly opposed by her people. But her husband had some means, and was the wife's brother of a wealthy money-lender, Tapidas. So Mr. and Mrs. Tapidas patronized the match and installed Manchha and her husband in a new milk shop at Nanpura, so that they might be out of harm's way. But here the pair were no better off than they might have been elsewhere. The rival shop-keepers kept aloof from them, spreading all manner of rumours to their discredit. The new shop was virtually boycotted. When this came to the knowledge of the Parsis of Nanpura (including schoolboys) they swore a big oath to befriend Manchha. They transferred their patronage almost in a body from Dullab and Vallab, hitherto their favourite milk-sellers, to Manchha. Thus Manchha's shop was besieged every morning by scores of Parsi customers in search of milk and cream and curd and butter. Well do I remember her smile of gratitude as she dispensed the products of her dairy. She was particularly kind to us schoolboys, because it was we who had brought her case to notice. For a time all went merrily with Manchha and her spouse, as merrily as a marriage bell. But all this while their enemies were hatching a plot against their peace. Now Manchha was a big strapping body, not particularly proud of her lord. She was handsome, too, and extremely sociable in an innocent sort of way. So, unhappily for her, she made friends with an elderly Parsi who monopolised her afternoons, whom she served with *pan supari*, and with whom she discussed local scandals. There was nothing wrong in all this. Manchha was not to her husband what Anarkali was to Akbar, whom the old stupid is said to have ordered to be buried alive for having unconsciously returned a smile from Mirza Selim. Manchha flirted with her venerable beau in open day, as the jolly milk-maids and the malans and the tambolans of Surat often do. But in this case her caste people made it too hot for the poor girl, and one morning we found Manchha's shop deserted by her and her husband. Whither they went we could never find out. For months we grieved over the loss and thought it was a shame that *our* Manchha should have *eloped with her husband* without taking friends into confidence. Her aged lover took to bed the day after the elopement, some said from unrequited love, others said because Manchhabai had forgotten to return sundry ornaments she had borrowed from him. This latter was, I think, an invention of her enemies.

My next lesson was in match-breaking, or rather an attempt at it. An old tamboli (*pan supari* seller) one day surprised his customers by bringing up from the district a girl whom he repre-sented as his wife. She was about 15, whilst he was over 50, besides being a morose, taciturn, miserly beast whom nobody liked to exchange words with except by way of teasing. The school-boys of Nanpura found in the girl an excellent handle for perse-cuting her husband. Returning from school they would go up to him, and one of them would ask—"Kaka, where is your— daughter?"—and he would reply—"you fool, she is your mother." Then would the boy retort—"very well, Kaka, I'll inform my forgetful father about it"—at which the outraged husband would shriek like mad, flourishing his chunam stick.

Many were the annoyances to which the boys subjected him— they sang songs in his wife's honour, they praised her beauty, they advised her aloud not to throw away her charms on a scare-crow, a mumbling opium-eater, and so forth. One evening they collected copper pieces amongst themselves, had them converted into a four-anna silver piece, and then went to the tamboli's shop. The spokesman went forward, and holding out the silver coin, said:—"Kaka, let us have four annas worth of pan, supari, chuno and katho—look sharp there is to be a singing party." The tamboli executed the order cheerfully, advising the boys in a fatherly spirit not to be truants and not to tease elderly men like himself, &c., &c. They listened to him with bowed heads, but as soon as he held out the packages, asking for the coin, the leader of the gang remarked:—"Not this way, Kaka, I must have the packages from Kaki's hands." A shout of cheers from his companions greeted the remark. This was too much for the unsuspecting tamboli. "You son of a she-demon," he yelled, "why were you born to be the plague of my life?; at your birth you ought to have been turned into a stone. Have you no shame in speaking thus of an honest man's wife?" "Don't I pay for it?" replied the young profligate, with an insolent leer which maddened his opponent, and exhibiting the silver coin. "But you black-faced villain, she is in the kitchen above," explained the tamboli half relenting. "Send for her, Kakaji, send for her—shall I call her down?"—that was the boy's rejoinder. The tamboli again lost his temper, and remarked sulkily, "go away, I don't want your custom." "Very well," said the boy, "I'll go to the other shop." Then followed a struggle in the tamboli's breast between jealousy and avarice, and in a minute or so avarice, the stronger passion, triumphed. He called out his wife, abusing her as the cause of his misery, and so on; she came down, half crying, half smiling, protesting against the old man's injustice. In answer he thrust the packages into her hands with the injunction—"give these to that dog." The boy reached out his hand eagerly, but as the fair tambolan's hand approached his, he slowly withdrew his hand, till he made her lean more than half her body forward. He then pretended to kiss her hand, took the packages and gave her the four anna bit with a smile she could not help returning. The old man sat all this while grinding his teeth and cursing everybody before him, including his innocent wife.

It may be mentioned here that the boys were too young to be serious. But light-hearted as these frolics were, they were a terror to many a jealous husband or cruel father. The young women, as a rule, encouraged their little gallants.*

FAST AND FURIOUS FUN.

These merry-makings were innocent enough, but I can't say the same thing about some other achievements

---

* *Indian Spectator*, p. 533.

of Behram. For example, he and ten or eleven of his school-chums going early to school see a Bania shop-keeper snoring away on a cot lying outside his shop. Instantly they put their shoulders to the cot and re-move it to the Killa maidan. That was too bad—for the Bania was sure to think his house was haunted by hobgoblins or perhaps start some equally beautiful theory to account for his translation. Curious to say, the policemen on the beat often enjoyed this fun. One of them was a special friend of Behram, and I am sorry to say taught him some questionable songs.

Another amusement of these little imps was to tease Borah Jamalji—" one of those noble fellows, you know," Malabari told me, " who seldom dun you for debt." But woe unto the poor old Borah if he ever dunned Behram and his merry band. Early in the morning before he was up from his bed, they would stealthily remove the little ladder used by him for getting down from his shop, and place it against the stall of his rival on the opposite side. Jamalji coming to the edge of his shop would, as usual, make for the ladder and have a fall to the delight of his tormentors awaiting this event in a corner. Then there would be a ringing volley of curses upon all and sundry, but the Borah, not much hurt, would soon pick himself up and seeing the boys would inquire about the lost ladder. " Have we the ladder in our pockets, Jamalji?" the ringleader would ask " look about you and then foul your tongue." He would look about him, and noticing the ladder at the opposite shop-keeper's would kick up a row with him, and the naughty boys would then hasten to school, having had enough of mirth for the day.

A Caning and What Came of It.

But of all the naughty deeds of our hero perhaps the naughtiest was his treatment of the new head-master of his school. It happened in this wise. Behram was a good pugilist and a good wrestler. He had strong muscles and strong bones, and his animal spirits, as the reader might have already concluded for himself, were abnormally high. While studying for the Fourth English Standard Test, he was one day, during the half-hour recess, challenged to force open a door held from the other side by four or five other boys. None of the boys knew that the hinges were rotten, and none therefore anticipated the catastrophe that ensued. Behram accepting the challenge, pressed against the door with all his might when the hinges gave a creak, and the door all of a sudden gave way and fell down upon the poor boys on the other side with his own weight upon it. Fortunately, no serious injury was done, but the crash frightened the school masters. The new head-master, Mr. Jevachram (the old one had been transferred) was a rigid disciplinarian, though not an unjust man. The boys were marched up as criminals before him, and after a long trial he sentenced them to receive each a dozen stripes on the hand. But Behram would not submit to this order. His other masters tried their influence with the head-master in his favour. But Mr. Jevachram being a stickler for his authority adhered to his decision, while Behram, equally obdurate, adhered to his own. At length Mr. Dosabhai procured a concession that the school-peon should not inflict the punishment on Behram—but Mr. Dosabhai himself. This was something, and Mr. Dosabhai in his most persuasive tone came up to the culprit, and "now my boy," said he, "you won't feel *my* caning you, would you? Do be a good boy, and hold out your hand." Behram held out his hand—but with the first stroke, the over-sensitive lad was in a tremor and was about to fall down in a swoon. The masters were frightened and did their utmost to revive him. The boy did revive, but the first thing he did on coming to was to throw his books at poor Mr. Jevachram and bolt. He had to descend a staircase of about thirty steps, but three or four plunges brought him to the landing, and he rushed frantically home to complain to his mother.

An Irreparable Loss and Its Lesson.

But his mother was laid up with cholera. She had had an attack some time previously and had recovered, but that day she had experienced a relapse. To this day Malabari remembers the revulsion of feeling—call it rather a mental cyclone—which swept "the offending Adam" out of him and sobered him down to the gravity and stillness which have since then been his main characteristic. I do not think that there was much dross in his nature. Those who know him as he is now can never believe that his instincts could have been other than good even in his boyhood. Boys of course will be boys—and who is there among us who can blame him for being often up to a lark? But unless I have misread him egregiously, I am sure he was a loveable boy. Indeed, the man who could not have loved this frank, genial, gifted little one, singing like a bird and pouring out his melody so freely, must have had little "music in his soul" and still less of human nature. Let us not, therefore, uncharitably judge the remorse-stricken boy for disobeying his master. Let us rather give him our best sympathy, while he is standing, shame-faced, crest-fallen, and almost dazed, beside his mother's bed.

Behram ministered to his dying parent as only such an affectionate son could for two nights and three days. She was all in all to him, and she was dying. He could not go to bed even though his mother would implore him to take rest. He sits there fascinated—rubbing her feet and watching—watching—watching! At four o'clock in the evening of the third day her head and feet grow cold, then the chest, then the hands one of which holds Behram's to the last. She hovers between life and death for half an hour, and then the boy first sees the sight of death. He does not weep —for the tears have frozen at their fount and there is a mist before his eyes. He is not able to realize for some time that his mother, who had just now passed her hand over his head, is no more. He sits like a statue until the neighbours come and the body is removed. He follows it and returns with the neighbours, and sits again like a statue. "Next morning," he tells me, "I became an old old man. All my past associations were discarded."*

---

* There is a touching allusion to his mother's death in the *Indian Muse*, p. 86-87.

> " One day the sun as his decline began
> Declin'd the sun of this my earthly span !
> Her latest breath below my safety sought:
> To bless her orphan was her dying thought!
> No tear I shed, when first my loss I view'd;
> My sense was smother'd, and my soul subdued.
> She'd clasp'd a child, with sad emotions wan ;
> But when the clasp relax'd, there was left a man."

She was only thirty-three when she died.

C

CHAPTER II. YOUTH (1866-1876.)

Malabari's life may well be divided into three periods. The first period is one of play and song ; the second of study and poetry ; the third of politics, literature and social reform. The third thus overlaps the second to some extent. But the division is convenient.

MALABARI A PUPIL AND A TUTOR.

With his mother's death the orphan boy of twelve found himself utterly friendless in the world, for Merwanji in his old age had become cantankerous and was in straitened circumstances. Fortunately the people in his street and thereabouts knew of the lad's astonishing powers, and so it came about that although he was yet in pupilage himself, he found no difficulty in securing pupils some of whom were his seniors in age. He, however, devoted only his mornings and evenings to their tuition, for he was himself now hungering and thirsting for knowledge and was anxious to go to school again. The Anglo-vernaculr School would have been only too glad to take him back, but he preferred to join the Irish Presbyterion Mission School, then under the supervision of the Revd. Mr. Dixon. Mr. Dixon, an exemplary Christian and a gentleman in the best sense of the word, took the boy by the hand, and gave him every encouragement. The head master of the school, Mr. Navalkar, and also Mr. Motinarayan thought highly of the newcomer and were very friendly. Thus, under sympathetic guidance, Behramji commenced his study of English in real earnest.

Mr. Dixon as head of the school used to teach Shakespeare to the boys in the first class. Behramji

Chapter II.

YOUTH.

The prize is in the process! knowledge means
Ever renewed assurance by defeat
That victory is somehow still to reach :
But love is victory, the prize itself :
Love—trust to !   Be rewarded for the trust,
In trusts' mere act.—BROWNING'S *Ferishtah's Fancies.*

" As if there were sought in knowledge a couch whereupon
to rest a searching and restless spirit ; or a terrace for a
wandering and variable mind to walk up and down with a
fair prospect ; or a tower of state for a proud mind to raise
itself upon ; or a fort or commanding ground for strife and
contention ; or a shop for profit or sale ; and not a rich
storehouse for the glory of the Creator, and the relief of man's
estate. —BACON'S *Advancement of Learning.*

Half grown as yet, a child, and vain,
She cannot fight the fear of death.
What is she, cut from love and faith,
But some wild Pallas from the brain

Of demons ? fiery hot to burst
All barriers in her onward race
For power.   Let her know her place ;
She is the second, not the first.—TENNYSON'S *In Memoriam.*

had been put in the third class and was at this time in
the second, but was, nevertheless, allowed the benefit
of these lessons. This was a great privilege, and the
boy was grateful for it. He made very rapid progress
in speaking and understanding English, and one day
surprised Mr. Dixon by giving a lucid explanation of
a very difficult passage in Shakespeare which had
puzzled the master himself. His admiring teacher
foretold the boy's greatness and heartily helped him in
his pursuit of knowledge.

MALABARI'S STRUGGLES.

But the pursuit of knowledge was no easy task
to one situated as the poor boy was. Imagine a lonely
orphan who, in his thirteenth year, has to earn his own
livelihood, who has sometimes to cook for himself, who
has none at home to speak to but a snappish old man,
who has to attend his school from 10 a.m. to 4 p.m., and
to school others often from 7 to 9 in the morning and
6 to 8 in the evening ; and you have an idea of Malabari's hard lot in those days. He seldom slept more than
four hours, for his nights alone were his own, and he spent
many an hour in poring over the pages of Shakespeare
and Milton, Wordsworth and Tennyson, Premanand
and Akha, Samal Bhat and Dayaram. He was given
to musing, and would often take up a scrap of paper
to jot down those "short swallow-flights of song" which
come so naturally to born poets. It is a remarkable
fact that most of the Gujarati poems in the *Niti Vinod*
and several in the *Sarod-i-Ittifak* were composed
about this time. On the whole, though chilled by
poverty, Malabari at this period of his life was not

quite unhappy, and he often longs to move again in those "shadowy thoroughfares of thought" and imagination, amidst which his prime was passed, to weave again those wreaths of poesy which were the delight of his youth, and to prove himself what Colonel Olcott once wished him to be " the song-writing redeemer of his country."

Schoolboy-Ambition.

This, however, is the dream of his after-life. In those hard days when he was toilng for bread his one ambition was to matriculate. This may look like an anti-climax, but it is a fact. Matriculation in 1866 was considered by many a young scholar as the be-all and end-all of study, and as an unfailing portal to preferment in Government and private service. Behramji set his heart on matriculating and studied all the subjects prescribed for this examination with commendable assiduity, except arithmetic. He could not conquer his aversion to arithmetic, and used often to despair of passing the test on this account. But his teachers used to hearten him to his work by assuring him that he would make up the necessary marks in other subjects, if he only succeeded in securing the minimum number in the intractable science of calculation. This minimum number, however, proved tantalisingly unattainable for several years, as we shall see.

His Guardian Angels.

" I have somehow had more sympathy from the angels than from the brutes of my own sex—begging *your* pardon." So wrote Malabari some time ago. He speaks of many women, European and Native—Hindu,

Mahomedan as well as Parsi—who " have been kind to me, kind as mother's milk." This was, I presume, in early life, for Malabari is not now a society man. He studied in the Mission School for about two years only, as he went up for his matriculation from the second class, but I have no doubt that the example of the good missionary who presided over it, and of his noble wife, deeply influenced the young student's life. This is clear from his first book which abounds with the loftiest sentiments, and from the tenour of his own life. Malabari still corresponds with Mrs. Dixon, now at Belfast, with her son who is studying for the Bar and whom Malabari still remembers as the " little Willie " of the happy mission-house. Mrs. Dixon had another child—a little girl who died in her infancy at Surat, and whom her father followed shortly afterwards lamented by the whole town. I have sometimes speculated as to what Malabari would have been if those benevolent men who founded the Irish Presbyterian Mission had never thought of India, and provided no mission school or closed it on seeing no visible, tangible results. I feel little doubt that his good instincts would have asserted themselves sooner or later ; but I have as little doubt, that Mr. and Mrs. Dixon evoked and fostered these instincts much sooner than would otherwise have been the case.

There were other lady friends who often cheered the sadness of the lonely boy. He fondly recalls the days he spent at Munshi Lutfullah Khan's. Munshi Lutfullah, whose "Autobiography" is well known, had a son, Fazal, who studied in the mission school and be-

came a fast friend of Behramji's. The two boys used
often to spend their evenings together, and on those
nights when Behram had not to attend to his pupils,
he enjoyed the pleasure of hearing Fazal's sister sing
and play. She had a sorrow of her own, and perhaps
felt drawn to the the pensive orphan. The accomplished old Munshi was himself particularly fond of
entertaining Behramji, Vijiashankar and other school-
boys who frequented his house. Malabari gratefully
remembers the friendship of two of his own cousins
as also of several Parsi and Hindu ladies.

JIVAJI, THE GENEROUS JEW.

Nearly two years have now elapsed since that
" dark day of nothingness " when Malabari's, mother
breathed her last. He is now fairly ready for his
matriculation, though he is doubtful about his
arithmetic. But there is no money forthcoming for
his passage to Bombay where the examintion is to
be held. Mr. Dixon tells him " mind, don't fail to prosecute your studies after you matriculate. Draw upon
me for money, if need be ; " but the good Padre does
not know that his favourite pupil is almost despairing
of going to Bombay for want of money. The boy is
too proud, too sensitive to take a loan ; but he is the
admiration of his class, and his class-mates know his
circumstances. Curiously enough, help came to him
from a quarter the least expected. There was an old
Parsi gentleman, Jivaji, at Nanpura—a remarkable
man who had burnt his fingers in the Share Mania
of 1864-65, but who had sufficient money to lend,
especially to butchers. He was, however, by reputa-

tion such a tight screw to deal with that he had himself come to be nicknamed after the class with whom he had business relations. He was Malabari's opposite neighbour and one of his sons was in the mission school. Learning how the case stood with the boy, old Jivaji behaved with a generosity which few would have given him credit for. He sent for the youth, wormed out his secret, and thrust Rs. 20 upon him. This was all that was wanted. "Don't be sad, my lad," said the good old Jivaji, "your honest face is security enough for my money," and he actually took no bond or note of hand. His confidence was eventually well rewarded. Meanwhile let us follow Malabari to Bombay. He had to pay Rs. 10 for the usual examination-fee, and he required the remaining Rs. 10 for his passage. So with this little amount in his pocket, and with a little bed and a few books he left Surat for the capital of the presidency.

At the Door of a Bombay Dives.

Behramji was barely fifteen when he came to Bombay, and so green was he that he did not realize the enormous gulf between the rich and the poor in that great city. He knew how Jivaji had treated him, but he forgot that Jivaji had started in life with perhaps a couple of rupees, and had known what it was to be poor. Our Surati *ingenue* had heard of a rich Parsi at Bombay, and had read some of his public utterances and of his public charities. Surely such a man would be but too glad to help an orphan. Old Merwanji was very unhappy owing to the mortgage of his house. He had found out the sterling worth of his adopted son, and this latter on his side was anxious to see the house redeemed. It was a matter of Rs. 300 only, and surely a boy ready for his matriculation, with such excellent testimonials from Messrs. Curtis and Dixon, could get this trifle on his word of honour from a sympathising benefactor. He would pay it back with interest. So one day, pocketing his pride for the sake of old Merwanji, Behram presents himself at the door of the public-spirited Parsi Dives. He is called in, and modestly states his case. The reply is a withering smile and an offer of a cup of tea. But the young man, who had thought so much of his word of honour and read so much of the brotherhood of men, finding his cup of hope dashed to pieces, turns his back on the man of the world and is off. This was one of his first experiences at Bombay. "I felt too stunned even to be able to give him the parting salaam," writes Malabari. "I never met him since but once, when he was in need of my good offices. Little did the poor Sheth know that the man whom he paid such lavish attentions was the same as had come to him for a little loan to help his adoptive father. I do not blame him now; perhaps he had been deceived by others before I appealed to him."

Arithmetic Revenges Itself.

But a sadder disappointment was in store for him. He failed in arithmetic on going in for the examination. He did well in all the other subjects, but had to give up in despair some of the hard nuts from Colenso which he was asked to crack. Had it been possible to solve a puzzle of decimal fractions with Gujarati or English poetry, our hero would have easily scored the highest number of marks. But there was as little poetry in arithmetic as in the Parsi Dives he had encountered. He had a bulky bundle of poems in English as well as in Gujarati, but then who would believe that a mite of a boy could be a poet. He had no patron and no friends. He had put up at Bombay with a relation of Merwanji's, and must now either return to Surat, or make up his mind to draw on Mr. Dixon. He was however, soon helped out of these embarrassments.

A Good Samaritan.

While at Surat, Behram had given free lessons to several boys. One of these was a son of a Parsi lady who was his mother's friend. This lady had a brother in Bombay, Dr. Rastomji Bahadurji, and had commended Behram to his care. Well Dr. Bahadurji, who rather liked this shy little stranger from Surat, came to the boy's rescue, and introduced him to the owner of the Parsi Proprietary School in the Fort, who was so pleased with the boy's English and general acquirements that he formed a new class for him. He had to start with only Rs. 20 a month.; but after a few months he was promoted to a post of Rs. 40, and then to one of Rs. 60. The young man also took pupils privately, and was able soon to make between Rs. 100 and 150 from tuitions alone. Behramji was no longer oppressed by poverty.

A Narrow Escape.

But a new danger turned up at this stage. Having now a moderate income, he was an eligible son-in-law ; and the wife of the relation with whom he had lived for a year from the date of his arrival, was a great match-maker. She had a widowed sister older than Behramji, and she didn't see why these two should not be a happy couple. But Behramji was not quite a greenhorn now, and had eyes to see and understanding to judge for himself. He declined the offer with thanks and quietly removed to other lodgings.

Matriculates—at last.

Mr. Kavasji Banaji had offered our poet-pedagogue Rs. 40 a month for teaching his son, and Behramji now became a lodger in his house. He was also for a while with Mr. Cowasji Bisney. After some time he commenced to live on his own hook in a house in Dhobi Talao rented for Rs. 20 a month, and then in another in Hanuman Lane, Fort. All this time he had not forgotten his matriculation. He had failed first in 1868 ; he failed again in 1869, and for the third time in 1870. But at last in 1871 the goddess of integers and fractions had pity upon the persevering young votary and pulled him safely through his ordeal. He was no longer an orphan now in the educational service.

The Revd. Van Someren Taylor and Dr. John Wilson.

If sorrows come in battalions, joys also sometimes come in a goodly band. Behramji had borne the shock of the battalions bravely. Poverty, the loss of his mother, his repeated failure in the matriculation test, were all so many "blows of circumstance" which he had courageously breasted. And now a better day dawned upon him, and he emerged from his obscurity.

One of his examiners had been the Revd. Mr. Taylor whose name is still a household word in Gujarat. He was the author of a standard Gujarati Grammar and some Gujarati poems. Behramji had heard a great deal about him, and one day mustering courage took his own Gujarati poems to him. They were in a neat manuscript written like print, and Mr. Taylor turning over the pages and struck with the beauty of the verses exclaimed :—" Do you mean to say you have had this for three years and it has not yet been printed?" No, of course, not. It had not been printed, and was not to be printed for some years yet. But Mr. Taylor's encouraging words put new life into the author, and by Mr. Taylor he was introduced to one who moulded his life and shaped his ends in a remarkable degree. This was the great linguist, the devoted missionary and the enlightened educationist—the Revd. Dr. John Wilson.

Dr. Wilson read Behramji's little volume, found the versification " remarkably good," and the ideas expressed indicative of " poetical imagination,"—stood sponsor to the book, named it the *Niti Vinod* (or the Pleasures of Morality), and exerted himself in its favour. The Government subscribed for 300 copies, Sir Cowasji Jehangir Readymoney for 75, Sir Mangaldas Nathubhai for 50, Sir Dinshaw Petit for 25, and several others followed these gentlemen's example. The book nevertheless came out only in 1875. This requires an explanation, and I give it with reluctance, because I shall have to say that Behramji carried as little of the spirit of calculation into his life as he did to his examination ; in other words, to praise him for what he does not wish to be proclaimed or praised. The truth is, his earnings, except what he sent to Merwanji and what he spent on books and sometimes on good cheer, went to others—some of them, I am afraid, idlers who imposed upon the young donor. He had even borrowed money to relieve their necessities. This was one cause of the delay. Another was that he was shy and knew nothing about printers and publishers. At length, however, he overcame these difficulties with the assistance of his friend, Mr. Shapurji Dadabhai Bhabha, but before the first born of his genius came into the world an important event took place, which I must not pass over.

MARRIAGE.

This was his marriage in his twenty-first year. My fair readers, if I should have the good fortune to have any, will ask several questions, but they had better put them to Mrs. Malabari, for I cannot answer them. I shall, however, try to satisfy their legitimate curiosity. Was she pretty? Yes. Was she young? Yes, only nineteen. Where did the two meet? Why, in the house of Malabari's landlady, close to Malabari's own lodgings. Was there any courtship? A short one. Was it an affair of the heart? Both thought so. At any rate it was not a question of money—there was no dower and no settlement. All that could be gathered now is that it was a matter of intense devotion on one side and intense pity on the other. Was the marriage celebrated in the orthodox style? Yes. I think this much ought to suffice.

The "Niti Vinod."

By a fortunate coincidence, Malabari brought out the *Niti Vinod* about the time his first child was born. In a short time a second edition was called for. It was the first work of the first Parsi Poet ;* but it had other merits.

The Gujarati of the *Niti Vinod* is not Parsi Gujarati, but Hindu Gujarati. The two in many respects differ as much as Hindustani and Hindi. Malabari, thanks to his association with the *khialis*, and his study of pure Gujarati poets, had obtained a wonderful mastery over Hindu Gujarati. His favourite authors were Dayaram, Premanand and Akho, "the last for aphoristic wisdom and manly spirit, the second for dignity and true poetic sentiment, and Dayaram for his luscious sweetness and captivating imagery."† He was also very fond of Kabir, Nanik, Dadu, Mira and other minor singers. A natural gift so diligently cultivated could not but produce the very best poetic style.

There is another thing remarkable in the *Niti Vinod*. It is the bewildering number and variety of the metres employed. I am afraid the title of the book is forbidding. It would lead Englishmen to suppose that it is something like Pope's *Moral Essays*, or Tupper's prosaic verses, or at the most, like Roger's *Pleasures of Memory* or Campbell's *Pleasures of Hope*. But the *Niti Vinod* is almost wholly lyrical. There are few pieces in it which are not pure songs.

---

* *Rast Goftar.*
† Private letter.

The book is divided into five parts—moral subjects, miscellaneous subjects, questions and answers, short lives of great men, and religious subjects. The first part takes up only thirty-seven pages out of 215 and deals with such subjects as Youth, Friendship, Flattery, Jealousy, Swearing, Procrastination, Idleness, Drunkenness, Sensuality, Worldliness, Suicide, and Death. But even this purely moral portion is full of gems such as the piece which tells us what things are good to buy in the market of the world, and that other which shows how to prepare to meet death patiently. In this part also there is a faithful and artistic translation of the Indian schoolboy's favourite—"You are old Father William." —Father William becomes "Kaka Karsanji" in Gujarati, but acquits himself in it as well as in English. There is also "a word of advice to the body" which is worth reproducing as a whole. I quote the refrain of the song which may one day pass into a popular saying, at least with the Salvationists.

Dunyá ulat sulat che khel
Sátún mukti nún múshkel *

The third part contains pithy answers to such questions as "Why God gives happiness," "Who is truly happy" "Who is the true hero," "Where is God," "Who is the true God," "Who should weep," "Who should laugh," Whose wife is a widow," and so on.

The "Short Lives of Great Men" commence with Mr. Dixon whose untimely death is deplored in pathetic verse.

---

* The world is a game of ups and downs,
The bargain of salvation is a difficult one.

Garíbo bhanáve, suníti shikháve
Pashú bál ne je ghadímán rijháve
Gayo svarga sádhú kharo úpkárí
Vidiá máta rotí pharéche bichárí*

Then follow the first Napoleon Buonaparte, Karsandas Mulji, Lady Avanbai (the first Lady Jamsetji
Jijibhoy), Nelson, Wellington, Sir Jamsetji Jijibhoy
(the first Parsi Baronet,) Prince Albert, Jagannath
Sankarsett, Rustomji Jamsetji Jijibhoy, the great
Anstey, and lastly Dr. Bhau Daji. There are also a
couple of other poems, one on the murder of Lord Mayo,
and the other on the calamities which befell the third
Napoleon.

The fifth part treats of salvation, devotion to
God, prayer and like topics from the point of view of
a pure theist. The language is very terse, limpid and
musical, and the thoughts are as pure as Keshub
Chunder Sen's.

But decidedly the best poems in the book are to
be found in the second part, and of all his best poems,
the pathetic ones on the woes of enforced widowhood
and the horrors of infant marriage† are the very best.
Here is one of them :—

---

* He who taught the poor—inculcated morality—won the
hearts of little children in a moment—he, the true saint and philanthropist is gone to heaven, and the bereaved Mother Learning
wanders about weeping.

† The headings of some of the pieces on these subjects may bo
mentioned :—

"How to relieve Bharat Khand (India) of the curse of woman ;"
"Contrast between the condition of Hindu women in ancient and
modern times ;" "Advice to the leaders of Hindu caste ;" "A heart-

He hína-hathílá, jama játílá, hilatíla kema karó ?

Shubha avasara páse, ve'mo ná'se, kàn jítaáshe, jútha
varo ?

Sau dukhí abaláne, marada-bhaláne, satapáláne, sonpì do,

Jagasukhahin nárí, garíb bichári, bedí akárí, kápí do.

A-'desha sudharshe, ridha sidha vadhashe, pápa utarshe,
chút didhe,

Dinabandhu ke'she, desha videsha, kírati re'she, ám
kidhe ;

Je hashe akarmí, puro adharmí, vipati garmí, nahi
talashe,

Jo ishwarjáyá, karshe sáhya, to ishmáyá, jhat malashe

Pashu bála kapáye, ùdarmánhe, nahi nikláe, mána vatí,

Baní máta niráshí, niráshaphánsí, ghále trásí, krúra matí

---

broken lady's lament;" "A supplication to the Hindu Mahajan."
"The sorrows of a widow on the death of her husband;" "A sinful
widow's prayer to God;" "A widow's prayer to her father;" "The
sorrows resulting from Infant Marriage." The first four lines of
this last song run as follows:—

> Pita bachapanthí ná parnavo re
> Jaldí kháo na lagan no lávo
>
> Pita, &c.
>
> Prabhu kero didhel hawálo re, tene dhíraj thí sanbháló ro
> Pachí vá'lí hoe ke vá'lo
>
> Pita &c.

Fathers, do not marry your children in infancy;

Do not be in a hurry to enjoy the pleasures of a marriage (in
your family.)

(Children are) a sacred charge from God

Rear them with patience, whether they be daughters or sons·

Manamá bahú lágé, baltánáge; vidhwá máge, sukha radí,
Béhrám vicharun, chále márún, to ugárún, áya ghadí.*

To appreciate the beauty and melody of this
piece, as also its warmth of denunciation, one should
have it sung, and then he would see what deep
earnestness has been infused into it. Indeed, it is the
young poet's depth of feeling, almost phenomenal,
which is the most salient feature of his work. This

---

* Read á as in all, o as in lo, a as in attempt, u as in bull, ú as
oo in fool, i as in British, í as ee in eel,

The verses may be loosely translated as follows :—

"Oh ye God-forsaken, perverse fiends of caste, why make
you these shuffling shambling excuses ?

Good times are near, superstitions must now flee, why (at
such a time) do you wed untruth to obtain a (fictitious).
victory (over truth) ?

Entrust all unhappy women to the care of men good and true.

Cut off the miserable fetters of poor weak woman desirous of
worldly happiness

This country will improve, (its) weal and bliss will increase,
sins will go away, if you liberate (widows from their
thraldom.

He who does this will be called the friend of the poor, his
fame will spread in his country and in foreign lands.

He who is an evil-doer and utterly irreligious, *his* fire of
misery will never be removed.

But heaven-born beings rendering help (to the helpless) will
soon attain God's grace.

Poor (innocent) infants are cut off in the womb—cannot see
the light of day with any welcome.

The mother, becoming hopeless, casts the noose of despair
(on the infant) through fear, and with a hardened heart

Burning in the flames (of sorrow) the widow, with her heart.
in distress, weepingly asks for relief.

I, Behram, think, if I had the power, I would save her this
very moment.

(The mention of the poet's name in the last line is usual in
such songs)

D

will not appear at all surprising to those well acquainted with Malabari—for he is, by nature, extremely
sympathetic, and his is not a "painless sympathy with
pain." "When I see a lame person," he once wrote,
"I feel lame for a moment; when a blind person, I feel
blinded. I feel corresponding pain or loss in witnessing
it. When I first look at a leper or other foully diseased
object I feel a shiver, but the feeling passes off, and
I have tended many diseased patients."* We have
seen how quick his mother's hands were unto good, and
there is very little doubt that Malabari inherits his
ready benevolence from her.

In this second part there are numerous other subjects discussed. For example, we have a graphic but
chaste description of what an innocent Hindu girl saw
at a sensual Vaishnava Maharaja's; a touching lament
by a husband who has lost a good wife; an amusing
analysis of the thoughts of the superstitious regarding
the Kali Age; an appeal to Banias to educate their
children; a scathing condemnation of the high-pressure
system pursued in children's schools; besides, several
purely English topics, like the bravery of the English
sailor and our Queen's sorrow on the death of her
Consort. This last is a most spirited piece of composition.

It may be asked why Dr. Wilson named the book
"Niti Vinod" when the bulk of it dealt with other subjects than morality. But the truth is that a profoundly
religious and moral tone pervades the whole work, and
its tendency is certainly to bring home to the reader the
delights of virtue and the miseries of vice. Even

* From a letter.

before he came in contact with Dr. Wilson, Behramji was a "prayerful animal,"* and it was his earnestness, as much as his precocious genius, that made him so attractive to Dr. Wilson. The burden of many of his songs is a simple lesson—"*Do* good," and in various ways, and with considerable originality and freshness, he enforces that,

> "The gods hear men's hands before their lips
> And heed beyond all crying and sacrifice
> Light of things done, and noise of labouring men."

HOW THE 'NITI VINOD' WAS RECEIVED.

The *Niti Vinod* appeared with some capital testimonials. One Hindu scholar certified that "the poetry was without prosodical defects;" another that "the language was natural and the style graceful;" while the Parsi High Priest went into raptures over the "pure Gujarati verses" and stated that they had "no precedent." The book was received by the Vernacular Press generally with equally hearty praise. The *Rast Goftar* welcomed it as the production of the first "genuine poet" among the Parsis, who had expressed his sentiments "in pure Gujarati" and in "sweet and beautiful verses." The *Shamsher Bahadur* was struck most with his "sweet and harmonious versification" and his "deep moral tone." The *Vidya Mitra* wrote: "We are glad to see that, though a Parsi, the author has succeeded in writing such polished and harmonious lines in Gujarati. The different metres seem to us to be faultless in their construction; and most of the lines smooth and graceful. Some passages are really of the highest order.

---

* From a letter.

Some subjects have been most graphically treated; while in some lines the author displays the powers of a painter." The *Gujarat Mitra* was likewise very appreciative. "There is hardly a page," it said, "in which we do not meet with lines which are very good and creditable, and the metre is faultless. Looking to the composition and the language of the verses, one would irresistibly be led to believe that they were the production of a learned Hindu writer; he would hardly think a Parsi capable of such chaste and classical language. We pray that this gentleman may go on making the same laudable use of his pen."

The reviewers in the English papers were no less eulogistic. The book was "an agreeable surprise" to the *Indian Statesman*, and recommended by it "as a fit text to be placed in the hands of students and introduced as a reading book in families." The *Bombay Gazette* noticed that the young poet had "displayed an amount of observation which is seldom to be found in works of native authors," and that he was equally "at home in didactic, humorous and pathetic poetry." The *Times of India* regarded the book as an attempt "to infuse into the Eastern mind something of the lofty tone of thought and feeling which distinguishes the most approved literary productions of the West," and in reviewing the second edition that journal wrote: "These verses display, to great advantage, the author's wonderful command over pure Hindu Gujarati. But that is not their only merit. They evince considerable originality and reflect a lofty tone of moral teaching. We cannot withhold our admiration of Mr. Malabari's success in the line of study he has adopted." To crown all these plaudits of the press two living Gujarati poets welcomed him heartily to their ranks. Kavi Shivlal Dhaneshwar wrote :—" Such wide acquaintance with Gujarati, such beauty of versification, and such a delightful combination of sentiment and imagination would do honour to the pen of an accomplished Hindu poet." And Kavi Dalpatram Dayabhai wrote :—" It is a general belief amongst us that Parsis cannot excel in versification, through the medium of correct and idiomatic Gujarati; but Mr. Malabari's *Niti Vinod* effectually dispels that belief. It will be a proud day for Gujarat, when the odious distinction between Parsi Gujarati and Hindu Gujarati ceases to exist. I concur with the opinions that several competent critics have given of the book, and hope it will meet with greater success than before." There are pieces in the *Niti Vinod* which will live so long as the vernacular of Gujarat endures. Among their special merits may be mentioned a striking originality, both of thought and expression, and a simplicity and spiritual grace in which Gujarati literature appears to be very poor. I believe many of these poems will bear an English translation; they ought certainly to be introduced into the school curriculum.

IN THE BOMBAY SMALL CAUSE COURT.

The *Niti Vinod* was a success,* and one would think Malabari was happy. But his life has been truly

---

* There must have been some critics who could not have found anything good in the book; but I am sorry I have not been able to get at their reviews.

a "pendulum between a smile and a tear," and just when he was drinking in the delicious compliments of the press and of his brother-poets, he found himself summoned to answer a suit in the Court of Small Causes. It was brought by a person who was under deep obligations to Malabari, and who should have been the last to bring it. He had been a teacher at the same school where Malabari was still teaching, and having a large family had often been assisted by Malabari. But he was a nettle who ought not to have been so tenderly treated. He had been made to leave the school, and now filed an action to recover Rs. 200 as commission for the sale of the *Niti Vinod*, for the collection of subscriptions, and for other services rendered in connection with the book, including the revision of the verses themselves. This last count almost maddened our young poet, and, though extremely shy, he resolved to contest the claim. Moreover, Rs. 200 was a large sum, and Malabari following the biblical maxim that the love of money was the root of all evil, and having an itch for giving away which amounted almost to a disease, was unable to pay even one-half of it. Fortunately, the judge was a discerning and patient man, and saw through the plaintiff as he gave his evidence in the witness-box. His witnesses also deserted the plaintiff, when they found the case going against him. The revising charge was withdrawn, and the plaintiff got a decree for Rs. 30, and a reprimand for his sharp practice. The thirty rupees were awarded by the court for service rendered in obtaining subscriptions, a service for which Malabari had offered him Rs. 60

before the case was taken to the court. Thus our author tasted his first and last law-suit, to which the reader of *Gujarat and Gujaratis* is indebted for the very amusing " Scenes in a Small Cause Court."

The Mehtaji, however, had his revenge. He prompted a Hindu paper to repeat the calumny he had withdrawn. Malabari had had a plentiful share of the ills that assail the life of a struggling poet ; he had had toil and want, the garret and a Small Cause Court suit, and he was not to escape the worst of all these ills—envy. He, however, silenced his adversaries by offering to compose as good verses as could be found in the *Niti Vinod*, under any conditions prescribed by them. The challenge was not accepted, and Malabari was left in peace to bring out a second edition, and to publish his *Indian Muse in English Garb*.

" THE INDIAN MUSE IN ENGLISH GARB."

I have said that Malabari when he came to Bombay had some English poems with him in manuscript. To compose verses in a foreign language is no easy feat, but Malabari had natural gifts. He has an ear for rhyme and rhythm which few have. He is extremely responsive to good music, and bad music frets his nerves, and makes him unhappy. He had read a good deal of English poetry, and had his favourites. " Wordsworth," he writes,* " is the favourite of my soul and intellect ; Shelly, Byron and Burns of my heart. Shakespeare and Milton *I admire* most, but there is something savagely practical in the former, and something awfully

---

* In a letter.

stilted in the latter that keeps one from *loving* them quite." Malabari studied the works of these poets and of Tennyson,* but he read many more. English numbers, he found, came to him almost as easily as Gujarati, and so in 1876, he published his *Indian Muse*, and dedicated it to one who had done so much for her sisters in India—Miss Mary Carpenter. Before rushing into print, he showed some specimens of his poetry to Dr. Wilson, whose loss he keenly deplores in the verses headed : "To the memory of one of the noblest friends of India." Dr. Wilson's opinion was that the lines " displayed an uncommonly intimate knowledge of the English language", and were " the outcome of a gifted mind, trained to habits of deep meditation and fresh and felicitous expression." The good doctor also spoke of the author as " a young man of most excellent character and talents, and of rare literary accomplishments." Few knew the young man so well as this venerable scholar. Even in his boyish days, Malabari used often to sing to himself in a meditative spirit, and though he gave up singing after his mother's death, he did not give up meditating. The influence of Dr. Wilson on his character was very great. He was already earnest, but Dr. Wilson made him more so. He was already prayerful, but Dr. Wilson chastened his prayers. The two used at times to pray together, with another young Parsi, and whenever Dr. Wilson was ill or fatigued, he loved to hear his young friends read to him the Psalms of David, and some of Bishop Heber's beautiful

---

* There is a beautiful translation of the song in the " Princess," "Home they brought her warrior dead," in Malabari's *Sarod Ittifak.*

poems.* They had had many religious discussions, and Dr. Wilson had put forth all his learning, eloquence, and zeal to win over his favourite to Christ. And looking back to those days, Malabari often wonders how he escaped becoming a Christian. His main difficulty was, he tells me, the need of a Saviour. He believed in salvation by faith and by work, but did not think the mediation of another absolutely necessary for salvation. I imagine his heart was as much against changing his religion as his understanding. Bunsen places Zoroaster at least 6000 years before Christ, and the oldest Gatha of the Avesta says about this great Prophet—"Good is the thought, good is the speech, good is the work of the pure Zarathushtra," and quotes a saying of his, "I have entrusted my soul to Heaven, and I will teach what is pure so long as I live." A pure, ancient, hereditary creed, with its hallowed associations, its historical grandeur, its touching memories of persecution and tribulation, would naturally have a greater attraction for a poetic mind than a foreign faith. Zoroastrianism, like its sister (some say its mother, and others, its daughter) Vedism, has been debased by later corruptions, but Malabari looked to its essence and not to its accidents. He did not care for ceremonials of any kind, and his real prayer was "to think well, to speak well, and to act well." He bowed to that Truth which includes all creeds and transcends all. He read or recited, five times a day, little gems of thought which are commentaries on the original texts, and the under-

---

* "A dying man to his soul," at page 24 of the *Indian Muse*, was suggested to Malabari, when so employed.

lying sentiment of which is the worship of the Creator through the noblest of His works, like the Sun and the Sea. Malabari is still the prayerful poet he was in 1876. He has still the same habits. He is not an orthodox Parsi, but a primitive Zoroastrian. None, therefore, need feel surprise that he withstood Dr. Wilson's powerful attempts to convert him. His companion and class-brother, Shapurji Dadabhai Bhabha, embraced Christianity after fearful persecutions, and is now a Doctor of Divinity as well as Medicine, practising in London. Shapurji and our Behram were like twin brothers. The latter stood by his friend amid all his trials. " If anything *could* have made me a Christian," Malabari once told me, " it was Shapurji's example." "His faithfulness to Christ and his fortitude were most edifying. Dr. Wilson loved Shapurji as a son, and I myself owe much of Dr. Wilson's kindly regard for Shapurji. I look upon Shapurji's family as my own. His father is one of the worthiest, and yet one of the most unlucky men I have known. "

But though Malabari did not become a Christian in form, he is not one of those who think lightly of Christ, or who take a gloomy view of the work of Christian missionaries. This is what he said about them in replying to a passage in Mr. Wordsworth's letter on Hindu social reform :—

. And how much do we owe to Christian missionaries ? We are indebted to them for the first start in the race of intellectual emancipation. It is to them that we are beholden for some of our most cherished political and social acquisitions. Our very Brahmo Samaja, Arya Samaja and Prarathna Samaja are the offshoots, in one sense, of this beneficent agency. And, apart from its active usefulness, the Christian mission serves as a buffer for the tide of scepticism usually inseparable from intellectual emancipation. At a time when doubt and distrust are taking the place of reasoned inquiry among the younger generation of India, I feel bound to acknowledge in my own person the benefits I have derived from a contact with the spirit of Christianity. But for that holy contact I could scarcely have grown into the staunch and sincere Zoroastrian that I am, with a keen appreciation of all that appeals readily to the intelligence and a reverent curiosity for what appeals to the heart, knowing full well that much of what is mysterious to man is not beneath but beyond the comprehension of a finite being.

A similar generous feeling inspires his poem—"To the Missionaries of Faith" in the *Indian Muse.*

Malabari is himself a missionary. Turn to his poems, turn to his prose, turn to the life he is living; and you feel he is a missionary with a definite mission. The *Indian Muse* has something to say on the celebrated "Fuller Case," on the treatment of Malharao Gaekwar, on the time of famine, on the glories of the West, and on the British character. But the poet is at home when describing the woes of widows, and social tyrannies. He has a stirring poem in imitation of Campbell's " Men of England, " which can only be fully appreciated by those who know what Rajput chivalry, what Aryan "chastity of honour " was in days of yore, and how low their descendants have fallen in these days. His own ideal is a very high one, and he has kept true to it through all his troubles and sad experiences. This appears from the last poem in his book,"Manhood's Dream, " and it forms a fitting conclusion to this chapter. Here it is :—

" O life is but a stagnant sea, a weary trackless main ;
Its waves asphaltic, undisturb'd, the soul with poison
stain.

The glory of good work it is our better part can save ;
I'll rush to glory deathless, then, to glory or the grave !
The ice of silence will the soul to selfish languor freeze ;
While mine is yearning for some work of merit here
  she sees ;
So fly to works of charity and love, my spirit brave !
To glory bear me on thy wings—to glory or the grave !
There's Pleasure luring me to ruin ; I'll ne'er the
  siren heed ;
If once my soul is wreck'd, she's naught but shame
  to wed indeed.
But no ! I'd honest death prefer to being Pleasure's
  knave ;
So up and on to glory, soul !-to glory or the grave !"

CHAPTER III.—MANHOOD.

The *Indian Muse* made Malabari famous, and se-cured him many friends. Professor Wordsworth praised his "skill in versification" and "the sentiments expressed" in his verses. Mr. Gibbs congratulated him "on having produced poems superior to any I have yet seen from the pen of a native author." Mr. E. B. Eastwick, the veteran scholar and Orientalist, "hailed the appearance of a true poet and master-mind in India." William Benjamin Carpenter acknowledged "the tribute of affectionate respect" paid to his sister, and Mr. J. Estlin Carpenter wrote :—

I have often been surprised at the knowledge of the English language and literature displayed by some of your countrymen ; but your verses indicate an even completer mastery, and exhibit

Chapter III.

MANHOOD. ,

How well in thee appears
The constant service of the antique world,
When service sweat for duty, not for meed!
Thou art not for the fashion of these times,
When none will sweat, but for promotion ;
And, having that, do choke their service up,
Even with the having.—SHAKESPEARE'S *As You Like It.*

~~~~~~~~~~

And he, shall he,
Man, her last work, who seem'd so fair,
   Such splendid purpose in his eyes,
   Who roll'd the psalm to wintry skies,
Who built him fanes of fruitless prayer.

Who trusted God was love indeed,
   And love Creation's final law,
   Tho' Nature, red in tooth and claw,
With ravine shriek'd against his creed.

Who loved, who suffer'd countless ills,
   Who battled for the True, the Just,
   Be blown about the desert dust,
Or seal'd within the iron hills ?—

TENNYSON'S *In Memoriam,*

Thronging through the cloud-rift, whose are they, the faces
Faint revealed, yet sure divined, the famous ones of old ?
" What"—they smile—" our names, our deeds so soon erases
Time upon his tablet where Life's glory lies enrolled ?
Was it for mere fool's play, make-believe and mumming,
So we battled it like men, not boy-like sulked or whined,
Each of us heard clang God's ' come,' and each was coming :
Soldiers all, to forward face, not sneaks to lag behind !

BROWNING'S Ferishtah's Fancies.

Lives of great men all remind us,
    We can make our lives sublime,
And, departing, leave behind us,
    Footprints on the sands of time.—LONGFELLOW.

a quite remarkable power of fulfilling the numerous and complex requirements of poetical composition. * *

Your lines to Wordsworth prove that you have found your way into the secret of perhaps the deepest poetic influence of this century, and I rejoice to learn that his profound teachings thus make their way into wholly new modes of thought and feeling with penetrating sympathy.

Throughout your verses I recognise the same high tone of aspiration which your dedication leads your readers to expect; and I heartily congratulate you on this early and rich promise of poetic skill.

Miss Florence Nightingale was touched by many of the pieces and ended her letter with a blessing—

May God bless your labours! May the Eternal Father bless India, bless England, and bring us together as one family, doing each other good. May the fire of His love, the sunshine of His countenance, inspire us all!

The late lamented Lord Shaftesbury bore witness "to the excellence of the work, the high character of its poetry, and its sentiments." Mr. Bright read the book with interest, and wrote:—

Though you write in our language, I note that you abound in Oriental compliment.* I thank you too for your good wishes for myself. I fear it is not possible for any Englishman to do much for your unhappy country. The responsibility of England with regard to India is too great—it cannot adequately be discharged.

Max Müller acknowledged a copy with the following letter:—

I am much obliged to you for your kind present. It is certainly highly creditable to you to be able to write English verse. To me also English is an acquired language, but I have never attempted more than English prose. However, whether we write English verse or English prose, let us never forget that the best service we can ren-

---

* This applies only to the first three or four poems welcoming the Prince of Wales to India, &c.

der is to express our truest Indian and German thoughts in English, and thus to act as honest interpreters between nations that ought to understand each other much better than they do at present.

...... Depend upon it, the English public, at least the better part of it, likes a man who is what he is. The very secret of the excellence of English literature lies in the independence, the originality and truthfulness of English writers....... It is in the verses where you feel and speak like a true Indian that you seem to me to speak most like a true poet.

Accept my best thanks and good wishes, and believe me

Yours Sincerely,

F. MAX MÜLLER.

The Poet Laureate also sent a most encouraging little note.

My dear Sir,

I return my best thanks for your "INDIAN MUSE IN ENGLISH GARB." It is interesting, and more than interesting, to see how well you have managed in your English garb.

I wish I could read the poems which you have written in your own vernacular; for, 1 doubt not they deserve all the praise bestow'd upon them by the newspapers.

Believe me

Your far-away but sincere friend,

A. TENNYSON.

The Crown Princess of Germany and Her Majesty the Queen-Empress communicated to him their gracious thanks, and the Princess Alice, through her Secretary, wrote as follows:—

Dear Sir,

H. R. H. The Grand-Duchess of Hesse has ordered me to express Her Royal Highness' most sincere thanks for the copy of your "INDIAN MUSE."

Her Royal Highness has read a part of the poems with deep interest; and it afforded Her Royal Highness great pleasure to see a foreigner write English with so much taste and feeling, and the expression of such loyal sentiments.

Her Royal Highness equally appreciates the motives which prompted you to dedicate to Miss Carpenter the work which Her Royal Highness accepts with the greatest pleasure.

Believe me to be, dear Sir,
Yours very Sincerely,
BARON KNESEBECK.

All these honours brought our poet into great prominence. Sir Cowasji Jehanghir Readymoney had become his friend long before the publication of the *Indian Muse*, and by him and by Dr. Wilson, Malabari had been introduced to the highest functionaries as well as to influential citizens. Had the young poet been ambitious or sordid-minded, he could have easily made a name for himself and won a fortune in other walks than those of literature or journalism. But Malabari prized his independence, and was proud of his poverty. He lived altogether by his pen, and has up to date faithfully adhered to his vocation. He contributed to newspapers and periodicals, and cultivated his genius for poetry. He was always at the disposal of the poor and the aggrieved, and spent no small portion of his time in writing memorials and appeals for the latter, with a tact and ability which seldom failed with the authorities. His reputation as an adviser and interpreter brought him into close acquaintance with some of the Native States, but he was often cheated by unprincipled officers in their service. Once he went to a State on the sea-coast during the monsoons, at the risk of his life. The Parsi Diwan had implored him to come and promised him a large sum for a representation to Government; but this worthy did not scruple to trick him by giving him an empty bag supposed to contain currency notes. Malabari was so trustful and so careless in money matters, that it was not until he reached home and opened the bag that he discovered the fraud. He wrote to the Diwan, and the Diwan made an apology and begged for time. Malabari replied by sending him back the promising letters and releasing him from all obligations. He has done this in several other cases. If his constituents had been honest he would have been today worth at least half a *lakh*.

MALABARI AS A JOURNALIST.

Early in 1876 a couple of enterprising schoolboys and a clerk in the Bombay Municipality started a cheap weekly under the name of the *Indian Spectator*. Malabari used now and then to assist them. Later on he was made a co-editor with another friend who went in for politics, while Malabari was all for social subjects. There is a humorous account of this undertaking and its termination in *Gujarat and the Gujaratis*. While this strange literary partnership continued, Malabari fell in with a proposal of Mr. Martin Wood, who had then left the *Times of India*, to start a new paper devoted to the advocacy of the rights of Native States and of the masses at large. He had been introduced to this veteran publicist by Sir Cowasji Jehanghir, after the publication of the *Indian Muse*. Mr. Wood took very kindly to him and gave him his journalistic training. He became now Mr. Wood's coadjutor, and at his own expense undertook in March 1878 a journey to Gujarat and Kathiawar, in order to interest Native Princes in the enterprise, and to secure their support. *Gujarat and the Gujaratis* was the result of this tour, besides about Rs. 2,000 in cash, and promises of some Rs. 15,000 more, which were never fulfilled. Mr. Wood started the *Bombay Review*, a small weekly of the size of the *Pall Mall*, in which many of the descriptions of places and people that are to be found in *Gujarat and the Gujaratis* were first published. The Editor set a high value on Malabari's writings, and paid him at the rate of Rs. 20 to Rs. 25 a column. Malabari has had offers of the same rate of remuneration from other proprietors, but has seldom or never contributed for money. The *Bombay Review*, in spite of the great abilities and experience of its conductor, was financially a failure, and after a couple of years ceased to exist. The *Indian Spectator*, too, had had its struggles, and eventually the proprietors became so sick cf it as to be glad to sell the plant as well as the goodwill to a Bori, who some time after sold the goodwill to Malabari for Rs. 25 ! Thus, about the beginning of 1880, Malabari entered upon his journalistic career with plenty of brains, but a plentiful lack of the sinews of journalistic enterprise—money. In fact, he would not have undertaken the task but for the promise of pecuniary aid from a wealthy and enlightened Hindu gentleman. The two entered into a contract, the one to supply brains, the other money. The profits were to be shared in equal proportion. But here arose a difficulty. To make the story short, Malabari was startled by a proposal to send his sub-editor twice a week to the Seth for instructions. On objecting to the proposal, our journalist was curtly told : "You see, two men have to ride one horse. One of

E

us must ride behind." "Well," replied Malabari as laconically, "I am not going to be *that one;*" and without further parley he left the astonished sowcar. Unfortunately, he had borrowed one month's expenses in advance from the partner that was to be. But he sold a trinket and paid off the debt. "For the first few months," writes Malabari, "I struggled with the *Spectator* only to show that money was not everything. It was a cruel hardship, and there were moments when I almost felt the Walpolian theory to be correct. But I struggled on, writing, editing, correcting proofs, at times folding and posting copies and even distributing them in town, going the round in a buggy with the driver to deliver the copies as instructed by me." Malabari had started on his tour with borrowed funds. He never had recourse to professional lenders, but though his creditors were his friends, the money had of course to be repaid. The *Indian Spectator* added to his embarrassments. It had hardly fifty *bona-fide* subscribers. Only a couple of ornaments were left, and these were now sold to pay at least the interest due to the clamorous creditors and to support the paper. There were many to whom Malabari had given pecuniary help; some who had used him as their security for loans which he had to liquidate. None of them came to his aid, and it was at this time that Malabari realised fully why prudence was counted one of the cardinal virtues. His devoted wife and children (he had a daughter and a son now) shared his privations. But there is a silver lining to every cloud, and although Malabari had found many for whom he had toiled and even borrowed, ungrateful, he came across one as unselfish as himself at this crisis of his life. This was the Parsi gentleman to whom the *Sarod Ittifak* is dedicated, and who acted like a brother. He helped the young journalist on hearing from a friend of the struggles he was undergoing. " Though he lent me the money, he showed as if he were borrowing it of me," writes Malabari. Some years after, the money was thrust upon him by force ; and he had to take it back, though with great reluctance and with even bitterness of feeling, as Malabari was unwilling to keep it when he no longer needed it.

Malabari, before he was relieved, was in a very pessimistic mood. He thought he was unfit for town-life and had better be in the jungles. But he could not retire on nothing a year, and there was his family to be maintained. Moreover, there was a vast field of usefulness open to him in his new career. He had taken up the *Indian Spectator* to make it " the people of India's own paper."

He was " a people's man " himself, and understood the poor—the great majority of the nation—as very few have understood them. He could also do justice to the acts and motives of the rulers, being in touch with official opinion. He wanted to be a political, social, and even religious reformer. There were moments when he thought his songs and his poetry would be a better lever, a better organ for this purpose than a newspaper. But the *Indian Spectator* was alive, and like Frankenstein, refused to die. The little paper that was a rag in 1879, after a creditable early career, rose into fame, and compelled its editor to remain in harness. To kill the work of one's own hands is very much like killing one's own children. That has been Malabari's feeling at least about the *Spectator ;* otherwise, I am afraid, he would have preferred the obscurity of a village with his muse than the celebrity of a city life with its attendant evils.

The *Bombay Review,* shortly before its surcease, spoke very favourably of the new journalist.

"The editor," it wrote, "is peculiarly fitted for being a trustworthy interpreter between rulers and ruled, between the indigenous and immigrant branches of the great Aryan race. It is easy to see that he thoroughly understands the mental and moral characteristics of those two great divisions of the Indian community, not only as presented in Bombay, but in other provinces in India. We have always felt confidence in the sincerity and independence of its editor. His knowledge of the various castes and classes of society in Western India is full and exact, while in aptitude for discussion of social questions he displays a discrimination and aptness in picturesque description and a genuine humour, sufficiently rare."

When it is noted that the *Indian Spectator* has often had to try conclusions with Anglo-Indian and English contemporaries the compliments paid to it by these journals may be better appreciated.

The *Indian Mirror* praised the " brilliant and pithy paragraphs" of the new paper, and the *Hindoo Patriot* " its refreshing and trenchant style, " and " the force and independence " of its views. The *Amrita Bazar Patrika* passed even a higher encomium :

In wit, humour and satire, and in the complete mastery of the English language, our contemporary stands pre-eminent. His smart and playful sayings, so full of meaning, pass current in the country. Week after week the columns of our contemporary are filled with the treasures of a rich and versatile mind.

The *Indian Statesman* called it in 1882 "the best paper in India." The *Pioneer* called it "the ablest native paper in the Bombay Presidency." The *Englishman* bore testimony to its "idiomatic English" and its "bold trenchant style." The *Indian Daily News* eulogized its remarkable ability and fairness.

"In politics," said this paper, "its tone is moderate, and it is thus a very safe guide to native readers, its criticisms having mostly a practical turn, and showing a ready acceptance of facts as they stand. Looking at its very varied and often clever contents, the *Spectator* is a marvel of cheapness. It often gives a sketch of some typical class or caste, which, by reason of the special information it affords, as well as by its piquant style, is alone worth the small subscription to the paper for the whole year."

The London *Times* in 1882 wrote :—

A considerable portion of the English Press of India is written by natives ; and many of these so-called Anglo-Native papers are written with great ability and in excellent idiomatic English. Such are the *Indian Spectator* of Bombay, the *Hindoo Patriot* and the *Indian Mirror* of Calcutta.

The *Academy* considered the *Indian Spectator* "no unworthy rival of its London namesake," and *Allen's Indian Mail* spoke of it as

a journal representing in the highest degree not only the intelligence but also the moderation and liberality of educated natives.

The *Revue Critique* of France in 1883 wrote as follows :—

The *Indian Spectator* has rapidly assumed a foremost place in the Indian Press and is not wanting in interest for a European reader, although unluckily it *comments* on the events of the week more than it *shows* them. Its language is remarkable for its brilliant strokes, its vigour, and *pungency* of style, and is very *idiomatic*.

And the *L'Economiste Française* in 1885 wrote :—

The Indian Press, notwithstanding its infancy, counts in its ranks men remarkable as much for their abilities as writers as for their sagacity and courtesy. In support of what we say it will be sufficient to cite the Editor-in-chief of the *Indian Spectator* of Bombay. By persevering efforts he has to-day become one of the most influential men of the true Indian liberal party which, while maintaining the general tendencies of the policy of Lord Ripon, is not slow to recognise that this latter sometimes erred through excess of liberalism in wishing to move too fast. This political party, which does the greatest honour to the good sense of the Indian race, demands earnestly the gradual enfranchisement of their country.

The fame of the paper travelled even to America, for in 1883 the *New York Sun* said :—

There is many an American newspaper written less correctly than the *Indian Spectator;* and there is probably not a British scholar living who could use any of the Indian vernaculars with the ease and idiomatic precision displayed by Mr. Malabari in dealing with the English tongue.

The highest officials in India have recognized the merits of the journal. Lord Ripon admired it, and Sir E. Baring wrote :—

I always read your paper with interest for two reasons—first, because it represents the interests of the poorer classes ; secondly, because it is opposed to class and race antagonism. The last point is especially important in this country.

The Hon'ble Sir Auckland Colvin, his successor, called it some time ago " the leading native journal," and in a resolution of the Government of Bombay it has been styled " the foremost native paper in the Bombay Presidency." General Sir LeGrand Jacob, Sir Erskine Perry, Sir George Birdwood, Colonel Robert

D. Osborne, Sir Arthur (now Lord) Hobhouse, and others also warmly praised the paper for its high character and its ability. But what perhaps Malabari prizes most of all is a letter from the late lamented George Aberigh Mackay (Sir Ali Baba) in which he wrote :—

I have read a number of your paragraphs and short sketches with the greatest interest and pleasure ; they have point and humour and are charmingly expressed. I heartily wish every success to the *Indian Spectator.*

Thus the *Indian Spectator* has grown to be one of the ablest public journals in the country, certainly the most influential Native journal. Its voice penetrates into the Councils of the Empire. The secret of its success lies mainly in its rigid impartiality between class and class, as also between the rulers and the ruled. It may be mentioned that in conducting the paper Malabari was valiantly supported, till lately, by one of his intimate friends and advisers, Mr. Dinsha Edulji Wacha. Mr. Wacha contributed some of the most notable articles in the *Spectator*, displaying an amount of political and economical study, and an aptitude for thinking which are most creditable to him. "But for Dinsha," writes Malabari, "I would have been nowhere, and so also the *I.S.* He not only gave us most valuable literary assistance, but brought us more than once pecuniary help from friends as disinterested as himself. My own money affairs are even now managed entirely by Dinsha."

MALABARI AS A TOURIST.

The *Indian Spectator* did not absorb all the energy of its editor. He was very fond of leading a kind of

Bohemian life at least for a month in a year, and had his tours. This is how he describes his peculiar system of travelling.

I am now and then asked by European friends how often I have been to England, and how long I have stayed there altogether. And when I protest that I have never been out of India, my friends look at me in blank astonishment. The fact is, I have my own ideas of travel, as more or less of everything else. The first tour I remember having made was round grand-mother's kitchen. Thence I transferred my attention to the front-yard of the house, thence to the street, the neighbouring street, the whole suburb of Nanpura, and the surrounding suburbs—Rustampura, Salabatpura, Gopipura, and many others ; next the Camp and the villages beyond Umra and Dumas, and so on. The climbing of trees and roofs in search of paper kites was another round of useful tours. (Kite-flying is one of the best Indian sports, and I am sorry to find it discouraged. I think it is an aid to the sight, and it undoubtedly steadies the hand, and sharpens presence of mind). Well, then, next to climbing of trees and roofs, swimming or fording the Tapti, and running over to Bhatha, Rander, Adajan and other *gaums,** was also a means of touring. My early local tours were often extended to Udna, famous for toddy, and some miles from Nanpura. My last long tour from Surat was a walking match to Nowsari when poor Mr. Rustomji Jamsetji gave his savoury and succulent *malida†* feast. From Surat and its districts I have passed on to Gujarat generally, and from Gujarat, of course, to Kattyawar and Kutch. I have seen much of India during the last seven years, but Gujarat and Kattyawar I know best. Much of these two provinces I have done on foot and with my eyes open. I know so much about them, that if I were to sell my knowledge at retail price, so much for the page, I think I could make an honest penny out of it. And I tell you again, my dear respectable Bombay reader, that much of my experience is the result of good hard tramping. If you want a real guide, one who would make you profit by your travels, consult me. One peculiarity about my travelling is that I seldom return the same way I have gone.

* Villages.

† A confection made of flour, ghee, sugar, and spices.

This is a somewhat inconvenient habit, but it has grown upon me, and I think, on the whole, I have gained by it. I hope one day to finish India from end to end ; and then, who knows that I may not go to Europe, America and the rest of the world ? Less likely things have happened.

But whether I go to Europe or not, I will never give up my habit. In study, as in travel, I wish to begin at the very beginning, and to proceed by slow stages, gaining something at every stage, and that something such as to be of immediate practical use on the next stage. This is the best way of travelling and studying. Your globe-trotter will laugh at my antiquated method, but he cannot deny its advantages. When you travel or study by degrees, every fresh step or item of knowledge is a keen enjoyment. You are prepared to receive it, and thus received, your knowledge will fructify. But when knowledge is thrust upon you without previous discipline, that is, without your being made fit for it, it will be inert and unleavened. What is the use of visiting foreign countries when you know nothing of your own ? When you go to Europe, ignorant of your own national life, you will miss those thousand points of comparison and contrast, those thousand shades of difference, those thousand beauties and blemishes that modern European civilisation presents. At the best, you will *look at* things, not *see* or *see through* them. Knowledge is best acquired, take my word for it, by the comparative method. And what will you compare your new acquirements with, when there are not half a dozen home ideas in that empty head of yours ? You go to see the Windsor Palace and are lost in admiration at the sight. Have you seen Agra ? Had you seen some of the architectural glories of your own country, you might at any rate have controlled your faculty for admiration. You might have been quite at liberty to admire the modern structure, but at the same time you could have seen what beauty it has which the palaces of India do not possess, and *vice versâ*. The same is the case with study. If you learn Greek after learning Sanskrit, Persian or Arabic, you will enjoy the process, recognize the advantage of one over another, and though you may admire the European classic as much as you like, you will have no reason to be ashamed of your own. I honour you for your desire to examine the arts, sciences and philosophies of the West, but you cannot do this with advantage to yourself and the world, unless you have already made yourself familiar with the national systems. The worst result of this method of travel and study that I am complaining of is, that it gives a man poor ideas of everything in his country, in proportion to the exaggerated notions he imbibes about other countries. This is a charge from which very few of our England-returned men can escape. It makes me sick to hear a man rave about this thing or that 10,000 miles away, when a much better, perhaps the original thing, is lying unnoticed in his own land. Bah! I hate your Anglicised Aryan.*

It must be admitted that no Anglicised Aryan has yet produced a work like *Gujarat and the Gujaratis* or the charming sketches, so brimful of humour, which Malabari sent to his paper, when with Max Müller's "Hibbert Lectures" on his brain, he went about collecting funds for translating them into the principal vernaculars of India. He travels with a small quantity of luggage, but always with a chest of homœopathic medicines. In 1878 while at Wadwan, he was snatched from the jaws of death by a Hindu practitioner, Dr. Thakordas, who gave him his first lessons in homœopathy, and ever since Malabari has gone in strongly for it, and done his best to popularize it in Bombay. He was instrumental in starting the largest Homœopathic Charitable Dispensary in that city, and is its Honorary Secretary. The medicine chest is extremely useful to him in his travels. It has often served to give relief not only to him, but to many a fellow-traveller and to many a patient in the places visited by him. Malabari on tour is at his very best. A keen lover of nature, with observant eyes and a sympathetic heart, he finds true poetry in the homeliest

* *Indian Spectator*, 1-7-83, p. 411.

scenes and every-day incidents. Many of his sketches are bright little idylls in prose, not unworthy even of Wordsworth. *Gujarat and the Gujaratis* has won great fame, but to my mind, the free and easy "round-about papers" which are to be found in the *Indian Spectator* of 1882 and 1883 are far better. They abound with sparkling and incisive sayings, witty anecdotes, humorous comparisons and charming observations. One example of these last might be quoted. At Rutlam, Malabari put up at the Musafir Bunglow, and he writes :—
" Musafir Bunglow was a few yards from the Dharamsala. Khansama an old man. I have never known a young Khansama in these parts. The explanation is that when a Saheb cannot afford to pension his old butler, he provides a place for him in this manner. The Khansama had a large family of children and grand-children, all ready to serve ; but he kept a very spare table—only curry rice for breakfast, the town being so far. Had to make shift with milk. About 2 p.m., came Khansama's little grand-daughter, with broom and duster. She moved sofas and lifted chairs with an agility that would horrify Bombay girls of twice her age. ' What is your name, child ?' ' Pyari' —Darling. What a name ! ' Whose darling are you, *betta ?*' * 'Ajisaheb† I am God's darling, my mother's darling, my father's darling, whose else ? ' So God before mother and father. Not bad for a girl who has never attended the Alexandra School.‡ Whatever their failings, the Mahomedans are remarkable for their

---

* Child.
† Oh Sir.
‡ At Bombay for girls.

ready wit, and for those amiable accomplishments which Hindus and Parsis find it so difficult to acquire or exhibit. Pyari sang one or two little songs at my request, which were decidedly more intelligible than the pathetic buffalo-song I had at Indore." *

It is this familiarity with the poor, and his heart-felt sympathy with them, that endear him to the reader.

MALABARI AS A LITERARY MAN.

After suffering "twitches, aches, swellings, rawness, thirst and hunger" during a twenty-six hours journey by a Dák Tonga to Kolhapur, Malabari wrote :—"Motion is the poetry of life, and so long as you are within an inch of suicide, you can enjoy motion. And much good may it do you." I don't know whether it did him much good, but I have no doubt that he enjoyed writing poetry as much as living it and walking it. In 1878 he published his *Wilson Virah, in memoriam* of Dr. Wilson, and dedicated it to the Revd. Mr. Taylor. Its contents may be described in the words of the *Bombay Gazette :* "It opens with a pathetic lament of Saraswati,† and its interest is throughout maintained with great power. Under the heading Satishiromani‡ is given a picture of the amiable and accomplished wife, Margaret Wilson. He then tenderly touches the period of Dr. Wilson's marriage, and recounts the united efforts of Dr. and Mrs. Wilson for the good of the people. Much of what follows is taken up by a spirited descrip-

---

* *Indian Spectator,* 5-8-83, p. 491.

† The Hindu goddess of learning.

‡ The best of virtuous wives.

tion of Dr. Wilson's services to Bombay—his visit to Scotland, his return, illness and death. Then follows a series of eulogistic verses devoted to the enumeration of Dr. Wilson's erudition and personal merits." " Altogether," concluded the *Gazette*, "*Wilson Virah* is a remarkable work of its kind, and we hope that the setting forth of this great man's life in a captivating form, and in the author's own vernacular, may not be lost upon all who may read it."

Wilson Virah is mainly lyrical, and it moves its reader to feel keenly the sorrow of the poet at the loss of his friend and benefactor, and to appreciate fully the worth and virtue of the great philanthropist and *savant*. " Dr. Wilson was the patron of thousands of the poor, the supporter of the unfortunate indigent, the advocate of the people, the adviser of the State."* Malabari had enjoyed his friendship for three years, and could do justice to his exemplary life in all its manifold relations. The result was a work occupying a unique position in Gujarati literature, as it was the very first which gave an attractive picture of a true Christian with almost an unapproachable standard of duty, a marvellous amount of solid learning, a genuine modesty, and a rare sense of self-sacrifice. It was received by the Press with a chorus of compliments which were certainly not undeserved.† Malabari's next

---

Rast Goftar.

† " The language of *Wilson Virah*," wrote the *Jam-e-Jamshed*, " is simpler and more racy than of *Niti Vinod*, and its original thoughts, descriptive power, and genuine poetic expression reflect credit on the author's genius." " His readers," wrote the *Gujarat Mitra*, " are not only loving Parsis, but admiring Hindus. And no wonder. For Mr. Malabari's language is not only pure—it

attempt was in English verse. It was a series of sonnets, in memory of the late Princess Alice, in which he
drew a noble picture of her womanly excellence with a
" pathos and sympathy very warm and deep." He
received the following appreciative acknowledgment
from Her Majesty the Queen-Empress :—

Captain Edwards presents his compliments to Mr. Behramji
M. Malabari, and begs to inform him that he is commanded to
acknowledge the receipt of the sonnets which accompanied his letter
of the 7th instant. They have been laid before the Queen. Her
Majesty sincerely appreciates the very kind expression of sympathy
conveyed in Mr. Malabari's letter and thanks him for his condolence
on the death of her dear daughter, the Princess Alice, Grand
Duchess of Hesse.

Osborne, 30th January 1879.

" This," wrote the *Bombay Gazette*, " is a great
compliment to a young Parsee author, and will prove
a stimulus to him to assiduously cultivate the great
talent which he undoubtedly possesses, and strive to
achieve greater triumphs."

The Calcutta *Statesman* wrote in the same strain.
" This is a great compliment to the poet's genius and
character. From what has been written by Mr.
Malabari, and from what has been written of him, we
believe him to be a genuine poet ; and his writings
certainly evince all the earnestness and enthusiasm
of a poetical temperament. The youthful poet and
journalist has our best wishes for his future success."

---

is the purest of the pure." " His language is very pure and
simple, his poetry is very sweet and readable," wrote the *Shamsher
Bahadur*. " Mr. Malabari's poetry is so touching and impressive
that we are tempted to read it over and over again. His works
are the ornaments of our libraries."

The *Madras Athenæum*, the *Madras Mail*, and several other papers noticed the sonnets very favourably, and the Calcutta *Englishman* in its issue of April 5, 1879, had these generous words about him :—

He is, we understand, a constant contributor to English newspapers and periodicals; and his writings are characterised by great felicity of diction and vigour of expression. He takes keen interest in the moral and social progress of his countrymen; and his earnest and manly endeavours in that direction, as also in faithfully interpreting the relations of India to England, ought to be appreciated by both countries. Such men are all too few in this country.

In 1881, Malabari published his *Sarod-i Ittifak*, and dedicated it to his "dear Jehangir," the friend who had helped him in sore need. It contains a number of beautiful songs. The *Gujarati*, a critical Hindu weekly, wrote rapturously, of " the best harmony and the best poetical spirit " it displayed, and thus dilated on its merits.

When it is seen that many of these verses were written some fifteen years ago, it will be granted that Mr. Malabari was born with all the powers of a first-rate Poet. The fire of Religion, the aspirations of Love, the strengthening of Virtue, the yearning after Friendship, and contempt of this false World......these subjects have been treated in spontaneous language and in metres that could be rendered into music......What heart will not overflow with enthusiasm and delight by a perusal of the dramatic romance, *Pakdaman* (Lady Chastity) and *Shah Narges* (*Prince Narcissus*) ?......The lines on Fortune may adorn the Musician's art and may breathe hope into those who are discontented with their lot. *Bioga Bilap* and *Prabhu Prarthna* will prove refreshing to two intoxicated souls—the love-intoxicated and the faith-intoxicated......These noble lines will work powerfully upon the singer as well as the hearer...... In short, the highest forms of Poetry abound in these verses, and they are sure to fascinate the student of Nature with their deep meditative spirit like that of Wordsworth or Milton. The work is got up in the best style, contains the highest thoughts and the finest poetic expressions, is dedicated to some excellent friend "Jehangir" —an admirable work altogether, tending to do credit to the author and to strengthen the powers of Friendship.

The *Deshi Mitra*, the *Gujarat Mitra*, the *Jami Jamshed*, the *Dnyan Vardhak*, and several others wrote almost as admiringly. The language of *Niti Vinod* and *Wilson Virah* was what is called Sanskrit Gujarati ; that of the *Sarod* in many pieces was Persian Gujarati, and the little work contained some *ghazals* (odes) after the Persian model, and also some pieces in Hindi. The book was financially a greater success than either the *Niti Vinod* or the *Wilson Virah*.

MAX MÜLLER'S HIBBERT LECTURES IN THE VERNACULARS
OF INDIA.

In 1882 came out the first of a series of translations of Max Müller's celebrated Hibbert Lectures on the Origin and Growth of Religion as illustrated by the Religions of India. In 1880 Malabari had undertaken to bring out this series after several Indian scholars who had been invited by Max Müller to translate the lectures into one or two only of the vernaculars had declined the honour. The purpose of the Lectures was thus explained by Max Müller in a letter to Malabari, dated Oxford, February 2, 1882.

" As I told you on a former occasion, my thoughts while writing these lectures were far more frequently with the people of India than with my audience in Westminster Abbey. I wanted to tell those few at least whom I might hope to reach in English what the true *historical* value of their ancient religion is, as looked upon, not from an exclusively European or Christian, but from an *historical* point of view. I wished to warn them against two dangers, that of undervaluing or despising the ancient national religion, as is done so often by your half-Europeanised youths, and that of overvaluing it and interpreting it as it was never meant to be interpreted—of which you may see a painful instance in Dayananda Sarasvati's labours on the Veda. Accept the Veda as an ancient *historical* document, containing thoughts in accordance with the character of an ancient and simple-minded race of men, and you will be able to admire it and to retain some of it, particularly the teaching of the Upanishads, even in these modern days. But discover in it steam-engines and electricity and European philosophy and morality, and you deprive it of its true character, you destroy its real value, and you break the historical continuity that ought to bind the present to the past. Accept the past as a reality, study it and try to understand it, and you will then have less difficulty in finding the right way towards the future."

Why Malabari considered the translation of these Lectures a necessity was interestingly explained by him in the following maiden speech delivered · by ¦him at Jeypore on May 5, 1882, at a meeting presided over by Major Jacob. The speech is well worth reading, and I therefore make no apology for reproducing it :—

I must thank you in the beginning, Major Jacob and gentlemen, for your interest in the passing visitor, or, it may be, in his project. That interest is implied by your kindly presence here this evening. It may be as well, gentlemen, to tell you here that I am

F

not going to give you a lecture or an address; all that I have agreed to do is to make a general statement before you of matters connected with my scheme of translations. I am not given to speaking in public, and am opposed to it on principle. My idea is, that a young man, and a young woman too, for that matter, are best judged by silence. Silence is golden in their case. I have always acted up to this principle, gentlemen, and if I deviate from it now, it is to show to you that I may stop at no sacrifice in popularising my project. I hope this may be the last time, as it is the first, when I have to address a public meeting. I assure you, gentlemen, that if any of you were to write to a friend at Bombay and tell him of my perpetration this evening, it would be taken either as a hoax, or as one of those phenomena which now and then tax human credulity. (Laughter.)

Max Müller's theory of Language and Religion I may place before you in a line. Language, he thinks, has arisen out of four or five hundred roots or germs. These roots have been developing in number and in strength since the beginning, with the result that the human race possesses this day so many different and copious forms of speech. Religion, Max Müller thinks, may be gradual development or elaboration of Sense and Reason into Faith, that is, the power to comprehend the Infinite. Gentlemen, you will observe that there is nothing gross or revolting in this view, whatever may be our estimate of its value. This is called the theory of Evolution, or, what I would call by preference, the theory of Historical Development. You will forthwith see, gentlemen, that my little scheme too, which I have the honour of submitting to your consideration, is the result of a series of evolutions. It is now seven years since I published a book of Gujarati verse. It was well received, among others, by my venerated and all-worthy friend, the late Dr. Wilson. The main feature of the book was that in it the author had attempted to infuse the spirit and tone of some of the most approved literary productions of the West. Here I am quoting the *Times of India*. Well then, gentlemen, you see that this infusion of something of the modern Western thought into Gujarati verse marked the beginning of my literary career. Some time after I published a little volume of English verse. That book, though a very indifferent performance, proved a blessing in its way. Gentlemen, it brought me acquainted with some of the nob'est Englishmen and Englishwomen. The Earl of Shaftesbury, Miss Nightingale, Tennyson, Gladstone, Max Müller, Le Grand Jacob, Erskine Perry and many others wrote to me approving, suggesting, correcting, and advising. It is no business of mine, gentlemen, to tell you how a local critic decried our ambitious young versifier! Take that as granted! Many of the English worthies sent me their works in return; and it was then that I began to realise what doing public good was like! (Cheers.) Gentlemen, if there are any saints treading God's earth, we may fairly take that venerable nobleman, noble in birth and in life and conversation, Lord Shaftesbury, and such incomparable Englishwomen as Florence Nightingale and Mary Carpenter, to be such. (Hear, hear.) The other notables you know better than I do, except, perhaps, General Sir Le Grand Jacob, whose nephew and heir here has done me the honour of presiding on this occasion; and Sir Erskine Perry, whose death only last week all India deplores and will ever deplore. Their enthusiasm of humanity was something phenomenal, gentlemen: but India was their first and best love; it was the object of their constant, lifelong love. (Applause.) But I must not wander. Well, gentlemen, some of my English verses were liked, because therein I had expressed myself as an *Indian* thinker. I was true to myself and my country. Pray observe, gentlemen, that in my Gujarati verse I had tried to introduce some element of Western thought—in my English verse I introduced more or less of purely Indian interest. In this fact, good friends, you may trace the germ of my theory, my pet theory,— that the means thus silently suggested are among the best calculated for a true and lasting union between West and East. Max Müller seems to have grasped this idea, though in me it was lying crude and inert. He wrote to me very kindly, and sent me a copy of his Hibbert Lectures. A perusal of his letters and his Lectures breathed life into that inert idea of mine, and made it a definite tangible entity. My latent purpose was roused, and I longed to realise it. The Hibbert Lectures came as a godsend to me! You all know who and what Max Müller is. In our parts we call him a *Muni*, a *Rishi*, an inspired sage. Gentlemen, the *Rast Goftar* calls Max Müller a prophet. I dare say there is some amiable exaggeration in that; but you will grant, that the man's

intellect is luminous; that his powers of investigation and expression are equally marvellous. At times one feels that that
man almost penetrates the mysteries of our life and birth ! (Cheers.)
Then, he possesses keen catholic sympathies. He is as much in
request with the Archbishop of Canterbury as with the Hottentot
priest. He had laboured all his life to bring about a union amongst
nations. That union has long been aimed at. A marriage between
East and West was arranged even before the days of the illustrious
William Jones. Even the silver wedding is gone and past. In
that work of union you trace the hand of a higher power than of
man. Modern Indian history teaches you that. But I may say
that Max Müller and his contemporaries have contributed largely to
bringing to the surface the practical results of that process of, let us
hope, progressive union. By his *Rig-Veda Sanhita*, and other
works Max Müller has given new birth, so to say, to Sanskrit : he
has resuscitated, I say he has helped to regenerate, the language
and literature of our land. (Loud cheers.) He has his faults, too,
I allow. You often wish that a man in his commanding position
could be a little more decided, a little more assertive. But,
worthy critics, let me tell you that the more a man knows, the
more ignorant he will feel; knowledge does not breed confidence
so much as ignorance does, believe me. And thus where you
and I will blurt out what we feel to be the truth, this man will halt
and hesitate and discriminate.

For these reasons, and others, I felt that the Hibbert Lectures
were just the thing for me to begin with. In these splendid dis-
sertations the author gives us back our own, modernised, if I may
so call it, and spiritualised. We badly want "character" in our
modern vernaculars. Here you have as much character and originality as you may wish for. You will readily grant that, by reason
of his special study, Max Müller is best fitted of all his contemporaries for a work of this nature. And let me tell you, gentlemen,
that he is decidedly better qualified than the best of our Indian
scholars, because he is unbiassed and disinterested. (Hear, hear.)
His chief recommendation is his catholicity. Different systems of
faith are so many paths leading to the same goal, namely, to the
source of Truth. Well, gentlemen, I have proposed to myself to

have these Lectures translated into Sanskrit, Gujarati, Marathi, Bengali, Hindi, and Tamil. The Gujarati is already done by my friend, Mr. Nowrojee Mobedjina, and myself; the other translations are more or less advanced. The work is entrusted to the best available hands, and their labours are to be revised by competent scholars before passing on to the printer. And I trust that, when published, these vernacular versions may do some good. If I succeed, it is my ambition to form a standing association for purposes of translation from and into Indian languages—a service peculiarly acceptable to the *unlearned*—the people. And now you will have seen, gentlemen, that, like Max Müller's theory, my little scheme too has grown up after a series of evolutions, and that all I have just told you has not been evolved out of the depths of my own inmost consciousness! It may be that I am growing a monomaniac on this subject; but pray see, there is some method in the madness. Besides, the mania cannot be so very rabid after all, since I have some of the best European and native friends in sympathy with me, as also the Press of the country. It is no less encouraging than significant to know that my respected friends Messrs. Wood, Wordsworth, Ryan, Birdwood, Macnagten, Candy, the Hon. Mr. Kemball, Hon. Mr. Gibbs, the Hon. Major Baring, the Hon. Mr. Hunter, Babu Keshub Chunder Sen, Babu Rajendralala Mitra, and others have, from the beginning, evinced a common interest in my experiment. The Government of Bombay have generously strengthened my hands with a pecuniary grant, and I reasonably expect similar encouragement from the other Governments. I cannot, of course, be sure that the scheme will succeed. Upto now very little practical success has attended my arduous itinerary save the Maharani Shurnomoye's munificent *little* gift of Rs. 1,000. But I have sown the seed, and in good time I hope to reap a harvest. I have spared no effort and no expense; will spare none. Others too have been working, especially my brothers and friends of the *Hindoo Patriot* and the *Indian Mirror*. And now, gentlemen, I appeal to you to work with and for me. Make my scheme your own, I beg. It is no more my scheme than yours, of the nation; yes, gentlemen, it has been described as a national project. Life is a precious blessing. What is impossible, with that blessing in us and around us? With you living, and I living, and the world living ; with the English language moulding our thoughts, and the English rule moulding our destinies, why despair ? Nay, let us hope for the best. I am not one to despair; then why should you ? I thank you all, gentlemen, for your patient hearing, and I thank my Bengali friends here,to whose enlightened efforts this beautiful city, beautiful at least from outside, is not a little indebted. I must also thank the Principal of this well-endowed and excellently managed College, which is only one out of the numerous monuments which the late Maharajah has raised unto himself for all time. Maharajah Ram Singh was a Prince in every and the fullest acceptation of the word.

Malabari followed this up, at the President's request, with a speech in Hindi which he speaks almost as fluently as English. Major Jacob then said a few words to mark the sympathy of the meeting with Malabari's efforts, and the meeting broke up.

These proceedings took place while Malabari was on his way from Calcutta to Bombay. He had visited almost all the important centres of Bengal, and had received a great deal of praise. The leading newspapers in Bengal, Native as well as English, recognized his venture as a " national enterprise," and called upon the Government and patrons of literature generally to support it. The *Indian Mirror* and others went so far as to recommend the establishment of a permanent national fund to help Malabari in his undertakings. The project was viewed with equal enthusiasm by Keshub Chunder Sen, Rajendralala Mitra and other leaders of thought in India. But no substantial support was given to the scheme in Bengal, except by the Maharani Shurnomoye. The work was extremely expensive, for it was quite clear that these translations would not be *popular*. Malabari knew this well enough, but his object was not gain or popularity, but a gradual religious revival. "India wants nothing so much as a religious revival, or rather a restoration. There is no real unity for the nation except through one faith ; political unity is always uncertain. The struggle lies in future between a new religion for the people and a revival of the old. And to a consummation of the latter, which will be through a natural process, I believe that the labours of Max Müller will contribute more than of any other living authority."*

This scheme of translations has cost Malabari no end of trouble and sacrifice. Not dispirited by his indifferent success in the North-West Provinces in 1881, and in Bengal in 1882, he started, in January 1883, for Central India, and, travelling very rapidly, was able to interest many princes and chiefs in his enterprise. He saw the " Merchant Prince of Indore," the father of the present Holkar, on the 7th of June, reached Dhar, the old capital of Raja Bhuja, and Mandu, that " eloquent sermon in stone on human vanity," on the 11th, passed on to " Mhow and Misanthropy" and the fat bugs of Mhow "as healthy and full of blood as Bhattia millionaries," on the 13th, missed the train for Rutlam, and went to Ujein, the capital of Vikram, and thence travelled to Rutlam where he met the little Pyari, and Raja Ranjitsing (the pupil of Aberigh Mackay) with whom he had a most interesting conference. This tour was not so disappointing as the Bengal one; but it was not a success. Malabari said as much to an English friend on his return to Bombay, and this friend advised him to

---

* *Indian Spectator.*

try the Southern Mahratta Country. No sooner said than done. On July 3, he left for Poona, and thence starting post-haste for Kolhapur on July 5, reached his destination after a most fatiguing journey of twenty-six hours. He saw Colonel Reeves and the Regent, and passed half a week at Kolhapur, and thence discoursed on "that licensed assasin," that "poisoner-general of the population"—the liquor seller—on pottery and poetry, on the Gujri fair, on High Court Judges, military politicals, and secret despatches. On July 9, he left for Sangli, got a handsome little donation from the Chief, and wrote about the water-famine on the G. I. P. Railway, "the insolence of office," "the autocratic obstructiveness of some Collectors, and the " naikins (dancing girls) reciting the mantras of the 5th Veda." On July 10, he left for Miraj, and thence on the next day he proceeded to Bombay, after a short but not unsuccessful expedition.

In August 1883, he published the Mahrathi translation, and in the cold season again set out to plead the cause of " Bhat Max Müller." This time he wanted to attack the Scindhia ; and so passing a couple of days at Agra (this was his third trip to this famous city), he started for Morar, where, unfortunately, he was laid up with fever. Nevertheless, on November 11, he had an interview with the Gwalior prince—a fruitless one—for H. H. Jioji Rao Scindhia knew nothing of literary charity or of Max Müller, and quietly

> " Smole a smile
>
> A quarter of a mile"

at his young visitor's enthusiasm. The enthusiast returned to Bombay, nothing discouraged, and pushed
on with the translations. The Bengali version has
come out already, and the Hindi as well as the Tamil
is in the press. The Sanskrit is the most difficult
one; attempts have been made costing much labour
and money, but without satisfying Max Müller. But
this Sanskrit translation will not be long delayed.
Malabari himself translated about one half of the
Lectures in Gujarati—the other part was done by Mr.
Naoroji Mancherji Mobedjina, Manager of the *Indian
Spectator*—and prefixed to this translation a lucid essay
of his own on Religion. The rest of the translations are
the work of Hindu scholars employed by him.

"GUJARAT AND THE GUJARATIS."

The only other literary performance of Malabari,
excepting fugitive poems like the elegy on the death of
Lady Fergusson, the sonnets in memory of Aberigh
Mackay, the " Lines addressed to a Photograph," the
poem on the retirement of our noble ex-Viceroy, that on
the unholy gains of Commissariat contractors, and so on,
is his "Gujarat and the Gujaratis." This had the honour
of being published in London by the well-known firm of
Messrs. Allen and Co. at their own risk and cost.
It has already gone through a second edition, and the
third would have been out three years ago but
for the author's absorption in the social reform crusade.
This third edition will appear shortly. The merits
of the book have been acknowledged by almost all
the leading journals in India, by many in England, and by some even in France and the United

States. One of the best reviews appeared in the
Civil and Military Gazette of Lahore which, though
it perceived in a few places the faults of "over-
smartness" and "vivacity occasionally lapsing into
vulgarity," heartily praised "the genuine humour"
of the writer, "the sincerity which seems inseparable
from the gift of humour", his "unforced vivacity and
frankness of style", his "unmistakeable strain of comic
faculty and sound moral intentions." "The result,"
it summed up, "though English enough in form, has a
fundamental independence, a national idiosyncracy
which is its best feature, and is as characteristic and
piquant as though it had been written in the flexible
Gujarati in which Parsis delight. The fiction, then,
that a native of India loses his national characteristics
by English education is not true. Nor is it true that
his moral sense is blunted. Nor is his affection for
the poetry and learning of the East in any way lessened,
but rather it is intensified. It would be mockery to
ask whether the M. O. L's., B. O. L's and D. O. L's. of
our new University are likely to produce anything in
Sanskrit shloka or Persian ode with half the vitality
and direct bearing on the difficulties that beset
national development, as this little book possesses."
The London Press wrote strongly in favour of the
book. The *Saturday Review* alone was of a different
opinion. But then critics, like two of a trade, seldom
agree.*

---

* The following passage from a review well describes the
varied contents of the book :—

"The writer is truly a humourist in the best sense of the
word. He "professes", to quote Thackeray, "to awaken and

MALABARI AS A POLITICIAN AND PUBLICIST.

We have now only to glance at Malabari's politics and then pass on to his last labour—his campaign against social abuses. Of a retiring disposition by nature, we do not find his name among the political

direct your love, your pity, your kindness, your scorn for untruth, pretension, and imposture—your tenderness for the weak, the poor, the oppressed, the unhappy. To the best of his means and ability, he comments on all the ordinary actions and passions of life almost. He takes upon himself to be the week-day preacher, so to speak. Accordingly, as he finds, and speaks, and feels the truth best, we regard him, esteem him—sometimes love him." No one who reads "Gujarat and the Gujaratis," will fail to have a very high admiration and esteem for its author. It awakens and directs our love for men like Karsandas Mulji and Rustomji Jemsetji, the Rev. Robert Montgomery, Mr. Taylor, and Mr. Birdwood. It rouses our pity for the slaves and victims of caste, the blooming brides married to baby husbands, the youthful widows cut off at an early age from matrimonial bliss and consigned to the tender mercies of a heartless soulless society. We learn to think kindly of the " primitive peace-loving Surtis" and of prodigal Mahomedan nobles of the type of Mir Bakhtawar Khan, ...
The untruth, pretension, and imposture of the Vaishnava Maharaj, the Parsi Dastur, the Mahomedan Mulla, are here most trenchantly and effectively exposed—and we are made to feel intense tenderness for those misguided creatures, who, bred in perverted faiths, expect salvation from sensual or superstitious cults. The book is full of pictures from life, whose " photograhic fidelity" we cannot praise too much. The prudish milkmaid of Broach who angrily refers her customer to her " *this* " (husband), when asked what she would take for a seer of her beverage—the bullock-driver who " kisses, embraces, lashes and imprecates" his animal by turns, ... the snobs with their ' reserved seat' etiquette, their ' purse-pride' and ' power-pride'—the naikin with her inseparable appendage who serves as her bear-leader, music-master, and go-between— the wrestlers making their make-believe bows and rubbing,

orators of Bombay, and it is noticeable that he has seldom, if ever, made a political speech. Once indeed he
intended, at a Town Hall meeting, to contrast Mr.
Justice Bayley's position as President of the Society
for Prevention of Cruelty to Animals, with his attitude

---

scrubbing, currycombing and kneading each other—the ultra-
patriotic native politician with his maxim, 'Let a hundred
people die under native misrule rather than ten of them be
saved by British interference'—the bloated Banya Railway
passenger giving vent to imbecile cries on finding the train
was about to move from the station at which he had to alight
—the 'loyal' sneak who curries favour with the Collector in
order to terrorise over the people, and is rewarded with a Khan
Bahadurship—the Parsi Shett, prim, old, well shaved, well
washed, well scented, sitting down with a grimace, standing
up with a yawn, walking as if he were a basket of newly laid
eggs, and sleeping with a stout cotton pillow tied under his
chest—the Hindu *paterfamilias* inviting his young hopefuls,
after swallowing plenty of substantials, to pommel and prome-
nade on his capacious stomach—the orthodox Parsi crying out
" Defeat defeat to Shaitan" after giving a flap to his " triple
cord" at daybreak, "mumbling over an extent of jawbreak-
ing jargon" near the seashore, and having even while at
prayer an eye to business and the main chance—the Parsi
graduate flattening his nose against the Agiari altar, on the
sly—the Parsi reformer who in the public is honey-sweet to
his family, but does not mind pulling his daughter by the hair
if his shoes have not the requisite shine after blacking—the
Parsi fashionable wife who insists on having a wet-nurse, a
dry-nurse, a cook, and a hamal, though her husband earns only
100 rupees a month—the guests at a Borah marriage ogling
the bride according to the Borah custom with extreme unction—
the Marwari with his policy of the " long rope" and " *centum
per centum,*" lending and lending till his victims are completely in his meshes—the village Hajam, barber, torch-bearer,
herbalist and procurer, all rolled into one, retailing scandal
while plying his razor or his tweezers—the mofussil Vakil, that
" column of vapour issuing from the ocean of emptiness", with
his *brass* and his bluster, and his combative and obstructive
tactics—the terrible Aghori besmeared with ordure, with eyes
on fire, the nostrils wide-distended, the tongue protruding, the

as one of the opponents of the Ilbert Bill ; but his design miscarried. Here is a funny account, in Malabari's own words, of what transpired :—

Pray do not ask me to attend a public meeting, much less make a speech at it. I am a fraud upon three-fourths of the committee meetings I join. What can a fellow do if you put in his name without so much as asking him ? People seem to have no conscience in the matter. I love peace, except where the weak is being trampled by the strong. I love silence, except where the wrong cause is triumphing over the right. In such cases I may strike a blow, and even " make a speech" for a few minutes. But these are spasmodic efforts, the result of a momentary impulse or loss of temper. The only set speech I remember having made was at the Town Hall last year. Having been pressed hard by Mr. K. M. Shroff, I weakly consented. I did not ask about the subject, feeling sure it was the annual meeting of the National Indian Association. So I went over Miss Carpenter's Life by my good friend, her nephew. From it I took a few strik- ing passages and happy thoughts, and inscribed a neat little speech upon the tablet of my memory. Never being able to give out the exact wording of a quotation, I stuck a few choice flowers of speech on my note-book, and turned to them now and again with the longing of a thief who is also a miser. The day came. I went to the Hall, big with half- stolen fire. On the way I learnt by an accident that I was

---

hair full of vermin, and the nails an inch long—the Vaid with his Mantras and Tantras, his charms and his amulets, and his doses "pottle deep"—the mannish ' mother-in-law', a plague to her *dear* daughter and her dear daughter's lord, stern, med- dling, and mischief-making—and last but not least, the Hinduani " saturated with sweet silly domestic legends", singing the garba with her companions, round " a bonny youth and maiden fair"——all these are graphic portraits with the un- mistakable lineaments of truth, and tell us much more of native life than your bulky gazetteers and heavy books of travel.

going not to a meeting of the National Indian Association but of the Prevention of Cruelty to Animals' Society. Oh my poor similes and metaphors! My picture of perfect woman-hood! All blown off like soap bubbles. But cheer up—nothing is impossible to the genius of adaptation. What was to be said of one association might as well be said about another. What is in a name?—especially when you change it. Entering the hall with friends I again forgot the resolution I had to speak to, namely, a vote of thanks to the Committee of management. Now, the Committee being a vague sort of a thing I took Mr. Justice Bayley, the President, in hand. Yes, Sir, I made a speech that blessed evening on the Hon. Mr. Bayley. It was quite to my taste. Mr. Bayley had poured ridicule over the Ilbert Bill some time ago, and here was a chance to pay him off. I began by paying him all the compliments of the season, thanking him for his generous interest in the lower creatures of earth and hoping to wind up with the remark—how curious that an English gentleman who loved *animals* so well as to make them the equals of human beings, should grudge equality to his fellow-creatures and fellow-subjects in India? That would have been a good hit. But fates were against me. Before I was half way I saw that there was a division in the camp. The party which did not understand English cheered and applauded the speech loudly. The others appeared to be doubtful. The subject of my oration, Mr. Justice Bayley, grew red and white by turn. The Governor moved uneasily in his presidential chair. What could be the matter? Were the audience hungry? But there was no time to speculate. Go on, brave heart. This, however, became impossible. Sir Jamsetji looked at me with a scared face. Mr. Dadabhai Naoroji pulled at my sleeve. My Hindu friends kept up cheering. Was ever speech-maker in such a fix? At last His Excellency got up and said—"Pardon me, but you have to propose a vote of thanks *to the Secretaries.*" I did not feel very friendly towards him then, but saw immediately after that he had meant it all for the best. May he feel the same towards me! And now I wheeled round by main effort and concluded my speech, mangled and discredited, amidst the applause of an enlightened audience, the majority of whom were in blissful ignorance of the byeplay above referred to. Fancy my victim getting all the praise and myself overwhelmed with self-reproach! May that be the fate of every intriguer! The dailies were merciful next morning, and Bombay has no doubt forgotten the little incident. Can *I* ever forget it? No —that was my first and my last speech pre-arranged. Any one who asks me to make another speech is my natural enemy.*

But though not a noisy politician, Malabari has had no small share in moulding the political history of the last seven years. He was the right hand of Dadabhai Naoroji, and by his moderation, as Editor of the leading native paper, and by his influence with the Native press, did yeoman's service, in critical times. When the *Voice of India* was started in January 1883, at the instance of that earnest friend of the country, Sir William Wedderburn, Malabari became its Editor while Dadabhai Naoroji found for it the sinews of war. The scheme of sending periodical telegrams to newspapers in England to counteract the effect of those sent by Anglo-Indian politicians owes its success, in no small measure, to Malabari's exertions. Malabari was one of those who kept their heads cool during the agitation which followed the introduction of the Criminal Procedure Code Amendment Bill and the Bengal Tenancy Bill. He was in correspondence with the highest in the land, and in touch with the best thought of the country. His services as a thoroughly honest and judicious inter-

---

* *Indian Spectator* 15-3-85.

preter between the rulers and the ruled, cannot be too highly spoken of. How well his labours as a politician and a public journalist are appreciated may be seen from this testimony given by an English friend of India, who has done more than any other Englishman in shaping the character of what is called the National Party:—" But for him Bombay during the late great crisis (the agitation on the Criminal Jurisdiction Bill) would have had positively no voice outside her own narrow limits, and her distinguished citizens, left to the tender mercy of hostile or at best, in *our* cause, lukewarm European journalists, would have found her position widely different this day from what it is...... Many brave men, we are told, lived before Agamemnon, but unsung by any Homer, have sunk into oblivion. Mr. Malabari has not only been in this Presidency the voice of the National Party, a voice which has ever been a credit and an honour to the province, but has been the Homer, to whose vaticinations, quite as much as to their own high intrinsic merits, our political leaders owe the wide-spread and distinguished reputation they bear." The same Englishman, writing later, on to a friend, says: "Lord Ripon, who had the highest possible opinion of Mr. Malabari personally, considered the *Spectator* the best of the Indian papers, devoted to the National Cause. And at home I was pleased to find, that amongst the comparatively small section of intelligent politicians who are interested in India and will stand by us, the *Spectator* was the one Native Indian paper, read and respected."

Great as are Malabari's literary merits, his scrupulous regard for truth is even a greater merit, for a public man. In his editorial capacity he acts more like a judge than an advocate, and that is why he is trusted equally by the Government as he is respected by the thinking public. During the heat of the Ilbert Bill controversy, for instance, Malabari was the means of preventing a very hostile demonstration against that measure as finally compromised. Distrusting the version of the compromise as telegraphed to Bombay by partisans, he telegraphed to Simla for correct information, and was requested to " suspend judgment" for a time. That message was passed on to responsible politicians in town, who were thus saved from the suicidal tactics of their countrymen elsewhere. Authentic information came in time from the seat of Government, and Malabari submitted the proposals to some of the soundest jurists and administrators of law in the country, only to find his own opinion confirmed.

It goes without saying that a publicist occupying such a unique position enjoys opportunities of usefulness all his own ; and it is equally unnecessary to add that Malabari always uses his opportunities for the public weal.

Although Malabari's name is as good as that of any of his contemporaries to conjure with, he is personally little known even to the Bombay public. The reasons are not far to seek. In the first place, he is as shy as a schoolgirl before strangers. He has no taste for the small talk of society, and is generally pre-occupied. Want of time is Malabari's usual complaint, and those who know the life of untiring beneficence he is leading will readily understand it. Besides, he is far from being a

G

methodical worker, and you often find on his table "copy" and "proofs" for the press, lying cheek by jowl with poems and petitions, and pamphlets and papers and currency notes mixed up in admirable confusion with flowers and photographs and a score of other sundries.

Another reason why Malabari is so seldom seen in the public is his failing strength. For years he has been more or less out of health, suffering from loss of appetite and of sleep. And in this state, with his nerves often on the rack, he has had to meet an increasing strain of work. No wonder that this genial and ever obliging man is so little in evidence.

The politics of Malabari are, what may be called, the politics of the poor—not the politics of the rich. He was one of the very few who supported Sir Auckland Colvin's Income-Tax Bill rather than see the Salt-tax raised. He approaches every political question mainly from the point of view of the masses, the great agricultural population and the labouring class, being fully convinced that in their welfare lies the stability of the British rule. Read his "Ramji *bin* Byroo of Mahableshwar, Bhisti and Guide, Naturalist, Malcontent and Political Economist," and you have not an unfair idea of the opinions Malabari holds regarding the beneficence as well as the defects of English administration. " As for an united India," he writes, "a national India, an India kept in peace and order, it is not among the possibilities of the near future." English sovereignty is indispensable to the progress of India ; but this original publicist would have men like Lord Ripon and Sir E. Baring to come out to India as Assistant Collectors and not as Viceroys and Members of Council. He thinks we have had enough of good legislation, and that what is now necessary is good administration of the laws. He is not blind to the faults of educated natives, and has had a great deal to say on the educational policy of the Government. He believes that there is too much of *head education*, and too little of *heart education*. Referring to Poona, he wrote in July 1883 :—

" Its educational activity is as great as of Bengal, and I think, more real. Bombay is nowhere. And yet, what has Poona done for its people ? It may be a craze with me that the intellectual elevation of some of our best men has removed them from the sphere of general usefulness. But if this be so, what is the use of a hundred highly developed intellects, where millions upon millions of their fellow beings live only a degree removed from monkeys ? I will not go the length of saying that education breeds selfishness ; but in this country, especially in Bombay, it does seem to me to tend to exclusiveness. We are raising an intellectual aristocracy which owns to no concern in the fortunes of the vulgar herd. Under the British Government this class must necessarily grow in wealth and influence. Will it ever give us a Shaftesbury or a Stansfield, a Howard or a Pen, a Nightingale or a Fry ? And unless college education quickens sympathy with the mass, is it worth imparting at a high pressure ? I know that almost all the friends whose opinions I value are in favour of education to begin at the top and to filtrate. The theory is sound and consistent with the law of nature. But though here I am in an inglorious minority, I cannot help saying that the peculiar conditions of life in India require consideration. Mr. Ranade, for instance, is perhaps the ablest Native judicial officer in India ; few know as I do what marvellous sagacity and acumen that man possesses. His judgments would be no way unworthy of a Westropp or a

Sausse. Mr. Bhandarkar shines equally well in his line ; he may not yield even to Max Müller in his special branch. These are "the forlorn hopes" of the people. Could they do no more for the people than at present ? Poor Ganesh Joshi was just showing the way when his invaluable life ran short of a sudden. India wants more people's men. The country cannot rise unless its millions are lifted to a higher moral atmosphere and social responsibility. And this will not happen till we have a system of heart-education side by side with head-education. Can colleges give heart-education ?"

I believe, they can, but the best heart-education can only be imparted in the family and at home. This is the opinion of the best Indian thinkers, and holding this opinion Malabari commenced his crusade against social evils.

Malabari as a Social Reformer.

" It was the widow," wrote Malabari in 1885, " who first set me thinking about the whole question. And though I find that her cause is very difficult to win, and that the cause of the girl-bride, on which her own fate largely depends, is comparatively easy of success, still I really cannot give up *my widow*. And I am sure every Irishman, at least, will sympathize with me." We have seen with what deep feeling Malabari pourtrayed the sorrows of Hindu widows in his *Niti Vinod*. He knew that there were many exemplary widows, and personally he was in favour of strict monogamy for both the sexes. But then, was it just to enforce widowhood on a girl who became a widow before she had known what it was to be a wife ? And was it just to shave her head, to make her a scarecrow among her playmates and companions, and to rule her life, as it were, with the iron rod of custom and superstition? Was it just, again, for the male to marry as many wives as he liked, and for the female to be prohibited from marrying again after her first husband's death, even though she might be a child in her teens? A great Hindu Pandit—Vidiasagar—had challenged his brother Pandits to prove that enforced widowhood was at all sanctioned by the Shastras. He had fought out his battle almost single-handed, and succeeded in moving the Legislature to pass an Act enabling those who conscientiously believed that widows could remarry, to translate their belief into action. That declaratory Act had done very little good, for caste had proved too much for remarried widows and their husbands. It had, on the other hand, emphasized the curious anomaly that though unchaste widows could not be deprived of their husbands' inheritance, remarried widows could be. The position of Hindu widows was most unsatisfactory, legally and socially. There was not the least doubt that most of them were unhappy. Their misery was not sung by Malabari alone in pathetic verse. I have said before that the Hindoo widow is almost a stock topic in Vernacular literature. The Native papers often came out with very sad tales of their sorrows, and in 1883 an orthodox journal llke the *Gujarati* actually proposed that all Hindu widows should be called upon by Government to show cause why they had remained unmarried! Malabari was a constant reader of Native papers, and often noticed the cases brought to light by them. Let me quote a couple of these from the *Indian Spectator* of 1883.

THE HINDOO WIDOW AND HER WOES.

The *Gujarati* reports a case of infanticide at Jetpur in Kattywar. A 'high-caste' widow, long suspected by the Police and closely watched, gives birth to a child. The new-comer's mouth is immediately stuffed with hot kitchen ashes. Thus 'religiously disposed of' and thrust into a basket of rubbish, its loving grandmother deposits the child into the nearest river. The village Police THEN come to know about it.

A very similar case is reported to us from Viramgaum; high-caste widow, new-born baby and hot ashes, though no mention is made of the loving grandmother or the basket of rubbish. Three persons are implicated in the former case. It must be remembered that the mother is very seldom a party to the 'act of merit.' After all it is her child, flesh of her flesh. Woman's love shines best under trials. The wife of a thief or murderer will cling to him all the closer the more he is shunned by the world ; the mother of a bastard will love him more intensely, perhaps, to make up for the father's neglect. In the Jetpur widow's case, we may say she is no more a murderer than is the head of the local Police. The father of her unclaimed child, whom your humane English law never thinks of calling to account, is the prime mover, with the widow's parents and caste-people as his accomplices. So cleverly is the affair managed that hardly one case out of twenty can be detected. In most cases the child dies before birth. The patient is removed far from her own home, on a visit to a friend's or on a pilgrimage, and there she is absolved of the burden of sin. She is lucky if she escapes with permanent injury to the system' for the village surgeon is but a clumsy operator. If less lucky, she succumbs under the operation. But least lucky is the widow whose case does not yield to the manipulations of the *Dái*. And woe be to her if she belongs to a respectable family. Then they get up a ceremony in her honor, what they call a *cold Suttee*, they serve her with the best of viands, they ply her with sweet intoxicants, and they cap her last supper on earth with something that will settle their business. The widow is soon a *cold Suttee* and is forthwith carried off to the burning ground, (the pious Hindu can't keep a corpse in his house for ten minutes). This 'cold Suttee' means a double murder. Let us hope it is a very rare practice. But a case is known where the widow suspected foul play in the midst of the nocturnal festivities in her honor. She turned piteously to her mother and asked to be saved, but she was thus urged in reply :—'Drink, drink, my child, drink to cover thy mother's shame and to keep thy father's *abru ;* drink it, dear

daughter, see I am doing likewise'!

...   .

The only remedy is to dispossess Caste of its power of excommunicating the widow who marries again. Government sanctions remarriage and Caste opposes it. What a position for the Government of an Empire ! It is all very well for English Officials to say that the widow and her friends ought to defy caste. They do not know the terrible effect of the Mahajan's curse. The widow and her husband, and very often her and his families, are shunned like poison. Thus some forty people may suffer for the courage of two. They suffer in life and in death. No casteman joins them in any domestic ceremony ; none of them can take part in the social affairs of any casteman. So cruelly rigid is the discipline,. that it drew tears of anguish from that most patient Hindu martyr, Karsandas Mulji. He used to cry helplessly when his wife wanted to know when her family was to be re-admitted into the Caste. Englishmen can have no idea of the bitterness of this social seclusion ; it is worse than the bitterness of death. One result of the persecution is that few remarried couples live happily. They are hunted out of caste, out of profession, and if we are not quite wrong, out of part of their inheritance. And not being sufficiently educated to take to new modes of life, husband and wife pine away in despair, accuse each other of folly, and under a sense of injury they sometimes take to evil courses. What a triumph for Caste ! That the widow marriage movement in India is making head in spite of such crushing opposition is a proof of its necessity and its ultimate success. If the Government only rules that Caste has no right to prevent remarriage ; if the public prosecutor is instructed to lay heavy damages against the

Mahajan for putting a remarried widow out of caste, the reform will have an easy victory over prejudice. Is there no Englishman to put down this unnatural interference with a movement sanctioned by the law of God and man? Is there no Englishwoman to plead for the rights of her unfortunate sisters in India?

An eminent Mahratta Shastri had followed Vidiasagar's example at Poona and Bombay ; but though Vishnu Shastri spent himself in the cause and did much solid work, he had had scant support. At Madras in 1871 or 1872 a "Widow Marriage Association" had been started by M. R. R. T. Muttasamy Iyer, and in 1880 this was revived by Rajah Sir T. Madava Rao, Dewan Bahadur Ragoonath Rao, and others. At Bombay a Hindu gentleman, who had married a widow, used to afford shelter and support to all poor creatures who wished to remarry, and had by his unostentatious friendliness helped not a few widows to happy homes. There was, however, no active sustained organization, and the problem of Hindu widowhood was as far from solution as ever. Malabari had thought about it for at least ten years, and knew well its difficulty. But he felt no doubt on one point, and that was this. Infant marriage had a great deal to do with unhappy widowhood. *Infant marriage!* Infant *betrothal* might be tolerated, but Infant *marriage*—irrevocable so far as the bride was concerned—and leading to the widowhood of children who in some cases had hardly cut their milk teeth, was certainly most unnatural. The Native Press was on the whole alive to its unnaturalness, and often condemned the practice in no measured terms. Here, for example, is a translation of an article in the *Hitechhu*, which appeared in one of the *Spectators* of 1883.

THE HORRORS OF INFANT MARRIAGE.

A Brahmin betrothed his daughter in her infancy. The girl never saw her husband or the husband's house. On reaching years of discretion the husband turned out to be worthless and diseased. But knowing all this, the father, bound by caste rules, &c., to save the honor of the family, married his daughter to the same man. When without free choice one cannot pass a single day happily, how can one pass a whole life! The girl lived all along at her father's house. Now, when even ascetics at times long for social happiness, how could this young woman restrain herself? She managed to have private meetings with somebody in the village. But secret intercourse means deception for the woman, and thus shortly after our heroine felt *embarrassed*. What to do now? In spite of amulets and threads, and even drugs, her condition continued to grow worse. Then they took her to her father-in-law's house. People there found out the secret. They, therefore, hesitated at first, but agreed to receive the daughter-in-law on condition that her parents should pay hush-money to the outraged husband. Where could the wretched parents procure money from? They brought back the girl. Days after days passed by and her secret was made public by every waft of wind. The crisis approached nearer, and just a little while before all would be over, the dear mother started with her in a cart with the required amount for her father-in-law's. But unfortunately, whether through the jostles on the road or otherwise, the girl was overtaken by labour. Where to turn now?—without house or home, without relations or friends. But the shrewd mother, telling the driver she had to obey a call, at once made for an adjoining thicket with the daughter. The spot was scarcely reached when the latter gave birth to her child. O! thou unfortunate intruder, thou little knowest thou hast to leave this world within so short a space of time, to be born only to be killed! In a moment the fragile little thing was despatched and buried, and the heartless woman returned to the cart. Oh *Shiva! Shiva! Shiva!* What unnatural cruelty! But wait, reader, say, is this not the result of child marriage?

A man like Malabari, full of sympathy and tenderness for the suffering, could not but feel the acutest pain on reading all such tales of wrong and misery. This custom of Infant Marriage had worked havoc for a long time among the Parsis who had imitated the Hindus, and it had its votaries or rather victims even among Mahomedans. It sometimes led to evils the very mention of which would make one's hair stand on end. For instance, Malabari knew at Surat of a rape on a Parsi girl of ten by her husband. Of course, according to law, the husband was not punishable, for such rape was not, and is not, a crime. But the heart-rending shrieks of the outraged child still ring in Malabari's ears. The Parsis—thank God—have succeeded in making such cases impossible, for under the Parsi Matrimonial Act no Parsi husband can force his wife, who is under fourteen, to live with him. But as the law now stands, no Hindu girl at least can deny herself to her husband, if she is ten years old.

Malabari was not a Sanskrit scholar, like Ram Mohan Roy or Vidiasagar, and he was not a Hindu. But he felt vividly the sin, the folly, the unnaturalness of this custom of Infant Marriage, and traced the woes of widowhood to this cause. How this pernicious custom could be abolished was a question which long perplexed him. He knew full well the internal economy of Hindu homes. He was not unaware that many of these were happy homes in a way. But was there not a large amount of misery which could be easily avoided? And was not this practice a dead obstacle in the way of female education and of national progress? The evil was admitted all round. And surely it could not be an evil without a remedy.

Diffident and distrustful of himself, Malabari did not make his *debût* as a social reformer with any quack nostrums warranted to cure the distempers of Hindu society. He was willing, to quote his own words, to be a "mere camp-follower," if a Hindu leader would but lead the way. But he was thoroughly familiar with the tremendous difficulties of Hindu reformers and the fate which had overtaken some of them. A Hindu sovereign could have easily put an end to such practices, if convinced of their illegality from the Shastric texts. But an alien Government was a Kumbhakaran in social matters, extremely difficult to awake to its responsibility, while the stronghold of Hindu usage and superstition was harder to conquer than Ravan's Lanka.

What, then, was an outsider to do for the victims of these baneful customs ? Was he to fold his arms and do nothing because he was an outsider ? Had humanity as a whole any outsiders *within itself*? Was not this a patent contradiction in terms ? Had those great and good men who had abolished negro-slavery ever felt any hesitation on the ground that they were outsiders ? Was it not the plain duty of every man to do what lay in his power to mitigate the hard lot of his brothers and sisters ? Were not the suffering Hindu widows, the suffering child-brides, with their heads shaved for the sin of losing their husbands, his own sisters, though he was a Parsi ? He had not a particle of vanity in him, but he knew that earnestness was a power in itself, and that as he felt keenly the sorrows of Hindu women he could plead their cause with eloquent directness and moving pathos. Still there was the question, "what would people say if he placed himself in the front in this fashion"? Would they not attack him as a presumptuous youth, and credit him with no other motive but self-aggrandisement and vain-glory? Yes, they would. He had won golden opinions, as a poet and a journalist. His life had been pure and self-sacrificing. But the world at large knew him only as the editor of a prominent paper and an able writer, and the world at large would listen easily to those who would attribute worldly motives to him. It was an enterprise "of great pith and moment." It would tax all his energy and resources, and would bring him probably nothing but abuse and defamation. But was it manly at all to be afraid of consequences—when the finger of Duty pointed clearly to one direction only and to no other? Was it not clear that female education would never make any appreciable progress so long as girls had to be married away in their tender years? Had not Keshub Chunder Sen proved, by the opinions of medical experts in India, that Infant Marriage led to an unnaturally early development of sexual functions, and that such development was in the long run ruinous to the physical and therefore to the mental strength of the nation? Was it not Infant Marriage, again, that led mainly to enforced and unhappy widowhood? And were not unhappy widows as great an object of pity and sympathy as any other unhappy creatures? Was there any religion or morality, any reason or sense, in shaving and degrading them, and subjecting them to a hard, almost merciless, discipline, as if every one of them was sure to go astray without it ? The picture of poor widowed children undergoing the slow invisible torture of a ruthless custom, bred of iniquity and un-naturalness, was ever present to Malabari, and gave him at length the courage of a hero and the meekness of a martyr. I am using these words advisedly. Few know how sensitive is this noble Parsi's heart, and how much he has suffered during these three years and a half. He is not likely to live very long. He has been judged most uncharitably by some of his contemporaries ; but posterity will do him justice.

Having resolved to devote himself to the eradication of these evils, Malabari next thought about the ways and means, and about the plan of his campaign. He had studied the question for a long time, and he knew the *pros* and *cons* of every remedy that occurred to him so well, that it was impossible for him to be cocksure about any of them. His main object was, as so often explained by him, to draw the attention of wiser and cleverer men to the two evils, to see if a national association could be started, and thus to place at its disposal all the ability that he could command. But how could many minds be brought to bear on the problem ? If he merely went on describing the evils and suggesting the remedies that occurred to him, there might be some academical discussion, but there would probably be no results. Malabari well knew the formidable difficulties which had presented themselves when female education was first taken in hand by a previous generation, and eq well knew how these difficulties had been overcome

through official co-operation and sympathy. He had no
horror of officials. He knew them too well to suspect
them of evil motives. He knew what help he had
received from them in carrying out his scheme of
vernacular translations. He knew how official guidance
had served as a *kamarband* for the invertebrates of
society in many matters necessary for the well-being
of the people. He knew who had abolished Suttee and
Infanticide, and introduced Vaccination and Sanitation.
He was averse to legislation on the subjects which had
interested him so deeply, but he thought the moral
support of the State was essential. Jotting down his
thoughts, therefore, in the form of Notes, he presented
himself one day in May or June 1884 to Lord Ripon
at Simla.

These Notes will be found in the present volume.
The one on Enforced Widowhood is liable to be misunderstood as advocating legislative interference. But the
truth is, Malabari was not well acquainted with technical
legal language, and he has several times disclaimed any
such intention. There is also a paragraph at the end
of the first note regarding marriages brought about by
widowed fathers or brothers of infant boys for their own
nefarious purposes. This last has been severely criticised
as a gratuitous slander. But anyone who reads the paragraph carefully will see that the practice condemned
is expressly stated to be "limited in area." Malabari's in-
formant on this subject was one who is the idol of educated natives, and the life and soul of their national
progress. The fact is, that the custom is not unknown
in some parts of the N.-W. Provinces, and Malabari

meant as much.* His critics, however, forgetting the words "limited in area," ran amuck against him for traducing the whole of Hindu society, and raised a considerable prejudice against him,

But I am anticipating events. Lord Ripon, Mr. Gibbs, Mr. Ilbert and the other members of the Supreme Government were struck by Malabari's fervour, and promised to consider the Notes, and they of course kept their promise. Lord Ripon, on August 20, 1884, wrote to him to say that the two questions of Infant Marriage and Enforced Widowhood were "practically branches of one and the same question, the position of women in India," that the question was "perhaps the most pressing, at the present moment, of Indian social questions," that the practices undoubtedly led to great evils, but did not in themselves involve crime nor were so necessarily and inevitably mischievous as to call for suppression by law, if they were sanctioned by the general opinion of the society in which they prevailed ; and his Lordship concluded his letter as follows :—

"In such a case the Government cannot take action without having before it full information as to the sentiment and opinion of the community interested ; and in consulting, as I understand that you are doing, influential persons throughout India on this point, you are, I believe, taking the most practical step, which is at present possible, towards the attainment of the objects which

* Compare the opinion given to Government by Mr. Denzil Ibbetson, Director of Public Instruction, Punjab. "The form of marriage by which a woman is for purposes of cohabitation the wife of A., while her children by him are for purposes of inheritance reckoned as the children of B., in the next generation, is common enough among semi-civilised races, and is by no means necessarily criminal or immoral. *But where it is the exception, it probably does lead to immorality.*"

you have at heart. I shall rejoice if the result of your inquiries should show that there exists an opening for the Government to mark in some public manner the view which it entertains of the great importance of reform in these matters of Infant Marriage and Enforced Widowhood. "

The other members of Government wrote in the same strain, but every one expressed his sympathy with the cause.

To obtain the opinions of other influential persons, official and non-official, Malabari had a large number of his Notes printed, and on August 15, 1884, submitted them with a modest printed letter for consideration. The result was their discussion by the press, and their translation by the native papers in almost all the vernaculars of India. The criticisms were generally favourable at first, and on September 11, 1884, the Supreme Government forwarded the Notes to the Local Governments and Administrations for their opinion, and also for consulting representatives of native opinion. It would have been much better if the revised notes published by Malabari in October had been so referred, for these latter notes contained much more practical suggestions than the first. It is curious to find that in November 1884, Sir F. Roberts, the then Commander-in-Chief of the Madras Army, directed that no recruits would be allowed to marry until three years after their enlistment. This was in effect a recognition of the principle laid down by Malabari, that the State could prefer unmarried to married men for its services, in order to discourage premature marriage. This suggestion, however, met with no favourable reception. The suggestions which were most approved were (1) the formation of a national association, (2) the introduction of lessons on these subjects in educational books, (3) and the enactment of a regulation by the Universities that after a certain number of years none who were not bachelors would be admitted to the degree of B. A. This last suggestion was supported by a gentleman who was an out-and-out opponent of Malabari in other respects.—I mean Mr. Chiplenkar, the able Secretary of the Sarvajanik Sabha, Poona—and by several other distinguished Hindus who admitted that, according to the Hindu Shastras, as well as Hindu traditions, marriage should succeed the completion of the long period prescribed for study.

It is unnecessary to dwell on the events that have followed the publication of Malabari's Notes—the Surat widows' appeal to the Nagar Shett in January 1885—the Nowsari widows' appeal to the Gaekwar in April—the campaign of Malabari in the Punjab in September and October—the effect produced in India by the revelations of Mr. Stead in November—the strong advocacy of legislation on the subject of Infant Marriage by Mr. Ranade in December, in the preface to the publication of papers bearing on the enactment of Act XV of 1856—the speeches delivered by Malabari at Agra, Alighar, Bareilly, Allahabad, Benares and Muthra in February 1886—the memorial of Sir T. Madhao Rao and other leading citizens of Madras to the Viceroy in March 1886, for fixing the marriageable age of Hindu girls at ten—the Viceroy's reply that the prevailing customs were "deleterious to morality" and that the

H

movement had " his sympathy and approval " *—the
Meerut memorial in August 1886 praying that the limit
of age might be legislatively fixed at 12 for girls and
16 for boys—the Madhava Bagh meeting in September, 1886, to protest agains any contemplated interference, legislative or executive,—the interview of the
Shastris with Lord Reay on September 13-1886—the
publication of a paper in the September number of
the *Nineteenth Century* on the Hindu Widow by Mr.
Devendranath Dass, and another in the October number of the *Asiatic Quarterly Review* by Dr. Hunter—
the final Resolution of the Government of India on
Malabari's Notes in October 1886—the publication
of the opinions of Hindu gentlemen consulted on
the subject in the form of Government Selections in
January 1887—the attacks on Malabari and Ranade
by some of the Poona lecturers in February—and lastly

---

* " H. E. the Viceroy said he was very glad to meet the deputation.
The subject which they brought to his notice was a very important one.
There was nothing so well engrained in the British system of government as a fixed determination, *as far as possible*, not to interfere in the
established national customs of the people.' That was the policy of his
predecessors and to it he meant strictly to adhere ; *but it did not follow
that there should be no departure from that policy*, and that the present
Viceroy and the members of his Government should not watch with
sympathy and approval any movement that had for its object the reformation of social customs. Personally he thought that no customs could
be more deleterious to morality, and fraught with greater evils, than that
mentioned in the address. Every European nation would look upon it
with horror, and for his own part he would not like his child to enter
into so momentous a contract under such conditions. If native opinion
was not absolutely unanimous, there should at least be a general
consensus of native opinion in favour of the movement. He had not yet
been sufficiently long in the country to gauge the character, force, and
extent of native opinion on the movement. More than that he was not
disposed to say at present, and they would not expect him to say more.
At all events, they might go away with the satisfaction that their
movement had his sympathy and approval. He was much gratified to
see so many men of position and intelligence taking interest in so
important a movement."

the publication of the opinions given to Malabari, in the form of a companion volume to the Selections. Besides these may be mentioned the extremely thoughtful pamphlet of Mr. Ardesir Framjee and several other interesting publications. Thus those brief notes of Malabari have gathered round them a vast amount of literature, and Malabari has certainly succeeded in bringing the best and wisest intellects to bear on the question. This alone is no small achievement, and his worst detractors cannot but admit that this achievement is to his credit. On the other hand, they ought also, in fairness, to admit that they have been guilty of the seven mistakes which Malabari has enumerated in the following extract:—

"It may be remembered that every paper I have written upon the subject of marriage reform in India has been marked "Submitted for Consideration." The first Memo. was so marked, and it was for the reader to approve the contents or not, without questioning motives and entering into other personal details. Some people did the latter, solely and simply because I happened to be a Parsi. That was Mistake number One, since magnified a hundred-fold by a hundred false steps, at each of which the man was assailed and his measures almost entirely kept out of sight.

(b.) It may also be remembered that I have invariably spoken of the two specific evils as *infant* marriages and *enforced* widowhood, and that my hypercritical opponents have made a point of mistaking them for *early* marriage and widowhood in general. This has in most cases been done on set purpose, and it has exposed me to great annoyance, as it has greatly obscured the points at issue. I have often tried to explain incidentally in the course of the discussion, that it is *infant* marriages alone that I object to, and that it is the prevention by social conspiracy of widow marriages, declared valid by Shastras and by the British law, and the endless persecution of widows intending to remarry, that called for a protest. But the opponents knew that their only chance was to mislead the ignorant, and so they went on repeating that I wanted Hindu girls to remain unmarried till 20-25 and *all* Hindu widows to be remarried ! This was Mistake number Two.

(*c.*) The third mistake was that I had grossly exaggerated the evils. Now this is a matter of difference of opinion. The opponents say I have over-stated the case. I say I have understated it. Let it be noted that the evils are scattered over a vast area and that all throughout they cannot be the same in extent and intensity. We have to judge of the matter by caste as well as by tract. Thus, what obtains in one caste or in one part of the country may be more or less absent from another caste or another part of the country Those belonging to the latter, therefore, find it easy, perhaps necessary from their point of view, to charge me with exaggeration, libel &c., when I am describing evils as they actually exist in the former. This seems to me to be the secret of the Exaggeration theory which is shared even by two or three European friends. The European is naturally more sceptical than the Hindu, because the former cannot conceive of irregularities which do not occur in European society. The charitable Hindu would be equally sceptical as regards some of the social enormities prevailing in European countries. But because one is not personally acquainted with a particular phase of social evil, is it fair that he should charge another who knows, as libelling him and his people ? My statements are generally made on accurate first-hand information, acquired by personal contact with the victims themselves or a study of the literature of the subject as relating to particular localities. Not to say anything of marriage before the babies are born and while they are at breast, I ask if Hindu girls are not usually married at about 8 ? If a mean average were taken all over the country I fear it would not go beyond 7. If in some parts marriages take place at 11, in many they occur before 9. Where a marriage is postponed, it is done out of sheer necessity, the absence of a suitable match or want of means. Where marriages, as a rule, take place so early, a good deal of harm must necessarily follow. I admit that in some cases parental control may avert this harm. But such enlightened parents in India are in woeful minority. If you advise an uneducated friend to postpone consummation till a proper age, he will turn upon you with the unanswerable question——what were the couple married for ? Then, as to unequal marriages, those between 50 and 10, for instance, are they so very rare in all parts of India ? And what can be the result of such unions, with lifelong 'widowhood staring the brides in the face ? What are we to think of the public opinion of a country in which such marriages are possible ? On the other hand, there are cases in which the boy-husband is younger than the girl-wife. The latter grows rapidly, while the former has a comparatively slower growth, and sometimes does not grow at all. Is not this a great wrong to both parties ? But I will not pursue the subject. Let the critics go over different parts of the country and study the different customs, and then come forward to confirm or contradict my statements. They have never done so nor attempted to do so, but have contented themselves with ignoring facts not within their personal observation. This is Mistake number Three.

(d.) Another mistake on the part of my critics is that I have been clamouring for legislation. As a matter of fact, I declared in the very first Note my aversion to legislative interference. I " submitted" other methods for " consideration," which were approved by some and objected to by others. As the discussion went on, I " submitted" more suggestions made to me by friends, mostly Hindus. It was for the community concerned to accept or to reject those suggestions. Too much stress is being laid in some quarters on the draft bills sketched by Messrs. Melvill and West. It is needless to refute the assertions of mischief-makers in this regard. The drafts are still before the public, who can see that they were not at all meant for immediate adoption by the whole community or by sections of the community, but were intended to guide those who might in the future think it necessary to appeal to the Legislature. No one, who has read the drafts and the remarks prefacing them, or who has any acquaintance with their authors, would think them amiss for a moment. Let us hope this too was only a Mistake, Mistake number Four.

(e.) But why did you at all consult the officials and publish their opinions ?—ask my indignant critics. Because I knew my critics too well to trust only to their co-operation. In consulting official opinion I had the example of others before me, What

would have been the fate of the agitation against Suttee, Infanticide, Compulsory Widowhood, Hook-swinging and other pastimes,
but for official co-operation? How far would Ram Mohan and
Keshub Chunder, for instance, have succeeded without the moral
support of Bentinck and Lawrence? As to publishing official and
non-official opinions, surely they were not intended to be pigeon-
holed? Those who think so make a bad mistake, Mistake number
Five.

(f.) The sixth mistake has regard to my motive; that I
undertook this work for cheap popularity. The absurdity of such
a supposition is self-evident. I was one of the most popular men
in India, if not the most popular of my years, when I took up the
question. I took it up with a full knowledge of the sacrifices it
would entail. I took it up as my life work. It is scarcely three
years now since I began when people are talking about my having
become "thoroughly discredited" and abusing me as never was the
worst enemy of the country abused before. All this does not look
like popularity, and it constitutes Mistake number Six.

(g.) The last and the worst mistake is to threaten to "crush
that Malabari." Here the opponents have entirely mistaken their
man. There is only one way of silencing him, by showing honest
work. He does not care for their respect or estee ; he never
cared for favours from them, has ceased to care even for common
justice from such quarters. But can nothing make these gentlemen see that less than half the labour and ingenuity they spend in
attempting to crush a solitary well-wisher might, if otherwise
employed, bring about the reformation of a whole community?

What is the moral of Malabari's crusade ? It is
that earnestness, like faith, can move mountains, though
not in company with high Sanksrit scholarship or scientific or philosophic acquirements ; that there is wisdom
in guiding and utilizing such earnestness, but crass
folly in allowing it to spend itself in vain, if it
can ever be in vain. No one can say that Malabari's
exertions have been futile or fruitless. He has succeeded

in engaging the sympathies of the ruling class in favour of Hindu widows, and against the practice of Infant Marriage. He is not an iconoclast or a revolutionary patriot. He is not for introducing European customs wholesale, and has repeatedly stated that by infant marriage he means only the marriage of children under twelve, and that he would be quite satisfied if this modest reform could be carried out. It may be that in certain parts of India no such reform is required, though that remains to be proved. But then the educated men of these parts should be the last to say that because it is not required among them, it is not required elsewhere. One of the most disappointing features of the opinions given to Government is such fallacious generalisations. The educated natives have had some hard hits at Malabari's hand. But they should remember that their treatment of him was not generous or just. I am myself, I am afraid, generalizing wrongly when I say that the educated natives have been ungenerous or unjust to him. I believe that no educated Hindu in his senses can fail to perceive the single-heartedness and the conspicuous ability with which his Aryan cousin has launched this scheme of social reform, and I believe that, excepting a few noisy and irresponsible editors, the bulk of educated men are on the side of such reform, however they may differ as to the ways and means. Malabari is not a man who would desist from doing what he feels is his lifework simply because of unpopularity, and it would be a thousand pities if his agitation were not kept up. The educated natives ought now to form themselves into a strong organized Social Reform Association, or start a Mission with the necessary propaganda. The eyes of our rulers and of the ruling race, and I may say, of civilized people generally, are upon them. They at first thought of achieving political progress and then trying their hand at religious and social reform. But by this time they ought to see that social reform would no longer wait upon their sweet pleasure, that they are challenged on all sides to show themselves worthy of higher political rights by adopting more natural and enlightened social customs, and that the advice of their best friends—men like Lord Ripon and Mr. Wordsworth—is to the same effect. If Malabari has done them any wrong, they ought to show they can forgive him. We ought to rise above petty spite, envy, and jealousy, and ought to band ourselves in the holy spirit of self-sacrifice to do our utmost to bring about the social regeneration of India, remembering that our fathers in the days of our grand epics knew of no such " anthropological curiosities " as baby-brides and virgin-widows, and that the reform sought for is after all a mere return to the customs which prevailed in the palmy days of Aryan India.

SELECTIONS.

NOTE I.

INFANT MARRIAGE IN INDIA.

The British Government put down Infanticide by law. That was a great gain to society, apart from higher considerations. But we find Infant Marriage in practice a more serious evil than Infanticide. For, whereas the latter was one short struggle, in which the victim was almost unconscious, an ill-sorted infant marriage entails lifelong misery on either or both parties. Infant marriage is the cause of many of our social grievances, including enforced widowhood. The argument, that such an arrangement forbids the exercise of free will on the part of those most concerned, may not commend itself readily to all practical reformers. For, parental control is necessary and mostly beneficial even when the parties have come to years of discretion. Absence of choice, therefore, is not my only complaint. But the area of selection is so narrow where society is split up into numerous castes and sub-castes, that practically Hindu parents have to make Hobson's choice of it : to accept the first boy or girl available, or to buy one who comes the cheapest, all things considered. There may be physical defect or moral taint on one side or the other. But so long as this, and no other match, is to be secured, why, it must be secured at all risks. What wonder, then, if many of these forced unions turn out unhappy ? The physical defect may increase with age, the moral taint may grow into a malady. The wife may outgrow the husband, or "the husband may become fit for the grave when the wife becomes fit for his home." There may be total or partial absence of physical adaptability or hopeless disparity of temperament. In any of these events the "married martyrs," as they have been aptly described, are

1

socially alienated from each other, though perhaps living under the same roof. These are some of the many dread contingencies.

But let us take the union to turn out happy, as it no doubt turns out in a large number of cases. What follows? A too early consummation of the nuptial troth, the breaking down of constitutions and the ushering in of disease. The giving up of studies on the part of the boy-husband, the birth of sickly children, the necessity of feeding too many mouths, poverty and dependence; a disorganised household leading perhaps to sin. In short, it comes to a wreck of two lives, grown old almost in youth, which might, in favourable circumstances, have attained to happy and respected age. That this is not an overcharged picture will be admitted by those who have even a superficial acquaintance with the domestic affairs of our people. Last of all comes Death to the relief of the husband or the wife. If the former, it adds one more widow to the forty million and odd, and two or three orphans to the fraternity of unprotected infants. Here we are confronted with that grave economic problem—over-population in poverty. If over-population is felt as an evil in advanced and wealthy countries, where natural and artificial means exist to hold it in check, what must be the effect of over-population in a poor and backward country, where the evil is actively stimulated by unnatural means? Can the State take no cognisance of this economic phase of the evil ?—apart from the social aspect with which a foreign Government may well hesitate to meddle.

We are often told by benevolent Let-Alone-ists that the only remedy possible is to educate public opinion on the subject, and then to set this educated public opinion to cope with the evil in operation. This is no doubt a very sound doctrine. But where such a very small portion of the population of India have received elementary education after so many years, the chances of bringing educated public opinion as a force to bear upon the question are extremely slender.

The higher classes of Hindus, the more educated amongst them, feel the necessity of discountenancing child marriage; and most of these would undoubtedly act up to their convictions if they only could. But caste is too powerful even for men in that position. Where the girl's parents are enlightened, the boy's may be the reverse; and as that is the only eligible boy *in the caste* the former are obliged to sue for terms. Amongst the illiterate mass early marriage obtains most widely, and amongst them, least able to bear the strain, the consequences of such marriage are most far-reaching. They tell disastrously on the physical and social well-being of not only the contracting parties, but even their children and their children's children. We occasionally hear of a debt incurred by a man towards the marriage expenses of his youngest son having to be repaid by his grandson or great-grandson.

I have never heard an argument in favour of infant marriage as a national institution, except that it is enjoined by the Shastras. But so far as I have been able to see, no Shastra enforces marriage proper on a girl under 12 years of age, when presumably the boy must be between 15 and 20. So much as to the social or so-called religious aspect of the practice. In India every custom that is unintelligible, or actually indefensible, becomes a religious question, the merits of which we are not supposed to appreciate in this *Kali-yuga.* But taking infant marriage as a purely economic question, as a source of over-population and consequent disturbances, can the State do nothing to check it? I would not propose a legal ban to be placed upon it. But an enlightened Government might well show its disapproval of the practice indirectly. To begin with, the Educational authorities might rule that, due notice being given, no married student shall be eligible to go up for University examinations, say five years hence. This would be some check. Several other departments of the State might also devise similar means to discourage this pernicious custom of modern India. I have little doubt that some such expedient would be welcomed by leaders of Native

Society in all parts. An enlightened Hindu friend writes to me from Bengal cordially approving the proposal.

Our educated young men can do a great deal to strengthen the hands of authority in this direction. An excellent suggestion was made only the other day, that University graduates and others should form themselves into an association and take a pledge not to marry under a certain age. To which another suggestion, equally good, has been added as a rider, namely, that no educated man should marry a girl too much under his age. This would be a fair beginning for the educated class.

It appears to me that the State has a right to insist upon having the best available servant, if not the best available citizen. If so, the head of a department may prefer the unmarried candidate to the married, all other qualifications being equal. I am not blind to the risk to which this proposal is open; but the advantages far outweigh every possible inconvenience. Then, again, the Educational Department may give a few chapters in its School Books, describing the evil in its various forms. The State may offer indirect inducements to students remaining unmarried up to a certain age. There are ways in which the Executive can do a great deal towards the mitigation of social martyrdom, without invoking the aid of the Legislature. Let the officer evince personal interest in the matter, keeping his official position in the background. It is such friendly sympathy, in my opinion, more than anything else, to which we owe what little progress we have made socially during the last fifty years, especially in the matter of female education. And I suspect that something very like gentle moral pressure had to be exercised by friendly officials when Girls' Schools were first opened in the mofussil and pupils were hard to find. Parents would not allow their daughters to be out of sight for a few hours every day. But the thing had to be done, and we have now a Girls' School in almost every large village. Shut up these schools to-day, and I dare say the villagers will make a grievance of it.

The most obnoxious amongst early marriages (which are often unequal in point of age) are : 1, the marriage of an infant girl with an old man—the object generally being for the bride's father or relatives to secure money from the bridegroom. This is much the same as selling the child, selling her into slavery and worse. Now the State may not directly interfere with the transaction. But indirectly, I think, it can aim a deadly blow at the practice itself. For instance, by ruling that the money received from the bridegroom, the price of the girl disposed of, is not to belong to the seller, the parent or relative of the victim, but to be safely deposited in her name and for her exclusive use. Some such ruling will discourage marriages of the kind. And where the marriage does take place the money paid by the bridegroom, the cost of the bride's sacrifice, will be a comfort to her in widowhood. For, in all human probability the girl must become a widow, in which case she has at present to be solely dependent on her male relatives. This suggestion was made to an English friend by a competent Hindu authority at Madras about a year ago.

2. Another objectionable form of marriage, so called, is —a girl of 12 to 15 married to a boy of 8 to 10. When we know that the marriage is brought about by the father or the elder brother of the boy, who (the father or the elder brother) is a widower, we may guess the object. It is a criminal arrangement, leading to sin all round, and to much suffering for the unfortunate girl who must in name remain the wife of the boy. When the boy-husband realises his position, he may murder the wife, the father or the brother. For proof positive the reader may search the records of a Magistrate's Court here and there : of presumptive evidence there is no lack. The evil is limited in area, but it is none the less a horrible thing. How long will Society and the State put up with it ?

BEHRAMJI M. MALABARI.

Bombay, *August* 15th, 1884.

Submitted for consideration.
<u>Submitted for consideration.</u>

NOTE II.

ENFORCED WIDOWHOOD.

I may begin this Note by saying that personally I do not approve of Remarriage in either sex under ordinary circumstances. Nor do I endorse the vulgar prejudice that the Hindu widow is necessarily a social danger and must therefore be remarried by force. As a matter of fact the Hinduani is, by blood and tradition, an excellent type of womanhood in all relations of life. But in modern India woman seems to have become, as if by common consent, the inferior of man as a social unit. She is married in infancy. In case of early death of the husband she has perpetual widowhood before her, even though still an infant. Her life is a social failure. In most things she is at the mercy of others, because the average Hindu widow is not able to appreciate and protect her rights as a member of society. To many it is a wonder that the world hears so little of the results of such social inequality. I believe this is so because woman is the sufferer. It is not in her nature to publish her wrongs, however great. A Hindu woman complains little. But that little, in the present case, is too much for those who know. The widows of Gujarat and of Maharashtra, of Bengal and North-West, of Punjaub and Madras, have often set forth their grievances, in prose and verse, in odes and elegies, in piteous appeals and memorials to the Collector of the district, to their Mother-Queen, and to their gods and goddesses without number. To be sure there are thousands of young Hindu widows leading pure, if not happy, lives. We hear of a case now and again in which the widow is the guardian angel of the house and the street ; who, having lost the sharer of her joys and sorrows while yet a girl, consecrates her womanhood exclusively to works of charity, cherishing the hope of union in a better world. But if there are thousands of such saintly beings in Hindustan, there must be millions of simple misguided creatures, exposed to all sorts of trials and temptations, whose lives are a curse to themselves and, in some instances, a standing menace to society.

Hindu parents deplore no misfortune so much as they deplore the widowhood of a young daughter. But it is a common misfortune. And its consequences are generally so inevitable, that exposure is a rare occurrence. When every village almost may be covering its shame, or may be in daily dread of having to do so, connivance is the only hope of the community. Direct evidence being nearly impossible in a suspected case, the policeman finds free scope for the exercise of mercy or cupidity. Yet, how many cases of infanticide do we hear of every month? And these are only exceptional cases that come to be known. The unknown ones may be twenty times more. There is a regular system of freemasonry maintained for the purpose—the removal of the widow in trouble on visits to distant relations or on pilgrimage—which baffles detection. When all attempts fail, the mother's health is ruined for life, or she dies with the babe unborn.

It is sometimes urged that enforced widowhood must be accepted as a necessary evil. If so, the question arises—is Hindu Society reconciled to the evil? No; Society is and has long been in revolt against this inhuman custom. Educated young men, and many of the orthodox old, are anxious to be saved from its demoralising effect, if for no higher purpose, at least for their own interest. Why don't they, then, shake off the evil? Because the Hindu is hard to move. Caste exercises overpowering influence. Caste is more potent in its secret persecution than was the Inquisition of Spain. Not only are the offending couple excommunicated, but their relations and friends too may become outcasts henceforth and for ever (unless they can afford to buy readmission) in life and in death. They are shunned like a moral plague. No European can have an idea of the operation of this dread award: it is more bitter than the bitterness of death.

Such are the results virtually of the abolition of Suttee by the British Government. Had Mountstuart Elphinstone and Lord William Bentinck anticipated them, they would have paused before enforcing the law without its legitimate corollary. For, whereas Suttee was one single act of martyrdom or heroism, as the victim conceived it, and an act of religious merit popularly believed, the life which caste imposes on an unwilling widow is a perpetual agony, a burning to death by slow fire, without any chastening or elevating effect on the sufferer or any moral advantage to the community at large by way of compensation.

Now, my contention is, has caste the power to punish an act which the State recognises as legal and natural, and for which, in fact, the State has presumably rescued the widow from the flames? The plea as to re-marriage of all widows being forbidden by the Shastras has long been known to be untenable. The only rational objection that is urged against remarriage is based on the theory of over-population. But all remarried couples do not necessarily transgress the laws of population. Caste has no objection to the widower marrying again, as often as he likes, and more women than one at a time if he so wishes. Its cold-blooded philosophy is reserved only for the woman who has lost her husband, that is her all in life. Here, then, is a conflict between State and Caste. Who is stronger?

It has often been asked—why does not the remarried widow or her friend seek the protection of the Law against her persecutor? My answer is a simple question—why at all do you allow the oppressor to oppress the weak and the innocent? Government saves the widow from compulsory immolation. Henceforth the widow becomes a ward of the State, and has the power, if she have the will, to enter into another honour-

able contract. And yet, caste condemns her to an unnatural
if not an ignoble course of life, may be for its own purposes,
and tramples upon her finer instincts. Why should caste be
allowed to do this ?

We are again told that the custom has a purely religious
bearing. No such thing. It is more a freak of the priestly
class and of a set of social monopolists. At any rate, this is
what it has come to. And how many bad customs and usages
have already been put down which were all alleged to have
had their orgin in religion ? Suttee, infanticide, the rolling
of the Juggernaut Car: the suppression of these raised a
howl of indignation at the time. Government were threatened
with mutinies and rebellions. What became of those hostile
national demonstrations ? By all means, let us respect and preserve all that is good in a custom. But the British Government belie their cherished traditions in putting up with what
is harmful, simply because it is sanctioned by that custom.

Now, I am not one of those who are for violent interference
by the State or for abrupt reforms from amongst the people
themselves. We must move with the times, carrying the
people with us. *And I say that in this matter the people are
ready to go a step further.* Our progress, since the abolition
of Suttee, has not been quite perceptible. But still I hold
that a move forward has been maintained all along the line.
There have been a number of remarriages in Bengal, Madras,
Bombay and elsewhere, in spite of the stringent prohibition
of caste. But this progress has been far too slow. And there
are so many obstacles in the way, that those who have watched
the movement closely apprehend a re-action if the people
are left much longer to struggle on by themselves. Karsan-
dass Mulji, our foremost social reformer on this side, died
broken-hearted under implacable persecution. Happily we have Societies and Associations working in aid
of this particular reform. The widow's cause has enlisted the
sympathy of notable men, official and non-official, European
and Native, who think it cruel to take full cognisance of the
errors and irregularities incidental to enforced widowhood.

2

All that now seems to be needed is the interposition of authority to a small extent. Let Government rule :—

> (I.) That no Hindu girl, who has lost her husband or
> her betrothed, if she is a minor, shall be condemn-
> ed to life-long widowhood against her will.

Here I need not be reminded of Act XV. of 1856. It is
a fairly adequate provision in itself. But what has it done
for the re-married widow and her friends in the course of the
last 28 years ? Practically it has remained a dead letter.
I ask for little more than that the existing provision be made
known to the victims and enforced in their favour by all .
possible means. That the secret opposition of caste be met
by some indirect encouragement to them from the Government. Show your dissatisfaction at the prevailing state of
affairs and your anxiety to do something on proper representations being made. At present there is a struggle between
caste and the code. It is an unseemly encounter. The practical impunity—the feeling that Government cannot and will
not interfere—encourages the aggressors quite as much as it
discourages the aggrieved seeking redress from the tyranny of
caste.

> (II.) That arrangements may be made, in suspected
> cases, to ascertain whether a widow has adopted
> perpetual seclusion voluntarily or whether it has
> been forced upon her.

> (III.) That every widow, of whatever age, shall have
> the right to complain to the authorities of social
> ill-usage (over and above excommunication), and
> that proper facilities shall be afforded her for the
> purpose, such as the gratuitous service of counsel,
> exemption from stamp duty, attendance at Court,
> and so on.

> (IV.) That the priest has no right to excommunicate
> the relations and connections of the parties con-
> tracting second marriage, besides excommunicating
> the principals.

Unless some such protective measures are adopted in time, I repeat there is fear of re-action at least on this side of the country. What little progress has been achieved after thirty years of arduous struggles may be washed away by one wave of the returning tide of fanaticism. If Government fail, as guardians of the unprotected, to rescue the widow from this terrible thraldom, they will, in no small degree, be responsible to the Supreme Authority above, and to the civilised world for the results of a vile custom in working.

For, there is scarcely a village in India, scarcely a hamlet, whose shrine is not desecrated by murder; where the blood of the innocent does not pollute the sanctuary of its God. Emancipate the woman of India, ye English rulers! Restore to the widow her birth-right of which she is robbed by usurpers who owe no allegiance to God or to man. Give her back the exercise of free will. Is it meet that in the reign of the most womanly Queen the women of India should remain at the mercy of a foul superstition? Raise the status of our women, and in time England shall be furnished with a Volunteer Corps a million strong. Win the blessings of India's women, —the most grateful amongst a grateful nation. You are following in the steps of your predecessors. Then complete the reform inaugurated by them, carry it to its logical conclusion. Declare that the widow, being the State's adopted daughter, shall not be wronged by caste, and that even if custom allows the wrong to be perpetrated, the victim shall be avenged by law.

But I am afraid what I ask in the last paragraph is a question of time. Government may not at present go beyond the four suggestions made above. Nor would it be advisable to press the authorities. I believe an advance would have been made before now by the people themselves, but for certain conditions which have always operated adversely on the progress of the Native community. In the first place, it is a mistake to trust entirely to the educated agency. Education by itself has failed to secure influence in the country. Our educated young men want position. They are no match for the priestly class, who are, in a sense, better educated. Nor are the orthodox Pandits so devoid of sympathy as young reformers seem to fear. Be that as it may, it is a fact that the mass of the people look up to the Pandits and Shastris as their guides. The priest is a friend of the caste, the custodian of its honour and integrity. He directs the affairs of many a household, and is instrumental in maintaining the patriarchal relations between old and young, rich and poor. The priest is an institution whom the poor man worships, and the rich man thinks it a privilege to bow to his teachings. Besides, of long has this priestly class been on the defensive against attacks from within and without, that organisation—that is the power to work together—has become the law of their very existence. Has the average educated man, the young reformer, any two of these advantages to offer for our purpose? Modern education has made him impatient and offensive. He has no hold on the popular mind. Not only have his orthodox neighbours no confidence in the educated young reformer, but they look upon his doctrines with positive distrust. Then, again, in many cases his acts fall short of his words. Last of all, the educated class lacks the means for organisation—the different elements are generally so incohesive. I hope and believe that these are only temporary difficulties. But there they are, and one is obliged to recognise them as seriously interfering with the usefulness of the educated class in matters social.

If an earnest reformer, therefore, wishes to carry the mass with him, he finds the support and co-operation of the priest indispensable. And such support he may not seek in vain. The priest is not so bigoted as to deprecate social progress. But he is rather shy of outside light and wants gentle handling. The reformer must go to him as a friend, and perhaps as a suppliant.

At this stage I would propose the establishment of a national association for social reform, with the existing societies as branches, and get most of the prominent members of Government to join as sympathisers, from the Viceroy and the Governors downwards. I am not without hope that our cause would interest them so far. Indeed, we might look further up, going to England for similar countenance. An institution like that would have a certain prestige—people would deem it an honour to be associated with distinguished members of the ruling race. Besides its direct practical advantage, the presence of English friends might deter Native members from backsliding when the time came for action. This wealthy and influential association may then try the usual plans of operation, lectures, tracts, &c., *for the people*, under the sanction not only of their secular rulers, but also of their spiritual guides. All such attempts in the past have been all but useless as directed upon the small educated class who knew the evils full well but had no power to remedy them. Let the people be addressed directly in their own vernaculars. Let the poet and the pandit go hand in hand, scattering the seeds of true knowledge broadcast amongst the mass, to bear fruit in time. Let Government move to some extent under a sense of humiliation that a hundred years of British rule could do but so little towards the amelioration of the social condition of the subjects. And let the people, too, now move for very shame, remembering that there is no hope of political elevation for so long as we live, and apparently love to live, in such social degradation.

BEHRAMJI M. MALABARI.

Bombay, August 15th, 1884.

THE PROBLEMS EXPLAINED.

Some of the suggestions offered in my Notes on the above questions are apt to be misunderstood. It may not, therefore, be quite useless to examine them here one by one. I shall do so briefly and plainly, leaving it to Hindu friends to come to a practical conclusion. In the first place people seem to have very vague ideas about Infant Marriages in India. An infant marriage generally means nothing better than the making over of girls into matrimonial slavery. It is the *girl* whom the *Shastras* wish to be so disposed of, and not the boy necessarily. The boy has often to be married before 10 on account of the compulsory marriage of the girl before 9. But caste is not called upon to excommunicate the parents of a boy, as in the case of the girl, if they do not marry him before a certain age. A Hindu male can marry at any age from 10 to 60. But the female becomes unmarriageable after reaching puberty, and parents who are unwilling or unable to marry her off before that, have to lose caste. The rule is most rigidly enforced amongst Brahmins. I believe Rajput girls marry at a comparatively later period. Banias, Bhattias, Shrawaks, and other classes also generally wait till 11, by which time children are believed to have survived all infantile ailments, before going out in search of suitable husbands for their daughters. Thus it will be seen that the custom is not so universal as outsiders are led to suppose, nor does it apply to boys. At any rate I do not think infant marriages amongst other classes than Brahmins could be counted at more than 40-50 *per cent.*, whilst amongst Brahmins they reach the proportion of 70-80 *per cent.* of which full 20 *per cent.* are *kajodás*, that is ill-sorted marriages, with wives older than husbands. With the spread of education the feeling has grown strong against infant marriage. Young men pledge themselves not to marry before getting through the B.A. course. But the parents of the girls do not wait. "Are we to keep grown up daughters on hand on your account?" they ask. "We would rather bestow them upon the poor and illiterate. What do we care for your education?" Some brave young fellows tried to put up with this social ostracism. But what about their families?—the old father and mother, elder brothers, sisters and *their* families? Must they all suffer with the young reformers? At Ahmedabad they started an Association some years ago, and leading reformers pledged themselves not to give or take girls in marriage under a certain age. But practically it came to nothing. One by one the signatories fell away. We may be sure the poor fellows did not do it without a struggle. Only they could not help themselves. The people of India have been morally crippled. It is cruel on the part of Englishmen to say, let the educated class fight out the battle. The struggle is unequal in point of number and influence. Give them a helping hand, and our young men will do their duty. It is in this sense that I suggest a gentle well-directed action on the part of the Universities. If they make bachelorship one of the qualifications for the Entrance examination, the battle will be half won for the struggling minority. Such action no way involves interference with the religious or social prejudices of the people, because the *Shastras* do not compel a boy to marry before he is quite prepared to undertake a householder's duties. On the contrary, the Hindu scriptures insist upon the boy studying up to at least 25. The present form of marriage before that age is obviously meant as betrothal. If boys refuse to marry before 16-18, girls will have to wait. But this refusal can be based only upon a ruling of such authority as students cannot set at naught. It is quite true that the Hindus cherish the greatest respect for traditional doctrines. But that applies, if at all, only to the orthodox and the illiterate classes. Manu, the ancient sage, is a great authority, and is, no doubt, recognised as such by every Hindu graduate. But the authority of our modern Manu, the Vice-Chancellor of the University, for instance, does not carry less weight with the average B.A. and M.A. A Universty degree is indispensable. To the majority of young collegians it is their means of livelihood. I am convinced the University can do us great service in this way. And I am equally convinced that the educated class would be profoundly thankful for the relief. Whether it is practicable to make such a rule it is for the authorities to determine. But I am supported by the general approval of Hindu graduates. And they know what is best for them. I make the same appeal to the Educational Department and to the other departments of the State, also to private offices and firms. Give a long notice, 5, or, if you like more years—after which you will prefer the unmarried candidate for employment to the married one, all other qualifications being equal. " Why should the children suffer for the parents' sins?" they ask me. But there will be little to suffer save amongst fools and idiots, if you give fair warning. And even if the arrangement does cause suffering or inconvenience, what are we to do? Is it not in accordance with the Divine law that the son must suffer for the father's sin ? And in this very instance, do not children suffer for the sins of their parents—the ignorance or cupidity which leads the parents to keep their children in lifelong bondage ? This custom entails much more suffering than would be caused by the arrangement I suggest. And then let it be remembered that once the University Senate has laid down the rule, Hindu parents will be only too glad to avail themselves of it. Even the more ignorant among them will, in their own interest, prefer that their sons should obtain a degree before entering upon the trials of married life. The Hindu father cares quite as much for his son's income as for his marriage. Under this head I make other minor suggestions such as offering inducements to girls remaining longer at school than at present, of describing the evils of early marriage in school books, and so on. *None of these suggestions need legislative interference of any kind whatever.*

In the seventh paragraph of my Note I refer to the marriage of girls of 8-10 to old men of 50-60. The parents or guardians of the girls make money out of these nefarious transactions. Let this money be set apart for the victims. I am told that the money paid by the bridegroom is supposed by law to belong to the girl. But in practice it is appropriated by the father. If this is fraud it must be so declared, and the fraudulent parent must be made an example of. Sometimes the bridegroom may present his father-in-law with 10,000, Rs. of which the latter may appropriate 9,000 and set apart the remaining 1,000 as the bride's *palla*. In this case it may not be impossible to find out if the father sold his girl for a thousand rupees only when there were other buyers in the caste offering a larger price. The bribe at times amounts to Rs. 50,000 and even more. Let caste be called upon to regulate this matter.

In the 8th and last para. I refer to another kind of infant marriage. I need not here dwell upon that scandalous arrangement. Can no power prevent it?

Side by side with efforts in this direction, the people must also be roused from their apathy of ages. Every locality ought to have an Association in aid of social and domestic reform. To begin with home—more value ought to be placed upon the life and liberty of woman. She must be treated in practice as the exact equal of man. The idea of inferiority, which always places the girl next to the boy in the Hindu household, ought to be gradually effaced. Woman's first duty is doubtless at home—but she is not therefore to be treated as a drudge and an encumbrance, to be got rid of the soonest that could be. Then some of the habits of the people require to be changed—the sleeping in the same room, talking about forbidden subjects in the presence of girls, foul language and filthy jokes, insane ceremonies at marriage, pregnancy, birth. The studied segregation of women in their monthly trouble, and other stupid practices, ought to be slowly got rid of. Local Associations could be of immense service in the matter. The school-master, too, can co-operate with advantage. Schools are a hotbed of the vices of youth. Many of these evils will, of course, continue so long as human nature remains the same. But not a few of them are pre-

3

ventible. Rome and Greece suffered from the same social pests as India now suffers, in a more or less intense form, till Christianity softened and humanised a population of very little better than beasts. India is under a Christian Government. Can the Government do nothing to prevent the outward manifestations of man's animal nature, in the form of obscene songs, abusive epithets, and indecent speech and gesture? I dare say the policeman is under instruction to arrest an offender, if he is found disturbing the public peace. But the policeman in India scarcely comes up to his work in such matter. The school-master must take his place if he is at all worth his salt. Who has not heard the language used by our school-boys? For the slightest difference of opinion, and often out of mere wantonness or force of habit, we hear striplings of 8 and 10 treating each other's female relations to language quite incredible to the European in its gross suggestiveness and amplitude of resource. The schoolmaster ought to exert himself, though in the face of the parent's own default he cannot do much all at once. After all the evil is traced home to the domestic circle, and the father of the family is responsible for it. He must set his house in order. Let him try his best to free his home of such foul atmosphere. Let him take a vow not to marry his sons before 20 (his religion does not force him to do it), nor to attend foolish ceremonies, including the performance of an early marriage, nor to countenance them in any way. The Hindu is too sensible not to know that infant marriage is a crime against nature, against manhood, and more especially against womanhood, and that deterioration of a noble race is its direct outcome. It is for the Hindu to profit by the knowledge so far as he can help himself.

The problem of compulsory widowhood appears to me to be more easy to solve either by the people or otherwise, although it is quite true that this wretched custom is of a much earlier date than infant marriage which is a comparatively modern growth. Is it possible for any man of sense to believe that the ancient Hindu sages, who prescribed a protracted moral and intellectual discipline for the male student, if not also for the female, could have enjoined or even suggested a practice so destructive, as early marriage is, of national development? The noble institution of *Swayamvara* gives a lie to advocates of infant marriages, if there are any such advocates. With enforced widowhood the case seems to be different. No Hindu widow in early days could re-marry. But what was the object of the prohibition? Only to keep the property of the deceased husband in the family. The younger brother of the deceased husband kept his place till a son was born to the widow. That arrangement then went out of vogue and Suttee was substituted. Suttee has been abolished by law, but the Hindu widow, though nominally allowed to remarry, remains in the same position as before without any of the advantages above referred to. I do not ask for a new law even here to ameliorate her condition. All that I seek is that Act XV. of 1856, passed in her favour, may be made fairly operative. If the three suggestions I make in this connection are impracticable it is for my Hindu brethren to treat them as they deserve, and find out other means for themselves. They need not be discussed here at length. An important suggestion was made to me the other day—that the State may rule or the caste may arrange that the widow shall have a handsome personal allowance made to her out of her late husband's effects. One reason why she is forced to remain in widowhood is that it enables her parents or protectors to appropriate what is meant for her own comfort and independence. If she remarries the widow forfeits her late husband's property. Now, if her protectors have actually to make her a liberal allowance, they may very likely think it good business to part with the widow and keep her money. Thus a door would be opened to remarriage. In the case of widows without property—a most pitiable condition of life—the temptation is far greater to enter into another alliance. But the victim has few friends and a large number of enemies, beginning with parents and relations. The marriage ceremony includes costly formalities and tedious details. The Brahmin refuses to officiate unless heavily bribed. In such cases could it not be ruled that two or three declarations at intervals before, say the Registrar or the Magistrate, should constitute remarriage? The widow and the man of her choice may go to the official and declare that they wish to remarry. This is merely a suggestion. Another suggestion that I would respectfully submit to the caste is that in case of crime, the betrayer of the widow as well as the unfortunate woman herself should be visited with its displeasure. Abortion and infanticide—more prevalent than people have any idea of—will never decrease unless the betrayer is made to bear his part of the responsibility. I know this is not done even in England. But the law of the Caste can reach where the law of the Court cannot or will not. My last suggestion is about a National Association with numerous local branches. I have great faith in the power of such an Association both as a medium of education and as an interpreter between the people and the State. But Hindu leaders can best initiate such a movement; they alone can make it popular. There will be no lack of sympathy from those whose sympathy is worth having. I think I have shown that much at least. Let a dozen Hindus of talent and influence stand up, and let each of them declare before a public meeting that his life shall henceforth be lived for the restoration of woman in India to the position for which nature has designed her, and which the *Shastras* have themselves determined.

WIFE MURDERS.

It would be interesting to know how many cases of wife murder happen in Bombay every year, and how many of these cases are due to ill-sorted child marriages. The immediate cause is said to be "infidelity" which includes the unwillingness of the girl-wife to render conjugal duties to some hulking ruffian of a husband whose ideas of the matter are sometimes less natural than those obtaining amongst animals. Such is the history of the last two or three cases reported.

The "wife" dreads coming in contact with the "husband." She is dragged "home" from under the parental roof and there slaughtered with as little concern as if she were a domestic fowl. Her parents are helpless : it would be a "shame" unto them to interfere. In other cases the wife may go wrong. Is a young woman, married against her will, so very much to blame if she deserts the miserable old skunk who will lord it over her and force her to find a living for himself and family? When she cannot bear the *zulum* she yields readily to temptation. Then the husband murders her in cold blood and his friends clap their hands—*vah shabas.* The Government at last hangs the husband and goes to bed, satisfied that it has done its duty to God and to man. Let us have a return, giving the number and history of wife-murders amongst the lower classes.*

˙COMPULSORY WIDOWHOOD AND THEOSOPHY.

I am reminded of a correspondence which passed some time ago between two Theosophists, a Native and an Englishman. The former seems to have asked his English friend to prescribe some remedy for the woes of widowhood in India —the sins committed by, and often on, the helpless widow ; and the consequences. The English friend prescribed a non-stimulating diet, rebuked his "brother" for his impudence in having asked for checks, and then read to him a scathing sermon part of which I quote below:—

" But, please, don't write to me about your erring country-*women,*—who are altogether more sinned against than sinning. It is you, or your country-*men* who. err and who are the

---

*On 27th March 1887 Malabari wrote : " Girls of 11 are assaulted by their husbands in a fit of jealousy or anger, and the matter sometimes comes before the Court. We had a case last year, in which a man was accused of having murdered his wife of 11 at Parel. Girls of 11 married and living with their husbands, twice, thrice or four times their age, now and then to be killed when they are not sufficiently obedient or hardworking, according to the husband's ideas of obedience and hard work ! And yet, we are assured that infant marriages do not occur amongst the lower classes, that they do no harm wherever they occur, and that they are a "sacrament" leading to holiness and happiness."

persons really to blame for any slips of the weaker sex. Not only does your opposition to widow-remarriage, which is clearly authorized by the Shastras, tend in a climate like that of India to sin, but by refusing or neglecting to develop and cultivate the minds of your women, you retain them in the position of animals, and are directly and distinctly responsible for all the sins into which they are led by their animal instincts.

Some of you think that by living, yourselves, chaste lives and otherwise raising your own mental and moral status, you will attain *mokhsha*—but I warn you that it is not so. That *karma* covers all the effects, all your acts and omissions, and that each and all of you who aid to maintain and keep in force wicked and injurious customs, which result in impurity and sin in the persons of your weaker fellow-creatures, will most assuredly share in the reflex vibrations of those evils things.

It is all very fine for you men to reprobate the unworthiness of your poor, untaught, child-like sisters—they at least, even if they do in their ignorance sin, suffer for it here. But you—you who by your supineness in this most vital of all questions, by your prejudices or selfishness, are the real source of all this evil—are *you, think* you, to get off scotfree? Believe me this is not how the universe is arranged—this may be *human,* but it is not *divine* justice, and all this evil blots its inevitable stain on *your* KARMA, and, although you escape here, you will elsewhere pay to the last jot the penalty for that sin of which you are in reality the origin and cause.

Do not deceive yourselves—the *Karma* of the most unworthy of your untaught, semi-animal sisters, will be a protecting angel, compared with the retributive demon that will scourge you, pure living, highly intellectual Brahmins, who through indolence, selfishness, prejudice, and what not, aid to keep in force a monstrous system which, as a necessary consequence, leads the poor women too often into evil ways.

Let each man who does not resolutely stand up against this system, which degrades half the children of his motherland to the position of animals, remember that his *karma* shares all the *animality* that results, and when he pretends to lament over the depravity of his injured sisters let him take to his heart the answer of the prophet to David, ' Thou art the man !'"

A SINGLE SUGGESTION.

A Madras friend thinks it would be better if I made one comprehensive suggestion instead of the half dozen already made. Well, there is no harm in trying. The other day I was closeted with a veteran jurist, who is as conservative and as much a stickler for the law as any Hindu Shastri could be. As he pulled to pieces some of my suggestions, he threw out a hint which struck me as worth serious consideration. I have already made use of some of his suggestions for which I must disclaim credit. The cause may suffer by plagiarism of any sort. Now as to the principal suggestion. Suppose a majority of Hindus say that child marriage being a religious institution (which is not true) they cannot practically question its sanctity, the Hindu reformer may meet him somewhat in this wise. Granted, for argument's sake, that his Church obliges every Hindu father to marry his children at an early age. But like the Church the State also has some claim upon him. In justice to society, therefore, there ought to be a civil ceremony besides the so-called religious ceremony. Marriage is a contract of assent, and having come to the age of discretion (say 18 and 16) the contracting parties may be called upon to make a declaration before some public officer, that they are of one mind. Two children may be married at 6 and 4 respectively, but on arriving at puberty, both of them must declare their willingness to abide by the contract made by the fathers or guardians. Circumstances may occur in the interval which forbid the possibility of a happy union, and in that case either or both of the parties may repudiate the marriage, as Mahomedans do now, according to Mr. Maccce, who wrote on the subject to the *Times of India* last week. The declaration may be made privately, if not before the Magistrate, say before a

Native and an English member, of the Council. To avoid fraud, births, adoptions and marriages may be registered. Thus the object of a progressive society may be easily gained, without any State interference with the "religious" usages of the people. This is a mere suggestion, and I know there are difficulties in the way of working it, especially parental coercion and perhaps a forced consummation of the marriage vow. But these could be obviated. At any rate, it seems to me that the dread of the exercise of free will on the part of their children would prevent eight-tenths of Hindu parents from marrying off infants. As it is they consider child marriage to be a very doubtful investment. The new arrangement would make it a dangerous experiment altogether. No Hindu would court a public scandal such as is inevitable on his son or daughter refusing to carry out his wishes in the most important concern of life. But let me say again, this is a mere suggestion for Hindu reformers to consider. As to compulsory widowhood I said last week—make a fair allowance to the widow from the husband's property, and in many a case you either ameliorate her position as it is, or compel the selfish parent or guardian to get rid of her by remarriage. Hard is the lot of the young Hindu widow and it draws tears of blood from those who watch her career of agony and shame !

THE NECESSITY OF GOVERNMENT CO-OPERATION.

The weekly *Subodh Patrika* of Bombay writes without hope. The writer is afraid of any action either on the part of the University or the State. The argument is that inviting the co-operation of Government shows weakness. I contend that it shows strength. Here is a nation suffering for centuries from a disease. If there is a prospect of the chief physician curing the patient, in consultation with the family doctors, is there any shame or harm in applying for an operation? I have observed one peculiarity about the Hindu mind. It spends itself on speculation and stops at the threshhold of action. In this matter the evils are acknowledged on all hands as leading to the deterioration of a splendid race. Are the Hindus wise in trusting too much to their own unaided efforts? Modern education is not likely to help them much in this direction. And a religious revival under the circumstances is out of the question. It may be worth mentioning that the custom of infant marriage has spread from the Brahmans to the other Hindu castes, and I am told it is now becoming fashionable amongst the Musulmans. Compulsory widowhood, too, began with the Brahmans and has been borrowed by the " lower " classes. The fashion will never go out so long as there is a strong intellectual class ruling the masses socially. And even supposing that five hundred years hence the masses may be sufficiently " educated " to help themselves, are we to do nothing for them in the meantime? The least that the State can do is to ascertain the popular feeling. I believe not one out of ten Hindus will deny that the customs are ruinous. That done, the State may take the representatives of the people into confidence and devise practical remedies, keeping itself as much in the background as possible. Luckily, circumstances seem to be very favourable to this plan of action. There are so many classes affected by the evils. Reform may begin with one or more of these classes least affected, that is not hopelessly wedded to the fashion. The Brahmans, who suffer most, but who are the least willing to be relieved, may be left to themselves. I do not want coercion of any kind. If we can move the people ourselves, well and good. But have we been able to make an impression after a struggle for so many years? And is there any real chance of success in future? I know of no Hindu paper so jealous of external pressure as the *Gujarati*. And what does the *Gujarati* say? Something to this effect—Hindu reformers have done their best to shake off the evils, but they could not succeed without some authoritative arrangement to lean upon. The *Indu Prakash*, true to its traditions, observes that the time has now come for a combined action on the part of the

4

people and the State. I am myself entirely of that opinion, though I do not wish to force it upon others. But for God's love don't tell me it is " all right " with the people, and that leaders of society as well as the State have done their duty by the victims of social tyranny. Officials have some excuse for want of spontaneous action, not so our enlightened Hindu brethren."

WHY NOT TAX CHILD-MARRIAGES?

An esteemed correspondent writes to ask why a tax may not be imposed on child marriages. This suggestion, I am told, was made some years ago by a Native gentleman of great judicial experience. I do not know what valid objections may be urged against the proposal. But personally I see no reason at present why a formal ban may not be placed upon a practice which results in such widespread mischief to public interests, and which is so noxious to the best cultivated sense of the community. At any rate, if the Finance Minister promises to apply an Infant Marriage Tax to the education of unprotected widows, he may count upon my support—and my blessing. The point is worth considering.*

*This suggestion was first made on 12th November 1857 by Mr. Pestanji Byramji Dantra to Lord Elphinstone, Governor of Bombay, who brought it to the notice of the Government of India in the following words on 21st November 1857, " The scheme under notice seems to the Right Honourable the Governor in Council to be open to fewer objections than most of those which have been proposed for raising new taxes." At that time a License Bill had been introduced and was one of the burning questions of the day. Mr. Dantra's suggestion was probably not accepted as besides a tax on marriages he had also recommended a tax on the religious ceremonies of baptism, circumcision, assumption of the Janoi (sacred thread) by the Hindus or of the Sadra by the Parsis, and on other initiatory rites. A Madras Civilian in March 1887 advocated the taxation of infant-marriages as follows :—

" The Salt Tax is already, to all intents and purposes, a poll tax, and a poll tax of the most iniquitous kind, as I pointed out at some length (but quite in vain) in your journal, some years ago. Why should not the money raised by it be levied on marriages instead ? No one need object to pay a fee for his marriage, and those who choose to spend larger sums on pompous ceremonies merely for the sake of display might fairly be made to contribute part of their voluntary expenditure to the State ; while those barbarians who choose to condemn helpless children to a life of misery might at least be fined heavily, if they cannot be punished as they ought to be. What sort of ideas of liberty can they have, and how far can they be qualified for self-government, who will not even allow a woman to wear her own hair or marry if she wishes to do so ? If the Hindu religion really sanctions any such restrictions on liberty it is high time that our educated Brahmin friends began to reform."

SIGNIFICANCE OF CORONERS' INQUESTS.

Government decline to interfere with the social or religious concerns of the people in this country. How, then, do they defend Coroners' Inquests? In order to detect crime or trace foul play? But why insult the victim who is dead in order to punish the living offender? That is because, I suppose, human justice is imperfect. Then how about holding Coroners' Inquests on the bodies of those who have died from accident? Natives are extremely sensitive on this point. The Parsi especially will give everything he possesses to avert the scandal of the corpse of a friend being ripped open by a *Feringhee* in the presence of other gentiles. A Coroner's inquest follows every sudden death from whatever cause. Is not this adding sacrilege to misfortune? That it is a sacrilege may be gathered from the fact that a Parsi corpse handled by the Coroner has small chance of being deposited in the consecrated Tower of Silence. The orthodox section of the community have to this day been denouncing the inquest as *Zulum*. How does Government justify it?

WHY VIDIASAGAR FAILED.

The *Bengalee* cannot brook the very idea of State action of any kind. Do I understand my friend to be of the same mind as regards action on the part of the Universities? That would be unfortunate indeed, coming from an advanced thinker. My brother reminds me of the efforts of Pandit Vidiasagar—how he worked without official aid in any form. I am not quite sure if the venerable Pandit scorned friendly co-operation from the rulers. But it is certain that he did not get it publicly. And what was the result? That Pandit Vidiasagar practically failed. The veteran champion, who has had no equal in point of learning and personal influence over the people, breaks down in mid career, never to rise again. He struggles with the evil genius of the nation till completely exhausted. He spends his strength and his substance. And now we find him almost broken-hearted, with scarcely ten followers to keep up the crusade. What is the cause?—the people is an inert mass whom it is impossible to move without some sort of extraneous action. And let me ask the patriots of Bengal—what have you done for Vidiasagar? You ought to have furnished him with lakhs of rupees and thousands of men. Have you so much as made a serious effort to stand by him? What then, becomes of your boast about helping yourselves? I should like to know the number of University Graduates in Bengal and to be told what each has done towards bettering the condition of women? There are 7,400,000 widows in the province. Has anything been done for their education, let alone other social benefits?

WHAT PANCHAYETS CAN DO.

It is truly gratifying to see that the subject of marriage reforms amongst Natives is occupying the attention of benevolent English friends in all parts of the country. Amongst these silent workers of good we may name Mr. C. W. Whish, C.S., of Shahajehanpur, who has drawn up a programme which is likely to meet with general approval. We must say here at once that Mr. Whish has confined himself merely to the public aspects of the question. He wants the people themselves to regulate marriage expenses, dowry and polygamous connections; also to obtain an extension of the limit of age in the marriage of girls.

"It is well known that the scale of expenses in marriages has been forced up by a spirit of emulation to such an extent, as not only to lead to almost universal indebtedness and the ruin of numbers of old families, but actually to prevent poor people from marrying their daughters at all. The rates of dowry to a bride are also unregulated and excessive, and as a reciprocal expenditure is expected on the part of the bridegroom's family, a further impulse is given to keeping up the excessive scale.

This evil, combined with the unreasoning contempt which has sprung up for the relationship of the bride's father and brother (these terms being used as expressions of abuse) is clearly the root of female infanticide. Among some castes marriage assumes the form of a trade and brings infamy."

Along with these matrimonial customs Mr. Whish also appeals for the suppression of intoxication and the use of noxious drugs, of gambling and other forms of social immorality, the moral training of youth, and improvement in the intercourse between Natives and Europeans.

As to means Mr. Whish suggests the formation of local and district committees, composed principally of delegates from each important sub-division of the Caste. He gives a number of practical rules for consideration, and is so confident of success, if the Panchayet works with zeal, that he thinks these Panchayet bodies may eventually obtain the sanction of the Legislature to the solemn decisions of a sub-committee ratified by a district committee, and if need be, by a provincial committee. That is to say, it could be made penal for any individual to transgress the rules laid down for the benefit of the entire community. Such, we believe, were the Panchayets of old, but the life has gone out of them, and the social interests of the people are presently at the disposal of selfish and irresponsible monopolists. We commend the scheme under notice to every well-wisher of India. It is for the people to make it a success.

GOVERNMENT NEUTRALITY.

The Government of India professes to be neutral. Why then, does it allow cattle-killing on such an enormous scale ? (This is one of my pet grievances). The cow is sacred to the Hindu; and a foreign Government is bound to respect his religious scruples. But it is not on this account only that I protest against the slaughter of kine. India is an essentially agricultural country, and the value to it of its cattle is much greater than to other countries. It is true that Mahomedans use beef; but if the enlightened British Government sets them an example they are sure to desist. Will Government rule that the army is not to be supplied with beef after due notice? Let the men have good vegetable and other diet with a ration of mutton once or twice a week, if necessary. I am prepared to prove that this would be better for the army and for the country, and what is more, it would end an interminable strife between Hindus and Mahomedans, which may lead one day to serious results. Will Government do its duty both from the economic as well as the religious point of view? To my mind the "cow-question," which is so often made light of, involves grave political issues.

I said last week that Rajputs do not marry too early now-a-days. This is due, at least in part, to English influence. The Resident at a Native Durbar is at times guardian of one or two minors. And whenever he can, he prevails upon ladies of the zenana to put off the young fellows' marriage. So long as boys do not marry girls must wait. The latter cannot go out of the clan. And what the Chiefs do will be done by the Thakurs and other dependents, though the people, not being of the same race, are slow to follow. If leaders of Native communities set the example, the other members, especially of the same sect, are sure to follow. But where is the example?

Referring to the proposed Infant Marriage Tax a friend says the people will not mind it. That they will borrow from the sowcar. I doubt this. The sowcar would be very slow to lend money for an unproductive investment (in point of money, of course!) as the marriage of paupers.

IS CONCERTED ACTION POSSIBLE?

It is an instructive fact that no Hindu correspondent has yet denied the existence of the evils to which I have adverted. A few of them say that I have over-painted the picture of misery; but many seem to take the picture as faithful, if not faintly coloured. This is so far a gain—it is half the disease cured. The difficulty is about concerted action. Such action seems to be impossible where society is split up into innumerable sects. The number of educated men is pretty large. But they have their way to make in the world. Besides, we must remember that though taken together the number is large enough to be a "force," still when divided into sects and centres of action, as it is necessary to do for practical work, the force becomes useless as a national regenerator. For instance, Messrs. Mandlik and Telang appear to work together as brothers and yoke-fellows in political matters; but for matters social they stand as far apart from each other as I stand from either of them. Neither they nor the ladies of their families could be induced to be of one mind where social amenities are concerned. This is *the* difficulty. It is all well to blame "lip-reformers" and denounce their "hypocrisy." But men cannot be more than human (though some of them do abuse me with superhuman energy). The best plan of action, therefore is, as I suggested some time ago, to take up one or two castes readiest for reform and to help such from inside and from outside.

The Hindus, as a people, are the mildest and most law-abiding race in the world. And I cannot adduce better proof of this fact than the way in which the nation has been clinging for centuries to a "corrupt and corrupting" social law. In some of its bearings the law of marriage amongst them appears to be not only a one-sided law, but one generally unsuited to the times. The people know it to be an unequal law, one which has sapped the vitals of society, which has partly demoralised it and split it up into a thousand sects (from the original four) wider apart from one another than is Zoroastrianism from Judaism or Christianity from Islam. And knowing this to be so, the people still cling to this old law, the mere carcase of the law that was. Now, I say, help these "children of a larger growth" to a new law, a living, wholesome law, a law suited to the wants of the age and based on humanity and common sense, and the people will thankfully discard the old law. Who is to do this? The Government are wringing their hands in despair. The social leaders of the people won't do it, because it is to their advantage to keep up the "corrupt" law. The intellectual leaders of the people, our only "forlorn hopes," seem to be placed at a disadvantage for the desired reform. Whatever their profession at College in favour of reform, they have to modify them largely on entering upon public life. Our educated young men have to make a position for themselves, and for this they have to depend more upon "the natural leaders" of Caste than upon their own merits and the good sense of the community. Thus, owing to the timidity of the State, the selfishness of the "natural" leaders of society and the helplessness (?) of its educated leaders, the people are condemned to lasting stagnation.

WIDOWS FOR WIDOWERS.

The *Bombay Samachar* lights upon a point which will be very useful just now to those who are frightened at the idea of widows displacing virgins in case they remarry freely. To such alarmists the *Samachar* points out that Nature intends widowers for widows. But even supposing that in some cases widows do displace virgins, there is this consideration not to be lost sight of—that whereas the virgin hopes to marry some day, the widow has no hope. The result is that the virgin conducts herself well because it is open to her to obtain a husband some day. But the widow, in her desperation, is apt to go wrong, disregarding her finer instincts, because she knows she has no chance of remarriage. Make remarriage optional for the widow and see that she does not suffer for taking a second husband ; and you greatly reduce the amount of sin and misery incidental to widowhood. The very hope that she may marry again one day will keep the young creature from harm. She will then know how to respect herself.

WIDOW SHAVING.

A friend asks why the barbarous practice of shaving widows, is not put a stop to ? The widow is shaved, I understand before the body of her husband is removed, and thereafter she is shaved periodically by the street barber. I cannot say whether this practice is general amongst all classes: But it is one of the cruelest indignities offered to a woman, to deprive her forcibly of her crown of glory. Surely, the widow does not love to be shaved by the street barber ? My friend says that this shaving is not enjoined by the *shastras* ; what what is wanted is only a tress of the hair: But Caste will have the head shaved clean, to render the victim hideous to look at, and thus to prevent her from thinking of social amenities. Confound these fools who pique themselves so much on their worldly wisdom ! The indignity only drives the girl to desperation ; it kills her self-respect. The woes of widowhood are so keenly felt that if the British Government were to leave India to-day, they say, Suttee would be thankfully revived in the country. Now cannot our reformers rescue the widow from the barber's hands? If the hair must go, cannot the mother or the sister clip it with a pair of scissors ? Why heap indignity upon indignity till you almost brutalise a human being ? Well has Altaf Housein of Delhi said:—you lock up the girl in a coal room, and still want her to come out spotless !

CAUSES OF INFANT MARRIAGE.

One tendency of the present discussion is to show that child marriage is a custom of modern growth and that it has little to do with caste or religion: Is it not so much the easier, then, to shake off the custom ? I believe early marriage is opposed to the spirit of the Hindu *Shastras*. It may have been forced upon the people under the first Mahomedan inroads. But whatever its origin and extent in previous times, it is conceded on all hands that the evil is peculiarly harassing in our present circumstances. The theory of climate calling for early marriages has exploded. The inhabitants of Africa and of the islands of the Pacific do not marry early. One cause of the prevalence of the evil in India, as a friend explained to me the other day, is that we Natives attach primary importance to marriage ; we look upon it as *the* event

5

of life, the be-all and the end-all. Now a rational being ought to be prepared for marriage, with its heavy responsibilities, before he even thinks of it. He must first acquire the necessary education, moral and physical. He must also learn to make an income and a provision for himself and the future family. And then alone has he the right to marry. Most young men would take this course if left to themselves. But the matter is taken out of their hands by parents or guardians. The dread of caste, the love of display, the desire for progeny—these are amongst the causes at work. And as a result marriage is an all-absorbing topic in the Native family. The home atmosphere is saturated with silly notions about marriage. No sooner is baby born than the elders of the family begin thinking about its disposal. Poor little soul! Born in bondage and in bondage to remain all its days! So all-pervading is this pernicious idea that it enters largely even into children's play. Little boys and girls playing with their dolls marry them in form and in effect, perform the previous and the subsequent ceremonies, carrying the farce down to the birth of doll's baby! How can you save these children from precocious development? Here we come home again. We must purify the home first of all. We must think of our country more than of ourselves. To say that a man will be absolved of all his sins merely by begetting a son, is preposterous. By doing so before his time he will only incur more sin and be open to more suffering. A good thought, a good word, a good deed in the cause of the country are more potent to save you than any number of sons and daughters. To marry and beget before the season is very much like suicide and murder rolled together.

THE UNNATURALNESS OF INFANT MARRIAGE.

What could be more unnatural than that an intelligent Hindu, knowing that widow marriage is impossible, should give away his daughter of three or four in marriage? We hear of widows of three now and then. And there is a large number of widows under 9. I believe it was Khanderow

Gaicowar who celebrated the "marriage" of two favourite pigeons with all the pomp and circumstance of a royal wedding, including dinners and *dakshnas* to Brahmans. Brahmans officiated at the ceremony, and the people turned out in large numbers to witness it. In fact, no Raja could have married himself or his children with greater *èclat*. I suspect His Highness took the pigeons to be his cousins in a previous *avatar*. But were not all educated Hindus in the country shocked at his barbarous joke? And now I'll give you my opinion—I think poor old Khanderow was not so much to blame for "marrying" pigeons as some of my educated Hindu friends are for "marrying" little mites of humanity. Khanderow could afford the luxury. The feathery bride or bridegroom had no idea of unhappy married life or perpetual widowhood. In the latter case you have no excuse, nothing to recommend the coupling together of babes in the presence of grim uncertainty. Child marriage leads to manifold evils, and yet the educated Hindu cannot foreswear it. Who is more to blame—the illiterate Maratha Prince or the educated Brahmin Pandit?

THE PRIEST, THE PANDIT AND THE GRADUATE.

Mr. S. Ragonath Rao, Assistant Commissioner of Kolar, suggests that the Hindu priest and the graduate must be induced to work together in putting down child marriages. And he says that this could be easily done, as such marriages are not religiously enjoined. I have proposed something like it at the end of my second Note. Let the priest, the pandit and the graduate work in concert. The latter two may do so, especially if friendly English officers and the more enlightened Native Princes take them in hand. I am not [so sure of the priest. But who will move the prince that he may move the pandit and the graduate? The Raja is not a Brahmin, and in many cases he will be only too glad to defy modern Brahmanical teaching. But a Raja or Nawab cannot be

moved at least under a Member of Council. He needs some
incentive. Mr. Ragonath Rao says that if we only give the
Hindu girl her own option as to the time of marriage, the rest
will take care of itself. There is much sense in this proposition. The marriageable age is quite optional with Hindu
boys—they can marry at any age. The same was the case
with Hindu girls in former days. The *Shastras* say nothing
against the marriage of girls at a mature age. It is only in
modern times, and I believe under peculiar circumstances, that
child marriage came into fashion. It seems to me to have
been merely a precautionary measure at first; and then as
Caste went on being divided and sub-divided, and marriageable girls became fewer, the custom became established.
To-day, no Hindu in any part of India can keep his daughter
unmarried long after having attained puberty. "A grown-up
girl is to the household a serpent cherished in one's bosom."
"As the elephant is kept best at the Raja's Darbar so is the
girl at her husband's." To these idiotic and one-sided sayings
the priest adds his shibboleth, *tarta dana maha punya*—the
sooner given away the greater the merit. The fact is, as Mr.
Deshmukh observed the other day, woman has no status in
society. She is man's inferior in every respect. She is
allowed no will of her own, no power to act. In not a few
relations she is treated worse than menials. She is married in
childhood unconscious of the pledge. Now even if this union
turns out happy, there is a chance of her becoming a widow.
And that means her complete obliteration. Henceforth she
has no hope of happiness ; and either she suffers herself
to be misled, or what is more frequently the case, to be killed
by a process of starvation. The only plausible reason given
in support of infant marriage is that the girl is thereby
saved from mischief and her parents from prolonged responsibility. This is false reasoning. The sexual instincts in
woman are almost invariably quiescent. This appetite of
the unmarried woman is infinitely less strong than of the
unmarried man. Even in the married state woman yields to
the sex-passion more under a sense of obligation than indul-

gence. This is a physiological fact. It is man generally who is the cause of mischief. The fellow makes laws for himself and for woman, breaks them at will in his own case, and in the case of his sisters he not only enforces the laws with rigour, but has the impudence to justify the course on the ground of woman's supposed weakness. This one-sided law obtains more or less all over the world—in India it is universal and inexorable. Why we Hindus are so slow to reform society, when we know that reform is urgently called for, is because we do not care to treat woman as man's equal, at least socially.

There is nothing in Nature, and nothing in the *Shastras* making child-marriage compulsory. Then why practise it to this frightful extent ?

Mr. Ragonath Rao further hopes that if infant marriages gradually go out of fashion, they may, to that extent, make room for intermarriages. This latter will be a very wholesome change if introduced. I must not be understood as advocating intermarriages between all castes—the day is too distant for that. But why, for instance, should not all the Brahmin castes intermarry ? The Brahmins are sub-divided into a number of sects ; and though many of these eat together and have other dealings in common, still they avoid intermarriage. Nothing could be more unreasonable. In the same way all the other castes which are closely allied may extend their intercourse a step further. Intermarriage was generally practised in India before till each of the four communities broke up into sects and clans. The *Shastras* do not object to intermarriage within a certain area, the want of which is a serious drawback both to the growth and the unity of the people.

INFANT MARRIAGE IN INDIA.

NOTE II.

[WITH SUGGESTIONS REVISED AND AMPLIFIED.]

In continuation of my notes, dated 15th August, on the subject of Infant Marriage and Enforced Widowhood, I have now to submit the following points for consideration:—

I. That my statement has been accepted as being generally correct, and that several of my suggestions have commended themselves, partly or wholly, to some representative Hindu gentlemen and responsible Hindu journalists. It may be added here that a few of these have actually suggested direct legislative action as chief remedy for the evils under notice.

II. That it has been shown that Infant Marriages contribute very largely to compulsory Widowhood.

III. That Infant Marriages form no part of a religious institution in India.

IV. That the nominal marriage of a Hindu girl is not insisted upon either by her religion or caste much before puberty ; and that even after that period the girl is fit to be married on performing certain expiatory rites.

V. That according to Shastras no Hindu male may marry before he has gone through a prolonged course of moral and intellectual discipline. This condition places him between 20 and 30, and it also naturally implies that his wife should be much above 12.

VI. That in spite of this salutary rule the fashion of child marriages has become " all but universal" in modern India— in some castes as many as 60 to 80 *per cent.* of girls being found prematurely married.

VII. That the educated classes and all sensible Hindus generally deplore the evil results of the custom, but in the absence of some AUTHORITATIVE REGULATION they are quite unable

to help themselves. It is too much to expect individual reformers in India, with their peculiar habits and usage, to
discard a deep-rooted and wide-spread custom where the area
of selection in a caste is extremely limited, and where both
parties to a contract of marriage are seldom or never of the
same mind as regards the disadvantages of the custom. In
some caste the leading members have tried corporate action,
but without avail. For instance, a society was formed at
Ahmedabad a few years ago, the members of which pledged
themselves not to marry their children under certain fixed
limits of age. But as there was no binding agreement, no
real and uniform *bandobast*, and as breach of faith involved
no inconvenience, the volunteers, many of them earnest and
sincere men, fell away when their turn came for action.

VIII. That this being so, it is desirable that the State
should co-operate with Society to some extent, at least in
the initial stage of reformation; that it should lend the
cause the weight of its moral influence, should invite the
confidence of representatives and otherwise aid them in their
struggles for self-improvement. Such action is quite competent to the State; in public interests it can and ought to co-
operate with the people so far without resorting to any form
of "Interference" rightly understood.

IX. That Infant Marriages lead to a variety of mischiefs.
They may lead to unhappiness, and they do lead to suffering
in the case of women and to early widowhood; they lead to
pauperism and to deterioration of the race. I submit that
the State is bound to deal with at least some of these public
aspects of the evil.

X. That I propose two methods of action—*first*, to discourage the practice, and *second*, to encourage reform in the
matter. With regard to the former (*a*) I propose that, after
due notice, the University (which is not a State department)
may declare the married candidate ineligible for Matriculation, and that Fellowships and Scholarships may be likewise
refused to married students at College. Further, that heads

of Public Departments may prefer the unmarried candidate
to the married, all other qualifications being equal. This
second proposal might need longer notice. And then, too, I
would gladly avoid it if a more feasible alternative could be
found. At the same time, I cannot help observing that even
this proposal, as it is, does not fall within the legitimate de-
finition of the word Interference. If parents and guardians
claim to be free to marry their minor charge at any age, is
not the State also free to exercise its patronage to the best
advantage consistently with its principles of public morality ?
Government do not employ physically or morally incompetent
persons, however pitiable their circumstances may be. In
the case of girls who are minors, and not a few of them orphans, the duty of the State to protect their interests becomes
imperative. It is not, therefore, on grounds of justice, but of
practicability that I am induced to view this proposal with
diffidence. A practical suggestion elicited in the course of the
present discussion is worth mention here—that children may
be betrothed at any time, but that on coming to years of discretion they may be given the opportunity of ratifying the
contract previously entered into without their assent.

My other method (*b*) is that special inducements may be
offered to grown up pupils at school, especially to girls, in the
shape of scholarships, prizes, medals, &c.

Referring again to suggestion (*a*) I may be permitted to
enumerate a few cases with which the British Government
has been constrained to deal in a public manner. And though
all these cases are not exactly parallel, still they fall more or
less under the same category, the difference being more of
degree than of kind. The results of a child marriage, are
almost as inevitably mischievous as of many other social customs in India which the British Government has already
put down: in some points the result of such marriage are
indeed more mischievous. We have, for instance, Compulsory
Vaccination. Defiance of the Vaccination Act, or even
neglect or omission to take the benefit of it, has been made

penal. Students and applicants for State employment are required to produce the Vaccinator's certificate. Then, during epidemics, patients, of whatever caste, are forced to take hospital medicines. Again, we have the Coroner's Inquest in cases of accident and of suspected crime. All these measures are extremely repugnant to the religious sense of the community, and none of them was asked for by them or their representatives. On the contrary, their introduction was bitterly opposed by the majority. And yet, in the interest of the people these measures had to be forced upon them under specific penalties. There was State action of the same kind, apparently more arbitrary, in the suppression of *Satti*, infanticide, self-torture, lotteries, gambling on holidays, and other religious practices, so-called. Slavery and the traffic in human beings had similarly to be put down with a high hand, though we know that in some cases the slaves themselves, no doubt under inspiration from their masters, declared for bondage in preference to freedom, and though such selling and buying was alleged to have the sanction of religion amongst some nations. A Government, which has done so much for the happiness and advancement of mankind, shows strange inconsistency in declining to act in the present case as supreme guardian of the interests committed to its care. If it waits for the entire population to be sufficiently educated to help themselves, or to apply for aid from without, it lays itself open to the same charge of inconsistency. The Parsi Act, the Brahmo Act and other legislative measures to regulate inheritance, succession, &c., were not undertaken at the instance of entire communities or even all their leaders. Thus, then, guided by the light of its own past experience the least that the State should do in this matter is to co-operate with enlightened public opinion to the extent above indicated. The practice of Infant Marriages has taken deep root in the soil, and the efforts of private individuals by themselves will never dislodge it. The custom is like a chronic disease too obstinate to yield at once and to single remedies. Combined and sustained action alone will cope with it successfully.

6

At the end of my first note on Infant Marriage I have called attention to two seriously objectionable forms of the custom—young girls married to old men and grown up girls married to boys. Is it too much to call upon Society and the State to protect minors from such obvious injustice ?

BEHRAMJI M. MALABARI.

Bombay, 23rd *October* 1884.

ENFORCED WIDOWHOOD.

NOTE II.

[WITH SUGGESTIONS REVISED AND AMPLIFIED.]

As to Enforced Widowhood it is in some points a more difficult and a much more delicate question to deal with. Nobody wishes the young widow to be remarried by force. Only let second marriage be optional with her. This justice has already been accorded to woman under Act XV of 1856. But though the British Government in India has made the remarriage of widows perfectly legal in theory, practically the enactment brings little relief to them. In effect it leaves the widow very nearly where she was before; and by betraying its own weakness, it upholds the pretensions of caste. The struggle between the two parties, as unequal as ever, has now been rendered doubly sharp. This conflict appears to be incompatible with the avowed object of the Legislature, and it may ruin the cause of reform. The Code sanctions the remarriage of widows. But Caste tears up the sanction with vindictive zeal, and visits with its severest displeasure all those concerned in an act sanctioned by the law of Nature and confirmed by the law of the land. Europeans cannot realise the full meaning of " excommunication " in India. It means the snapping of cherished domestic ties, the upsetting of close social relations for an essentially home-loving people, the forfeiting of everything that makes life bearable. Let the Courts call upon the Punchayet to show cause for its action wherever it is found to be vexatious, affording some facilities to the victims at the same time; and excommunication will lose half its terrors. Such a step, necessitated by the ineffectual advance made in 1856, will curb the recklessness of the strong and breathe a sense of security into the weak. To add to the difficulties in the way of widow marriage there are the expenses. The priest will not officiate at the ceremony for his usual fee. In view of these and other difficulties I now submit the following revised suggestions :—

I. That, if possible, the widow be helped to a handsome allowance from her husband's effects, so as to make her independent of those whose interest it is in many cases to keep her a widow all her life.

II. That in the interests of widows ill-provided for, the marriage ceremony be made as inexpensive as possible—for instance, by ruling that two or three declarations before the Registrar may constitute marriage.

III. That Government may be pleased to make annual grants for a few years to a Widow Marriage Fund in aid of the movement.

IV. That special educational facilities be provided for widows, to enable them to qualify themselves as school mistresses, midwives, medical practitioners, and so on.

It would be wrong, I submit once more, to trust entirely to the unaided efforts of individuals. Such efforts may have succeeded in European countries where society is more or less compact and homogeneous. But in India, with its innumerable sects cut off from one another by wide difference in locality, language and other bonds of national unity, and where social life is regulated by the *ipse dixit* of an intensely conservative and irresponsible priesthood ; where men's minds cling to the glories of the past too tenaciously to be diverted to the more glorious possibilities of the present or the future ; spontaneous and self-helping progress is, to my thinking, impossible. It is necessary, no doubt, that social leaders should pave the way for action on the part of the State. But at the same time it is equally necessary, I hold, that the State should brush away obstacles in the path of progress, listen to the reformers' call for succour, approve and encourage their appeal, and in short, show itself ready to guide the steps of a nation struggling in second childhood. This has been the character of British administration in India, and this spirit of statesman-ship shall have to be maintained if Britain wishes to vindicate her moral supremacy. Let me not be misunderstood again as throwing the burden of responsibility on the rulers. The sum total of my demand on the State is for *temporary aid and co-operation*, such as it has more than once extended before to less urgent reforms. This friendly action is of vital impor-tance to the cause, and I cannot therefore lay too much stress upon it or repeat the demand too often or in too many forms.

Now whatever the attitude of statesmen, it does not absolve social leaders from their liability which is comparatively heavier. But in the case of the latter it must be remembered that most of them, as individuals, are far from being free agents. And though anxious to take the initiative, they dare not do so unless assured of combination from within and co-operation from without. As to the people I observe that the national conscience is being slowly awakened to the urgency of reform. Signs are visible in some parts of earnest inquiry and discussion. Encouraged by these signs of the times I am arranging to publish in book form all the opinions received for and against my proposals. This compilation will be largely distributed in India and elsewhere. It will also be translated into the principal vernaculars and scattered far and wide over the country. The next step will be to start an Association. If this Association is subsidised by Government, by Native Princes and other friends of the cause, it may do much good by means of pamphlets, lectures, appeals, and other modes of popular education. In the meantime practical suggestions will be gratefully received. If correspondents wish their letters to be treated as private, they have only to express the wish.

BEHRAMJI M. MALABARI.

Bombay, 23rd *October* 1884.

THE WEAK SIDE OF THE NATIVE REFORMER.

If India is to reform herself, she ought to have an army of martyrs scattered over all centres of activity. Now we know that martyrdom is the highest development of the purest form of patriotism, a spirit of absolute, unconditional self-denial. And what is the present phase of Indian patriotism in this connection? Whenever a defect is pointed out the first impulse of our average patriot is to protest, to justify and to conceal. He thinks it a shame to confess his weakness, and acting upon this principle it is but natural that he should resent other views than his own. How can he bear witness to a cause when he is so anxious to hide the truth of it from the world's gaze? The only way to reach perfection is by getting rid of imperfections at any cost.

OUR PATRIOTS.

The *Subodha Patrika* has a hard hit at our patriots. These lovers of their race argue that as in the tropical climate girls cannot be trusted to themselves after puberty they must be married. Otherwise they are sure to go wrong. But in the same breath the patriots oppose the remarriage of young widows! How consistent! If maids of 15 are apt to go wrong (which assertion is an unmanly libel on the sex) widows of that age are more likely to err. And yet, while the patriot is anxious to marry away girls before twelve, he cannot brook the idea of widows marrying a second time at any age from 12 to 30.

THE EAST AND THE WEST.

The *Reis and Rayyet* publishes some skilful remarks against my "theories," in which remarks I trace the cunning of a well-known hand perceptible in many a pungent paragraph and learned leader. There is nothing wrong in such criticism, and 1 am bound to notice the arguments. To begin with, the writer says that infant marriages in India "are scarcely anything more than mere betrothals." I respectfully ask—are not these "betrothals" binding for life on both parties? Can either party break the contract? In fact, is not the "betrothal" a *pucka* marriage in every sense? Does not the girl become a widow if the boy dies? How, on earth, then, can you call such unions "mere betrothals"?

As to going to Europe and America to find fault with maids, wives and widows, I must really decline the invitation. I am concerned with the affairs of my own countrymen. I know that they are in a very bad way. Sufficient unto the day is the evil thereof. It is true that knowledge of other people's misery partly reconciles us to our own. But in this respect I will repeat, at the risk of offending social philosophers, that there is very little room for comparison between the West and the East. Europe lives in the present, with an eye to the future, at the same time remaining true to her past traditions. India, on the contrary lives only in the past and even therein she is not true to her best traditions. Child marriage was no more a fashion in ancient India than was the drinking of raw brandy and the eating of forbidden food. Europe is far from perfect in her social laws; but just look at the status of woman there and of woman here.

There is no harm if marriage in India takes place earlier than in Europe; but as the *Behar Herald* shows, the question was thoroughly threshed out some years ago, when the highest authorities in Bengal fixed the limit of 15 for girls and 20 for boys. And to-day I do not find even twenty Bengalis to confirm this declaration, though there must be hundreds of thousands who accept it. After all, am I not "only a Parsi"? As to the charge that boys and girls often reach maturity before 20 and 15, the *Herald* shrewdly remarks that this is quite likely when we have a custom in force to induce this ruinous precocity. Precisely so. I myself trace this premature development of the sexual instincts more to custom than to climate. And if the fashion of coupling infants continues, why may we not have fathers and mothers at 12, a few generations hence? We already hear of mothers at that

age, even at 11, and those who know the law of adaptation
and are guided by practical experience will not set down my
proposition as an idle scare.

THE ATTITUDE OF "NON-POSSUMUS."

I am very far from flattering myself with the hope
that success is within sight. But it is something to have
roused the official Kumbh-Karana. Now that the evil has
been acknowledged as "all but universal" we are bound to
find out a cure. Nature provides a remedy for every disease.
I do not insist upon the value of all or any of my own suggestions. Let men of greater experience take the matter out of
my hands. But many of these seem to delight only in opposition. This is a general tendency—the easiest way to assert
your superiority is to say that your neighbour is wrong.
I am not surprised at such opposition local or personal. But
what really puzzles me is the attitude of *non-possumus*
assumed by some of the oldest friends of the cause. If this
be due to the apprehension that my attempts may take away
so much of their fame so well-earned in the same field, I
hope still to win them over, showing that mine shall be the
work and theirs the credit. May Wisdom guide those
gentlemen to whom my notes have been officially submitted!
But if she won't, I trust they will give *me* the opportunity and
the privilege of doing so. As to officials let them by all
means ascertain public opinion. But let them go about it
with tact and discretion. Public feeling is very strong
against the practice. You have only to fraternise with
Hindu friends: sit on the *otla** any fine evening and hear
how they curse caste, how they curse custom, how they curse
themselves in the bitterness of despair. But if they are
asked to confess publicly, knowing that they will, after all, be
left to the tender mercies of caste, the poor fellows cannot
help "retiring into their inner shells."

* A raised earthen platform in front of Hindu houses in Gujarat.

WHY UNITY OF ACTION NOT POSSIBLE.

For unity of action there is absolutely no hope in this matter. A million Hindus may be ready this day for the reform. But each of the leaders may have his own views. They are not likely to agree, and even where they agree they are not likely to work together. The Brahman may not work with the Khshatri, the latter with the Vaishya, and so on. Nay, the Brahman of one part may not work with the Brahman of another. There are numberless sects in the country, and what commends itself to one sect may not commend itself to another. It needs but a small knowledge of human nature to see this. The opposing forces are too many and too strong—there are the local jealousies, the personal, the social, the religious. What power on earth can cope with these adverse forces except a uniform regulation which shall meet with the wishes of the majority and at the same time strengthen the hands of individuals ? At present a Brahman may be anxious to follow a Vaishya reformer— but the very idea that he has to follow another, apart from social consideration, prevents him from adopting the course. Brahman gentlemen like Messrs. Deshmukh and Ranade, who have studied the problem in all its bearings, have lost faith in the reforming power of Caste. No wonder, then, that they call for co-operation from outside.

OTHER SIDES OF THE TRUE PROBLEM.

Mr. Muzoomdar is quite right in saying—" we cannot afford to have love letters, flirtations, rejections, and amorous fancies in our households." Most of these pastimes are certainly undesirable in India ; and I believe they are impossible in our climate and under our social conditions. Now having agreed so far with the Brahmo reformer, may I not put in a few words *for* the usages—poor undefended clients? Are courtship and engagement always so objectionable as we Asiatics conceive them to be? After all the purest and holiest love on earth is the love between the sexes. Such love is the

7

making of a life. The hope of obtaining it one day, of winning and wearing it next one's heart in one's passage through this vale of tears, elevates the moral nature of man and often leads him to the path of glory. These are positive gains. The negative benefits of courtship and engagement are not insignificant. They serve as a useful test, and they give the would-be partners an opportunity of withdrawing in time from a venture which might lead to social bankruptcy and ruin. Flirtation is a naughty little amusement. But I suspect (not without some fear and trembling) that it is often a healthy exercise for the heart : it nerves and steadies that incontrollable little rebel. As to "amorous fancies" let them by all means be made over to the moral hangman. But are not these plaguy things more likely to haunt the inmate of the zenana than the flirt? The flame that scorches and consumes is the secret flame. I do not think a genuine flirt is ever troubled with "amorous" or any other fancies. And now to wind up judgment on these ticklish topics, I may add that with all its drawbacks, marriage after courtship is generally to be preferred to enforced marriage or marriage in which the parties most concerned are least thought of. I must not be misunderstood as sanctioning the usages (for India) which Mr. Muzoomdar so frankly condemns. But the idea that adult marriages—marriages of choice—are seldom pure, is based purely on that Oriental jealousy which can never dissociate woman from sin. I see no earthly reason why the father of a "bevy of undergraduate girls" may not let them alone—to marry or not to marry. It is not every father in India who is blessed with educated girls—so there is no fear of a universal spinsterhood.

I cordially agree with Mr. Muzoomdar that there ought to be "an appreciable number of men and women, disentangled from the anxieties and trials of matrimony for the ministry of sorrow, suffering and other wants of general society." I also heartily concur as to there being numerous sisters of mercy amongst Hindu widows. This is a most satisfying idea. But sentiment apart, are our widows, a decent majority of them, capable of benevolent usefulness ? Are they not generally debarred by their very status in society from such usefulness ? How can they be better when even the rights of a human being are seldom allowed them by the ignorant and the orthodox? We are all agreed that the life of the average Hindu widow is not at all enviable. It is mere euphemism to talk of " men and women " together. The life of the two is extremely unequal—its sweetness and light reserved for men and its sufferings for women. Mr. Muzoomdar seems to be in error when he places the number of Hindu widows between fifteen and nineteen at 28,369. The number of Hindu widows up to nine only is 63,557. Up to 14 it is 240,181. The number up to nineteen is 550,732. And the number up to the mean maximum of twenty -nine is 21,22,877 (keeping the vast number of elderly widows out of count). Are these 21 lakhs of souls all expected to be happy or to bring happiness to others, leading the cruelly unnatural life prescribed to them ? I do not plead for remarriage so much as for social emancipation. The mere sense of freedom would spread sunshine over their hearts, and consequently over half the heart of our humanity.

Mr. Muzoomdar's letter affords an instructive insight into the operations of the marriage law within the pale of the Brahmo Church. Young Brahmos " will not marry widows when their turn comes," although " they theoretically uphold widow marriage as a reform." And this because "all the notions on the subject of the holiness of the marriage tie are absolutely and constitutionally puritanic amongst Hindus." But it is a noteworthy fact, which should not be missed in this connection, that our " puritanic notion " always operates *in favour* of men and *adversely to the* interests of women ! A man may marry ten times over and over in spite of this "puritanic notion." It is only when a woman, even though she be a virgin widow, seeks independence, that our "puritanic notion" comes in the way of progress. Mr. Muzoomdar may declaim as much as he can against this unrighteous system of monopoly ;

but what can an individual even in his position do? I can never bring myself to blame individual reformers.

IS THERE NO *ENFORCED* WIDOWHOOD?

Mr. Chiplonkar's present contention seems to be this :—that out of the 21 lakhs of Hindu widows of a marriageable age (letting alone Musulmans, Parsis, and others) full 15 lakhs are at liberty to remarry. This is Mr. Chiplonkar's latest discovery. But in spite of his " fact " the real fact remains that there are in India at this moment 21 lakhs of women under thirty, made to remain widows. Will any man in his senses believe that the majority of these unhappy creatures, more than 5 lakhs of them in their teens, are allowed to marry, but will not do so? The liberty is only nominal. Talk of " liberty " when the exercise of it means social ostracism of the victim as well as all her friends ! Is not excommunication the unfailing result of widow marriage in all save the lowest castes ? If the widow is always a willing victim, if her widow-hood is not compulsory, what prevents the Widow Marriage movement from growing ? Many widows are no doubt happy. But does Mr. Chiplonkar dare to assert that *all* these 21 lakhs of young women live happy in their enforced solitude, often neglected and half-starved under the influence of a vile super-stition ? How does he then account for crimes and sufferings of daily occurrence? What is the *raison de etre* of so many Remarriage Associations in the country ? Has the venerable Vidiasagar been fighting only a phantom in Bengal for the last forty years ? Was Vishnu Shastri of Bombay a mere visionary? Did Dalpatram write an essay twenty years ago for nothing, depicting the horrors of enforced widowhood and proving by the weight of Shastric authority, under the patron-age of Parsi friends, that remarriage was allowable ? What have Durgaram, Deshmukh and hundreds of others been con-tending for ? In Madras have not Ragunath and his devoted band been struggling against the evil for years past? In Punjab and North West you have Altaf Hussein and others shrieking themselves hoarse. From Rajamundry comes the cry—give us the means and we can remarry hundreds of widows. At Lahore they have started the *Marriage Advertiser* in the interest of widow marriage. Fancy Hindu men and women advertising themselves. The idea is abhorrent, but what will not the desperate sufferer do? And what is the meaning of Hindu widows seeking shelter from Christians? Then, again, if this frightful extent of widowhood is not much felt by the people, what means agitation in the shape of newspaper articles, lectures, plays, pamphlets, odes, appeals and official reports? What is the meaning of a careful judge like Mr. Telang saying that the practice of early marriages and enforced widowhood is "all but universal"? Is all this mere hallucination? If so, if the widow has her choice, why can't you avert from her the curse of excommunication? Now, Mr. Hari Chiplonkar, do you really take me for a fool when you are gracious enough to call my views "foolish," "untruthful" and "false"? If these are the weapons with which you intend fighting your constitutional battles, I sincerely pity your countrymen. It is such attitude that makes me despair of progress from within. Your tactics seem to be to throw a sort of lurid light over Truth and to mesmerise her in half dark. Do you think you can ever succeed? But you are a man of mark, Mr. Chiplonkar, and you have your followers on the Marathi Press. The same is my trouble in Bengal—even outside of Bengal, in Punjab, N. W. and Sind where papers are under Bengali editors, though none of my Bengali brethren, I am thankful to say, has yet called me "false" and "untruthful." I may be weak and foolish, and if there is a combination it may crush me. But how long will it trifle with Truth? After all I am more or less a spectator and an adviser. Final action rests with you. You are the ultimate arbiters of your fate. It is a responsibility fearful to contemplate; and every man, however selfish, will have to account for it in his own person and the person of every one nearest and dearest to him.

WANTED—NOT GOVERNMENT COERCION BUT GOVERNMENT CO-OPERATION.

It is a pity some of my friends are still harping upon " Government interference." I want no such thing. It is co-operation from the State, and not coercion, that society stands in need of. And I am glad to find that such co-operation will not be withheld if duly applied for. Government cannot help sympathising with any well-organised movement in the direction of reform. Those who expect popular disaffection in the event of Government expressing sympathy, betray culpable ignorance of the state of enlightened public opinion. That opinion has pronounced itself emphatically against the evils now, for nearly thirty years. And if it has not had its way, it is chiefly because. of the absence of a uniformity of action. I am myself convinced that even the masses in India are disgusted with the customs ; but like their leaders they have no power in themselves to discard them. I should like to know of a single reform in the East, or for that matter in any part of the world, which the masses have initiated for themselves. It is the representatives who must take the lead, and these must be encouraged by a sympathetic Government. Child marriages are already in ill odour with the intelligent classes; they want only some authoritative regulation to be banished. As to the remarriage of widows, especially virgin widows, I am satisfied that the law shall have to go a step further. Government is only waiting for a suitable opportunity.

THE ATTITUDE OF SOME OFFICALS AND REFORMERS.

It would be amusing, were it not a melancholy sight, to see some of our best official friends holding back, or limping forward in a half-dazed manner, wistfully looking around for escape. The position is really trying, and it is not thought

likely to add to one's popularity. I wish I could convince
English friends that behind this show of opposition there is an
earnest wish for reform. The attitude of our educated friends
reminds me of the fair trifler who "whispering I'll never
consent, consented." And this is natural. They have to lose
everything by a bold avowal, and to gain nothing, not even
the countenance of men in authority to make up for loss of
position and prospects. What wonder if a reformer now and
then protests against the co-operation of the State? In his
heart of hearts I believe he will be only too glad to have some
friendly action. He knows that to be his only chance against
a combination of adverse forces. And even supposing that
this partial opposition is genuine, is it statesmanship, I ask, to
be so tremulously anxious to remain in the good graces of the
people? Why care so much for a brute majority when you
have right on your side? Thank God there is a very large
and intelligent portion of the community in favour of reform,
asking only for some regulating influence. But what if this
were not so? For my part I would rejoice in the glorious
minority of *one* provided my cause was just. It is justice, and
not popularity, by which men in power ought to be actuated.
The world would have known no progress if every step had to
be taken with the consent of the unreasoning rabble. Such
"popular" management of men may answer for a time, but
it is sure to fail in the long run. And, then, will the victims
of the hoax bless the memory of their paternal Government?

I have greater trouble with some of the reformers. They
know the evils to be serious, but will not cope with them
seriously. They suggest every abstract remedy conceivable
that shall not compromise their credit with caste. Most of
all they "trust to education," a delightfully vague expression
where 96 *per cent.* of the mass are unaffected by it, and where
even the two *per cent.* of girls are withdrawn from school at 9.
With this infinitesimal ray of hope, our patriot mounts the
platform ; and as he deprecates practical action, and denounces
those who differ from him, the audience emits a burst of
applause filling the hall with an aroma of onion and asafœtida.

Then they return home to sleep off the momentary fit of patriotism, and next morning the world finds no trace of this magnificent attempt at reform save perhaps a column or two of reports in the newspapers. The subject is laid aside for another year or two, and meantime the voice of the baby-bride and the girl-widow is drowned amidst the din of political declamation. Reformers have their clients to please, and their plaudits to win. Can they afford to say anything unpleasant to the mob?

ODIOUS COMPARISONS.

A correspondent signing himself "Mind your Business"—it is curious he does not mind his own business!—says that unequal marriages are common in Europe and that reformers can do nothing to prevent them. A similar difficulty was suggested to me some time ago by one of the highest administrators in the country,—the marriage of an English girl with her father's footman or of a French girl with an old and otherwise ineligible husband. This appears to be a serious matter, but if examined carefully it will be found useless for our purpose. Such argument can be urged only by those who do not understand the question at issue. Let us take the first case—the English girl is marrying her father's footman. Now remember (1) that *she is a free agent,* which the Hindu girl, given away in marriage by her parents, is *not.* (2) That the English girl is sufficiently well educated to put up with domestic persecution or even social ostracism. (3) That she is generally able to take care of herself in the way of freedom, amusement, &c. under certain circumstances. (4) That she can leave the partner of her choice. And remember that the Hindu girl cannot do any of those things. In fact *she cannot act for herself at any age.* She is not allowed to be a whole human being. Her marriage, often thrust upon her, takes away what nominal independence she may have enjoyed at her parents. Secondly, I do not deny that the French girl is often married under coercion. But look at the fundamental difference between the two married girls. To the average French wife marriage means *freedom*, going out into society, to balls, parties, &c., in short, making herself perfectly happy, whatever her idea of happiness. The husband is a non-entity at home or elsewhere when the two are together. With the average Indian wife the matter stands exactly the reverse of this. Marriage is, in all but name, little more than slavery. So for God's love don't drag in comparisons. Child marriages and enforced widowhood are crimes without a parallel in history, if not in themselves, most certainly in their general results.

HOW TO SET THE RIGHT FASHION.

I do not seem to have made myself fully understood as regards the suggestion to refuse the privilege of Matriculation to the married candidate. The proposal is based on the assumption—and a correct one—that young men are anxious to be saved from parental coercion, under pressure from an all but universal custom. These young men know that early marriage is disastrous to their prospects. But they cannot reason with their orthodox fathers unless the educational authorities, the most likely friends of progress, help them in an indirect manner. If this is done the boy will be able to tell his father—make your choice, Sir, early marriage or useful education. And I am certain, quite as much as my young friend is, that the good sense or the self-interest of the father will prevail. The girls' parents may grumble in the beginning. They may perhaps marry their daughters to elderly men rather than wait for suitable matches. But in a few years the horrors of unequal unions and the advantages of marriage with educated men of a suitable age will be realised. It was after deep thought that I ventured to put forward this suggestion. It amounts to this—save the rising generation from a practice which they are not socially strong enough to shake off and to which they may hereafter become quite as addicted as their fathers. There will be no injustice in the matter, if you give a long notice. After the explanation given above, I need not

8

reply to the argument as to punishing the son for the father's sin, &c. It is not loss, but gain; and the son, the principal party, at least appreciates the position. Many a sensible father, too, would be glad to be given this opportunity of ridding his race of this pernicious fashion. It is said that the results of such a rule would be very meagre. Yes, but it would be most valuable as an example. If you enable our educated young men to set the fashion, it is sure to spread. To those who urge that the rule might lead to dishonest practices, I have only to reply that the University enforces several other rules and is supposed to be strong enough to detect fraud.

WIDOWS AND CASTE.

Caste has no pity for the widow. Why, a woman of ill fame is often better treated than an honest widow. The former has her caste, she heads marriage processions at times, she gets proper funeral honours; whilst the widow, pure and guileless as God's mercy, is shut out of sight, shrouded in darkness and shame, half-starved and subjected to daily indignities. If she revolts, she is lost and undone for ever—so my Hindu friends assure me.

REFORM AND REFORMERS.

I must implore my Hindu friends to give up that unrighteous policy of justifying an evil because it is peculiar to us and has grown old; of protesting against remedies and deceiving themselves and others into a sense of security or of confidence that the evil will cure itself. This policy I should least expect to find favour with the educated. If the disease is chronic, the sooner you take it in hand the better. Because it will be long before you cure it. If the evil is widespread, better begin operation in various parts. If it is not widespread, why, then, it is best to check its growth at once. Let us find out remedies. A hundred may be suggested by a hundred men, and surely some of these ought to answer. It is a mistake, again, to trust to a panacea in such a case. I have myself a limited faith in education as a remedial agent. If education is to do real good it must be specially directed to this purpose.

And then, perhaps, a few hundred years hence the evils may give way. What in the meantime? Who is to be responsible for the sufferings of generations till then?

I must also implore enlightened Hindus not to consider the matter from their individual standpoint, but from the low level of the masses. For instance, when Mr. Telang said the other day that it is possible to keep away the married pair a good while, he was perfectly right. It is in the power of every student to resist temptation, and the longer our girls are allowed to go to school the greater the possibility of this salutary reform. I view this suggestion of Mr. Telang's with sincere satisfaction. But to how many of the social units will it apply? To a handful only. It will have no influence with the people who are sure to do mischief as soon as they are married. What do they marry for?—they ask. We must prevent these simpletons from early marriages if we can. And how can this be best done? By leaders of society setting them an example. The masses follow not the spirit but only the form of your actions. Well, the form is the marriage cere- mony, which educated Hindus must put off if they intend the people to profit by their example.

It is urged by Mr. Telang and other friends, whose word is a pledge of honesty, that widows are "willing victims." But my dear friends, this is what you *believe* more than what you *know*. It is *your* opinion and perhaps the opinion of widow ladies of *your* position in life. What about the mass of young widows, whose presence and very existence is consi- dered inauspicious by their relations, who have no education as a solace in solitude or as a weapon against tyranny and temptation? Think of these, my dear Sirs—of poor Dukhi, Bhagyahini and others. The difference lies here;—you speak from *your* point of view and of those widows who are blessed with certain advantages to make up for their misfortune. I speak for the poor widow, nominally allowed to remarry, but put out of caste directly she does so. I speak *for* the widow and *as* the widow. I not only personate her for the time,

but enter into the very spirit of her misery—verily *I am* the
destitude and deserted Hindu widow while pleading for her?
To you the widow is an abstract entity; to me she is a hard
horrible fact. Hence I may be betrayed at times into a
little warmth of expression. But upon my word it is not to
degrade you, but to elevate the widow, that I write warmly.

Some of my educated friends are opposed to the taking of a
pledge. This, too, appears to me to be a mistake, though
I fully appreciate their motive. To a refined spirit nothing
could be more unpleasant than binding itself down. One's
word must be taken at its full value. This is my own feeling.
But do not judges, barristers, solicitors and others take oaths
before they enter upon work? They are all *sworn in.* Besides, in the matter of popular reform I think the system of
pledge taking would be very useful. Remember it is for the
people that we have to do it. I doubt if the Temperance
movement would have prospered so well but for the pledge
system on which Father Mathew stoutly insisted. We Indians
are familiar with the idea of vow-taking. In this instance,
I have myself made a vow not to lie down to rest till something is done in the direction of reform. I know it is a pity
for a strong man to be weak. But from this very confession
of weakness do I derive the greatest strength in the hour of
temptation—when I feel tempted to throw up a thankless task
which exposes me to gratuitous abuse and vilification from
those in whose interests mainly have I vowed to sacrifice my
all.

FIGURES, IF YOU PLEASE.

Whatever my crosses and losses in connection with the
present crusade, I must not be unmindful of a great gain—
the power to understand and handle figures. There was a
time, and not so very long ago, when figures frightened as
well as baffled me. And now, the opponents be praised, I can
add, subtract, multiply and divide any row of figures, ay even
find out the ratios and percentages at a glance. Heaven
tempers the wind to the shorn lamb. Under this new inspi-

ration let us approach the shrine of the Imperial Census in a spirit of humble inquiry. Here we are told at the very threshold, without knock or cry; that the aggregate number of Hindu males in India taken roundly is 8,44,00,000; similarly that the number of Hindu females in the country is 8,16,00,000. The difference is immaterial so far. Now out of this number the number of males *found* married in 1881 upto 9 is 6,68,000 and the number of females married up to 9 is no less than 19,32,000, that is more than 3 times over. What means this enormous difference? If 6 lakhs of girls up to 9 marry the 6 lakh boys, whom do the remaining 13 lakh girls of 9 marry? I presume they are married to their elders, amongst whom there must be a considerable number of "venerable" bridegrooms. It would not matter much if a girl of 9 married a boy of 12, 15, or 18. But as we shall see hereafter, some of these 13 lakh girls are married to grown up men, not a few of whom may be widowers. What are we to say to such marriages? Let us now take the age between 10 and 14. Here married males stand at 18,08,000, and married females at 43,95,000 ! That is to say, more than 25 lakhs of girls between 10 and 14 are carried off by elderly husbands besides the 18 lakhs who marry husbands of a suitable age. Between 15 and 19 the number of married males stands at 27,40,000, and of married females of that age we have 53,23,000. Thus, again, do 26 lakhs of girls under 19 contract ill-sorted marriages. Between 20 and 24 the males married are 43,35,000 and the females are 66,51,000, a surplus of 23 lakhs given over to old men. Between 25 and 29 the males are 60,48,000 and the females 65,90,000, showing a surplus of only 5 lakhs. At the next stage, between 30 and 39, married males are found to be 1,08,10,000 and married females only 87,97,000, that is 13 lakhs less. Further on, between 40 and 49 married males are 71,89,000 and married females only 43,42,000 that is 28 lakh less famales. One step more, between 50 and 59, married males are 40,47,000 and married females 17,53,000, or 23 lakh less females. And at the last stage, 60 and upwards, married males are 26,72,000 and married females but 6,84,000, that is nearly 20 lakh less females. It will have become clear to mathematical reformers that the vast disproportion up to 29, between 1 and 29, is met by disproportion of a similar kind between 30 and 60, because elderly men have already been found married to young girls. In short, the latter is a confirmation of the former, showing that an unduly large number of girls of a tender age are married to grown up men, widowers included. The figures also bear out what I said some time ago, that by "infant marriage" we must understand generally the marriage of *infant girls* with men much older than themselves, besides those unions in which both parties are infants.

It may be worth while now to look at the number of the widowed and the unmarried. We have 44,05,000 Hindu widowers in India and 1,61,00,000 Hindu widows, that is more than 3 widows to 1 widower. And to make up this enormous difference we have 3,97,00,000 unmarried males and only 250,00,000 unmarried females, or 1,47,00,000 more of the former. Now, if some of the widowers and some of this excess of single males married from the enormous number of 1,61,00,000 widows, they would make themselves a comfortable home, afford sensible relief to a most unfortunate class and prevent sin and suffering the extent of which it is impossible for outsiders to realise. Again, let it be observed that the proportion of widowed males to married males is something like 1 to 9 whereas the proportion of widowed females to married females is something like 1 to $2\frac{1}{2}$; that is, to every 5 married Hindu women there are 2 widows! And yet, they say the evil of widowhood is not so widespread in India !

Look at another picture of widowhood, a more striking one. Between the ages of 1 and 9 the number of widowed Hindu boys in India is 21,000. But the number of Hindu widowed girls of the same age is 63,000. Between 10 and 14 widowed boys are 65,000 and widowed girls 1,74,000 ; between 15 and 19 we have 1,08,000 widowed boys and 3,12,000 widowed girls ; between 20 and 24 the number of widowed boys is 2,06,000 and of widowed girls 6,10,000; between 25 and 29 the numbers are 3,33,000 and 9,61,000 respectively; between 30 and 34 the numbers are 7,86,000 and 27,97,00,040; between 40 and 49 they are 8,77,000 and 36,01,000 ; between 50 and 59 they are 8,67,000 and 34,06,000; and at 60 and upwards we find 11,33,000 widowers and 41,77,000 widows. Taken for each of the nine periods the proportion of widowers to widows is 1·to 3 between the first four periods; nearly 1 to 4 and 1 to 5 during the next two periods and about 1 to 4 during the remaining two periods. And what is the meaning of only 1 widower to 3, 4, 5 widows? It is this, that so many girls *have* to marry grown up men, that these little wives *have* to become widows, and that they *have to remain widows.* To-day I have only scratched the surface of the figures. I could go deeper, but have no heart to do it. Suffice it to say that this enormous difference between the sexes in their civil condition shows that woman is often looked upon not only as man's inferior, but as his property, his goods and chattels: it also shows clearly enough that there are "vested interests " in the way of woman's emancipation. Here I am reminded of a question, not unoften raised during a friendly discussion—"Do you think our orthodox friends will ever agree with you, whatever their education ? These men have often to marry young girls in after life; therefore they *cannot* speak against infant marriage. And marrying young girls they are pretty sure of leaving them widows. How *can* they countenance widow marriage and thus throw temptation in the way of their young wives ?" The question has a peculiar significance which forms one of the stock arguments of the Anti-Remarriage party, namely, that if widows are allowed to remarry, there are so many young women mated to old husbands, that they would be tempted to do away with these lifelong encumbrances in order to have suitable companions. Here we see man beginning his married life in gross selfishness and ending it in gross cowardice. He suspects his wife because he is conscious of his own injustice to her. As a matter of fact the number of Hindu wives who get rid of their elderly spouses by means of poison and so forth must be extremely limited. The average Hindu woman is too good and unselfish to think of such a crime, and indeed too superstitious to attempt it. That is her pride and her misfortune. If the Hindu girl had a little more spirit she would make unequal marriages almost impossible. As it is, she does become desperate now and then ; and if she does not put poison into the husband's dish of rice, she may not scruple to plant a pair of horns upon his head. But I doubt if there is even one such wife amongst a hundred.

I have done with figures now. If they show one thing more than another, it is this—that the time has gone by for idle disputes about details. The evils are there; the victims are there, so there are the tyrants who are after all the greatest sufferers themselves. If my countrymen could but see that the injustice they do to women reacts upon themselves with terrible force, they would soon set themselves to the task of repairing it.

THE PARSAN AND THE HINDUANI.

Mr Chiplonkar* refers to the case of a Parsi widow at Bandora some years ago. Well, there are black sheep in every fold, and if once in five or ten years we come across a case like this it does not prove that Parsis cling to the custom of enforced widowhood. This woman, though she had a large family, might have married again. But her object was to be a "fashionable lady," and she became one. The crime was not forced upon her by custom, as in many a case, alas ! it is forced upon Hindu girls married to old men with a certainty of becoming widows and with a greater certainty of remaining at the mercy of others all their lives. If the Hindu widow errs it is because of her helpless, hopeless situation. She is condemned to suffer and is punished because she suffers. No Hindu girl will go wrong if she is treated as a human being. , She is pure as pure could be, and I believe

---

*Mr. Chiplonkar was not the writer of the articles here adverted to—though they appeared in his paper.

it is her *satta* that keeps the Hindu community afloat, and not education, so-called, of her brothers. If Brahmans have had any real education it is time they afforded proof of it. They are the guides and exemplars of the people. They owe it to others as much as to themselves to discard the common evils of which they have been authors and staunch upholders. If New India is to be blessed with a generation of free and enlightened sons, a nation able to manage their own affairs, the Hindus of to-day ought to rear in their midst a race of free and enlightened mothers. The spirit, the genius of nationality, is imbibed at the mother's breast much better than it is imparted by mumbling schoolmasters and potato-headed " patriots."

SILK BANDAGES.

Mr. Chiplonkar asks on what authority I say that only 2 cases of infanticide are publicly known out of 20. I would be bound to present statistics if these could be had anywhere. Will Mr. Chiplonkar give his "authority" for discrediting the statement? It is a widespread belief, quite rational, that such social crime must go mostly undetected. Abortion is not easy to detect; and as I have often explained before, it is the interest of all parties to shield the erring. Even the Police and the Magistrate will be instinctively merciful to the victim of man's injustice. Add to this the solitary pilgrimage to Nassik, Pandharpur, Benares, and other holy shrines. It is only when all this fails a widow that her shame is published to the world. Is it too much, then, to presume that only 10 *per cent.* of the crime comes to be known ? If Mr. Chiplonkar says so, I gladly accept his view so far as it goes, though unsupported even by presumptive evidence. But will he listen to no one else ? The *Hitechhu* of Ahmedabad, discussing the painful subject only this week, refers to *hundreds* of cases of widow murder and *thousands* of cases of child murder. The Editor is an orthodox Hindu, who seldom agrees with outsiders. Look, again, at the last number of the *Social Reformer* of Lahore, the Editor of which, after quoting a letter full of shocking details, writes :—" It is really strange

9

that a widower of 50, 60, or even 70 will not scruple to marry a girl of 8 or 9, but would not extend the same privilege of re-marriage to his widowed daughter 20 years old. It is wrong to say that the Hindu father is ignorant of all this. To give a widow daughter in marriage is considered much more dis. graceful according to prevalent customs than even her going wrong." I have been reading something like this oftener than I should like for the last 16 years. It is very unkind of my Hindu friends to charge me with wantonness and over-zeal. Besides, they must remember that I have not taken my stand only upon the question of immorality and crime. That Mr. Chiplonkar and others resent my writings shows that they feel on the point. And I respect every man's feelings. But they must make up their minds to agree as to the existence and the extent generally of this disease. We may differ as to the remedy. They may think it wise to cover the sore with a silk bandage. My treatment is to rip it open, so that it may at least stop festering.

THE EXTENT OF THE EVILS.

Cannot the extent of the evils of infant marriages and enforced widowhood be authoritatively determined once for all? The general opinion is that infant marriages are all but universal in India. At any rate, amongst the Hindus there seems to be no other form of marriage. Three of the four castes marry their girls *before* 12. The Census Returns, no doubt, show large numbers as "married" *after* 12. But it strikes me that the word "married" must in most cases be taken as meaning *found married* at the date of taking the census. I might be wrong and should be thankful to be corrected. But experience would show that save amongst the Shudras, girls are seldom kept unmarried long after ten, unless for want of suitable matches. Indeed, twelve would seem to be the period of consummation. And I will undertake to say that consummation immediately after puberty is as great a mistake as stuffing the mouth of a babe with *dalbhat* immediately after its birth.

As to remarriage of widows, though nominally optional with all but the Brahman, it is generally admitted in Bengal, Bombay, Madras, and the Provinces, that save amongst the lowest classes, remarriage is not at all a common practice, chiefly on account of the dread of excommunication. It is admitted that if widow marriage becomes popular it will be a gain to society generally and a relief to particular sections. Is it a common practice at all? The majority say it is not. But there are some who think it could not well be more prevalent than it is at present among all Hindus save the highest caste. It would, therefore, be very useful to have authentic information.

I. What percentage of Hindu girls marry *after* 12?

II. What percentage of Hindu widows under 30 are allowed to remarry?

Let us have figures only for one year. Will some of our Associations obtain them? If they cannot, they must appeal to the Government to procure the information.

WHAT IS LAW?

It is a healthy education which makes our graduates oppose " legislative interference" in social matters. But I have often explained in a variety of ways, and will do so now again for the last time, that I never have asked and never will ask for such interference. In fact, it would be a suicidal policy for one in my position. The utmost I ask of the Government is friendly co-operation which it has offered in many a similar case. And that intelligent men cannot see the difference between co-operation and coercion, shows that their education is but an indifferent success for practical purposes. Here we are beset with enormous evils, and struggling for centuries (since Akbar's time at least) to shake them off. If, with our present enlightenment we find an easy and effectual remedy, why should not we adopt it? A friend wrote the other day :—" You are our stoutest champion for Local Self-government ; and yet in your fervid zeal you seek State interference in social matters !" The answer to this is that I am perfectly consistent. I do not ask for "interference." Let us see what this great project of Local Self-government is. It enables representatives of the people to manage their own civic affairs. But can we say that because people are given the power to manage their local affairs, they will have it all their own way ? Do you mean to tell me that under the new regime a Brahmin member will have a *pucka* road made up to his own street, or that a Parsi will have the electric light introduced into his Fire Temple, at the expense of the public? Nothing of the sort. There is a *law* looming overhead, compelling every member to seek the *common* good. Members are independent of outside interference, but they are not independent of rules and regulations fixed by Government. Power is sweet, but it is inseparable from responsibility. In this sense no man can be said to be free. The same principle may be applied to the working of other reforms. Let us come to a general understanding, and then let us ask the State to lend it the sanction of law. Every such understanding without a legal recognition has been worthless. It is all very well for the patriot of New India to turn up his nose at the word Law. There can be no Order and Happiness without Law. Where would be the universe without Law ? Hindus must not forget the beneficent ऋत* of whom Vedic sages have sung so eloquently, raising her to the dignity of a goddess. I must decline to hold fellowship with those who scorn Law and Order merely to air their acquaintance with the heartless materialist.

A CRY FOR CO-OPERATION.

The *Gujarat Mitra* again indites a very kindly article about my proposals. He accords a cordial approval to my sketch for an Association for practical reform, and considers each one of the items of paramount importance. But giving me due credit for my intentions, and perhaps more than due he repeats his former conviction, that nothing can be done in the matter without the active co-operation of the State. He

---

* Literally " straight" but meaning "Law" or " Order."

enters into this part of the question at length and shows how popular movements have failed for want of the regulating moral influence of Government. It therefore earnestly calls upon Hindu reformers to accept my suggestions and ask the Government to help them in initiating practical reform in the absence of which the country has suffered so seriously. Such is the deliberate opinion of a Hindu journalist of large experience and who has had to do as much as any other public man in Gujarat with this and similar questions. The *Mitra* understands that with a few exceptions all practical thinkers of his acquaintance agree with him. This is the opinion of most newspapers of the province. And yet we can do nothing, because none is coming forward to set the example. The situation is very anomalous. Individuals are ready to sacrifice themselves, but they have others to think of. Europeans cannot realise the difficulties of the joint-family system amongst Hindus more than they can realise the force of social persecution. And after all, when once in an age a hero rises, like poor Karsandas Mulji, he is crushed by the majority, and has not even the consolation of having achieved something. The sacrifice is immense, but its results, for the success of the cause, are inappreciable. This is the reason why even the bravest Hindu hesitates and excuses himself. He loses all and gains nothing for himself or his people. Still, I do pray we may have a dozen Gujarati Hindus to lead the country. It is glorious work, and if my own Gujarat goes in the van, I will be all the more proud of my share in the work.

But there is little hope of success without benevolent co-operation from the State. The Sirkar must give us a lift or our cause will languish for an indefinite period, if it is not lost in this unequal struggle. The contest is hopelessly unequal between man and woman in India. Education may bring the sexes nearer. But the difference between the two in this respect is so vast that it will be ages before we can think of a near approach. And so far as I can see the education of boys will have to be proceeded with faster than hitherto ; whereas, in the nature of things, we can make but slow progress with female education, and that upto a certain point only. Does Government ever think of this? We must, no doubt, respect the majority. But let it be an intelligent majority, please, one which has reason on its side. A hundred men are decidedly ninety-nine more than one man; but I have yet to learn that a hundred fools make one wise man.

SOCIAL REFORM AND POLITICAL PROGRESS.*

It is a mistake to say that a movement affecting the Hindu population particularly has been started by a Parsi. I am no more a starter of the reform than is the *Pioneer* its opponent. The movement was initiated nearly half a century ago, and during the interval it has more than once had powerful impetus given it by *Hindu* reformers in many parts of the country. At this moment there are thousands of Hindus at work, but we outsiders know little about their struggles. Would it be fair, on that account, to say that the parties most concerned are indifferent to their own fate ? My contention is that a large majority of Hindus have recognised the evils of infant marriage and enforced widowhood, but that they are not so unanimous as to the remedies. The advanced section of reformers are for legislative co-operation. And their number is by no means inconsiderable. An equally large number, perhaps larger, are for indirect methods of reform. A larger proportion still would rather be left alone to work out their own regeneration. It is the minority, the priests, with their baneful influence on women, and others to whom the customs may be a source of revenue, who sedulously oppose progress. And as may be expected, this minority always present a compact opposition, while the majority are so divided and often so distrustful of one another, that in actual practice they are at the mercy of the former. The reformers complain of want of cohesion and want of a regulation to fall back upon. For, even supposing that a hun-

---

* This article is a comment on an extract from the *Pioneer.*

dred Hindu gentlemen combine and take a pledge not to
marry their daughters under a fixed age, they have no
means of enforcing the pledge in the case of a defaulter.
And considering the influence of women at home, the operation of the joint-family system and the secret persecution of
the priest, we must be prepared for numerous cases of
default. Such has been the result of the working of associations at Ahmedabad, at Poona, in parts of Madras and elsewhere. The Hindu reformer has not only to consult his
own conscience, but also the interest or even the whims of
an ignorant wife, mother, father, elder brother, of his relations and connections. Now, if the poor fellow had some
background to lean upon when the time came for him to
make good his word, he might be expected to stand. If there
is a regulation he might refer his relations to that. He
wants an excuse, in short. I had an intelligent Hindu journalist from Gujarat last week, who said—" *Mabap*, enough of
your associations and lectures ; let us . fix a rule amongst
ourselves, which we can have to-morrow again, and let that
rule be sanctioned by the *sarkar*, so that our women-kind
may be satisfied that we can no longer break through the rule.
As soon as my wife and her family know that I'll be fined for
breach of faith and thus become a disgraced man, they will
give up bothering me to leave the association when the time
comes for action. At the same time such a rule, sanctioned
by the State, will keep away hyprocrites and thus save our
sabha from future discredit." These are the views of a Hindu
editor who has been for years perhaps the strongest opponent
of official interference of any kind in municipal, educational,
and other administrative matters.

I am not surprised at an Englishman thinking it anomalous
that Indian reformers should clamour for political freedom,
and at the same time call upon the State to regulate their
social affairs. In Europe they manage social matters another
way. But we must not forget that the conditions of life in
India and Europe are very far from being similar. Look at
the position of women in this country, of the social divisions

without number : Hindus of the same caste and even in the same part of the country being often unable to break bread together, let alone intermarriage. Brahmans won't eat with Brahmans for most frivolous reasons, Vaishnavas with Vaishnavas, and so on. To expect the Brahman to sit at the same table with the Vaishnav, the Khshatri or the Shudra, is out of the question. There are many other considerations which forbid the hope for a long time of anything like a social amalgam. In the most backward country of Europe the conditions are much more hopeful. To compare Europe with India is, therefore, to my mind, a violation of the usual rules of comparison. But though broken up socially, the Indians, are not incapable of political union. Not to go far, the *Pioneer* will perhaps excuse me for referring to the wonderful unanimity which has marked the national demonstrations in Lord Ripon's honour, or the discussion of the Local Self-government Bills or the Ilbert Bill.

For administrative work, too, especially judicial, the Indians have shown remarkable aptitude, in spite of what appears to be their aversion to domestic reform. What, for instance, could be more satisfactory than the work done by the average Native Judge or Sub-Judge? And yet, the officer with whom Government have no fault to find may never come up to the ideal of an English gentleman at home. He may marry his children at 5, may immure the widows of the family into life-long seclusion, may worship metal gods, and wash the feet of the swarthy little priest whose presence oppresses intellectual freedom and keeps society tied down to indefensible customs. A Brahman may be as just and fatherly a man at home as one could conceive, and yet as an administrator he may be unjust, corrupt and grasping. The head of a Mahomedan family may lead a wicked irregular private life; and yet, as head of a public department, he may prove himself unexceptionable. I do not for a moment dispute the force of the general proposition, that reform must begin at home, and that a man who cannot order his household affairs in the light of truth and justice cannot be confi-

dently accepted as a true and just citizen. But, as I have
tried to explain above, it would be unsafe to rigidly apply
abstract principles of Western growth to practical politics of
the East. There are many circumstances in the way of such
application.

SUGGESTIONS, OLD AND NEW.

The feeling seems to gain ground every day amongst.
practical Hindu reformers that if Infant Marriage is to be
put a stop to, it will be best done by a brief Act, in consultation with influential leaders like the Maharajas of Benares,
Darbhanga and others. This may be preceded by something
like a Commission of Inquiry. If the inquiry shows that
there is a decided aversion to the girl's age being raised even
to 12 (there is little fear on this score) then the Legislature
may deal with the boy only. The boy's age may be fixed at
about 17. Against this there could be no valid objection from
the Shastras or the priest. And the boy's age being raised so
far it follows that the girl will be kept unmarried till at least 11.
This will be a vast advantage, so argue the advocates of
practical reform. I agree with them generally; but not being
a Hindu, have no right to *insist* upon the plan of action suggested above. I cannot, also, get over the suspicion that for
some time after the passing of the Act, there will be sullen
opposition from some quarters resulting in cruel injustice to
girls. The orthodox and priest-ridden father may decline to
keep his daughter waiting for a suitable match. He may marry
her to a grown-up man, even to a man already married. This
is a result I most dread. At the same time, I am satisfied that
parents will not act foolishly as soon as they see the results
of an ill-sorted union, such as we have here supposed. In
two or three years the people at large will be won over to the
side of reform. This being a moral certainty, I might yet go
in for a legislative regulation, if I only saw some chance of
obtaining the co-operation of the priestly class, or at any rate
an assurance that they would not actively oppose progress.

10

But if legislative action is generally disliked by the Hindu community, what is the next best remedy? I say let the Educational authorities come to our aid, especially the University. In the first place, this is not a State department. It has little to do with Government, and will have a less direct connection still in future. Education is closely allied to the reform under discussion. If this agency undertakes to remedy the evil, it will need no special law. It may also adopt tentative measures suited to different presidencies, with the view of paving the way for wide-reaching reform under the sanction of law, when the community is prepared for legislative co-operation. Let the University rule that married boys will not be allowed, after five years or more, to compete for Matriculation. Here I must once more explain on what assumption I base this recommendation. The assumption is that young Hindus are anxious to escape marriage till they have gone through the educational course, and will be thankful to have an excuse. Let them have this excuse, and they will know how to prevail upon their parents to defer marriage. It is said that such a rule will interfere with the progress of education, and after all will affect only a very small number. I submit that this objection is self-contradictory. If the rule is to affect a very small number; how can it sensibly impede educational progress? No, there would be some disturbance of this kind if I were to say—prevent married boys from entering Government schools. As a matter of policy I would not shrink from recommending even this extreme course. But I am well aware that under the present conditions of the country such a ruling would be exceedingly unjust and fraught with danger. Therefore, I say, let education proceed, but let a certain number of advanced students be helped to escape the trammels of matrimony. They need such help all the more as they have still to go through an academic course. Or, you may *matriculate* the *married* boy (what a contradiction in terms !) You may even admit him to the college and allow him—the *married* boy with perhaps a family, to become a *Bachelor* in Arts (what a contradiction again!) ; but withhold the degree from him.

You will say, this is unjust, after having made him spend five years at college. My reply is, you have done enough for him by giving him the privilege of a liberal education. He may turn his knowledge to account in the best manner he can. The forfeiture of a diploma means that he must not count upon the patronage of the State, must in any case wait till others are provided for. If the University considers child marriage to be an evil, she must mark her displeasure of it in some visible manner. Child marriage is only a fashion, one of recent growth. The University can easily, discountenance it—she is undoubtedly the best medium of reform. Why may not the experiment be tried for some years in one or two presidencies ?

Another suggestion is about passing an Act for the registration of marriages, and empowering the new self-governing bodies to fix a minimum age for persons to be married. As births are already registered these bodies will have no difficulty in detecting fraud where parents overstate the age of a child. And as members are elected by the people themselves, they will have no cause for complaint as to *zulum*, legislative or executive. In short, the reform is left to the people themselves. A good deal has been written of late in the *Pioneer* and other contemporaries throwing cold water over the scheme of what they heartlessly nickname *Lokil Sluff*. Now, if there is anything in this blessed ",Lokil Sluff," our educated and elected commissioners ought to show what stuff it is made of. In what direction can the representatives of the people show their capacity for self-government so well as in improving these ruinous marriage customs? I look upon the Local Board as the old *panchayet* revived and modernised. The dominance of Western ideas has been the death of the *panchayet* system. For good or for evil the *panchayet* is now a moribund institution. It has no power of action left in it. Let the Local Board take its place in this matter of vital importance to the local population. The registration of Births and Marriages may be entrusted to one of the commissioners, elected by the members themselves, who may be given an honorary title. There need be no executive interference of any kind. The Boards may also arrange for suitable text books for primary and secondary schools, translating scriptural verses for the students.

A further suggestion is this. Give Social Associations the power of enforcing a pledge. These bodies are at present unrecognized. If a member breaks the pledge, I do not know if any Court will entertain a plaint against him. The Association is unable to levy a fine. Can it not be empowered to this extent? That is a point for lawyers to settle. I think that social Association would work more effectively, if their hands were so far strengthened that they could enforce a fine on defaulters. These bodies might be registered, like literary Associations, and a certain status conferred on them for purposes of practical reform. As it is, their efforts generally end in *talk*.

THE AHMEDABAD TICHBORNE CASE.

The now notorious Bhabhutgar case at Ahmedabad has taken a new turn. We have watched its progress with some interest. Are we very far out in analysing it thus?:—After the death of his two wives an elderly Hindu gentleman, marries a third, a girl of 12 to 14. Soon after he dies, leaving over two lakhs of rupees, his last wife, and children by the first two. This woman, whom we may call "the old man's darling," seems to have much control over the family. She one day starts on a pilgrimage, taking with her the husband's two sons by the first wife, who are probably of her own age, their young wives, some servants, and of course a good deal of money. At one shrine our pious young widow is supposed as conducting herself in a manner which is not to the liking of one of her step-sons, a fairly educated, sensitive, high-spirited lad. And being unable to influence the pilgrim mother he drowns himself in a sacred stream. That brings us to a party of two young widows, one boy, and some servants. The party soon after returns to Ahmedabad, having duly mourned over the young fellow who wished

to save the honour of the family by drowning himself. Returning home the widow mother and the newly widowed daughter-
in-law compare notes. Alas! how are we to live in perpetual
widowhood? Can we think of no escape? It is impossible,
having enjoyed life so well, to have to depend upon others for
the barest necessaries of life. About this time a young man
crosses their path, a young man very like the boy who
drowned himself during the pilgrimage. Happy thought!
Why, that is *the* boy! Dear, dear boy, restored to the mourners
so miraculously! Restored to thy distracted step-mother
and thy stupified wife! Come sisters, come brothers, this is
our long lost darling! He is taken into the bosom of the
family and the widowed daughter-in-law becomes a wife again,
and in the nature of things she becomes a mother too. All
goes well as well could be with the widow mother, the
daughter-in-law and the strangely acquired son. *The
property of the deceased husband remains in the family.* Is
not the heir found alive? But there are others, who want
the property, ready to prove that the so-called heir is an
imposter. Master Bhabhutgar is hauled up. A protracted
lawsuit is the result, with heaps of money spent on both
sides, and no end of scandal. Such is the genesis of the
Bhabhutgar case. If there is any truth in what has transpired, what shocking revelations of social irregularities it
makes! And is this the only case of its kind? If young widows
were allowed to remarry such scandals would never arise.*

---

* On October 9th 1887, Malabari wrote as follows:—That notorious Bhabhutgar case, the last of which was heard recently in the High Court, shows how
eager a Hindu widow is to clutch at any chance that may restore her
to her husband. Here was a man who, upon the slightest acquaintance with the
deceased whom he personated, could be shown as an imposter. And yet
the wife of the deceased, that is the widow, welcomes Bhabhutgar as her
lost husband, lives with and has children by him.
Cases of this kind are not so rare as people might imagine, and parents
and neighbours are generally too humane to make a noise about such
mistakes. " What happens in his house to-day may happen in ours to-morrow"—thus the neighbours argue with themselves. They will do anything
to cover their own and their neighbours' sins. The stories that are told of
the contrivances to make widows " happy " without the " scandal " of a
remarriage are passing into proverbs. But so perverse is human nature
that men and women will risk their all, life and honour itself, rather than
approve of remarriage. .

HOW EDUCATION AGGRAVATES THE EVIL OF INFANT MARRIAGE.

In the course of the important discussion at the Conference at Madras two weeks ago, an influential member observed that far from giving way before the increasing spread of education, the practice of infant marriages has actually grown more popular of late years ! I have received the same version of the matter from a representative leader at Karachee. And the same may be said, more or less, about other parts of India. The Brahmins marry their girls early, from 5 years of age to 10. And the other castes cannot help following the Brahmins. Education is not necessarily a check in all cases. On the contrary, I do believe that in some cases education serves as a stimulant. The first thought of an " educated " man in India is to get employed and rise in social importance. He must make money, honestly, of course, if he can. And to what better use can a Hindu gentleman put his savings than to marrying his children as early as practicable, thus proving to the world that he is not less favoured than his fellows ? So long as he lacked the means he could not help the girls growing up unmarried to ten. At that age his relations or caste people had to come to his aid and save him from the torments of Hell consequent on a father allowing the daughter to remain unmarried after puberty. But now that he is the Collector's Chitnis, or a Mamlatdar, or a Deputy Collector, a Surveyor or a Medical officer, or, best of all, a lawyer, why it is open to him to marry the girl as soon as a suitable match is to be had. In fact, it becomes a point of honour with the average Hindu, who has secured the means, to dispose of his children before ten.

I know that there are thousands of educated Hindus in every centre who would give up the custom if they could. But they have the women to win over who are under influence of the priests, to whom, again, the custom is a source of income. The Hindu father is not a free agent. Let him be ever so enlightened ; but he is not the only party to a contract of marriage. The other party may be strictly orthodox: what is the educated man to do ? If he does not accede to the wishes of his family, of the priest, and, above all, of the family into which his girl has to marry, he may never again find a match for her ! She cannot marry out of a narrow circle. Even outside that circle, supposing that were at all possible, she will not be treated as an eligible bride after reaching the age. Whatever the causes, it is clear that infant marriages are "all but universal" in India, and that education, instead of discouraging the practice, in some parts actively encourages it.

It is amusing to see how my friends the let-alone-ists try to demolish me. At first they explained that the evils occupied only a limited area and that they were steadily disappearing. When convinced that facts pointed altogether the other way, they turn round and say that though marriages do take place very early all over India, still the consummation occurs seldom before 18 in the case of boys and 14 in the case of girls. This is a neat way of silencing opponents. But where are the proofs ? And if consummation takes place at 18 and 14, why should children be irrevocably "married" before 10 ? There is no escape from the "marriage." The boy husband may die at 10, leaving behind a widow of 6, who cannot be married again. So virtually the evil is there and has to be removed. Infant marriages and enforced widowhood, introduced by the higher classes of Hindus, have now grown into a national institution, and education can hardly cope with evils which in some cases it tends to aggravate. Such is the opinion of experienced Hindu reformers.

THE EVILS OF FASHION.

The Hindu population of India is so sharply divided by territorial distances and tribal and other differences, that it would be scarcely safe to lay down one uniform standard as to the prevalence of infant marriages and enforced widowhood all over the country, or to propose one particular set of remedies, regardless of local considerations. But the evils are

admittedly "all but universal," whatever slight difference
there may be in their operation over different tracts. Some
say that Bengal suffers most under the custom ; others believe
Madras to be the greatest sufferer. One authority gives the
unenviable award in favour of Bombay; while another contends that it is the N. W. Provinces and the Punjaub which,
by reason of their backwardness in matters of education, are
the chief victims of these social plagues. Ram Mohan Roy,
Vidiasagar, the Raja of Naldanga and others for Bengal ;
Ragoonath Row, Chentsal Row, and many other representatives for Madras ; Vishnu Shastri, Gopal Deshmukh, Ma-
dav Ranade, Mahipatram Rupram, Navalram Luxmiram and
numerous other reformers for Bombay; Ayodhya Prasad,
Altaf Hussein, Harishchandra (cut off, poor fellow, in mid
career) and a large number of Pandits, Shastris and scholars,
for the Provinces; all these have depicted the horrors of
infant marriage and enforced widowhood in language which
may be said to have reached the utmost limit of human expression. I could name hundreds of others, Hindu gentlemen of note, who have publicly denounced the practices; and
thousands have written them down, in prose and verse, essays,
odes, appeals, novels, plays, and millions of newspaper articles.
The whole country has been, in a sense, up in arms against the
evils for more than fifty years. Many individual reformers
have paid dearly for their temerity ; a few have been hunted
to death, some more have become outcasts. Their fate has
warned others. And to-day the boldest Hindu reformer
admits that to attempt practical reform in his individual
capacity is like cutting his own throat and courting the de-
struction of his innocent family. There is no hope of reform
in this matter without the friendly co-operation of the State,
at least without some authoritative regulation given in re-
sponse to the cry of the people themselves. To have an idea
of the misery of enforced widowhood let the reader turn to
Mr. Mahipatram Rupram's letter to the *Times of India* of
last week. His concluding remarks, though brief, are quite
to the point. Or, in order to realise the mischief caused by

infant marriages, let him read Mr. Navalram Laxmiram's *Bala-lagna Batrisi*. The picture given here is horrible in its expressiveness. Early marriage means early consummation in too many cases, which means the ruin of mind and body, poverty, sin, suffering; in a word, the deterioration of the race. The writer attacks the custom mercilessly, calls it thoroughly un-Aryan, and denounces its votaries as worse than brutes. Now, who and what are Mahipatram and Navalram? They are Nagar Brahmans, holiest of holy on this side, highly educated men, Principals both of the Training Colleges at Ahmedabad and Rajkot. They are veteran reformers, men who have suffered, and suffered grievously in their futile attempts to effectuate reform from within. And yet there are men who assert, without a tittle of proof, that the evils are neither serious nor widespread and that they are going out of practice of themselves !

It is useful to bear in mind that infant marriage and enforced widowhood are customs which stand to each other almost in the relation of cause and effect. As matter of fact, marriage is generally *forced* upon the girl at a time when she cannot realise its privileges and its responsibilities. And when she loses her husband, she has perpetual widowhood *forced* upon her. It is needful also to know that to every three women in the country one is shown to be a widow. And the Hindu widow is not only unfortunate in herself but " inauspicious" to all around her. She is shunned, neglected, at times ill-treated.

Here arises the question—Would Suttee have gone out of vogue but for State interference? I say, Never. Ram Mohan might have cried himself hoarse for a century. Bentinck might have written a hundred minutes appealing to the good sense of Hindu leaders. But that would not have availed. Suttee would have flourished with greater vigour if only to make a show of the "religious" zeal of the people. It was a usage introduced by Brahmins for purely selfish, or what philosophers call, prudential reasons. The usage soon after became a habit, and that grew into a second nature with

11

Hindu ladies of the higher class. They could not, dared not survive their husbands. A modest woman esteems the opinion of the world dearer than life. Well, what was at first only a Brahminic practice came in time to be followed by the other castes. The Khshatrya or the Vaishia widow could not help yielding to the fashion. It soothed the self-love of her family, it raised the family in the estimation of the Brahmin hierarchy. How could the Hinduani, whose wifehood is animated by the purest ideas of devotion, live on after her "lord" had departed this life, live in misery and privation, with the world pointing the finger of scorn at her for her unwifely selfishness? If Suttee had been allowed to prevail longer I believe even Mahomedans and Parsis would have borrowed the fatal custom. The idea is peculiarly attractive to the Oriental mind. And though Parsi and Mahomedan widows could not have burned themselves, as cremation is not allowed amongst them, they might perhaps have vied with their Hindu sisters in acquiring *sat* (the supreme result of devotion) by some other means. So much for the sway of fashion. My English friends may smile at this supposition; and my Native friends may shake their heads. But I say, withdraw the legal ban you have placed upon Suttee, and the practice may be revived without delay. This is not my own opinion, as Hindu friends will allow. So insupportable in many cases are the miseries of lifelong widowhood, that Suttee, which means instant and almost painless death *with honour,* would be preferred to widowhood, which means (God forgive me if I exaggerate) death by slow torture and not in a few cases *with dishonour.* Government have moved a step as regards widow marriage. Let them move a step further if they wish their action to prove a blessing instead of a curse. As regards infant marriage letthem co-operate with Hindu reformers, let them discourage the ruinous fashion and actively encourage those who seek to escape its trammels. It is not desirable that Government should do anything in the matter at their own instance. The initiative must be taken by the sufferers. But I wish it to be clearly understood that it is impossible for the victims to work out the reform unaided, without moral support from the State. But what can the State do unasked ?.

THE WIDOW IN TROUBLE.

The *Amrita Bazar Patrika* feelingly remarks that it is enough punishment for a widow to have to murder her unowned child. So it is. What with her helpless condition, the bodily and mental torture she has to go through in hiding her shame, the persecutions from within and without consequent on exposure, the victim has more than enough to bear for her momentary weakness and the deliberate villainy of her betrayer.

It is well-known that the law in England is more lenient to unmarried women under the circumstances than it is to widows in India. And its general tendency *there* is to be still more lenient. The Hindu widow deserves much greater consideration, I submit, than the English maid. The betrayer in the latter case has often to maintain the child, while for one reason or other the Hindu widow never seeks even that relief. She cannot do so, situated as she is. Now, as I have often urged, why cannot the seducer of a Hindu widow be criminally dealt with beyond being mulcted in a sum of money ? And why cannot the victim and her family be compelled to disclose his identity ? How is it that Caste never, as a rule, punishes the betrayer even when the widow is found to be in trouble ? At any rate the executive could insist upon a seduction being traced home. Some such vigilance would strike terror into a class of social monopolists who are about the strongest advocates of enforced widowhood. A systematic attempt may also be made for the establishment of Orphanages and Foundling Hospitals.

THE PANACEA OF BENEVOLENT VISIONARIES.

Let there be more education in the land and all will come right ! But what prospect will they hold out of female education in the right sense, when the infinitesimal proportion of our girls going to school are withdrawn at 10 and have to become mothers two or three years hence ? Before they have ceased to be girls, before even a preparatory training has been given them for the life they have to enter upon, our girls have to exercise the duties of wifehood and motherhood, in many cases, alas, of widowhood, too. Of what use your education for girls ? By all means give a vigorous push to female education, but that alone will do little under the social condition of the Hindus. It is these marriage customs which have to be improved before you think of real education for the mothers of the future generation. Why cannot my English friends see this ? It is hard enough to struggle with the sophistries of the Anglicised Brahman ; but the Brahmanic Anglo-Indian is too much for me, I confess.

THE REAL QUESTION.

Mr. Hume assures me that many infant marriages turn out happy. I have myself said so in my Notes. It is, indeed, a marvel that under the circumstances there should be so much of quiet contentedness amongst our women. I need not enlarge here upon the causes. Suffice it to say that if women in India are " happy " they are happy only after a fashion. The wife is a pretty little creature, a sweet thing, a dear inoffensive animal to be petted and got pleasure out of ; and when she becomes a mother she is of course a useful domestic drudge, God bless her. And that is all. She has no right or privilege save on sufferance ; she has no self-respect, no hope except what is reflected in the mirror of her lord's face. Can she be happy ? Well, yes, in a majority of cases our women are contented, because they do not know to be otherwise. The real question is, can these women, as they are, become the mothers of a great nation, of patriots, warriors, philosophers ? However, I must not dilate. Only let us remember that almost all the means of active happiness in life, in the real sense of the word, are wanting for India's women and therefore, necessarily for her men. Mr. Hume gives an instance, a most enviable ideal. I know a few exceptions like it myself. But these are extremely rare even as exceptions. And if we do not push on with female education in the right direction, the exceptions will become rarer still. Already our educated young men are longing for real wives, for spiritual more than physical partners. To turn to the ideal picture given above of a happy marriage, it reminds one forcibly of the numerous real pictures, girls of tender years torn away from the maternal breast, to be thenceforward at the mercy of the mother-in-law whom they have to serve as bondmaids, to be abused, half-starved, to be made at times the victims of a moral and physical outrage sanctioned by the law, to be forced into premature maternity—all this—the common lot of Indian girls especially of the lower order—all this, I submit, does not look much like *happiness*! As to the assimilation of the husband's nature, and the other beautiful theories, Mr. Hume does not seem to know that in most Native households wife and husband cannot sit together, talk together, eat together in the presence of their elders, even when they have come of age. I am sure my friend knows that the joint family system prevails more or less all over India, the head of the family living in the same house with all his brothers and their wives, all his sons and their wives and the children of both. But I must hurry on, having no wish to hurt the feeling of my brethren or of the impetuous and sanguine philosopher who champions their cause so chivalrously.

Mr. Hume is informed that consummation is deferred in many cases. Not so to my knowledge. That can occur only when the parents of both bride and bridegroom are sufficiently well educated. In the generality of cases, most so amongst the uneducated, parents long for the event which is held to be even more important than the marriage ceremony. And it takes but little knowledge of human nature to see that infant marriage super-induces precocious development in the case of the boy. This means the fellow's ruin. In the case of the girl it is worse, and almost all circumstances conspire to make her a willing accessory to what, on public grounds, I am constrained to denounce as a crime. The best way to prevent premature consummation is by putting down child-marriages.

Mr. Hume says infant marriage is becoming an anachronism. Competent Hindu observers assert that it is becoming more fashionable!

My friend says the questions raised by me are but two minor branches of the one universal problem in India, the Position of Women. Quite so. But I must remind him that my subjects are the real beginnings of the reform he yearns for. He seems to think the education of women is a more pressing necessity. I admit it. But real education, and in fact real national progress all round, is impossible till these two obstacles are removed. How can you educate a girl when she has to be withdrawn from school before eleven, and to be made a wife and a mother soon after? Besides, the spread of education in India cannot be accelerated by artificial means.

SOCIAL REFORM—WAYS AND MEANS.*

Here are the evils—(1) child marriages; (2) unequal marriages in point of age; (3) polygamy amongst Kulin Brahmins and others—a man of fifty marrying girls of 20, 15, 10, down to 5 years of age at times, for the dowries they bring; (4) too early consummation; (5) domestic irregularities, the results of the system; (6) enforced widowhood with its attendant horrors—shaving the girl-widow's head, depriving her of every hope in life, perpetual seclusion with protracted fasts and other privations. To these evils may be added a few minor ones—ruinous expenses on marriage, absence of intermarriage between classes practically the same, and so on. As to remedies—(1) Put a stop to infant marriage, taking a pledge neither to practise nor in any way to encourage it; (2) If you cannot do that, let the practice stand, but arrange amongst yourselves that child marriage is not invariably binding on either party; (3) Come to an explicit understanding that a wife may not be sent to her mother-in-law's till she is 15; (4) Pass a rule at a Mahajan meeting that a girl widowed before 14 is quite as

---

* This is the heading of an article commenting on the discussion at the Soba Bazar Debating Club, Calcutta, presided over by Dr. Hunter.

eligible for marriage as a virgin; (5) Make special arrangements to facilitate the remarriage of widows and to make their existence tolerable and less exposed to temptation; (6) Excommunicate or otherwise punish the seducer of a widow; (7) Prohibit the father or guardian from selling an infant girl; (8) Deal similarly with Kulin polygamists; (9) Encourage intermarriage between nearly allied castes, as was the case before; (10) Curtail marriage expenses. All this you could at least try to achieve; and though some such attempts have, to my knowledge, miscarried for want of a regulating bond, I do not see why you may not satisfy yourselves. At any rate, you can legislate for yourselves, and then ask the State to confirm your action. A number of other suggestions, more or less practical, have been offered. Make your own choice adapting each remedy to local requirements. There are three methods of work open to earnest reformers—(1) do the needful yourselves; (2) ask the Executive to strengthen your hands and guide your steps in the beginning; (3) ask the Legislature to sweep away the otherwise impassable barriers, as it has so often done before. The first method is the best in theory; my heart inclines to it naturally. The third method is the easiest in practice; my judgment approves it strongly. But the second method appears to me to be the safest. It is the golden mean favoured both by my feeling and my judgment. It neither exposes us to vain struggles and the risk of a reaction, nor makes us over, body and soul, to an irrevocable law. In our transitionary state of progress, this tentative and experimental method deserves consideration. If it does not do much good all at once, it will certainly do little harm, and we are at liberty to withdraw from it any day. But I have no business to insist upon this or that plan. If my Hindu friends are strong enough to do without outside aid of any kind, so much the better for them and the other classes who follow them. My only object in advocating the principle of *combination from within* and *co-operation from without* is to avert further risk of failure and of ridicule from outsiders who cannot realise the all-but-insuperable difficulties in the path of the Hindu reformer. It is indeed in a kindly, not in an unkind spirit, that I question his power to effect practical reform unaided. Suttee, human sacrifices, infanticide, self-torture, none of these cruel rites would have been suppressed had not Hindu reformers invoked and obtained the help of the State. Millions of innocent children would have been carried off by small-pox in the absence of *compulsory* Vaccination. And thousands of murders would have gone undetected, and the murderers unpunished, but for the Coroner's Inquest. The religious sense of the community is strongly opposed to these—even to-day. Would the people ever have accepted these obviously beneficent innovations? Could a thousand reformers, a hundred times more influential than they are at present, have popularised these exotic systems amongst a people so divided when progress is aimed at, and so united when the object is to stand still? From primary education up to the suppression of Suttee our staunchest reformers could do little without the sympathetic action of the State. A handful of men like the Parsis, decidedly the most progressive of the Asiatic race, had to seek the moral co-operation of the Government in matters of less importance. Leaders of the Hindu community have themselves more than once obtained such co-operation from the Government which it is foolish to shrink from as "*Interference.*" Government do not wish to *interfere*, and we shall take precious care they never do *interfere* in any of our private concerns. But once agreed, we have a right to the co-operation of the State, and the State owes it as a duty to us and to itself to take up the cause. Those who apprehend popular disaffection in the event of Government co-operating with social leaders in discouraging practices which have nothing to do with religion must be prepared to show that Indian society is less educated, less liberal, and less progressive to-day than it was half a century ago when practices intimately associated with the religious conviction of the mass were knocked on the head with the happiest results. By all means take the initiative yourselves. But pray do set about it in time.

THE SURAT WIDOWS' APPEAL.

I have noticed for some time past a sort of incipient revolt
in the ranks of Hindu widows, especially of Gujarat and
Hindustan proper. The feeling appears to be confined to
widows of the younger generation, who know reading and
writing. This is a hopeful sign in itself, and one might think
the widow could be left here to take care of herself. But
that would be a grievous mistake. The widow who has the
courage of her convictions is closely watched, and she knows
that she is completely at the mercy of social monopolists.
Her case has become desperate. This is just the time when
Hindu friends must stand by her; otherwise it will go harder
with the poor thing than ever before. Now, far be it from
me to encourage a spirit of disobedience or defiance. The
Hindu girl is all patience and charity. By nature, by tradition, and by training, she has learnt to look upon submissive-
ness as the crown of womanhood. This amiable weakness
of hers has been taken advantage of. But the world around
the Hindu widow is changing a good bit. She has begun to
realize that every one is personally responsible for his or her
action; that, however passive an instrument a human being
may be in the performance of a particular act, he or she will
have to bear the consequence of it all the same. In her
case the widow sees that she is wronged at every stage of life,
and made to suffer for other people's wrong-doing more than
her own sins. I am not surprised that she is beginning to
revolt. But what is to be the end of it?

Look at the appeal of several Bania widows of Surat to
the Nuggersett and the Mahajan. It is a formidable document occupying eight columns of closely printed matter in
the *Gujarati*. It gives facts, personal experiences, Shastric
authorities. It appeals for justice and nothing more. It
calls upon the citizens of Surat to consult their own interests,
their happiness, and honour. If this piteous appeal fails, the
writers threaten to go to Government, "the philanthropic
and merciful Sirkar under whose beneficent rule the tiger

and the lamb drink water at the same fountain"————" We, your infant-widow daughters will ask the Sirkar to judge between you and us."

Who are these bold young women? They do not give their names—for, "we are in momentary dread of ill-treatment, even death." But they give a tangible clue to their identity. They are girl-widows of Nanavat, Shahpura, and Gopipura. They give full particulars of their marriage—"We were sold for money into perpetual slavery, with a cord pressed tight round the throat, at a time when we knew absolutely nothing of the matter." Then "just at the time when the seed of knowledge was being sown on the soil of our hearts, we lost our husbands at short intervals; four died of cholera, two of fever, and one of consumption. Even at this time we were not quite conscious of the life in store for us." Here follows a terrific denunciation of the parents, of the priests and astrologers, who promised them all conceivable happiness, and a burning account of their wrongs—"Confined in pits of live fire, fire all over the body, fire all over the heart—our heads in the barber's grip, and the gimlet of terrible privations piercing our hearts—alas! in this world we are *nothings*, alas! the sun of hope has set upon our lives for ever, alas! our social freedom has been put under lock and key," &c., &c. Of the husband's age they say—"some were younger than ourselves, some older three times, four times, even five-and-a-half times, than we girls. Thus in spite of the strongest Shastric injunction against the selling of daughters we were sold for a thousand or fifteen hundred rupees. *Chamars* and butchers sell the bones and hides of *dead* animals; our parents sold our bones, skins and flesh whilst we were *alive* and too young to oppose the bargain."

Once more they set forth the horrors of enforced widowhood in the case of girls who are exposed to all kinds of temptations and powerless to resist them, the sins and scandals, crimes and miseries. They show on the authority of the scriptures that virgin widows *can* re-marry, that they are *required* to be re-married, that in fact, they are widows only in name, having been nominal wives, and that their second marriage is in reality their first and only marriage. The appellants again refer to their utter helplessness. They ask why men, with greater control over their impulses, are allowed to have any number of wives, whilst women, less able to control their feelings, are not allowed even one fair opportunity of indulging the bent of their sacred instincts. " The whole world denounces your injustice. Judges and Magistrates openly cry shame upon your system "............" You know that a brother now and then goes wrong with his widowed sister or sister-in-law; uncle with niece or niece-in-law ; nephew with aunt or aunt-in-law ; father-in-law with widowed daughter-in-law, &c., &c. —we are prepared to give names and full particulars. Again some widows seek relief in houses of ill-fame, some establish themselves as wives in other people's houses ; some run away and enter other castes. Then there are fœticides, infanticides, suicides, and murders of widows. Thus you seek happiness under the shade of a mountain of sins." And so on and on runs the widow's wail. Lastly, they ask why Kshatryas, Vaishyas and Sudras should follow the system of enforced widowhood, like Brahmins, on whom alone it is imposed by the Shastras ?

This is bad business altogether. Just look at what the widows assert as to the irregularities of households in which widowhood is enforced on purpose ! I have omitted reference to the grosser forms of misconduct they freely allege against some of their caste people. What has been quoted here is bad enough, and one's first impulse is always to suppress such things. But an ulcer is half cured simply by exposure; the light of Heaven has wonderful curative effect on it. Besides, the irregularities above alluded to are not unknown, and when Hindu widows have taken to giving publicity to such vices, we may hope that the un-Aryan system which has given birth to the vices is doomed. Let the "moderate" Native reformer, who has a morbid horror of "exaggeration," and with whom it is a point of honour to deny the existence of every evil he has not witnessed personally, or the publication of which he thinks will lower his social prestige, take this lesson to heart. If he looks about him and sees that the closest allied castes cannot intermarry, that, therefore, ill-sorted marriages are common in many castes, that in some castes marriageable girls are not available (some of the castes are becoming extinct on this account), and that in most of the castes widows, however young, are practically debarred from marriage; if he also realises, the extent of superstition which, in the name of religion, keeps men and women reconciled to the most abnormal conditions of life, he will find it impossible to escape the conviction that under such circumstances, the result of this marriage system in operation cannot but be undesirable. I have been denounced as a "slanderer" and a "libeller" for conveying the faintest impression of the evils here. What will our "moderate" reformer say to the widows' allegations? Thank God these social enormities are not common in any part of the country. But that they are known to most observers, felt by many and resented by not a few, will be denied only by those interested in the perpetuation of the customs and by their hirelings on the Press. How long will these mislead the public? Is everybody so hopelessly blind as never to be able to connect effects with causes? This arbitrary and unnatural prohibition against which the girl-widows of Gujarat have entered a solemn protest will have to be removed. If society does it, well and good; if it does not attend to an imperative duty in time, some other agency will have to interpose between the oppressors and their victims.

SAVE THE WIDOW!

Referring to the proposal that the Law should punish the seducer of a widow, an esteemed friend writes to ask—"when and how would you have the fellow hauled up—would it not be difficult to bring the charge home to the guilty?" As to

the *when,* my idea is that the man ought to be punished as
soon as the fact of the criminal intercourse is proved. As
regards the *how,* let the betrayer receive condign punishment.
It is an unsavoury subject, and one does not care to refer
to it in public. But those who have read the Section
on Adultery in the Indian Code (you see I dabbled with
law, some years ago, under the guidance of Dr. Maurice
Kavanagh, and gave it up in disgust and despair) must have
been struck with the exemption the Legislature has, for good
reasons, made in favour of the married woman found guilty of
the crime. The married woman, although she be the real
aggressor, a crafty, abandoned old thing, is let off by the law ;
but the paramour, however young and inexperienced, is invariably overtaken by legal consequences. When a married
woman, an active agent herself, is so carefully protected,
·how much more necessary is it for the helpless guileless widow
to be saved from the wolves of society ? It is wellknown that
these latter beasts of prey prefer widows to common women,
because they know they are safe from risks to person or reputation. Now, why could not these fellows be *puckrowed ?* *
The Police could be trusted to do it, and I feel sure the
leaders of society would heartily co-operate with them. They
would hail a law punishing the seducer of a widow. And
such a law enforced would indirectly pave the way for
Widow Marriage. The Secret Service Fund at the disposal
of the Police could not be applied to a better purpose than
detecting this secret crime against which Caste herself professes to be powerless.

WHO IS TO DO IT ?

A friend takes exception to the proposal made last week as
to an effectual mode of dealing with the betrayer of a widow.
He says :—" Upon my word you are far too decisive to suit
the slow-going Hindu. You know our difficulties, and have
been valiantly defending us from the attacks of Anglo-Indian

---

* Caught or brought to book.

writers. You are the stoutest opponent of Police interference
in any form or shape. And here you are suggesting the
worst kind of executive tyranny! Pray do moderate your
zeal. Government will be only too glad to take you at your
word."

Well, they say desperate diseases have desperate remedies.
The Police have already a good deal to do in this matter.
They pounce upon a widow on the least suspicion. And yet,
curious as it may seem, neither the Police nor the Caste think
of the betrayer! We first force marriage upon our little
girls; and when, as a natural consequence, they lose their
husbands, we force perpetual widowhood upon them. And
when this state of hopeless misery and exposure leads to crime,
we make over the victims to the Police. Thus are our
women thrice wronged in life, and we refuse to better their
position in any way. The Police are cruel and rapacious.
But are we, the natural guardians of our women, better
than the Police? It seems that we are decidedly worse in
some respects. If my proposal is inadmissible in one point
(and it was placed before me by a competent Hindu guide)
why don't you try to adopt it in a modified form? Why will
not graduates and others publicly declare that in every case
a widow has been betrayed, they will track the betrayer and
get Caste to make an example of the scoundrel? There will
be no need, then, for the Police to interfere even to the extent
they do now. Let educated Natives only do their part, and
there will be no call for action from without. But as a matter
of fact they have done little all these years, and do not seem
to be in the mood to do anything even now. My own idea is
that under these circumstances they *cannot* do much without
friendly co-operation from the guardians of public interests.
But the phantom of "legislative interference" haunts our
patriots, and hence their dearest interests remain neglected.
It is an awful thing, this intellectual pride of theirs. Sons of
India, are you satisfied that the splendid superstructure you
call Progress is not being raised on a rotten egg-shell?

AN EXPLANATION.

I am attacked by some whom I look upon as fellow-workers in the sacred cause of National Progress for having, as they allege, insulted and calumniated Native Society in the course of this discussion. They seem to assume that I desired it to be inferred that the immoralities alluded to *en passant*, as resulting from these two objectionable customs, were of constant and universal occurrence, that every household was tainted with such sin, and that the social life of the country was one seething mass of iniquity.

I wonder how any such monstrous idea could have originated. I never intended to imply anything so foreign to the truth. No doubt there is a vast amount of sin of this kind arising out of the customs. Millions of cases have occurred. If I wrote strongly it was in view to the prodigious amount of human sorrow and suffering entailed. But then the population of the country is infinitely more prodigious, and *the percentage* of the households in which such lapses occur must be very small indeed.

I only meant that but for these customs there would be far less of sin and unhappiness than there now is. I merely implied that, in *the aggregate*, the sufferings resulting from the customs was terrible in amount. That is all. If my words, no doubt, very strong at times, have ever implied anything more than this, I am truly sorry. I have more than once apologised before for any mistake of the kind, and now I frankly apologise again for the wrong impression of others.

The case against these customs stands complete without reference to any sin to which in some instances they may lead. As to the extent of the sorrow and suffering they involve there is no difference of opinion, and I only referred to the demoralization which in certain cases results from them as an additional reason for desiring their abolition.

SOCIETY AND THE STATE.

Here is Mr. Ragoonath Row's* picture of the typical Hindu widow, stronger than I have yet painted, but not so strong as it has been described to me in conversation by Hindu friends. The life of the Hindu widow, they say, is absolutely insupportable, having not the slightest element of hope in it :—

"Let us take the instance of a child, say of three years, which is declared by infernal custom to be widowed. This is not an exceptional, but a fairly general, instance. Of the fact that she had been once married and had become a widow, she knows nothing. She therefore mixes with children not widowed. Supposing there is festivity, children run to the scene ; but the sight of the widowed child is a bad omen to the parties concerned in the festivity. She is removed by force. She cries, and is rewarded by the parents with a blow accompanied by remarks such as these : " You were a most sinful being in your previous generations, you have therefore been widowed already. Instead of hiding your shame in a corner of the house, you go and injure others." The child understands not a word. Some jaggery is given her, and she is appeased. She should wear no ornaments. She cannot bathe in the manner in which other children bathe. Her touch is pollution. In the meanwhile, if the priest whose authority cannot be traced to the Vedas, Smritis, Puranas or any Shaster, happens to visit the place where the child is, she is immediately shaved and dressed like a widow in order that she may appear before the priest and get herself branded or initiated into mysteries. Only lately I saw a child moving about in such a garb to the immense sorrow of some and the amusement of others. She is then asked to eat only once a day. The lightest stimulant is denied to her. She is made to fast once a fortnight even at the risk of death. She often asks in vain why these things are done to her. During the earlier part of life, she is told

* An eminent Madrasi Brahman gentleman.

some story or other and appeased. When she reaches
eleven years of age, such devices fail. Then it is explained
to her that in her previous births, she was a bad woman,
created feuds between a husband and wife, and God (that
Merciful Father who is ever kind to all) being angry, was
pleased to ordain that she should, in this generation, be a
woman deprived of her husband. This is generally the first
correct intimation to the girl of her having been declared a
married and widowed female. She learns this with concern
and anxiety, but is not able entirely to realise her position.
Two more years pass away. Nature asserts her dominion. She
begins to feel that, for no fault of hers in this generation,
she is denied what her comrades are allowed to enjoy. She
becomes an object of suspicion. The hide-and-seek system
comes into play. If she be talking to one of her companions
who enjoys the company of her husband, she is dissuaded from
any conversation with her. The prohibition excites curiosity.
Respectable companions being denied, an evil one is secretly
associated with, who opens the world to her. Her passions are
roused. Feelings of shame cause her to struggle with them.
This life-long war begins, and in most cases passion prevails
over shame. She becomes pregnant ; she learns it generally
when she is advanced in pregnancy more than two months.
No respectable doctor will remove the cause of her shame.
Quackery must come to her help. Sometimes the object is
gained with or without injuring her constitution. A failure
is also possible. A series of attempts is then made for seven full
months to hide her shame. If all these fail, then a wretched
creature is brought into this world. The next step is to get
rid of it. A small conspiracy is formed. It is killed, and its
remains disposed of in the best possible manner. In this
attempt great danger is incurred. The Policeman, not having
much to do, considers it a piece of good fortune to discover
such a body. He secures it, and makes a list of young widows.
He exercises his detective cunning in finding out the culprit.
He often gets on a wrong scent. Many a widow, perfectly
innocent, is laid hold of, taken to the Police-station, and

13

marched off to a dispensary for medical examination. An examination is held, and some of them declared innocent. They pay presents to the Police and recover their liberty from the clutches of the criminal law. To the priest this acquittal is insufficient. His inquisition is set on foot, and is ended invariably by the infliction of a heavy fine payable to himself, on the receipt of which, she is branded as a mark of purification. She may have no money to do all this ; she is compelled to court any paramour who will furnish her with the necessary funds, and this money enables her to come out of purgatory. Her relatives, however, are not satisfied. She is shunned by them. It then becomes necessary for her to sell her body for the sake of bread.

No doubt there are cases in which the girl finds herself strong enough to combat with her passions. What a life does she lead ? Privation of food, of clothing, and of even necessary comforts ; observance of fasts, which at times extend to seventy-two hours ; enforced absence from every scene of festivity ; the enduring of execrations heaped upon her if she unwittingly or unfortunately comes in front of a man, a priest, a sovereign or a bride ; these, I say, become the daily experiences of her life which is often prolonged to a great age."

Mr. Ragoonath Row then enters upon the legal and moral aspects of the question. He contends that Goverment having prohibited Suttee ought not to have *stopped there.* This prohibition is based on the Shastras and on considerations of humanity, justice and public morality. So far well and good. But what business had Government to dispossess a widow, entering upon a second marriage, of the estate inherited from her first husband ? Government do not dispossess a widow even when she maintains criminal relations during her widowhood to a scandalous extent. But as soon as she seeks legitimate relief by remarriage she loses her property ! How can widows with means ever think of remarriage ? And how can the parents and guardians of young widows with properties ever think of re-mar-

riage for them ? Infant marriage often means the marriage
of a little girl with an old man for the sake of his money.
When the man dies the little widow becomes mistress of his
property. In her turn she is a slave of the parents and the
caste. If she remarries she and her parents lose the property.
So she, the little widow, may do anything with her life, but
must not contract an honourable alliance again. Any wrong,
any scandal or atrocity, is preferred to remarriage, which
means loss of property. This is the position in which the
enlightened British Government have inadvertently placed
the widow, in spite of explicit injunctions of the Shastras to
the contrary. Mr. Ragoonath Row holds Government responsible for this unfortunate state of affairs, and I am sure
Government will have to practically acknowledge their mistake.
Fancy the British Government sanctioning the marriage of
girls of 2 and 3 with the dread contingency of their becoming
widows before 10 and of remaining widows all their lives !
And all this when such enforced matrimony and widowhood
are opposed to the spirit of the Shastras, to the laws of morality, of health, of justice ; opposed to all considerations,
human and divine ! The attitude of some of the authorities is
truly exasperating. And when they wring their hands, like
one of these demoralised and thoroughly disheartened Hindu
widows, and urge in self-defence : " how can we help you ?"
—the case becomes hopeless. One looks in vain amongst
them for the sturdy sprits who, in much less favourable times,
put down much more serious evils. Compared with what their
predecessors have done we want so very little from the present
Government. We want honest inquiry and impartial action
based on the law of the land. We want such moral support
as the State is bound to render to society, and without which
it is impossible in India to attempt reformation of any kind
whatever. How long are the women of India to remain unre-
presented in all that concerns the nation most vitally ? Do
Government mean that their only duty is to raise the
revenue ? If they mean anything more for the political advancement of the governed they had better begin by raising the

status of its women. Education is a great blessing, but where are the opportunities for the spread of such education as may enable our women to assert their rights as human beings ?

Mr. Ragoonath Row makes seven proposals which he considers " absolutely necessary" for the mitigation of misery, sorrow and sin, and for the vindication of woman's honour according to the Shastras themselves. These proposals are that :—

"1.   Marriage is optional.

2.   Marriageable age for the male is from his sixteenth year.

3.   Marriageable age for the female is from her eleventh year.

4.   In the case of a girl widowed before sexual intercourse, the bride may be legally married to another, with Vedic rites ; and, without them, if she be a non-virgin.

5.   Their children are legitimate.

6.   Virgins widowed, whether re-married or not, have no lien on their first husband's estate, as they do not belong to his Gotra.

7.   Widows who have come into possession of their husbands' estate shall forfeit it, and it shall pass on to the next heirs, if they are proved to have had sexual intercourse during their widowhood.

These are the main provisions of an Act which, I think, the Indian Imperial Legislature ought to pass.

The first three sections are declaratory and contain provisions of the Hindu law. There has been, so far as I am aware, no decided case of the Privy Council, or of the High Courts to the contrary. The object of declaring these provisions as those of Hindu law, is to prevent too early marriages.

The fourth, fifth and sixth sections are also declaratory provisions of Hindu law. These, together with the seventh section, have been in a way declared to be law by the Widow

Marriage Act. There have been no decisions declaring these provisions to be no law. The object of re-enacting these is to shew them to be purely Hindu law, and as not based upon expediency.

The seventh section is intended to cancel the bad ruling of the Privy Council in 1880.* The latter enables an unchaste widow to retain her husband's estate which she obtained when she was a chaste widow.

Are these provisions revolutionarily aggressive ? Are they inconsistent with Hindu law ? Are they revolting to common sense, to morality, to humanity ? The first section will protect a female from persecution if she chooses not to enter into a married life up to any period of her life. Is this aggressive ? Is this tyrannical to her, or to anybody else ? The second section will save a great many girls from becoming widows ; for it has been proved from the experience of the world that deaths are more numerous below the age of sixteen than above it. It will make our children more robust and healthy than they have hitherto been. It will improve the physique of the nation. It will add soundness to the education imparted. It will afford opportunities for travelling, without which no education is complete. On the contrary, what harm can arise from such a provision ? Will the Hindu nation rise against the British Government for declaring such a provision to be law ? If I have correctly felt the national pulse, I am sure that the nation is fully prepared to welcome such a law.

The third section introduces no novelty. In Southern India I know, for a fact, that in some cases a marriage (in the sense in which the would-be-orthodox party uses the word), takes place when the bride is ten years old. It being so, what is the aggressive novelty in this third section ?

If the Widow Marriage Act was legal, these four proposed sections must be legal, as the former was based on the very

---

* Moniram Kolita v. Kerry Kolitany, 13th March 1880.

same authorities as the latter. These are only enabling clauses. They compel nobody to do anything against one's will, against conscience, against morality, against humanity, and even against the laws of nature.

The seventh section is an absolute necessity. The existing Judge-made law is opposed to Hindu law and morality, and holds out a premium to such of the widows as would lead an immoral life instead of getting themselves married under the provisions of the Widow Marriage Act. This Judge-made law was bitterly condemned by, I think, the whole of the native press at the time it was published."

ONE MORE UNFORTUNATE.

Jani, a little girl of nine, could not stay with her mother-in-law who ill-treated her cruelly—in ninety cases out of a hundred you hear of this ill-treatment, thanks to the custom of infant marriages. Well, Jani ran away from her mother-in-law to seek shelter at her mother's. But from the frying pan the poor little bird seems to have fallen into the fire. Jani's step-father took it to be a disgrace to himself that the girl should run away from the mother-in-law. So he branded her on several parts of the body and then "returned" her, like a bundle of rejected clothes, with two trusty friends. On her way back Jani met a policeman and appealed to him for mercy. The policeman took her to the chowky whence the Inspector placed her before the Magistrate. Mr. Dosabhoy Framji tried the case against Jani's step-father and gave him his due. So far so well. But how about Jani? Will she be better treated in future? The chances are otherwise. But what matters one more suicide, if the worse comes to the worst?

MORE SINNED AGAINST THAN SINNING.

A widow at Satara was charged with having murdered her new-born child of shame. The Judge found the charge proved and sentenced her to transportation for life. The widow appealed to the High Court for retrial. Here the sentence

passed by the Sessions Judge was confirmed. Some indignation is felt at this ; but we think the poor victim will be
happier in the Andamans than at home amongst virtuous
neighbours and moral law-administrators. In the course of
the hearing of the appeal two witnesses deposed that they
were present at the time the murder was committed, and that
they dissuaded the mother from such a crime. How philanthropic! Of course, the mother *would* kill her child, she
loved to do so. It is hard for us to be convinced that a
mother actually and with her own hands kills her child. At
the utmost she gives a sort of consent when half mad with the
agony of her situation. She is not responsible for her act
even when she does act in this manner herself. Will none of
our public Associations take up this point ? And, then, what
about the father of the child ? The man is known to everybody, and yet neither society nor the State could call him to
account ! If the Mahajan were to arrange for the maintenance
of the child and for screening the mother from public gaze,
as they always do in the case of the man, the chief incentive
to child-murder would be removed.

ONE RESULT OF SWAYAMAVARA (SELF-CHOICE).

If we do not read much about widow marriage in old times,
we must remember that infant marriages were very rare in
those days, that marriage was more or less a matter of choice
(*swayamavara*) with both sexes. Thus, there was greater
attachment between the pair, and when the husband died the
widow was not only more devoted to his memory than the
average widow is in our times, but she had probably children
by him or was at any rate old enough not to care for a second
marriage. Prohibit baby marriages to-day and restore to the
girl the exercise of her free will, and you will have very little
of the misery, the sin, the scandal that assail the ear .from
every part of India. But even in those days, when presumably there were very few girl-widows, there was the practice
of *Niyoga*.* What does this signify ? As to Shastras, we

---

* The lenirate.

must not forget that they are wholly binding on the Brahmins only. Why should the enormous majority of the other classes ruin themselves by aping the Brahmans ? We are sure they would not do so if the priests interpreted the Shastras to them faithfully. But thereby the priests would lose their occupation ! One peculiar misfortune of the Hindus is that they have not had anything like continued reliable *history*.

LORD RIPON ON SOCIAL REFORM IN INDIA.

In the course of his address at the annual meeting of the National Indian Association Lord Ripon expressed his high appreciation of the efforts made by a number of Hindu reformers towards obtaining an amelioration of the condition of Indian women, especially in regard to infant marriages and compulsory widowhood. His Lordship declared that he felt " the greatest interest" in these questions and that "great and signal evils *did* result from the present state of things in India with respect to them." But his Lordship was not quite sure as to how far it was advisable for the Government of India, *as a Government*, to move in the matter *at present.* We entirely agree that " Government could not and ought not to outrun public opinion " ; but in Lord Ripon's words, Government might do something " to guide and direct that opinion." Has the Supreme Government done that ? Have the different Local Administrations done so ? To be sure, individual reformers like Vidiasagar, Ragoonath Row, Ranade, Bholanath and others might do much in the capacity of " missionaries on the public mind." But the utmost they could do is to prepare the way for the co-operation of the State. And this they have already done. They now find that after laborious efforts for years the fabric of reform they have raised with valuable materials—correct interpretations of their scriptural writings, adapting them to the requirements of these times, holding up the laws of Nature, &c., does not stand firm for want of that authoritative regulation which can give it stability. This is the missing link, and the State alone could supply it. It is very little, indeed, that leaders of Hindu society want of the State, but that little they could, not do without. Lord Ripon seems to have recognised this difficulty. When Native reformers had done their duty, he explained, "then perhaps it might be possible for Government to do something to help on the work" if such help did not become unnecessary by the time ! This is a sly hit at the reformers and it reminds one of the familiar Bania story. A young Bania once asked his not over-liberal father *when* he was going to find out a suitable match for him. The worthy parent replied somewhat on this wise:—" My son, try and grow old and strong, and I'll marry you. If *I* don't marry you, my son, your uncle or some other relative will marry you ; if he don't, why, you will one day marry yourself. So, my son, try and grow old and strong for marriage." " But father,' asked the innocent youth, " what if I die in the mean time ? " " Then, my son," replied the Bania, " I'll be saved the marriage expense and the necessity of keeping a serpent (widowed daughter-in-law) in my house" !

BABY MARRIAGES AND PHYSICAL EDUCATION.

It is gratifying to see our Hindu friends beginning to recognise the value of physical education. But may we submit if it would not be better to begin with putting down baby marriages ? For a child to be strong enough to profit by physical exercise the parents must be fairly well-developed ; and this is not to be expected before they are at least something like 18 and 15 respectively. How many Hindu parents are " blessed " with children before the time ? To ask the sons of such parents to exercise their bodies, so as to be able one day to fight the Cossacks out of Central Asia, seems to us to be like adding insult to injury.

WHY HINDU WOMEN DIE EARLY?

Dr. Bhalchandra, head of the Medical Department at Baroda, seems to have written a book in Marathi, in which he inquires into the causes of the premature decay and death of Hindu women. This book is noticed by Mr. Samarth in last Journal of the National Indian Association. And what

14

is Dr. Bhalchandra's opinion? That early marriage is the principal cause of premature deaths amongst Hindu women. This has been the opinion of competent authorities for the last fifty years on our side. Medical Conferences have pronounced the same judgment in Bengal and elsewhere. Outsiders can have no idea of the number of girl-wives dying in child-bed. And even when the victims survive the shock, their life is a torture to many of them, certainly more painful than death. The evil was not unknown some years ago among Parsi families, "the most advanced section of the community," and in some cases doctors had to cry shame upon parents of the girl-mothers. Parsis have greatly improved since. They have given up bigamy, and the educated classes have given up child marriages too. Not so the Hindus. They are so conservative and so split up into castes, and so priest-ridden besides, that a thousand Hindu doctors preaching against infant marriages for fifty years have had very little effect upon moral suicides. On the contrary, we have "educated" Hindu gentlemen assuring us to-day that the practice of infant marriages is almost unknown amongst them and that so far there is no room for reform! Thank God the number of orthodox Brahmins who ignore the existence of the evil is extremely small and their opposition is becoming less effective every day. Their attitude just now reminds one of the misuse by the drowning Scotchman of the signs of the future tense—"I will be drowned and no one shall save me"? —with only this difference, that whereas the Scotchman suffered in ignorance, the Brahmin suffers with a full knowledge of his position, indeed takes pride in the ruin of his family and his race.

A STRANGE DEFENCE.

Babu Akhsaya Chandra Sirkar, Editor of the *Nabajibana*, delivered a lecture the other day, in the course of which he contended that the re-marriage of a Hindu widow is altogether unlawful ; first, because marriage is pre-eminently a spiritual relation among Hindus and therefore everlasting; and secondly, because a Hindu girl marries not only her husband, but also his whole family and clan. To his orthodox hearers Mr. Sirkar's argument must have appealed with all the force of a clencher, and the way in which it was put must have been found exceedingly pretty and pious. But in spite of its novelty, the argument is not worth a moment's thought. What does this "educated" journalist mean by investing infant marriages with the essence of spirituality? What spiritual relation can there be in a union, both parties to which are irresponsible? In most of these cases it is not the children who marry, but their parents. Can these be the marriages said to be made in Heaven? Marriages in India were, no doubt, spiritual unions in the days of the *Swayamvara*, and in those days I believe the re-marriage of either a widow or a widower was unknown. But how completely have the Hindus of to-day fallen away from those glorious traditions! Again, if marriage among modern Hindus is a spiritual contract, and therefore inviolable even after the death of one of the parties, how happens it that the widower can remarry at any time and to any extent?

Mr. Sirkar's second point, that a Hindu girl marries the whole family of the husband, cuts the ground from under his own feet. For, that means polyandry. And if widow marriage is bad, according to Mr. Sirkar, polyandry is a hundred times worse. A moment's reflection will show that in all polyandric connections there is the essence *of remarriage in the lifetime of the husband.*

I have heard many strange arguments against Widow Marriage, but none as queer as this. Probably the only honestly expressed objection I ever met with from an orthodox friend was that—if Hindu widows were allowed to re-marry, many a discontented wife would do away with her husband! I do believe this idea works upon the opponents of Widow Marriage more than any other consideration. What a libel it implies upon the women of India!

A SOCIAL PHENOMENON.

The *Indian Union* receives this letter from a friend at Bhatpore, a town in Bengal :—

" A social phenomenon has occurred here. One bridegroom was joined in matrimony to a string of four unmarried ladies. I cannot call them girls, because not even the youngest was below 35 years of age. This event took place here, on the last but one day of Baisakh. The happy bridegroom is a Brahmin of Khasbari in Halishahar, a man of 50 years age. He had before this one wife, and had by her several children. The brides hail from Vikrampore. Five of these were brought for marriage, their ages varying from 50 to 20. The eldest has her hair grown grey and her sets of teeth are not entire. Four of these brides were disposed of on that one occasion. The fifth has not been taken in as wife, but has been betrothed to the same individual. She will be married as soon as one of her cousins marries two unmarried daughters of her would-be husband shortly."

Such " marriages " are not unknown on our side especially among Anawala Brahmins. But when you remind "educated" Hindus of their revolting character, you are met with half-quotations from Bentham, Mill and the rest. When you appeal to the good sense of your orthodox countrymen, they take shelter under the purity and other virtues of their remote ancestors. Government is your last resource. But the utmost that the mighty *Sirkar* can do is to wring her hands in despair or to shed a tear of sympathy. A fine prospect for poor Ragoonath Row and his fellow-labourers !

AN UNEDUCATED HINDU REFORMER.

I received a call last week from Mr. Nathubhai Talakchand, a bookseller in town. Mr. Nuthubhai is not an "educated" Hindu, nor a very presentable one. He came up puffing and panting, and thrusting himself in an easychair, gave vent to his feelings in a series of violent ejaculations, stretching out his arms and legs, currycombing his neck and blowing his nose in a hearty familiar manner. I gave him time to settle himself ; and then asked for what high purpose Heaven had blessed me that evening with his society. " I am Nathu Talakchand, the bookseller," he replied sententiously. I pretended to make him out at once, thus obviating the necessity of introductions, references, &c., with which he appeared to have come well supplied. Asked about his business, Mr. Nathubhai began on this wise :—"I am a victim of our wretched marriage rules. Many years ago my father arranged for marriage with ——'s daughter at Ahmedabad. One day I was asked to go to that city, to stay there for some weeks, to give the necessary dinners to our caste, the *dakhshinas* to the priests, and the presents to the bride and her parents. I had lucrative business to attend to here at the time, and as I did not go up at once, the bride was given away to another. Soon after, I lost my money, and it is only after years of hard struggle that I have again built up a small competency. I have had a very miserable time of it, have suffered in health and in self-respect, as most men in my position do, and you see I am already an old man." "Why don't you marry now?" I asked, interrupting my visitor. "What is the use?" he replied. " I could marry a girl to-morrow, but such a marriage could never become happy. I have known hundreds of cases." " What prevents you marrying an honest widow?" I asked again. " Ah," he replied, " I would be put out of caste, with all relations and connections, directly I did so. I have my own arrangement now. And Caste won't interfere with *that*. Is it not a shame, and is not the Sirkar blind ?" I then explained to Mr. Nathubhai that the Sirkar had already turned a benevolent match-maker in the interests of the widow; but that if the match did not turn out happy, we could not blame the Sirkar. Thereupon Nathubhai, son of Talakchand, spoke bitterly of the ignorance and utter incapacity of Government to understand this question of widow marriage. He said that so long as Government submitted tamely to the defiance of Caste, their Widow Marriage Act would remain a dead letter. It was worse than useless. I could not quite agree with him, but asked to be furnished with his views in writing. Here Mr. Nathubhai took out an essay from his pocket and offered it to me with the remarks :—" Shett Sahib, I am not an educated man, and have put down my crude views here in imperfect Gujarati. Let any man in India controvert these views and I give him as reward Rs. 501."

I have gone through Mr. Nathubhai's paper much of which is terrible in its outspokenness. The writer has evidently become desperate under pressure of circumstances. But there is some force in what he says, and a brief substance of it may be given here with advantage:—

" Government says it does not wish to interfere with the working of Caste ; and yet it allows Caste to interfere with the personal liberty of unfortunate widows, which liberty has been guaranteed by the Sirkar itself ! Enforced widowhood is dangerous, not only to the Hindus of those classes in which it prevails, but to other sects, and also to non-Hindu communities. In fact, it is a national evil. Unprotected young widows, all whose sins are connived at by Caste (save the ' sin ' of remarriage), at times mislead maids and married women (especially young women married to old men). They ruin young men of all classes......They become in a manner teachers of immorality and crimes like fœticide, infanticide, and so on. They give incessant trouble to the Police, whose services are paid for from the general revenues. Thus, Government is bound, in public interests, to discourage enforced widowhood.

" 2. Government has made a mistake in policy in inviting the written opinions of representative Hindus on the questions of infant marriages and enforced widowhood. For various reasons these opinions cannot be *bonâ fide*. Most of your leading Hindus are unfit to give impartial opinions. In the first place all these " men of position " practise infant marriage and compulsory widowhood. Are they likely to disapprove the customs publicly, and thus proclaim their own hypocrisy or helplessness? Many of them, again, have widowed sisters, daughters and others at home. Can they be expected to denounce enforced widowhood´ publicly, and thus indirectly publish their own shame? Some of these men are living with other men's widows—with their own wives' sisters, with their......Caste winks at these things, because Caste is merciful to the rich. Can these men be expected to ask Government to put down the *zulum* of Caste against widow marriage? Some men live upon the estates of widows, whom they keep under their protection. Can they ever speak out against the custom which gives them a living? Then the religious heads of Castes, the family priests and others, derive their incomes mainly from widows in their life-time, and they often inherit the property of these widows on their death. Will these men approve widow marriage or allow others to approve the reform? Government has made a bad mistake in asking for written opinions from these men. The best way was to consult some of them privately in the light of such information as I give above. These irregularities are notorious.

"3. Enforced widowhood leads to most unnatural and fiendish cruelty. In populous cities like Bombay new-born infants are at times pounded to death or cut up in small pieces and then thrown into the sewers, mixed up with rubbish and so on. There is a class of women whose business is to do this.

"4. The real reasons for enforced widowhood are that some of our men wish to monopolise widows, some decline to think about other people's affairs, many are ashamed to confess their own weakness, or are too proud to do so; many wish to keep women as slaves, some old husbands are afraid of being killed by their young wives, if they approve remarriage of widows. However badly a young woman may be matched, it must be remembered that she prays to God every day to keep her husband alive—for the life of a widow, to an honest woman, is infinitely more painful than of an illmatched wife. The former has no hope and is at everybody's mercy.

The majority of men do not sanction widow marriage, because they think it a shame that their wives should one day pass away into other men's possession. But at the same time these men themselves can marry any number of wives. What justice !

5. Government must know that in India remarriage is more necessary for woman than man.

(*a*) Woman is weak.

(*b*) She depends upon man in all concerns of life and is not a free agent; for food, clothing, housing, for everything she is at the mercy of man.

(*c*) This being so, it is very easy for man to betray the poor creature. The result is bodily and mental torture to her, now and then untimely death. If she survives the crisis, she has to commit or connive at infanticide ; she then becomes answerable to law. Neither Caste nor Law holds anybody else responsible. Woman is the only sufferer throughout. The man, who is ten times more guilty than the woman (even granting she *is* guilty), goes free. He has no bodily or mental agony to suffer, and the law or the Caste can do nothing to him, although he may be known as the father of the child.

" 6. Then, look at the pitiable condition of the widow. She is condemned to an unnatural life of starvation all round. And when she tries to obtain that for which her nature hungers and thirsts, she is hounded by society and the State. The Government provides food even for a criminal. Does it know that many a poor widow goes without food and clothing, and is often compelled to sell herself for the necessaries of life ? . How is it that all Castes do not make provision for destitute widows ? "

Such is a substance of Mr. Nathubhai's views, for which he is responsible, and which I have tried to place before the reader as mildly as I could.

113

"A HINDU LADY"—AND HER WOES. *

"A Hindu Lady," I see, has not escaped the charge of "exaggeration" from her male assailants. 'How could she, poor thing? That is the only "argument" behind which the benevolent let-alone-ist can shield himself. Such and such social evil has been over-painted; therefore the evil *does not exist*—so argues our philosopher. Have I not suffered enough, and much more than any other friend of the people could put up with, from this theory of exaggeration? I have been denounced as a "slanderer," a "libeller," a "base," an "insolent" detractor, because I had "exaggerated" the results of these customs—that is, I had *referred to some of the evils which were not known to my worthy critics.* Now, this charge of exaggeration from an Englishman may be tolerated; for it is natural that a foreigner should be incredulous as to the existence of evils which pass all human forbearance. But what about Hindus who know of the evils personally? One unfortunate trait of the Hindu character is its horror of everything new or original. The Hindu cannot bear to look upon a woman who discovers some individuality of talent, some superior independence. Woe be to her—she will be set down as a bold woman, that is a bad woman. Can any decent woman ever think, much less talk, of re-marriage? Then, rest assured, this woman is—no better than she ought to be. So argues an orthodox Hindu. The coward! He deserves the word Coward to be written on his forehead in letters of blood, and thus branded he deserves to be driven out of society. No man who will not take woman's virtue on trust can be his mother's son. The whole fabric of domestic happiness rests upon man's faith in the purity of his purer half.

"A Hindu Lady" lashes her brother reformer with uncommon vigour. The Hindu reformer has no moral courage, she says. This is only partly true. It is unjust, in my opinion, to compare the Hindu reformer with the European or

---

* Rukhmabai, who wrote several letters to the *Times of India* and refused to recognize her marriage celebrated in her childhood as binding on her.

15

even the Parsi. The latter two can do much which the former dare not attempt. Why ask a man to do more than a man can do ? We have living instances of how the boldest spirits have quailed under the persecution of Caste. It is not for themselves that they dread this persecution—but what right have they to drag down the old parents, brothers, sisters, their families and connections ? I have known strong men— men who would stand any strain—sobbing like babies at the prospect of finding their elders dishonoured in life and in death. The Hindu's love of his parents is perhaps his noblest point; and much as I deplore this filial weakness, if I may call it so, and never as I would yield a principle to save myself and my whole race, I cannot help respecting his inborn veneration. By the way, it is a fact worth noticing that these are the very reformers who ask for Government aid most earnestly. They have done their best to help themselves ; they have failed ignominiously after repeated struggles; they now see only one hope of success to which they cling. So do not let us blame Hindu reformers. If Hindu men are wanting in their duty, let us remember that Hindu women are equally so. Why don't they throw off the galling yoke themselves ? An opponent may well ask this fair critic to answer him.

" A Hindu Lady " is right in deploring the general apathy of the Hindus in social matters. Contrasted with their political activity, this indifference appears to be criminal, and like all wilful omission of duty it will have its revenge on the nation. The writer is also amply justified in urging that this monstrous tyranny of custom tells more upon Hindu women than upon men, though virtually, the fools do not see, they are bound to be equal sufferers. The men of a nation will be mostly what the women will make them. In their own interests, therefore, should our Hindu friends free their women from social thraldom.

A good deal has been said of late about the " higher education " of Hindu ladies. But I have not noticed a more shrewd opinion about this so-called high education of girls of 10 than that so tersely expressed by the Hindu lady—it is like "putting the cart before the horse." Abolish infant marriages if you want to give suitably educated mothers to the future generations of India.

The picture of the mother-in-law, as given by this lady, is fairly accurate. I would warn English readers from mistaking the European mother-in-law for the Indian mother-in-law. Compared with the latter the former is quite an angel. In Europe it is the wife's mother on whom Benedici is fond of expending his feeble wit. The mother-in-law *there* is, at her worst, a well-meaning meddlesome friend, who insists upon preparing baby's caps before baby is born, who takes charge of the house, aids and abets the extravagant wife, and perhaps maintains her unmarried daughters partly at the expense of the son-in-law. This last is the most serious offence that could be cited against her. On the other hand, the ungrateful fellow often forgets how useful his mother-in-law is in many concerns of life. Blessed wife's mother! What is she to that terrible entity—the Indian mother-in-law?—that is, the mother of the *boy-husband* with whom the *girl-wife* has to pass the best years of her wedded life, commencing long before the honey-moon! On this mother-in-law I feel as if I could write nine volumes like Dr. Hunter's *Imperial Gazetteer* and still be in want of an appendix. Only my Native friends won't patronize the undertaking. And besides it would be superfluous, for in Gujarati literature itself there is quite a library bearing on the mother-in-law. There are books and pamphlets without number, some of them by eminent writers like Mahipatram Rupram and others, which throw light on the character of the average mother-in-law. In fact, there is scarcely any domestic institution, which has been so mercilessly assailed by Hindu poets, dramatists and pamphleteers, as the mother-in-law. What has she not been charged with? The mother-in-law has had to answer for murder, secret persecution, and corrupting the morals of her daughter-in-law,* who must do everything the mother-in-law does if she means to be in her good graces. Well did an orthodox Brahmin say the other day, with unconscious irony, that a girl-wife marries not only her boy-husband, but his whole family and clan. Quite right. And of this interminable nominal alliance the poor thing marries the mother-in-law most. She must walk about like the old lady's shadow, must be to her everything and anything she likes to make of her. The whole family, including the husband, cannot help her if she has fallen under the mother-in-law's displeasure. It may be mentioned in this connection that among Hindus there is no cousin marriage. As a consequence, the wife is invariably a stranger, with no tie of sympathy to bind her to the hearts of those for whom she has had to leave home at a tender age. Add to this the joint family system and the mother-in-law's firm resolve to rule her adopted daughter in every matter ; bear in mind, also, the fact that there are sisters-in-law in the house—husband's sisters as well as wives of the husband's brothers—and you cease to wonder if scarcely 5 *per cent.* of girl-wives are happy. It would not, of course, be fair to say that all mothers-in-law in India are so many demons. But the fact remains that the mother-in-law is generally supposed to be at the bottom of ill-treatment and suicide, a

* In his issue of July 26, Malabari wrote as follows :—" I have to thank the *Subodh Patrika*, whose visits, like the angels', are few and far between, for calling me to order. This friend, whom the *Indu Prakash* joins in a spirited note, says that he has never heard of a mother-in-law corrupting the morals of her daughter-in-law. And they agree that it was wrong of me even to refer to such a matter. I cannot help respecting these fair-minded journalists standing up for a woman, even though it be the obnoxious mother-in-law. On the other hand, may I ask if they have studied the history of Maharajism ? In such matters I go usually upon the testimony, oral or written, of Hindus themselves. But it is an unsavoury subject, and I have no wish at all to pursue it. I regret I should have mentioned it even in passing, and hope my friends will overlook the offence. To the mother-in-law, too, I have to express my sincere regret, though I did not use the objectionable phrase in the sense inferred by the critics. I must at the same time request my friends not to deny the existence of this or that evil simply because it has not come within *their* cognizance. India is a vast country, and my information comes from so many sources that it cannot but be news to the general reader who sees little beyond the visible horizon. I doubt if even friends like the *Indu* and the *Subodh* realize what painful restraint I have to impose upon myself in discussing the question. No man ever guarded himself more religiously against giving wanton offence."

common experience to those who have studied social life in this country. Parsi society is comparatively free from the plague of mothers-in-law, because, for one thing, the husbands are old enough to take care of their wives.

" A Hindu Lady" offers practical suggestions, some of which are worth considering. We cannot get better suggestions for relief than from the sufferers themselves. The writer has my best wishes for the success of her appeal. Let a few more Hindu ladies come forward to plead the cause of their countrywomen, and the battle will be won much easier. My sister need not despair,* there is something tells me that the problem of woman's position in India, as a subject and a daughter of Her Majesty's, is destined to be solved in Queen Victoria's reign; whether those interested in this national emancipation survive to witness it is beyond my power to predict.

Hindu leaders must, no doubt, begin the good work.; but they will not, cannot do it, till assured of all possible aid from the Government. In the matter of Widow Marriage Government has established the principle of co-operation, if you like, of interference. The scope of Act XV. of 1856 will have to be extended even without pressure from the party of reform. With regard to Infant Marriage full 80 *per cent.* of intelligent Hindus are, I believe, disgusted with the practice. But they look upon going to Government as a humiliation. Fatal pride !

---

* Regarding Rukhmabai's second letter Malabari wrote :—"It seems to have been finished with greater care by her English friend, presumably because her own expression was choked up by intense suffering. The cry of woe is more sharp and piercing than before. It is the cry of a full-grown woman—not of an infant girl—of one who might still be an honoured and a cherished wife but for a baneful custom overshadowing her existence. The cry will haunt us for many a long day, for it comes from a weary and desolate heart yearning after that perfect womanhood which is her natural heritage and of which she has been despoiled by selfish man, the maker and enforcer of law. Between the lines you may perceive how bitterly 'A Hindu Lady' resents, because she now fully realizes, this systematic starvation. She is writhing in the agony of despair, and is, therefore, more violent than is seemly. It is a hopeful sign, this daughter of Ind rising to plead for her sex, to plead for the motherhood of the nation. May her appeal move the (un)natural leaders of society !"

JOHN LAWRENCE ON SOCIAL REFORM IN INDIA.

I am indebted to a friend for the following passage conveying the official opinion of Lord Lawrence on social reform amongst the people of this country. The passage is taken from page 322 of Mr. Bosworth Smith's *Life* of *Lord Lawrence*. It may be mentioned that these views are expressed in the course of a valuable minute written as early as in 1857-58, immediately after the occurrence of the Mutiny. They are the views of, perhaps, the most experienced Anglo-Indian administrator, the soundest exponent of British policy in India, and one who was *strongly opposed* to Government interference in the social affairs of the subjects, as may be seen from the general tenour of this minute itself. Coming from such a ruler of men, one who has left the legacy of a glorious career for the admiration of his successors, these words will, I trust, have some weight both with the present Government and the educated classes of India :—

" There are, indeed, some branches of law regarding which the Native codes are incomplete, and in these departments it is very properly proposed to introduce the English law. In the Native codes, however, there are two points in which reform should be introduced whenever it shall be found practicable—namely—polygamy and contracts of betrothal by parents on behalf of infant children. It cannot be said that these practices are immoral in the abstract, as they were more or less followed by the Jews and the Patriarchs ; and the fact that they are not sanctioned under the Christian dispensation, would not, *per se*, justify us in prohibiting their adoption by our heathen subjects. If we, by legal force, interdict things on the ground that they are not Christian, we come to enforcing Christianity by secular means. But still polygamy and early betrothals are socially very objectionable, and in reality much affect the welfare of the people. The Chief Commissioner would, therefore, earnestly desire to see the law in these respects altered, if it could be. But it cannot at present, for the people cling to it, and in some places would shed blood for its sake. But if ever the temper of the public mind shall change, *or if we would succeed in raising up a strong party among the natives in opposition to these laws,* then the time for legislation will have arrived. Further, under this head it is to be remembered that Indian legislation has made two important steps in advance by legalising the remarriage of Hindu widows, and by removing all possible civil disabilities or legal disadvantages from Christian converts."

The minute was written more than 25 years ago, with the terrible events of '57 probably haunting the vision of the veteran statesman. This may explain the passing reference to bloodshed. At any rate, we expect no shedding of blood from the co-operation of the State in bringing about a reform the want of which was so keenly felt as far back as a quarter of a century ago. "The temper of the public mind," too, has undergone a marked change for the better. All that is now needed is an initiative. Who is to take the lead? The State calls upon Society to do it, and Society looks up to the State for an impulse. In my opinion both are right and both are wrong. The best course is for the two to combine. This combination alone will be able to overcome the *vis inertiae* of vested interests. Will the Government of the day kindly consider the force of the lines that I have taken the liberty of italicizing in this remarkably lucid passage?

It may also be noted that the disabilities of Hindu widows and Christian converts have not been removed by the enactments to which Lord Lawrence refers. These laws are now found very defective, and they leave the victims in some cases worse off than they were before.

THE ENGLISHWOMAN AND THE HINDUANI.

That letter of " An English Lady," contrasting the marriage customs of Europe with those prevailing in India, barely glances at the main issues raised by the Notes on Infant Marriage and Enforced Widowhood in this country. But as the English lady seems to have somewhat misunderstood the spirit of the discussion, and as certain opponents of progress have been trying to make out late marriages as an unmitigated evil, it would not be useless to briefly examine the leading points in the letter of "An English Lady." In the first place, our orthodox friends seem to ignore the fact that "An English Lady" does not approve of infant marriges, and that she positively condemns the system of enforced widowhood. This is a concession with which the Hindu reformer may be content. But, let us proceed. "An English Lady" thinks it a reproach to the social usages of England which leave so many maidens unmarried, and in this respect she thinks the Hindu girl is better off. May I ask here if the writer takes marriage to be the only salvation for woman, as it is held in this country? If that is her opinion, it is not shared, I submit, by the majority of her countrywomen. There are thousands of homes in England which are brightened by daughters or sisters who have no thought of marriage. If they are happy in their position, why should we quarrel with it? They are free agents, independent of surrounding circumstances, and have made their choice after coming to years of discretion. Then, viewing the matter from a higher standpoint, there are thousands of religious and charitable institutions which owe their usefulness to the voluntary labours of English ladies untrammelled by domestic ties the cares of a family of their own. If there is a patriotic career open to men, why should it be closed against women? It has been the fashion to talk of the young men of England as her pride and glory. But what would the country be without her maids?—I ask. Further, "An English Lady" seems to say that no provision is made by the parents for the English girl, single or married. I am not quite so sure of that, though, of course, the boy has the lion's share of the property in Europe as well as in India. I believe the English daughter gets something before her marriage. And where the parents have nothing to give, they generally manage to give her a sound education, which makes her useful and helpful to the husband, and not a burden on him. If unmarried, she has had enough of education generally to enable her to earn a living. Perfect happiness is not to be expected in this life; all that we can do is to cope with preventible evils.

Now, look at the position of the Indian girl. Marriage is indispensable to her; the sooner she is disposed of, the greater the credit of her dear parents, who seldom trouble themselves about disparity in age, temperament, &c. Surely, "An English Lady" does not prefer these doll marriages to spinsterhood. She, no doubt, knows that many of the marriages lead to weakness, physical and mental, to family feuds, misery, and sin—often to widowhood before the girl has become a wife. Does she also know that the Hindu girl has scarcely any recognised status in society—and that in not a few castes her birth is resented as an intrusion? As wife the Hindu woman is not much better off. At any rate, both as daughter and wife she is decidedly worse off than the European daughter and wife. As widow it would be absurd to compare her with the European widow. The Hindu widow is simply obliterated from the roll of humanity. I am sure "An English Lady" writes with the best of motives, and if she looks into the matter for herself she will see how piteously the fate of her Hindu sister appeals for sympathy.

HINTS TO HINDU HUSBANDS.

"A Native Thinker," no other than Sir T. Madhav Row, writes to a Madras contemporary :—

"Many reforms of great importance in view to the improvement of the status of Hindu women are sadly delayed, owing to the inveterate prejudices of the people and their irrational deference to custom; and their unconquerable adherence to the Shastras. But you can have no difficulty in acting up to the hints which I will now offer; by so doing you will considerably ameliorate the condition of your wives.

Hint No. 1.—If your circumstances allow of it, you and your wife should live apart from the family, in other words live separately.

Hint No. 2.—If you cannot do so, have at least a separate room for yourself in the house, so that you may have therein the company of your wife, without being seen by your elders.

Hint No. 3.—Let your wife at her pleasure go into that room and sleep during the day, or meet you there and converse with you, or represent her grievances, difficulties, and troubles, or at least escape from the persecution of the mother-in-law and other elder members of the family, whether male or female.

Hint No. 4.—In short, enable her to meet you often and freely, so that you may make her happy, you may comfort her, relieve her troubles and anxieties, and constantly afford her your sympathy and aid. She will often need your support and solace. Enable her freely to appeal to you for the same.

Hint No. 5.—Remember that a large share of the miseries of the wife is due to the restraints placed by the elders of the family on her intercourse and communication with you. Only take means to free her from such restraints, and you will greatly improve her happiness.

Hint No. 6.—In your separate meetings, try to teach her to read and write her vernacular. In due time give her interesting books to read.

Hint No. 7.—Give her small monthly money allowances to spend as she may like, without reference to the elders.

Hint No. 8.—In any quarrel between the wife and the elders do not blindly side with the latter. Your wife is as much entitled to your justice as your elders are to your respect. Moreover, by doing impartial justice, you will better set matters right than by indiscriminately identifying yourself with the elders."

The "hints" are meant, of course, for educated Hindus. What mockery of a home we find here for men of education! Mr. S. L. Sandaskar, M.A., LL.B., is brave enough when swearing at a public audience by Mill and Malthus, Bentham and Buckle; but his enlightened patriotism, which runs riot on the platform, evaporates in the presence of the elders at home. The chivalrous citizen, who flourishes his hands so lavishly, foams at the mouth and lashes the air with his tail, as he raves against the "odious" Arms Act, eliciting applause after applause, literally cowers before his mother's broomstick. Fifty years ago he said—let me have time and I'll see to domestic reform. Twenty years ago he was heard to repeat the same story. To-day, again, he assures us as coolly as ever of his intention to do the needful by-and-bye, and I am convinced by bitter experience that Rao Saheb Sandaskar will go on doing the same for the next three hundred years. He cannot, or will not, help himself in a matter which, he admits, calls for immediate action; nor will he allow others to help him, except it be done secretly.

THE SATURNALIA OF CARNALITY IN MODERN BABYLON AND THE SOCIAL REFORM QUESTION IN INDIA.

I already hear some of our Native friends harping upon the "evils of making women independent." To my mind the sins so graphically depicted by the *Pall Mall Gazette* are possible, not because Englishwomen have become independent, but because they are still kept dependent on men in the exercise of their most cherished rights. Make woman the equal of man generally ; allow that she can live, be happy, honest, useful, independently of man—just as all this is allowed to man—and you remove one chief cause of social immorality.

Then, look at the attitude of Society towards the fallen woman—Society always talks of *her* sin, of *her* shame, never troubling itself about the infinitely worse offender. The law, too, refuses to recognise the participation of the seducer as a crime against society.

But scandalous as these revelations are, India need not turn up her nose at them virtuously. Like London we have had our Delhi, our Lucknow, and other resorts, and are not quite without them even to-day. Temples and shrines, and halls of audience, are known to be polluted at times by mad orgies, and there may be centres of refined society reeking at this moment in the smoke of iniquities. Only we have no *Pall Mall Gazette* on the spot to show up the evil doers. What is the origin of the zenana system among us, and of infant marriage, too? To escape one evil we have probably rushed to another. If London boasts of its satyr whose depraved appetite has to be fed on three maidens every fortnight India can point to her historic Nabob, who claimed credit for sixty exploits every night—being carried, dead drunk, from bed to bed every five minutes, and thus grovelling in search of shadowy pleasures of the sense for which he had already become perfectly incapacitated.*

---

* In his issue of September 13, 1885, Malabari wrote :—" Had I known what pranks some of my Native contemporaries would play with the disclosures made in the *Pall Mall Gazette* regarding the criminal side of a certain phase of social life in London, I would not have welcomed those startling revelations so readily. No one who knows will deny that the constitution of English society is far from perfect; that at any rate, it does not suit the ideas and habits of the Asiatic. The inequality of the marriage law there, too, tells heavily upon the sex. But to argue from the vagaries of town life, that everything in the social system of the Englishman is corrupt is a travesty of truth which must not be tolerated for a moment. There may be forms of social vice in England unknown to us in this country ; but these are more or less adventitio usand temporary. They do not exist in the name of religion, nor are they ever defended under the cloak of usage and custom. If India is free from those particular vices, by all means let us be thankful. But nothing is gained by wholesale denunciation. England has no reason to sit in sackcloth and ashes because an Indian points the finger of scorn at her and refuses to borrow any material from her for a reconstruction of his own social fabric. I often doubt, at such times, if the average Indian gentleman is at all capable of realizing the purity and absolute loveliness of what is known as country life in England."

INDIA AND NATAL.

I have to apologise to Messrs. Chapman and Hall for long neglect in noticing their publication under the title of " International Policy," being six important Essays on the Foreign Relations of England. Each of the Essays claims a well-known specialist for its author. For the present I have been chiefly interested in the chapter on " England and the Uncivilised Communities" by Mr. Henry Dix Hutton, describing the social condition of the natives of Natal and the efforts already made by the British Government to obtain an amelioration of that condition, especially as regards the treatment of women. Mr. Hutton quotes a Report by the Secretary to the Government of the Colony for Native Affairs. Here is the full extract as given by the author:—

" Polygamy is an ancient institution among the native tribes. They say they were created with it, and it is still practised among them. It is a system with which, of necessity, all their laws, customs, habits, and ideas are bound up. It is one which time only can abrogate, because men and women would equally oppose any violent attempt to destroy it, and morality would suffer more from the effects of such violence than leaving it to the gradual extirpation which natural causes and *judicious but indirect measures will most probably soon bring about. The Lieutenant-Governor, in his capacity of supreme chief, has already made serious modifications in regard to it. One is, that every marriage shall be final as regards the parents of the girl; and the other that a widow may marry whom she pleases, without reference to her guardians.* These are two very important alterations in their old customs, and because they were reasonable the natives have quietly acquiesced in them. Further innovations will undoubtedly be made as opportunity offers, with the view of effectually but judiciously checking polygamy. One of these has for some time been contemplated; that is, to make the legality of every native marriage depend upon a full and clear declaration at the time by the woman of her personal consent. Practically, the effect has been the same wherever an appeal for protection has been made to authority ; but as yet it has not been thought prudent to base the legality of the marriage upon such specific declaration. The importance of this step will be better understood, when it is known that before the British Government took possession of Natal, a father had the power of coercing his child, even to the extremity of putting her to death, if she disobeyed him in the matter of marriage. Since then, however, no coercion has been allowed, and whenever brought to the notice of the authorities, it has been punished. The effect of even this check has caused the natives frequently to complain that the women have been made their masters."

I have italicized a few sentences for the benefit of my Hindu friends. Natal came under the British only the other day. Compared with that, the British Rules *in India* may be said to have become almost naturalized by time. And yet, while polygamy has been discouraged by the strong arm of law in a newly acquired territory and among an uncivilized people, here in India, under the most favourable conditions created by a century of liberal education and familiarity with Western ideas, the State finds itself quite unable to cope with this moribund institution, condemned by the highest and the most enlightened amongst its Hindu subjects. I really doubt if a thousand Hindu gentlemen of position would oppose the suppression of polygamy to-day. But Government seem to be waiting for a complete unanimity from end to end. It will be a weary waiting, and meantime thousands of poor little girls will be sacrified on the altar of Custom, married, half a dozen or a dozen of them, to one old man, to be cooped up like so many captive birds, and shortly after to be consigned to perpetual widowhood, a life worse than death itself. These remarks about polygamy apply almost equally well to Child Marriage. I anxiously await the day when the British Government of India may adopt "judicious but indirect measures" for the discouragement of evil customs. But to this end, educated Hindu opinion must continue to force itself upon the attention of the Government. For it would be unjust to the authorities here to forget that the people of Natal were mere children in civilization when their Government took some of their social affairs in hand whilst we Indians have become sufficiently " educated " to resent what appears to be a sort of interference. Every such attempt on the part of the benevolent ruler wounds our self-love. We will neither act for ourselves nor accept of friendly co-operation from outside. Looking at the matter from this view the Government of the present day might be excused for thinking somewhat unkindly of its predecessors for having left them to deal with a chronic evil, when they might have done so more successfully at a compatively acute stage. But this would be a mistake. The Hindus were never, in their worst days, a nation of savages, and each successive administration had, therefore, to deal with their social customs with due caution. But that they *did* take up social questions, each in its own way, on broad national grounds, cannot be denied for a moment, in the face of history. Let us see what the Government of our own day is going to do in the matter. The time is going by for *some* action: I wish I had strength enough to express my conviction that there is generally more danger in dawdling over a matter of necessity than in rushing upon an uncertain enterprise. But, after all, it is clear that a considerable body of public opinion must invite co-operation from the State—educated Hindus must meet the authorities half way. Is it too early for civilized India to do what Natal has already done without noise and much trouble?

WHY NOT A WIDOWS' HOME.

Poor Mr. Ragoonath Row! His zeal for the widow's cause has made him restless. He cannot be at peace without brooding over some project or other for her relief. His latest " fad" is a Home for erring widows, for whom he pleads eloquently, though not, of course, with mathematical precision. He refers incidentally to the number of Hindu widows, 21 millions. And for this his educated critics are down upon him. Does Mr. Ragoonath Row mean to say that all these widows are open to suspicion ! Now, every old woman in town knows that the veteran reformer could not for a moment have meant any such thing. But the juvenile reformer does not like action, and Ragoonath Row is in dead earnest. It is impossible, therefore, that the two should ever agree on the main points. But, surely, an orthodox Brahman like Mr. Ragoonath Row, old enough to be the father of two generations of speculative school-boys, may be allowed some measure of commonsense ? It would be more manly to try and improve upon his practical suggestions instead of making a point of ridiculing them every time they are placed before the public. I confess I do not like the principal feature of his proposal for a Widows' Home—where he wants it to be maintained by the Government. That is an objectionable feature. But what are we to think of the apathy of the higher classes, when an out-and-out Hindu is driven to such a proposal ! It probably means that Dewan Bahadur Ragoonath Row thinks the natural leaders of society too heartless or self-engrossed to adopt his suggestion. And this theory is at least partly borne out. For, no sooner does he make the suggestion than he is pounced upon by our little Benthams and Buckles. His proposal is examined from the legal and the economical points of view, and dismissed as impracticable and worse. It does not occur to any of these philosophical critics to consider the matter on grounds of humanity and social justice. They are scandalised at the mention of a Widows' Home. As if there was no such refuge of Hindu widows ! And, supposing there is none in Madras, I think it is high time to have one, if for no other purpose, at least to save God knows how many lives every year. What prevents our Hindu friends starting a Widows' Association under the management of Hindu ladies ? These ladies might open a day-school or an evening class where some widows might be trained as teachers, and others might be made to forget their unhappy lot or be reconciled to it. The widows of India are being starved for 'want of sympathy. It is all very well to talk of " beautiful home influence." Who exerts that influence ? Is it the barber who shaves the widow every eight or fifteen days or the priest who howls to her to keep out of his way lest her glance pollute his ceremonial mummeries ? The widow is supposed to be an unfortunate creature and one who brings misfortunes to all who are connected with her. Her touch and her very presence are shunned on auspicious occasions. She must eat once a day, use the coarsest cloth, and the worst corner of the house. And yet, they talk of " beautiful home influence" ! If people are too selfish or suspicious for greater concession to widows, let them at least organize a zenana system under which respectable Hindu ladies might visit and receive visits from them, passing a few hours in sisterly intercourse.

WHO IS TO DO IT ?

I had the honour of a visit, the other day, from Thakars Lukhamsey Ravji and Bhimji Ravji, brothers, of the Dassá-oswál caste. They trade in cotton, one of them living at Ahmednagar, the other in Bombay. Mr. Lukhamsey explained that he came that day to sympathize with me personally. He had heard and read so much about my efforts at social reform, that he made up his mind to have a look at me and to place himself at my disposal. In the course of our conversation Mr. Lukhamsey further explained that the Dassá-oswáls came from Cutch, and that formerly there was no social ban on widow marriage among them. He gave the names of a number of prominent members of his caste who are the offspring of remarried widows. It was only about forty years ago that some of the Dassá-oswáls who were in Bombay, and who had become rich enough to ape the Brahmins, entered into a league with those of their caste-fellows who had an interest in preventing the marriage of widows, and prevailed upon the Rao of Cutch of the time and his Political Agent to put down widow marriage ! For about nine years after this, there was no remarriage among the Dassá-oswáls, but a strong minority arose at that time and introduced the wholesome custom again. Mr. Lukhamsey said he had worked at the reform for nearly twenty years now, and he was happy to refer to no less than two hundred and fifty families of Dassá-oswáls to-day who practised remarriage. I congratulated him heartily upon his success, and hoped that the present ruler of Cutch would undo (if he had not already undone) what Rao Desalji was prevailed upon to do forty years ago by the priests and the dalals put up by Dassá-oswál Banias who wished to pass for Brahmins. Speaking of Brahmins, Mr. Lukhamsey explained that the Sáraswat Brahmins of Cutch allowed remarriage of widows among them even to this day, though the fashion now is to discourage the custom! He added that the Rajgors of Halar, Brahmins in H. H. the Jam of Nava-nagar's territory, also practise widow marriage. He exhorted me, before parting, not to give up the cause of the helpless widow, offering anything, his *tan, man,* and *dhan,* he said, by way of co-operation. His brother, Mr. Bhimji, then got up and said :—" We have no personal interest in this matter, as there is no need of widow marriage in our own family ; but we are for the principle. Here is our address, and if you want our help we are ready to do everything for you, up to giving our lives for the cause." I thanked them again for the offer and promised to write or to wait upon them whenever I should need information. I had a Parsi friend, a lawyer, sitting with me, to whom I remarked how wonderful it was that these rough, uneducated old men should sympathize with such a movement and offer practically to forward it, whilst educated young Hindus hung back as a rule when matter came to a point ! He replied that the same thought had struck him.

The fact of the matter is that infant marriage and enforced widowhood are mere fashions, and unless the Brahmins them-selves discountenance them, the other classes are more likely than not to be inveigled into these fashions. Take a Hindu clerk, or a merchant, or a pleader, for instance, one who is not a Brahmin. As soon as he is promised a steady income, he will begin aping the customs of his Brahmin neighbour. Why should he not carry his head as high as that beggar of a Brahmin? Is he not a Deputy Collector or a Sub-Judge? Could he afford to keep his daughter or sister unmarried up to 12?—or could he afford to think of a second alliance for the daughter or sister widowed at 15? What would his neighbours say? Why, his *abru* would be gone directly he attempted such a thing. Thus, as I have explained more than once, and as Thakar Lukhamsey explains for me to-day, the educated man has to rise in the social scale and to maintain his position. He cannot do this by setting up for a practical reformer. This is the secret of his apparent indifference or helplessness. Every consideration of self-interest makes him follow the Brahmanic customs, and if he gets the opportunity, which in most cases he does if he has received some useful education, he will rush to the very fashions his education is supposed to wean him from. How often have we heard, in the course of this discussion, of the evil of child marriage making way among those sections of the Hindu community whom it did not affect before, and of widow marriage stopped among those Hindus who once practised it freely within living memory? And have we not heard that education itself has in some cases encouraged these ruinous fashions? It is, therefore, doubly incumbent on the Brahmin, in his own interest and in the interest of the other classes, to give up the practices condemned by all sensible men. And this could be done only by combination.

RUKHMABAI'S CASE.

Mr. Justice Pinhey's decision of the case, in which a Hindu husband sues for restitution of conjugal rights, appears to my mind to be sound in equity and not inconsistent with common sense. This mode of hunting down an unwilling wife is un-

English. It is, or may be, theoretically legal in adult
marriage; but why enforce it in the case of unconsummated
infant marriage? In India the mere ceremony of nominal
marriage without intelligent consent of parties is, in my belief,
not binding even according to the Shastra. The wife becomes
of the same *gotra*, &c., with the husband after consummation.
It is a question whether she becomes widow according to the
Shastras on the death of the nominal husband. I for one
would devoutly pray that the judgment might be upheld on
appeal, so as to remain a worthy precedent to open our eyes
to the evils of the disastrous custom.*

RUKHMABAI AND DAMAYANTI.

It is distressing to find generally intelligent public writers
describing the defendant in the case of Dadaji Bhikhaji *versus*
Rukhmabai as wife of the plaintiff. How they make her
out to be plaintiff's wife, it is hard to understand. The marriage was nominal, the most essential part of the ceremony,
according to the Hindu and all other civilized marriage laws,
the consent of the parties, having been wanting. Rukhmabai
is less the plaintiff's wife than I am his first cousin. It would
not perhaps be so wrong if our conservative friends described
the connection as slave and slave-owner. In that capacity
they might insist upon the slave being driven home to the
owner, or rather the owner's uncle, to be suffocated, dismem-
bered and offered up on the altar of Custom. But in that
case, too, there would be a difficulty, for the British law no
more recognises slavery than it recognises sham marriages.

One writer, usually sensible and impartial, chides Rukhmabai for disowning her husband in name, because he has become poor and diseased. The preacher waxes eloquent on the
wifely sacrifices of Damayanti in the episode of *Nala Dama-*

* The judgment was not upheld in appeal and then Malabari wrote:—
Hindu reformers need not be cast down by the result of the appeal in the
case of Dadaji *versus* Rukhmabai. It is well the case has taken this turn.
The Judges had to administer the law as it stood; and on the whole, we think
they have shown some consideration in spite of themselves by sending the
case back for retrial.

yanti, and advises Rukhmabai to go and do likewise. Now, I
am a great admirer of Damayanti, and believe her story to be
a true one. But we cannot expect every Hindu girl to be a
Damayanti in this Kali-yuga. I am sure my conservative
friends will readily bear me out. For, they are never tired of
assuring us that Manu and the otherwise law-makers ordained
the present rigid injustice against women, because they knew
women would be dangerous enemies of society in the Kali-yuga,
if treated like human beings. But granting for a moment that
every true Hinduani of the day is bound to act like Damayanti, or any other of the heroines of goody-goody story-books,
let us see if there is a reasonable parallel between Rukhmabai
and her ancient prototype. There is none, so far as I know.
Rukhmabai was forced into marriage while in her infancy.
Damayanti accepted the husband of her choice, when she was
old enough to exercise her judgment. Rukhmabai never
lived with her husband since the sham marriage, did not
know him, had no opportunity of studying his character. Damayanti became Nala Raja's wife in fact, loved him with a
woman's whole love, worshipped him with a sense of passionate
hero-worship, taking him to be her all in all, her truest and
best. Rukhmabai's nominal husband is said to have gone to
the bad, ruining his mind and body for ever. Damayanti's
elected husband, her best beloved, whom she placed above
gods many and lords many, was overwhelmed with misfortunes
owing to the jealousy of others. What right have we, as
honest observers, to ask Rukhmabai to follow the example of
Damayanti? The two have nothing in common. But even
if the worse came to the worst, no law or authority can make
Damayantis of nominal Hindu wives.

Now reverse the case. Just suppose that, instead of Rukhmabai's husband, she herself had turned out incurably diseased and unacceptable. What would the husband and his
friends have done? Why, they would have discarded the
wife like a burnt stick, and supplanted her with one or more
new wives. It is only because the wife in the case has the
best of the bargain, a bargain struck without her knowledge or

consent, because it is she who is educated and virtuous and has prospects of a little fortune from her grandmother, that the discredited husband is urged, I believe, against his wishes, to destroy her life's happiness. She is asked to live with him under the roof of the uncle whom she naturally dreads with a mortal dread. Her friend and guardian is no longer by her, so they put the machinery of law into motion, conspiring to smother her *religiously*. How pious and chivalrous they are who sermonize upon the story of Nala Damayanti! It is my hourly prayer that Mr. Justice Pinhey's judgment may remain undisturbed and may be thus dignified into a salutary precedent. At any rate, I trust that no Englishman will be guilty of betraying the poor lamb into what may prove perhaps worse than a slaughter-house. Just fancy the sensitive little rebel delivered into the hands of Dadaji Bhikhaji his uncles, aunts, sisters and cousins. It makes one's blood curdle only to think of the outrage. If I had a child in that predicament, I would far rather she died before my eyes.

Dr. BLANEY REFORMING HINDU CASTE.

Nothing could be so encouraging to friends of reform as to see an Englishman of Dr. Blaney's influence with the Hindus of Bombay coming forward to strike a blow at the custom of infant marriages. I have always esteemed Dr. Thomas Blaney as a people's man, and if, as such, he keeps his eyes open and uses his own spectacles, he may one day lead his Hindu friends aright. And it is because I trust him that I venture to give him a little friendly advice. First, he need not trouble himself about contrasting the marriage customs of Europe with those of India. In this country we are likely to have early marriages for a very long time ; that is, early marriages according to the European standard. No practical worker thinks of opposing such marriages amongst Hindus, though for my part I should rejoice to see the age gradually raised amongst all classes. What we object to is *infant* marriages—marriages in which both parties are babies, or the bride is a baby and the bridegroom's age ranges between callow youth and drivelling senility. This sham contract is binding upon the girl for life, though the husband may marry again during the wife's lifetime, and certainly after her death. If for no other reason, at least for this, baby marriages ought to be put a stop to, and this is not very difficult, since the reformer has on his side all the best Hindu Shastras, as well as justice and common sense.

As to the method of reform, Dr. Blaney is quite right in suggesting that the more forward classes should take the initiative. This suggestion has been often put forth, notably by my friend Mr. Dinshaw Ardashar. But I have grave doubts as to there being "hundreds" of men among any of these castes able enough to act up to their conviction. There are tens of thousands who are convinced of the necessity of timely reform, and who will declare themselves publicly to that effect. They did so at Ahmedabad, at Poona, and I believe in parts of Bengal and Madras. Our reformers were all honest, earnest, influential men, and when they took the pledge in writing not to marry their girls under a fixed age, they each and all meant to keep the pledge. But what happened in practice? One by one the leaders of the movement fell away, and their followers did likewise, exposing the cause to the ridicule of the conservative party, and making further attempts at reform impossible at least for some years.

Let me place a concrete example before Dr. Blaney. There will be a meeting* of Hindu gentlemen next week, pre-

* There was a meeting of the Kapol Banias which was described in the issue of November 15th, 1885 as follows : "What a funny meeting! It first of all drove out the press reporters ; then while the promoter was addressing the audience he was encouraged by the enlightened president with—"Come now, that will do, proceed, what more, oh, do cut it short, take up some other point, finish, finish, we can't stay here for ever." Thus fared this speech of the principal, if not the only, speaker. Then our Kapol friends appear to have entered upon a discussion, twenty of them speaking at one and the same time, some of them grumbling, others jeering, and others making violent gesticulations. During the five minutes' lucid interval that followed there was some intelligible talk such as: "How can we have reform when the caste is divided ? We don't want any of your reform. We do not marry our daughters early, let us alone, &c." Only one bold Bania proposed "Let us form a Committee" (to go to sleep over the matter) but even this proposal was drowned in a chorus of

sided over by, say, Dr. Blaney. Dr. Blaney is in dead earnest, and so are most of his Hindu friends. They pass a lovely little resolution not to marry their girls under 12, and they mean to stick to the pledge. It is now six months after our memorable meeting, and one of the members marries off his daughter at 8. There is a hubbub in the community ; old men and old women are laughing, priests and priestesses and marriage dalals* are rubbing their hands in glee. All this makes Dr. Blaney furious. He rushes up to the delinquent and asks:— " Wretch, what is this you have done ? You have made me look ridiculous. " To which the mild Bania replies:—" O daktar,† don't be angrified. What could I do? My wife is such a *jalam*,‡ and you know her mother is so rich, and I am so poor ! *Hare-bápre*,§ please excuse me, I beg your apology " ! Dr. Blaney laughs broken-heartedly, and goes home wrapt in deep thought. He thinks at first of writing to the *Times of India*, but on second thoughts, forbears. Six months more, and another "pillar" of the association gives way. This time Dr. Blaney will have satisfaction—" or my name isn't Thomas Blaney." And the old defaulter gives him complete satisfaction:—"Doctor Sahib, I have listened to your remonstrance with respect, and am much obliged to you. But I beg to say that the girl we got married is not *my* daughter; she is my daughter's daughter. How can I control the action of my daughter and her husband ? You have no doubt read Mill, Buckle, Bentham, Herbert Spencer, &c., &c." Dr. Blaney does not wait for further explanation.

Now, far be it from me to blame Dr. Blaney's over-sanguineness. Such enthusiasm is always welcome. Nor will I say a word against the Hindu reformers. Dr. Blaney's only fault is that he is asking these men to do more than men could do,

---

condemnation. "The report winds up thus " The meeting broke up without coming to any resolution."

Those are the materials with which English friends want to reform Caste and Custom."

* Brokers.
† Doctor.
‡ Tyrant.
§ Oh my father!

and the only fault of the reformers is that they good-naturedly promise him to do what they know to be impossible for them. Dr. Blaney has no idea of the scenes enacted in the reformer's house :—મેર રડયા, ગુલામી ખત ઉપર સહી કરી આવ્યા; કાંઇ પુછ્યું ગાંછ્યું હતું કે નહી ? દીકરીના વિવાહ કરવા તેમાં મા તે કશાં લેખ્યાંમાંજ નહી કે ? હાય હાય, શું સહી કરીછ તે તને મારી લાખરો, શાંરી દેરો? મુવા ખટક આલા જધ ને ભાષણ કરી આવ્યા ને હાય મચ્ચકડા આપી આવ્યા, તો શું દીકરીને અઢાર વરશાનો સાંઢ કરવીછે? જોધ્યે તે થાય, મારે તો આ વરરા લગન કરવાછે. Dr. Blaney seems to know nothing about these domestic squalls.

What, then, is to be the remedy ? The very same as Dr. Blaney has suggested, with a very slight addition. Let the meeting be held, let the pledge be taken, and then let the Sirkar be asked only to ratify this voluntary compact, by ruling that marriages under the age fixed by the memorialists shall not be held legally valid in case of dispute. The delinquents are not going to be penally dealt with in any way. The Sirkar is not coming into our houses to carry away our girls to keep them unmarried by force. Government only do what we pray them to do—they save us from ourselves, from our clamorous wives and ignorant relatives and from the greedy priests. Practically, there is no difference between Dr. Blaney's method and the method suggested by Mr. Ranade. But the latter will lead to real reform, while the former may perhaps discredit the cause still further. Is Dr. Blaney prepared to incur a little odium from the ignorant, and the interested classes and their hirelings in the Press ? We must take the world as we find it, and make the best of it, such as it is. The State must be at the back of society for such a reform ; it must also adopt Mr. Dayaram Gidumal's proposal to register Reform Associations, so as to enable them to enforce their rules practically. These Associations have hitherto failed and become discredited, simply because they have not had the power of keeping men to their word. In other cases, again, Mr. Manibhai Jasabhai's suggestion will be found eminently serviceable.

SOME FACTS.

A correspondent of the *Gujarati* sends him particulars from Dhoraji in Kattywar, which the opponents of widow marriage would do well to study. The writer declares that five little ones, the fruit of unlawful intercourse, have been "religiously" disposed of "in two villages," in the course of four months. The suspected widows were placed under police surveillance when all attempts had failed to hide their shame. But the policeman could not save the infants from their unhappy mothers and unnatural relations. He, of course, insisted upon the mothers nursing their babes. This they pretended to do in his presence. But as soon as his back was turned, the infants were left to die of starvation or nursed on strong opium water. So badly had they been treated even before birth, that the poor things bore marks of violence inflicted while in the womb. So died the five orphans in four months. Two others were taken home by a kind-hearted Vakeel. But in spite of the best care, they too pined away and died. Did Caste do anything by way of chastising the widows, their betrayers and the murderers of the innocents ? Nothing.

Take another instance. A widow in the same district, finding herself inconveniently situated, went to the house of her lover (?) asking him to shelter her and the baby that was to be born. And for a wonder, the man took her in. Practical woman she, and a worthy lover he, however erring. In due course came the baby, and mother and father both resolved that they would not add to their sin by committing a murder. They would spare the infant's life. Now Caste, hearing of this, was scandalized. What, manufacture a baby and not kill it. So she excommunicates the man and the woman. Caste is willing to put up with unchastity and murder, but she cannot tolerate sin without the flavour of a good round capital crime. Such is Caste in India, whom chivalrous Englishmen serenade in the press, and whom they address sonnets and odes without number.

PROFESSOR WORDSWORTH ON SOCIAL REFORM IN INDIA.

Mr. Wordsworth condemns Infant Marriage as "an irrational practice" and as "seriously hampering any society that adopts it." He invokes "universal sympathy" for child widows, in spite of "all priestly casuistry" supporting compulsory widowhood. But he does not think the consequences of these "perverse and cruel practices" could be so disastrous as "eager reformers" would make them out to be. He appeals, and I think successfully, to compensating circumstances,—to the sweet devotion of women and their self-denial. But conceding all that, I venture to assert that infant marriages and enforced widowhood are productive of infinitely more harm than good. As to women in India being unconscious of their position at home and in society, is it just, is it wise, I ask, to avail ourselves of this purely fortuitous circumstance? In my opinion such a line of argument is like adding insult to injury. Let us consider if this domestic servitude, however unfelt by the victims, however gloried in, if you like, does not re-act upon the stronger sex, stunting the growth of the whole nation—of the male as well as the female portion thereof. Men must themselves suffer by selfishly entailing needless suffering upon women ; the former, in the long run, lose more than the latter. Such is the law of Nature. It cannot, indeed, be denied that Nature knows how to compensate herself. But she also knows how to revenge herself. And as every student of history knows, Nature will first revenge herself for any outrage or irregularity, before she attempts to compensate herself and to readjust her affairs. We cannot get out of this inexorable fact by seeking refuge under what philosophers coolly accept as the "necessary evils" of life. In this light is it not mere playing with the rules of comparison to liken Infant Marriage —an "all but universal" practice in India—to the immuring of certain noble ladies in medieval Italy, or to marriages of convenience in aristocratic France ? As well might you defend the system of Suttee by referring, for instance, to the conjugal fidelity of Porcia. One might put up with early marriage (certainly not infant marriage) where widowhood is not compulsory. One might tolerate enforced widowhood where early marriage is not the rule. But is it possible to contemplate, without a shrinking at heart, the two evils which have no parallel in history, as having worked together for centuries and threatening to work together for centuries more? With the domestic atmosphere thus reeking with injustice and wrong, with this gilded slavery which is at once the cause and the effect of our moral destitution, I must be pardoned if I cannot largely share the sanguine expectations of a revival of political independence, of an evolution of the patriotic virtues in India—of public spirit rising, on occasions, to the pitch of heroism, of self-denial sinking into absolute martyrdom. Mr. Wordsworth is much more sanguine than I am. I congratulate him upon this happy optimism, and honour him for his frank avowal of it, which may encourage hundreds of Indian reformers less diffident than myself.

And, what is the condition to which Mr. Wordsworth trusts for the improvement of society in India ? To " intellectual emancipation." On this subject he dwells with excusable enthusiasm. No other Englishman has done more for the emancipation of the Indian intellect. But I do not think Mr. Wordsworth looks upon his remedy as a panacea for all evils. He seems to suggest intellectual emancipation more as a means than as an end. And if I understand him aright, the question arises—is the Hindu intellect much in need of emancipation ? So far as that goes, I believe the high class Hindu is born with a full measure of intellectual freedom. What he seems to need is spiritual grace, that humility which controls the exercise of a subtle intellect, that clips the wings of idle speculation, and regulates the mystic rites of the mind. It is a fact worth noting that ever since the advent of the British rule, class after class of these intellectually emancipated beings have succumbed to the fascination of Infant Marriage and Enforced Widowhood and helped to raise the evils into a fashion and a merit. There is one other point in this connection which I may be allowed to notice in passing. "Religion and Habit," says Mr. Wordsworth, "were not created and cannot be destroyed by logic." To this proposition I cannot subscribe, at least as regards the more authentic portion of the Hindu Scripture. That religion is consistent with and based on logic. And consequently I hold that all illogical, that is irrational innovations (such as the two under notice) are essentially irreligious, as shown by Ram Mohan Roy, by Vidiasagar, by Ragoonath Row and Ranade, and as is now being shown by Mr. Telang in a course of admirable lectures. In these lectures before large Maratha audiences Mr. Telang insists that there is ample warrant in the Shastras themselves for a reconstruction of the moral and social fabric. We in India by no means look upon religion as a bundle of absurdities or hallucinations.

And this brings us to a consideration of the part which positive science and politics are destined to play in the future history of India. Here, too, it is my misfortune not to agree in full with Professor Wordsworth. Science and politics have undoubtedly a vital bearing upon the progress that has to be effected; but they will never be able to usurp the place of Religion. I think it is a mistake to ignore this religious aspect of life in considering the problem of national regeneration. Religion is not a matter of mere convenience with the Hindu, and he is not likely to subordinate it, except perhaps during the transitionary period, even to such mighty forces as politics and science. Whether it would be well that he should do it is a question which I am scarcely inclined at present to approach. Mr. Wordsworth himself no more than glances at the question, and that by implication.

THE PARSI GIRL OF THE PERIOD—AN ARGUMENT IN FAVOUR OF INFANT MARRIAGE.

The recent cases of elopement which have caused such a flutter in the Parsi community may be traced chiefly to want of honest occupation, and to spiritual decay, if we may use the phrase. With the spread of education, so called, more ornamental than useful, there has sprung up a sort of distaste for work at home, so essential to the happiness of domestic life. Parsi girls, not many of them, we hope, are becoming strangers to the dignity of labour and its saving grace. Hence we find something like a colony of Goanese and other Ayas in every Parsi quarter in town, and of Goanese cooks, "boys" and so on. What are we to think of young mothers who are ashamed or afraid of nursing their babies, and young wives who think it a hardship to minister to the wants of the family generally? More than 60 per cent. of the children of well-to-do Parsis at Bombay are, we believe, nursed and tended by Goanese women, and we should not at all be surprised if two of the three girls who have run away with Goanese boys are found to be practically Goanese girls themselves. This is the result of high living amid questionable associations. Leaders of the community will do well to see to this in time. Some of our elderly contemporaries think it is the result of English education. We beg to remind them that it is a result of want of education. Others there are who seem to say it is all owing to Parsis not marrying off their girls as fast as is done by their neighbours. To this class of thinkers, who are always ready with a joke at our expense, we need say no more than that their judgment is about as correct as that of the horse or the mule. That is the only plausible excuse we have heard in favour of infant marriages—namely, that it is dangerous to keep girls unmarried after ten. If this theory is to be accepted, it gives rise to two alternative results, either of which the propounders of the theory are bound to accept in return. Firstly, if a girl is likely to go wrong when kept unmarried after ten, it follows that her parents must themselves be living a very irregular life. Secondly, if the parents are themselves honest, they must be certainly most unparental, most unnatural, that they do not bestow ordinary care upon the well being of their child. The parents must be either immoral or unworthy the name of parents. We know they are neither the one nor the other.

Parents in India are quite as good as parents elsewhere. It is only the superstition—"a girl after ten is a serpent in the parents' house"—which makes them so ridiculous and exposes the child to the gibes and taunts of the vulgar. The girl cannot but be innocent—it is to the credit of the parents to believe so—at least so long as she remains under the parental roof. There is another way of meeting this stupid argument. If the girl is apt to go wrong as a girl, what sufficient guarantee is there that she won't go wrong as a wife or a widow?

DISTINCTION WITHOUT A DIFFERENCE.

As to working along the "line of least resistance,"* that is a matter of opinion. It may be right or it may be wrong. There is a good deal to be said in favour of it, but personally I cannot bring myself to endorse the view that heads of a community, its men of light and leading should be content with doing the easiest part of the work for the community, leaving the rest——to whom? To the mass of the people or perhaps to time. And what guarantee is there, for one thing, that political enfranchisement will lead inevitably to national unity for the eradication of moral and social evils? The reference to the palmy days of Shivaji, to show that political progress is not inconsistent with social stagnation, seems to me to be utterly untenable. What was the political progress of those times? Was there anything like national regeneration? Did the achievements of Shivaji affect the fortunes of all India for the better? With more justice might we point to the reign of Akbar. But even then it would be idle to talk of the political emancipation of the *people of India.* If that is the extent of political progress which satisfies our aspirations, why, we ought to be supremely happy as we are at present, provided, of course, the British Government affords a wider scope for material prosperity. Besides, there is the interesting question—would it not be easier to obtain the political

* This was the advice of the Hon'ble Mr. Telang.

rights and privileges we desire by trying to raise ourselves to the moral status generally of the dominant race, and thus establishing a bond of real sympathy between us two, than without any such attempt ? If we hope to have most of the political institutions of the West—and I am one of those who look forward to a timely realization of that hope—then, I submit, it is both our duty and our interest to assimilate our moral and social usages, as much as is desirable to that end, to those of the nation with whom our lot has been cast. And this is none the less desirable, since a revision of our social usages no way involves a breach of the most cherished traditions of the country.

The great mistake, and it is a fundamental mistake, is to distinguish this so called social question from other political questions, so called, and thus to brand the former with a sort of inferiority ; whereas, in point of fact, they are both one and the same question, equally important to the growth of the nation. Is not the question of Infant Marriages and Enforced Widowhood a national question—quite as much as the question of administrative reform in India—even if it is not more pressing ? We call it a social question merely for form's sake. It is as much a moral and a political question as it is social. What is politics but a branch of ethics, intimately concerned with public morality, with the sense of right and wrong as applied to society ? The question of infant marriages and compulsory widowhood involves the first principles, the very essentials of that moral law which governs the universe and which transcends the arts and sciences and philosophies of all the ages combined. It is a fatal mistake, I repeat, to dissociate questions which are absolutely identical both in their abstract and in their practical bearings. If politics is the science of government, then those who wish to devote themselves exclusively to that branch of national improvement ought at least to be able to support their responsibility. That most of our political reformers *are* able to do this I do not doubt for a moment ; but the fact remains that at home many of these are the conscious instruments of in-

justice and wrong. It is useless speculating about unconscious tyranny and unconscious slavery. ˙Both sexes are
conscious, at least they are becoming conscious, of what is
happening behind the curtain, the males decidedly more
conscious than the females, though virtually it is the tyrants
who suffer more than the victims. We are each of us living
a double life—one at home, another in public. As a public
man each of us is striving earnestly to realize national unity.
May not this exclusive devotion lead to the neglect of the
very materials which make such unity possible and beneficial ?

A PRINCIPLE VINDICATED.

I need not repeat what has been said a hundred times over
and over, that in advocating the co-operation of the State,
neither my Hindu friends nor myself have had the slightest
idea of coercion, interference, or any other action distasteful
to the most sensitive person. All that has been meant is
that Infant Marriages should be restrained (1) by individual
effort (which by itself can never succeed and which often
leads to discredit of the cause along with failure), (2) by
corporate action by means of representative Hindu Committees, and (3) with such assistance from the State as may
be found *absolutely necessary* by *the Committees themselves
for timely relief.* This is the programme, and I am glad to
find it commending itself to the approval of a daily increasing
number of thoughtful Hindu leaders. It is specially satisfactory to know that my friend ˉMr. Telang is prepared to
accept the principle of State co-operation, though in what
form we could best invite such co-operation remains to be
settled by him. Mr. Telang's present position, which, I
believe, has been his position from the beginning, ought to
re-assure many of our alarmist friends who trace the total
extinction of society to its contact with the State, whereas,
for a matter of fact, the two are as intimately connected as are
body and soul. I am glad to hear also that, in considering
Sir Madava Rao's proposal last ˙week, our Poona friends

19

accepted the principle of State regulation, provided it did not take the form of pains and penalties. This is a great gain to the cause. The suggestion of pains and penalties cannot but cause alarm. The best plan would be, as Mr. Ranade has shown, to make consummation the test of a binding marriage. Now consummation in Hindu society is not a hole-and-corner affair; it is a *sanskar* (sacrament) publicly celebrated with religious rites and festivities. There can be no dispute as regards the *garbhadhan* ceremony. Let the law simply declare that in case of disputes the Courts shall not recognize the marriages of minors as legal unless they consummate the connection, or ratify it by living as husband and wife after arriving at puberty. Such a declaratory law will serve as a self-acting leaven and discourage all too early connections.

A HARD CASE.

The Poona papers report another hard case. Kasi is a girl of twelve. She lives with a maternal uncle who proposes to throw her away upon a man old enough to be her father. Kasi has the spirit to rebel; she runs away from the uncle, but is overtaken by the police, and the Court compels her to return to him. Kasi returns to the uncle's under protest, urging that if the marriage is again proposed she will destroy herself. Virtually, then, Kasi is a slave, to be sold by a relative, for so much money, it is alleged, to be pocketed by the relative. The uncle is evidently a cruel man, but the law which recognizes and confirms his guardianship under such circumstances is decidedly more cruel.

THE WOES OF WIDOWHOOD.

The *Gujarat Mitra* is indignant that the " Local Governments, the Government of India and the Prime Minister of the Queen of England " have decided against my appeal on behalf of the widow. This is a misunderstanding on the part of the *Gujarat Mitra* and other friends of the movement. The authorities have *not* said "no" in the matter of Infant Marriage and Enforced Widowhood. What they say is this :— " Come to us in a body, and we are prepared to assist you ; only the initiative must be taken by yourselves." It is not a question of " yes" or " no "—that is settled so far. But who is to make the beginning ?—that is the question. Is the State to do it or society ? Some answer one way, others the other way. My own opinion is that the State is bound to meet society half way. As observed before, State and society are as intimately associated as are body and soul. It is no use society grumbling that the State does not come to its rescue. On the other hand, it is equally useless for the State to taunt leaders of society with inaction. In this country it is impossible for individuals to move with success except under an assurance from the State. The very fact that Government is ready to give them all possible assistance will induce hundreds to come forward, with thousands at their back. That, however, by the way.

Let us see just now how the orthodox *Gujarat Mitra* argues with the Government of India :—" You say you cannot interfere with our so-called religious customs. Then, who put down the " religious" custom of Suttee ? You answer that you were constrained to put down Suttee because it involved the crime of murder. Well, then, what does enforced widowhood involve ? What about the widow procuring abortions one to ten times, and committing infanticides? And when widows and their friends are caught in the act you hang and otherwise punish them. What is all this but crime, crime and crime. Thus, one instance of Enforced Widowhood leads to perhaps to ten cases of murder. What about that ? You hang and transport widows for murder, but infanticide is steadily increasing, and now young widows seem to have grown quite desperate and they stop not even at the excess of crime." So says the *Gujarat. Mitra* ; and it also gives some practical advice to the suppressors of Suttee, and the promoters of infanticide. Unless Government makes its Act XV. of 1856 operative, sin and crime and their consequences will never abate, says the *Mitra*; and further that Government will be responsible to God for this fearful state of affairs.

Fearful, indeed, is the state of affairs. What sin and sorrow Enforced Widowhood leads to ! Here is an instance. It is a simple record of facts, but full of pathetic interest for those who can feel. The case occurred recently in Bundelkhand—a loss of three lives, and under such tragic circumstances ! :—

Deposition of Narpat Singh, accused, dated 31st August 1885, before Munshi Dinkar Parshad, Magistrate, 3rd Class, and Tahsildar.

"Narpat Singh, father's name Gunjan Singh, caste Thakur of Kursenda, age 55 years, by occupation a zamindar.

Two years ago I went on pilgrimage. I returned home in the middle of Sawan on the Parwa or Dinj, *i.e.*, about 18 or 19 days ago. I arrived home at 1 o'clock in the day. My daughter-in-law, *i.e.*, wife of my son Barjor Singh, who had been a widow for the last 5 or 6 years and was aged 24 years, had gone to her father's house during my absence about a year ago. On the very day I returned she had also come back at 11 o'clock before noon from her father's house at Piprayan. She came with a barber and without having been sent for. Four or five days passed after she came. One evening at about 9 o'clock I was going out, after supper, when Barjor Sing's wife, who was sitting in a corner of the court-yard, laid her head on my feet and said that she had committed a mistake and that she had been in the family way for 3 months. I did not ask the name of her paramour nor did she tell it. I told her that I would give my answer in the morning. On the next evening, I told her that there was _a temple of Bhairow Dévta in Bagh Patharra in the Rampura State and that a midwife should come there and cause a miscarriage, and that I would bring her back after two days. I said this simply to deceive her. I had resolved in my mind to take her to some ravine and kill her. I told her in the evening, and she consented to go with me for the miscarriage. Early the next morning I took her away on foot. She wore a dhoti of Lattlia, one white covering cloth (chadar) with red borders and another of Garha, and one set of silver patelas (armlets). We left the road and went through unfrequented pathways through fields to Bagh Patharra, which is surrounded with forest, and below which the river Palinj flows. We arrived there at 9 in the morning. I took her to the temple of Bhairow Devta, and showing her the idol made her touch its feet (then said, Bhairow Devta is not in the Bagh, but at a distance of one mile from that place in the Rampura State). After worshipping I brought her to the Bagh Patharra, and then to the bank of the river, which is about 2 fields distant from Bagh Patharra. It is a forest, and not frequented. There I made her sit down under a Beri tree, and I told her that I was looking for the midwife. I went behind her and took out from my tobacco bag a bakai or knife, which is made in Ujjain, and is used for cutting sugarcane and vegetables. I took hold of her lock of hair and laid her on her back, and put one foot on her breast while I kept pressed the lock of hair under the other. I put my handkerchief (angocha) into her mouth, and taking the knife, plunged it into her throat and cut it, and she died. These spots which are on the chadar before the Court are of her blood. I washed it in the river there and again in the tank of Akbarpura. After her death I took off the chadar and patelas which are in Court, and let the corpse, clothed with the dhoti and another cloth of garha, float down the river, which was in flood, after taking it into breast deep water. Then I returned homewards, and threw the knife down on the banks of the river because murder had been done with it and it was not fit to keep it. It was 10 in the morning when I killed her. There was a heavy shower of rain when I was returning home. I arrived at Sarooli, and sent Chandi barber to fetch Mourakhan, a former lambardar of the village. He came and asked whether I had completed my agricultural operations and enquired, about my welfare. I told him that I wanted Rs. 2 worth of grain. He said that my son had taken one rupee worth and that he would give me the remaining one rupee worth in a day or two. The same day I reached my home at Kursenda a little before sunset. For five days I did not speak of this to any one except my wife, to whom I also gave the chadar and the patelas. On the fifth day I told how I had killed my daughter-in-law to Saik Sing, Pattidar, Gunga Singh, lambardar, Baldeo Singh, Pattidar, Thakurdas, Pattidar, and Manohar Singh, Pattidar, by night. They said, we know nothing, do as you see fit; the Court is open. They all went to their houses and I remained at mine. Next morning the Darogah and the Chief Constable of Madhogarh Police Station came with two Constables and put up with Gungah Singh, lambardar. They sent for me, I went and stated all the circumstances."

SOME RESULTS OF INFANT MARRIAGE.

My friend of the *Indian Mirror* is shocked to hear of a case in which a girl is found to be in the family way *before* attaining puberty. Her life is spared, thanks to a clever surgeon, who presumably cuts away the embryo from her unformed womb. What a narrow escape ! But the case does not at all surprise me. Do we not hear of girls of 12, at times of 11, becoming mothers ? Who ever thinks of their anguish, their perils, their death struggles ? A girl of 11 made over to a man of 30, 40, 50, shivering and perspiring even as the Brahman puts her hand into the husband's, is by no means a very rare sight. What follows can be imagined. I have witnessed some of the preliminaries. For instance, the husband comes to fetch his wife home. Her first impulse is to cling to her mother. But the father thinks the child-wife not accompanying her husband would be a disgrace to him. So he takes up a cane or a thong, and orders her to walk out. The husband takes the lead, followed by the little wife, now crouching at his feet, then attempting to run away, but prevented by the father who comes immediately after. The cries of the victim call out a number of spectators, which increases as the procession goes forward. Every five or ten minutes the child falls to the ground, panting like a hunted deer, as the thong or the cane is laid about. I remember having witnessed several processions like this at Surat, and every time I said to myself—"this is another form of Suttee." We need not enter the husband's house; but if we cannot realize what happens there, the *dai* or the *vaid* may enlighten us. It is a story of physical violence on one side and prolonged agony on the other. The thing occurs mostly amongst the lower classes. And what do our English law-makers say to that? "It is a marriage contract, we cannot interfere in its performance." A "contract" to which there is only one party—the husband ! Or a "contract" with which neither boy nor girl has had anything to do ! And even when the result of this precious "contract" is nothing short of violence still the man of law says he cannot interfere ! England is gaining much from her contact with India. She is also losing a good deal, and not the least of her loss is this spirit of demoralisation that is coming over the Englishman in India. When I find an English functionary putting up with such instances of wrong-doing, and attempting to argue himself out of his responsibility by pandering to the brutal prejudices of the mob, I cannot help thinking that the day of England's supremacy over the East is drawing to a close. *His* responsibility is only next to, if not equal with, that of the educated Indian representative.

And what is the main cause of this premature consummation ? Absence of widow marriage. About this we are told by Hindu friends that widows do not care to remarry, that as soon as a girl-wife loses her husband she becomes a saint all of a sudden. Now, I dare say there must be many young widows who have no wish to marry again. But I *know* that there *are* many more who, as human beings, living among human beings by no means given to a saintly mode of life, cannot but crave for the necessities of nature. This argument about widows being unwilling to remarry is the latest development of the seamy side of reform. It is worth noting that those who advance such excuses speak for themselves, not for the widows. I, on the other hand, speak *for* the widow and *as* the widow. No wonder, then, that I should be mistaken as exaggerating. If that is any comfort to Hindu reformers and English philosophers, I do not grudge it them. My own feeling is that I generally understate my facts.

WHY NOT BOYCOTT THE OPPONENTS OF REFORM?

It has been suggested that the votaries of Infant Marriage should be boycotted by the more intelligent of their respective communities—that is, these latter should not attend ceremonies and processions in case of infant marriages. The suggestion is as old as the oldest Pandit, but very few have been able, like Sir T. Madava Row, to follow it. " My wife (or mother or mother-in-law) forced me to attend the ceremony "—that is what the Hindu reformer has often had to confess to his friends. And when remonstrated with, he has often turned round waspishly with the question, " Do you wish me to be separated from my wife and family ? Why don't *you* begin ?" I do not blame the poor fellow much. The Hindu reformer can make no use of expedients until he is given a general regulation to lean upon. He will do the thing when " others " do it. Otherwise, he will not even attempt it. The Hindu is "discreet" above everything, and his position is a cruel one.

Bearing somewhat on this point I may mention the case of a friend in upper India. He is a Brahman, intelligent and public-spirited. He has a family of six children, the eldest, a girl of 11, being a widow. She lost her husband when only 7.

The father sought my advice some time ago. I had only one suggestion to make—that he should risk a second marriage. "But how can I?" replied the distracted parent. "I know that is the only remedy, though the child is too sensitive to speak of it. But the remedy is beyond my power. I myself am ready to be put out of caste, but what about the five innocent children and their mother? Really, it is too much for me to do, and then who can be sure of the result of the second marriage? The whole trouble and sacrifice might be in vain." I then gave him the next best advice—that he should leave the matter to the girl herself. To this, too, he demurs, and rightly, from his point of view. Were I in my friend's position I would certainly face a re-marriage. It would be the right thing to do. Whether it would be *wise* I cannot say, and therefore I am not prepared to blame my friend for what appears to be half-heartedness. There must be thousands who are in this predicament, and the State could extricate many of them by one stroke of the pen, by branding as conspiracy every united public action against them on the part of their orthodox brethren.

AS IT *OUGHT TO BE* AND AS IT *IS*.

In the *Pioneer Mail* of March 17, I read a very interesting and thoughtful article. The writer attempts to show that (1) "the prohibition of remarriage of widows is not general among the Hindus of these (the North-West) Provinces; that (2) the practice "is very much circumscribed even among Hindus themselves; that (3) "Hindu widows do very often remarry, and in the great bulk of the Hindu community widow remarriage is recognised and permitted"; that (4) "among the greater part of the Hindu castes in Upper India it (the prohibition of widow marriage) has never obtained acceptance." The gist of the argument throughout is, that with the exception of the Brahman castes the rest of the Hindu community do recognize and practise Widow Marriage. These assertions, as I noticed them at the time, appeared to be so utterly at variance with my own experience that they fairly startled me. Later I noticed some complacent testimony in a few Hindu journals confirming the theories of the *Pioneer*. After this I took up the *Pioneer Mail* again, and as, I studied the article para by para. I saw that the essay was right in theory, but in practice altogether wrong. What the writer means is, that considering the circumstances of the case, the prohibition against widow remarriage *ought not* to apply to more than one-fourth of the Hindu population. This is generally the way even shrewd and well-informed Englishmen think. But in India, unfortunately, what *ought to be* in such matters seldom *is*. The unexpected meets you at every stage, and your wonder never ceases till you have become an Indian in studying Indian life and character. I should be rejoiced if the generalizations of the *Pioneer* were found practically correct. For, then, the area of the evil would be considerably narrowed and Government might be forced to take action. Probably this is the unconscious object with which the writer in the *Pioneer* started on his generous mission to minimise.

Here let me once more revert to my old contention. Infant Marriage and Enforced Widowhood are both of them mere *fashions*. They began with the Brahmanas, but, like all fashions, they have since permeated the ranks of most of the other sections, till to-day these evil fashions, so ruinous to the national well-being, are followed by all classes of the Hindu community, save the lowest. All Hindus, of whatever caste, who expect to rise in the social scale, borrow the fashion if they have it not, those alone doing without it who have no hope of rising in the world. This is, of course, a general statement, open to exceptions due more to the relaxing of priestly discipline than to any natural cause. But one fact I have ascertained beyond doubt, namely, that a number of castes which did not marry their children in infancy and did not prevent young widows from remarrying only twenty years ago, are at present found to be as much the slaves of the fashion as the most fashionable twice-born. I have been told of a number of individual cases in which what the Brahmans call " low caste men " have set up for the Brahmanical practice directly on acquiring a small competency or a little position in society.

Coming to recent experience, what was the secret of my Hindu friends in Upper India dissuading me very strongly, at every centre I visited last spring, from making the slightest reference to Widow Marriage in the course of my public utterances? The friends were not all of them Brahmans ; a majority of them were members of the other castes. But all of them were men of position, social and official. What made them, one and all, speak of widow re-marriage with bated breath, as if the very mention of it would expose them to public obloquy ! This is practical proof of the extreme unpopularity of the cause which almost every educated Hindu is anxious, in his heart of hearts, to befriend.

But fearing lest this may be discounted as indirect evidence, I wrote to several representative Hindu friends in the principal towns of the North-West Provinces to which the article in the *Pioneer* referred. And I give below brief extracts from their replies. I have no wish to question the accuracy of the Census or of other official reports. But there are obvious reasons why inquiries into such delicate matters, by foreigners and officials, cannot always be satisfactory. At any rate, the results of such inquiries are generally apt to be misapprehended. My own case is different. I am neither an official nor an alien ; my inquiries have been at times made from door to door. I have now and again heard men and women, orthodox Hindus, describing to one another the horrors of Enforced Widowhood and cursing their leaders—officials of the Government among them—who help not, though they can. But for all that, it needs very little insight into human nature to understand that individuals in the position of our Hindu brethren will never move without a promise of aid from men in authority in case an unequal struggle ends n the social annihilation of the individuals.

Mr. Prahlad Sing, Pleader at Meerut, writes:—

"The feeling against Widow Marriage here is very strong, not only amongst the Brahmans, but amongst all. sections of the Hindu community."

Mr. S. K. Chatterji, Pleader at Meerut, writes:—

"Infant marriages are not only not on the decrease, but are actually spreading in large parts of the country............The same is the case with widow remarriages. In the Punjaub and the North-West Provinces widows among the lower classes marry as commonly as in any part of Europe. But widow remarriages are also becoming disreputable every day."

Mr. Baij Nath, Munsif of Agra, writes :—

"The feeling against Widow Remarriage is very strong amongst the uneducated classes.........It is tolerated amongst those who do not belong to the Brahman, and the Khatri classes with their sub-divisions. In classes in which Widow Marriage has been customary it has not decreased; on the other hand, in classes in which it has not been customary it is as rare as before."

Rai Peary Lal, Munsif of Barielly, writes :—

"With reference to your letter asking me, after consulting the principal residents of this place, to let you know if the feeling among the higher classes against Widow Marriage is strong, I am sorry to say that such is the case. They do not like even the question of Widow Marriage to be discussed, sentiment having entire sway over reason."

Mr. Ganga Prasad Varma, Editor of the *Hindustani,* Lucknow, writes :—

"In Oudh certainly the feeling against Widow Marriage is very strong amongst the upper 3 classes of Hindus. Sudras are the only class who are allowed Widow Marriage, but the pernicious example of the upper classes deters them too, and now I observe that they (Sudras) to a certain extent degrade their caste people in a Widow Re-marriage."

Pandit Badri Datt Joshi, Honorary Deputy Collector at Muthra, writes :—

"The feeling against Widow Marriage is strong only in the orthodox portion of the "twice-born" communities, namely Brahmans, Khsatryas and Vashyas......The distaste for Widow Marriage is not becoming general, though among the well-to-do of the lower classes there is a tendency to walk in the steps of the higher classes."

EDUCATION AND REFORM.

Here is a nut to crack for advocates of education as the only means of effecting social reform amongst Hindus. The Nagar Brahmans of Gujarat are the most influential community in almost every respect. And they are so well "educated" as to boast of 98 *per cent.* of educated males and something like 94 *per cent.* of educated females amongst them— this according to the Census Report, referred to by the *Gujarati.* Ninety-eight and ninety-four *per cent.* respectively ! It means progress beyond the dream of the most sanguine educationist. And yet, what social advance have the Nagars made of late ? Do they tolerate Widow Remarriage for instance, if they cannot practise it ? Nothing of the kind. Why, they have not yet made up their minds to allow young men of promise to go to England for study. They have been thinking about it for years. Two years ago the Nawab Sahib of Junaghar established a few Travelling Scholarships on behalf of his Nagar subjects. But the scholarships still remain unutilized. The elders of the community promised to consider the proposal seriously, with the aid of their priests, and the youngsters indulged liberally in tall talk—"everything has been settled, the candidates are ready, a steamer has been chartered, with Hindu crew and other servants. It is a glorious day for India"—so wrote some of the Hindu papers. Two years have passed since, but the reformers and the crew and the servants, the priests and the elders, are making no signs. The idea is no doubt alive, but its realization is probably as far off as it ever was. Our speculative friends are still speculating, dreaming, discussing—they are, in a word, *thinking*. When pressed hard, they turn round, covering their own weaknesses under the virtues of their remote progenitors —those " Aryan heroes " who did this, that and the other thing when the ancestors of the Briton " painted their skins " and otherwise lived as savages.

The Nagars of Gujarat are, on the whole, a splendid race, highly developed both in body and in mind. Sooner or later they *may* venture out on the seas under prescribed rules. They may also pick up cricket and cycling in the course of the century. But as for social reform and widow marriage especially, it is useless speaking to them. Individual effort is altogether beyond them, placed as they are at a cruel disadvantage for such effort. The pity of it is that they don't speak out, because they fear it would make them look so foolish. A race of born scholars and politicians, so to say, not able to mend their marriage customs when they are convinced of the necessity of reform! How odd! But how true, nevertheless!

OLD REFORMERS AND MODERN REFORM-MONGERS.

Probably the most solid amongst practical Hindu reformers on our side was Mr. Mathuradas Lowji, of whose death I heard last week with deep regret. This feeling is deepened further by the reflection that I never took pains to make his acquaintance, though living almost next door to him, so to say.

Mathuradas Lowji was an orthodox Bhattia. He was born in a sort of spiritual bondage, and lived all his life surrounded by moral environments which would have stunted the growth of any other reformer less earnest than he. But Mathuradas utilized these very circumstances to his advantage. In this respect he was like Ragoonath Row of Madras, fighting the Brahmans with their own weapons and thus depriving them of apparently their strongest argument—"you are a pervert." Mathuradas knew not a word of English, and consequently he had none of the monkey about him, none of those acquired habits and appearances to which one's inner conviction is often ruthlessly sacrificed. And yet he was a man of extensive learning, learned in several languages, and accomplished in debate. Mathuradas Lowji was not a professional reformer. He had his convictions regarding the social, religious and commercial improvement of his countrymen. And to the enforcing of these convictions, generally in public interest, he gave years of his valuable life. His career as a citizen was indeed a continued struggle with what we Parsis call the powers of darkness. Mathuradas was no respecter of persons. He hit hard when confronting the most powerful adversaries, and cheerfully received their blows as a necessary result. There was nothing of the whipped cur in him when attacked. In most of his dealings he showed himself a sturdy lion, though sometimes lacking the generosity of the lion. His private life was not quite in keeping with his civic reputation.

One notable feature of his life was that Mathuradas never troubled himself about politics. There may be more in this abstinence than appears on the surface. No less interesting is the fact that almost all our early reformers, the first fruit of Western education, our pioneers of progress, opened the campaign with social discussion. They did not, like the present generation of reform-mongers, seek to set right the affairs of the city, the country, and the whole world, before taking their personal and family affairs in hand.

HOW LITTLE THEY CAN *DO*.

I have been favoured with letters from Thana, Nasik and Katargam. The first writer thinks that the law should at once put down the shaving of widows' heads, the second thinks I ought to work with Hindu Associations, and the third advises me to take the Pandits and Shastris in hand. These letters may be published hereafter. In the meantime let us see what the Associations, the Pandits, Shastris, and Pleaders have done to put a stop to the personal disfigurement of young widows. There has been a very strong feeling against that practice for years, but our self-reliant reformers have scarcely yet made up their minds to take practical steps against it. I might point to a score of other matters which they could re-adjust with very little personal inconvenience. Here is a striking instance. One day, about seven years ago, a Bania gentleman, with whom I was on friendly terms, told me that he was thinking of disposing of his daughter in marriage. The girl was about 7 or 6 at the time, and as she used to read with me now and then I knew she was unusually intelligent. I could not understand why this bright little creature should be so soon given away in marriage. Her father was the head of his little caste, and the only man of means, the rest being petty shopkeepers. I asked about particulars, and was horrified to know that he was being pressed to throw away his daughter upon an illiterate young pauper. I asked if he could not find a better match. He explained that this was the best, unless he went out of his own caste, which he could not do. To be brief, the match was brought about, the marriage ceremony took place, and by this time, I suppose, my little friend is a mother, the wife of a do-nothing fellow whom she must feed and clothe, and to whose level she has descended long since.

The most curious part of it is that the caste to which my Bania friend belonged was only *one-sixth of a small section of the Bania community*. The six sections had free intercourse with one another down to eating and drinking together. But still they would not intermarry. The same state of things continues to this day. Now, if these six sub-sections married amongst one another, as they no doubt used to do at first, a marriage like the one I have referred to would not be heard of. Because in one sub-section there are more marriageable girls than boys, while in another the reverse may be the case. The misery that arises from confining marriages to the same sub-sections, (marriages between kindreds being at the same time strictly forbidden) can hardly be conceived by an outsider. And what has been done to mitigate the evil ? Absolutely nothing, and I doubt if anything will be done without moral pressure. There are many sub-castes like this, which could set themselves right with but a slight effort. But the effort is wanting. Some of these sub-castes have become extinct within living memory !

Let the reader observe that the Bania caste, which is one of the large divisions of Hinduism, is divided into numerous sections, of which that to which my friend belonged is one, and that again is divided into six sub-sections. Practically these sub-sections, and even the principal sections, are one and the same in everything. The sub-sections even to-day have free intercourse with one another. And yet, although they eat, drink and worship with one another, still they won't intermarry for some miserable squabble at a caste dinner, I fancy, or because one sub-section lives at Bombay and another at Surat ! Here was a Hindu gentleman, the head of his sect, one who could buy up all his other fellows, shrewd and sensible, loving his daughter as only a Hindu parent can love (because he may have to part with the child any day), confessing himself powerless before a handful of dependents. He could easily have found a suitable match for his daughter from the sub-section next to his own. But he did not, or rather he said he could not. What could be easier than to bring the six sub-sections together for purposes of intermarriage, as they are for all other purposes ? And yet, though unable to do this little for himself, your lip-reformer is ever ready with his " Yaw Yaw Yaw, we don't want outside advice." Who can tell what the result of this Yaw Yaw Yaw may be fifty years hence ? My Bania friend has gone over to the majority, and his son is now reigning in his place. Will he use his opportunities better ?

21

TRUE AND FALSE SATI AND FREE AND ENFORCED WIDOWHOOD.

Mr. Gadgil* seems to look wistfully back to the "good old days" of Sati, and thinks that the law against it is at times evaded even now. He is right in one sense. To the credit of human nature be it said that true Sati prevails in all parts of the world. No brighter instance of this form of Sati will ever be cited by History than that of Queen Victoria. She has been a living Sati all these years. This true Sati is no exclusive privilege of the Brahmins, nor can it be put down by human law. I would be the first to oppose such a desecration of our better nature. The Government of India did not, nor did it even intend to, suppress true Sati in the country. What Bentinck put his foot down upon was the false Sati, the forced Sati, involving poison, intoxication and murder in open daylight. The same may be said of widowhood. Let us rejoice that there are so many true widows in India, leavening the mass of society with their selfless devotion. But why should we tolerate enforced widowhood? I hope Mr. K. P. Gadgil will now see the difference between a voluntary act and that which is compulsory.

A SCIENTIFIC REFORMER.

Is there to be no end to this anonymous scribbling on the part of a few so-called "educated" Hindus who are a reproach to the education they have received and to the essentially grateful community to which they belong? Here is "Hope" writing to the *Times of India* of Tuesday last, Hope without Faith or Charity. A mixture of far fetched assumptions served up in the form of scientific or philosophical jargon, which is further marred by an attempt at mystification characteristic of writers of this class.

---

* A correspondent of the *Bombay Gazette*.

"Hope" examines the question of infant marriage "scientifically," and yet immediately after he passes on to the 120 cases of criminal assault on girls which are said to have occurred in England in six months. How logical and how charitable our "scientific" gentleman is! The swinishness of some Englishmen is held to be an excuse for Hindus cherishing infant marriages against nature and against their Shastras, thereby ruining the race. Opponents of infant marriage are then assumed to labour under the impression that "the very day the priest joins the hands of the bride and the bridegroom the marriage is consummated." How accurate! Does it need "science" to assure these silly reformers that a marriage cannot be completed between a man of 21 and a girl of five or even ten years? All this we knew very well, and "Hope" might have spared us his "scientific" explanation. We also know what our "scientific" critic feigns ignorance of, that infant marriages superinduce premature consummation, and that if even a day after the marriage ceremony the bridegroom dies, the bride is condemned to perpetual widowhood. How about that, sweet Hope, the inspired of science? Further on we are told:—"widows are not at all ill-treated by any." This may pass for a "scientific" proposition, but it won't stand the test of practical experience. Then there is a fling at the poor "Hindu Lady" who declined to incur the penalties, worse than death, of an ill-sorted marriage forced upon her in her infancy. Can these repeated attacks upon her be due to the fact that by her education the Hindu Lady has taken the shine out of some of her female acquaintances? Science is a good thing to swear by; but in India, more than elsewhere, she can be very narrow and bigoted when she likes.

We are then treated by "Hope" to the old old story about "education," "intellectual emancipation" of the masses, also that "the nature of man is intricate," that in the Asiatic Library there is a book on Caste system, and so forth. This is all very fine. But what use talking about "intellectual emancipation" of the people, when you know that *the people* at large can never and nowhere be really emancipated? If you, the leaders of society, are emancipated from self and the deadening influences it creates, that is quite enough for our purpose. Talk of " emancipation" where the youth of the country is being sacrificed to an unnatural custom, where boys and girls are tied together before they have scarcely commenced their school course, where the few girls that attend school have to be withdrawn about 10, to become mothers between 12 and 13 and old women before 33, and where young men are weighted down with the cares of family before they have seen the world or have found their own means of livelihood ! As to the discourse on things infinite, such as " the intricate nature of man " and all that, what has it to do with the plague of infant marriages condemned by God and man alike? But as a friend was telling me the other day—" your dunce who can't do his sums always has a taste for the infinite." And now I have done with these nameless scribes.

" WIDOWS ARE NOT AT ALL ILL-TREATED BY ANY."

" Widows are not at all ill-treated by any." Here are cases in point—very recent cases both of them :—(1) Gangabai, at present aged 16, daughter of————of Bombay, by caste Karada Brahman, was married at 11 to Vasudeva, son of —————in the Konkan. Twenty-nine days after the marriage ceremony the bridegroom died. Gangabai, the girl-widow, remained at her father-in-law's for about a year, and then returned to Bombay to her father's. Here Gangabai could not pull on with her step-mother—her own mother had died when she was only 9 days—so she went back to her father-in-law's. But she was told by her mother-in-law that she could not be kept there unless her father at Bombay provided for her maintenance, and unless she got her head shaved. Gangabai, therefore, once more came back to Bombay. Her father offered to take her in if she got her head shaved. This she did not like to do, and was therefore asked to do with herself what she liked. The unhappy outcast then went to her late mother's sister, but here too the shaving of the head was made a *sine quâ non* of admission. One more trial—Gangabai called upon her late mother's brother, who, again, insisted upon the head-shaving. In despair the girl left Bombay and engaged herself as a cook in the house of a Brahman Munsif at Baroda. For three months she found some rest there as a menial, but even this was not to last. The Munsif's caste people coming to hear of the matter told him that he ought to have her head shaved. The Munsif was somewhat of a tender-hearted man ; he put the matter before her, and seeing her firm on that one point, he paid her her wages and train fare for Bombay. Once more cast adrift, the little waif is seen by a fellow traveller—a Gujarati widow—sobbing in the carriage. To her Gangabai unburdens herself, and by her she is advised to go to Mr. Madhavdas Roognathdas who would treat her like his own child. Gangabai, the martyr, is now safe from further persecution. Such is her story, as it has been placed before me.

MORAL :—That Ganga's father is a good enough man, loving his motherless girl dearly; but he dare not incur the combined displeasure of his caste. He sees only one way open to give his daughter a chance in life and to save his own credit. Let her do with herself as she likes; if people ask me about her I'll say she has left my protection, she is a bad girl ! The story has another moral, too: the utter helplessness of Hindu reformers even in this matter of head shaving.

(II.) The other story is about a Gujarati Bania girl, very well connected. She too lost her husband while yet a girl, and has since been living with her father. When she sees that all her brothers and their wives are so happy, the girl naturally feels moping. She seeks corners and sits crying by the hour. In this state she is sometimes surprised by female visitors who are at a loss to understand why she is always in tears. If one of these friends sits by her side and tries to draw her out, she is at once remonstrated with by the relatives—"come on, come along, what's the use of talking with that crazy thing; she is mad." And forsooth her dear relations *are* driving her mad. One night the widow flies from home, no doubt seized by some desperate thought. But she is soon overtaken by her father and brothers who, though once they stood in the rank of reformers, take her back home, deal with her as a dangerous maniac and keep her in confinement.

MORAL :—" Widows are not at all ill-treated by any," but some of them are either *bad* or *mad* ! God forbid I should be understood to say that all widows are bad or mad, or that all of them wish to remarry. As I said in my very first note, and as I have repeated very often since, few widows in the real sense care to remarry. But there are the nominal widows, girls of 12 to 21, not a few of them entirely at the mercy of others. It is a most painful subject to dwell upon ; but those who look into the vernacular newspapers may have seen how frequent are the cases of cruel hardship and wrong which result from the enforcement of life-long widowhood on girls. These are only the known cases.

THE BEARING OF THE CRAWFORD-DILKE SUIT ON SOCIAL REFORM IN INDIA.

The other day we had occasion to refer to the extremes of wealth and poverty obtaining in certain parts of Europe and the consequences of such a state of things, especially where poverty has driven its victims to despair and where material prosperity only further debases what is base and brutal in the human animal. This ought, we think, to account for the scandals which now and then crop up in European countries, of which grossly exaggerated reports are sent out to India to be gloated over by a class of readers who excuse their own shortcomings by appealing to the existence of evils in other societies. This reminds us of the easy-going Indian

patriots who think that the credit of their society is established not by the removal of its own drawbacks, but the
existence of social evils amongst foreigners. They are now
furnished with fresh matter for self-complacency in what has
been called the Crawford Dilke case.

What has been said against the parties to this suit may or
may not be all true. We have little concern with it, as our
desire is only to get rid of social evils of our own and not to
adopt those of another people.* But the point which escapes
our shallow critics in India is that if European Society has
its black sheep and its shortcomings, it is not wanting
in courageous spirits who ruthlessly expose them and thus
bring about the requisite reform. It is their habit of publicity which magnifies their failings, and it is our habitual
reticence that hides us from the public gaze, that evidently
tends to blind us. Hence it is with us that the man who
makes known the sore is an enemy of his country; with
Europeans he is the benefactor of his race. How short-
sighted, then, and self-deluded, is our patriot? He admires
the Englishman who scorns the narrow prejudice or base
selfishness of his brethren and pleads for justice or generosity
to the Indian, but little does he dream of following him in
his conduct in regard to his own society. It is not thus that
strength of character and national greatness are attained.

A WORD WITH OUR MISGUIDED PATRIOTS.

There is one phase of the opposition, which needs to be as
often shown up as it makes head, namely, the intellectual
pride and exclusiveness of some of the cultured Hindus.

* In another place Malabari presented his philosophical and scientific
critics with the following passage in Felix Holt, Chapter XXI:—"Oh yes,"
said Felix scornfully, "give me a handful of generalities and analogies, and
I undertake to justify Burke and Hare (notorious malefactors) and prove them
benefactors of their species. I'll tolerate no nuisances but such as I can't
help; and the question now is not whether we can do away with all the
nuisances in the world, but with a particular nuisance under our noses."

This has been the curse of the race, and a few of its English educated members seem to be determined to perpetuate the curse. The people as a whole are tired of their social thraldom ; even orthodox Hindus are by no means unwilling that the marriage customs of the community be adapted to the requirements of the day. This is our daily experience, and any intelligent observer can see it by actual conversation as well as by following the drift of vernacular literature of the country. Our difficulty is with that important class of Hindus—important because they have a voice and can make it heard *as representing their voiceless countrymen*—who, though generally as denationalized as it is possible for Hindus to be, in habits, manners, language, even in their modes of thinking, are yet bitterly opposed to social progress, *in the name of the people* and on the plea that such progress will disintegrate society. I was convinced of this in the very beginning of the discussion, though I tried till lately to keep away the conviction as an evil dream. But after the repeated confirmations I have had during the last two years, and especially after the striking disclosures made by the *Indu Prakash*, it would be a sin to deceive oneself any longer. It is a handful of " educated " men who are at the bottom of this noisy opposition. Such men are hard to keep patience with. But even against these my feeling is a temporary one, and I hope that as a rule they may think as kindly of me as I think of them.

In this charitable frame of mind let us see what the promoters of the anti-reform movement are aiming at. They are trying to frighten the people with the notion that Government are about to force a law upon them. Now, this is a mischievous invention, and none knows it better than the inventors themselves. Government, as such, can do little in the matter, except with the consent and at the instance of representatives of the Hindu community. And, alas for the community, *these* are of their representatives and *this* is the way they represent popular interests. Afraid or ashamed of themselves coming forward boldly, they put up the masses from behind to impede progress by brute force. These are the reformers to whom we are asked to leave the work of reform. They first deny the existence of the evils ; when forced to admit that the evils do exist, they shirk their obvious duty, because it is unpleasant, by leaving the remedy to Education and Time, agents which have no power save what is infused into them by human effort. They themselves make not the slightest effort to cope with the evils, and abuse and misrepresent others who make the effort or advise it; and finally, they take to instigating the masses, themselves remaining in the background. What hope can there be of these " leaders" ever leading the people aright ?

Let my Hindu brethren beware of their sinister advice. What are they to the people or the people to them ? They have not a spark of sympathy for what they in their hearts despise as the vulgar herd ; they are incapable of offering personal sacrifice for those whom they look down upon as an inferior order of beings. They will use you as a mere convenience ; standing up on your broad shoulders these " leaders" will reach their goal and then kick you down as an encumbrance. It has been so always and will be so. Let the Banias, Bhattias and others of Bombay think for themselves. Do they believe for a moment that a Government like the British will be frightened by unintelligent clamours ? Such opposition might rather precipitate matters, which would be most unfortunate. They have every right to have their meetings, private or public, and to say their say. If they have facts and arguments they are sure to carry weight with Government. Even their wishes shall be consulted at every step, if the interests of the nation generally do not suffer thereby. But the non-Brahman communities will do well to resist the influence of their self-constituted leaders. In a matter like this may not an Englishman or a Parsi prove more disinterested than a Brahman ? At any rate, they will have sense enough to see that the drafts* prepared by Messrs. Melvill

* Of short bills to mitigate the two evils—*vide* p. 95 and p. 98 of Malabari's Collection of Opinions on " Infant Marriages and Enforced Widowhood."

22

and West are intended only for the guidance of practical reformers or Reform Associations, and not for immediate adoption by the community at large;

A BRIEF ANALYSIS.

The *Hindu*, of Madras, is in favour of legislative action towards raising the age of consummation and prohibiting disfigurement of widows. The *Sind Times* also favours legislation, suggesting that the girl's age be raised to 12, that municipal bodies be enabled to discourage infant marriages, and that Social Reform Associations be registered. The *Indu Prakash* strongly recommends permissive legislation to begin with and denounces the opposition as fractious and insincere. The *Subodh Patrika* is also for State action and bitterly complains of want of courage on the part of certain reformers and of their hypocrisy. The *Pandit* is for action somewhat on the lines suggested by Messrs. Melvill, West and Scott. The *Akola Vaidarbha* protests against the "littleness" of his countrymen in opposing me simply because I am a Parsi, and despairs of success so long as Hindu leaders do not do their duty by the people. The *Liberal*, of Calcutta, is not at all satisfied with the minimum ages of 12 and 14, but would have them fixed at least at 14 and 18, challenging any orthodox Hindu to show that such a proposal is opposed to the spirit of the Hindu Shastras. The *Promodh Sindhu*, of Amraoti, advises me to bring about the needed reform by means of lectures, tracts, &c. The *Indian Nation*, of Calcutta, does not like Government action, and is of opinion that respectable families in Bengal do not encourage infant marriages. The *Indian Chronicle*, of Bankipore, is heartily in favour of practical reform and protests strongly against my ill-usage by his contemporaries. *Young India*, of Calcutta, is also in favour of the proposals made by Messrs. Melvill and West. The *Gujarat Mitra*, of Surat, is strongly in favour of Mr. West's draft and suggests one or two additional provisions. It also writes cordially about His Highness the Gaekwar's advice to Hindu reformers. The *Gujarati*, of Bombay, also approves of State action with regard to the age for consummation, giving a general approval to the views of Messrs. Melvill, West and Scott. The *Ahmedabad Times* rejoices that the hour has at last come for practical action against these greatest of social evils. The *Ahmedabad Samachar* is equally rejoiced at the discussion having taken the present turn and hopes something will be done shortly to mitigate the evils of infant marriages and enforced widowhood. Both these papers write in high terms of praise of His Highness the Gaekwar's independence. The *Nyaya Darshaka* of Ahmedabad wants a stringent law against compulsory widowhood, and refers painfully to the results of such a condition, as witnessed almost every day. The *Broach Mitra* is equally well-pleased at the turn affairs are taking and thanks the Gaekwar heartily for his support. The *Rajputana Herald* is in cordial sympathy with the demand for State action. The *Praja Mata*, of Ahmedabad, is against all this noise and these European notions. The *Mahratta*, of Poona, is very uncertain. In one place he approves of Mr. Scott's advice, in other places he declares himself in opposition. The *Lahore Tribune* denies that either Professor Max Müller or the Maharaja of Baroda favours State co-operation! The *Dnyan Prakash*, of Poona, is decidedly in opposition, as also is *Native Opinion* of Bombay. Thus, then, of the 23 Hindu papers that I have been able to collect from all parts of India, 15 are in favour of State action. Of the remaining 8, 6 are for action on the part of the leaders of Hindu society whom some of them exhort strongly to move in the matter. The 2 papers that remain, *Native Opinion* and *Praja Mata* seem to be against action of any kind.

THE SITUATION REVIEWED.

NO LEGISLATION AT PRESENT.

I have no right, as an outsider, *to press for* legislation in regard to Hindu social questions, nor am I personally so sure that legislation is the best remedy, though looking to all the circumstances of the case it appears at present to be the only efficient remedy. Legislation seems indeed to have become a panacea with practical Hindu reformers, men who have done the battle single-handed or in small bands against the evils, and who confess themselves as defeated, and give up future struggle as hopeless and inexpedient. The only way that these men can adopt the proposed reforms individually is by *ceasing to be Hindus*, at once and for ever, not only themselves but their families, relations and connections. For, when a Brahman is put out of caste it is not to be supposed that he will be admitted into the fold of the lower class, the Kshatrya or the Vaishya. No, at the best he may be reckoned a Shudra, even if that. Those, then, who ask why such and such a Hindu reformer does not set the example, betray their ignorance of the rudiments of social reform in India. And so far the attitude of the English Government, too, is felt to be inconsistent with its liberal traditions. It asks the enlightened minority to accept what is impossible for their spiritual nature to accept—namely an absolute and irrevocable denial of the consolations of their religion. The marriage law of the Aryas is there, as pure and sensible as was ever made. But their modern descendants have departed from that law so seriously as to impede their progress in the race of life and to entail hardships and miseries innumerable. The Government is asked to restore them to their original law. This the Government declines to do, perhaps rightly as an alien Government. Virtually, then, a Hindu is left to sacrifice his religious aspirations and his worldly prospects *in order to be a true Hindu* following the law of Manu! To be a true Hindu he must cease to be a Hindu in these latter days!

ALTERNATIVES.

Now assuming that the general sense of the community is against legislation, what is the other alternative? Self-help. How far have our Hindu friends helped themselves in these matters, say during the last thirty years? To come to our own times, Mr. Goculdas Jagmohandas tried the other day to get something done through a caste meeting. He worked zealously and had the co-operation of several Hindu friends, and the moral support of Dr. Blaney, amongst others. The newspapers praised Mr. Goculdas's efforts ; and yet those efforts ended in a fiasco as soon as practical proposals were brought forward before the caste meeting. Poor Mr. Goculdas had to withdraw himself from an awkward position, and the bene-volent Dr. Blaney must have seen the futility of such efforts.

Let us take another instance. A few months ago my friend Mr. Chandvarkar delivered a most interesting lecture on the subject of reform. I was allowed the privilege that evening of proposing the formation of a Committee to draw up a programme of work. Mr. Telang supported the proposition strongly, and observed that the reformers ought not to have *a* Committee but *several* Committees. That was very cheering, and on return home I drank (tea) to the health of our Hindu reformers and the Committees that were to be. But where are the reformers and where are their Committees ? So many difficulties seem to have stood in the way that for the present at least the idea has been abandoned. People seem to be afraid of joining a Committee for *practical* reform. When it is so hard to *form* a Committee, what must be the difficulties of *working* it ? Speak of a Committee at the end of any lecture or conversation on social reform, and the most earnest of Hindus shake their heads. They have had too much of that nonsense, they think. Surrounding influences are too ·strong for them to work honestly on a Committee. They shrink instinctively from attempts foredoomed to failure.

TIME SPIRIT.

So that the only alternatives to fall back upon are Time and Education. What can Time alone do in such a case ? If people will only look into the matter carefully they will see that Time has actually aggravated some of the evils, and Education has made them more fashionable, though of course there may be cases in which contrary results have been obtained from the latter agency. But as I have so often urged, human effort is the first condition of success. This the people do not seem to admit. Mr. Wordsworth appears to have been thoroughly misunderstood on the point. Little did he know, dear innocent adviser, that he would be taken at his word literally when appealing to Time Spirit. " Orthodox reformers" find Time Spirit to be a capital excuse for inaction; while the unenlightened look upon Time Spirit as some hobgoblin of the intellect, who is to come to their rescue one day, if they will have but patience and let things alone *in the case of women.* Thus Sham-ji Dam-ji, who knows as little about Time Spirit as about the accomplished head of Elphinstone College, may be found expostulating with Mrs. Sham-ji of an evening, when, returning home from business he finds her breaking her heart over the misfortunes of her recently widowed child. " Come, come, what use crying, it is everybody's misfortune in the street. Time is our only cure. Better go and prepare supper, I have to attend a party." And Navivahu* does as she is bid. What is the good of crying about her widowed daughter when her husband is going out for a nautch? But do you think Shamjibhai will be guided by the same child-like faith in the omnipotence of time, if, for instance, he gets a boil on that fat little leg of his? Not he. He will go eagerly in search of the doctor and have the thing attended to.

SOME POSSIBILITIES.

Social reform implies effort, as does the supplying of any other human want. It needs honest, continuous effort. Have the gentlemen reformers of Bombay put forth any such effort of late? Have they tried to form themselves into an organization? Have they opened negotiations with caste in a proper manner and sounded the priest and the Punchayet? I am afraid they are too " respectable " to attempt anything of

---

* Literally ' new wife '—here used as a proper noun.

the kind. This sort of practical reform may be expected outside of the capital town. For instance, I referred the other day to certain Resolutions passed at a large meeting of the Khedawal Brahman caste at Vadtal near Nariad. The meeting was attended by Khedawalas from 52 different centres, and numerous letters of sympathy containing promises to abide by the resolutions to be arrived at were also received from all parts of the country. It was probably the largest and most representative gathering of the kind. What were the objects of the meeting? Let us quote the Report of the proceedings :—

(1). "To put down the wicked custom of selling girls" (in marriage).

(2). "To prohibit the painful practice of marrying a second, third and more wives while the first is alive and in health."

(3). "To prevent baby marriages brought about mostly in order to secure the largest amount as price of the girl babes disposed of."

(4). "To prevent constant breaking off of matches in order to secure larger prices for the girls."

Let us now glance at the Resolutions of the brave Khedawàlas :—

(1). "The whole caste entirely prohibits the shameful and sinful practice of bride selling......Whoever is found guilty of the offence shall be put out of caste for two years and shall have to pay a fine equal to double the amount he may have received as price of the girl disposed of in marriage."

"After the expiry of the period of excommunication the offender will be kept out of caste till he pays up the fine. The party who buys the girl shall remain out of caste one year and then pay the caste a fine equal to the money he has paid for the bride. Before paying up the fine he shall remain out of caste. Those who have aided and abetted the bringing about of such a match shall each be out of caste for six months, and pay as fine half of what the buyer of the bride has paid, remaining out of caste till the fine is paid up." Then follow interesting details as to how much money the bridegroom's parents may fairly allow to the parents of the bride (Rs. 501 *plus* Rs. 208). More than that would constitute the offence of buying and selling. A bridegroom whose age is 40 or 50 may pay about Rs. 200 more for the bride. But anything beyond that would be an offence. Then comes the rule saying :—" no man shall marry a second wife before satisfying the Caste Committee as to the absolute necessity of such a course and without making suitable provision for the first wife."

Here follow a set of significant Resolutions :—" The bride must be at least 8 before the marriage takes place " (which means that marriages do take place amongst Khedawala and other castes *before* 8, often from 3 to 6 and amongst Kadwa Kunbis at times *before* the bride and the bridegroom are born) " He who breaks this resolution shall have to pay a fine of rupees 101." " The bridegroom *must* be older than the bride, but if that is impossible in some cases, both may be of the same age. On no account, however, is the boy to be younger than the girl " (I have often been abused for hinting at this sort of marriage.) " A fine of Rs. 101 will be exacted from any one breaking this rule." Details follow as to how the fine is to be recovered and how to be employed.

It is a pity I cannot quote at greater length from this important Report. But the few passages given above will show (a) that the marriage law of the Aryas has been fearfully abused by their degenerate sons in India, and (b) that if a return to the primitive law is possible it may be effected at first not so much in "civilized" centres as in " backward " parts. Have our Bombay Hindus anything to show like this noble work of reform undertaken by the Khedawala Heetvardhaka Sabha? The Khedawalas are perhaps the most conservative class in India. What, then, cannot the educated

classes do if they set about the work in earnest, regardless
of worldly prospects and of what this mán or that woman may
say? If they have no Panchayet, or are too proud to recognize any, they might form a new Panchayet.

But no. Their present occupation seems to be to abuse and
to misrepresent opponents. They go the round of the
Press, trying desperately to obscure the main issues ; they
get up demonstration ; in short, they are doing what superstitious Native women do to shut out light. When a fire
breaks out in a street the women hold up iron or copper
sieves at the windows, so that the glare may not penetrate
their houses and thus pave the way for Agni-mata. The idea
is to keep the houses under shade, so that Agni-mata may not
see them nor make fiery overtures to them. The tactics of
some of our opponents seem to be equally intelligent and
beneficial. One of them, a particular friend of mine, is said to
have written to Poona friends, saying——" there ought to be
meetings all over India to crush that Malabari." What an
awkward thing to say for a reformer ! Nothing could be
more useful to the cause of reform than this crushing of the
obnoxious individual. For, from every drop of his blood
would rise up another agitator ten times stronger than he.
A second reformer tickets me about twice a week as " felon,
traducer, libeller, slanderer, defamer " and so on, presumably
quoting from Roget's Thesaurus. And how do I take all
this? Why, whenever I come across this string of "other
words" I bow my head in gratitude, exclaiming to myself,
Thank God so many things I am *not*! Equally disappointing
is the attitude of my young friends of the *Mahratta*, apparently playing into the hands of old advisers. The difference
between the *Mahratta* and myself is trifling ; for I do not
insist upon legislation as a *sine quâ non*. And yet what a
flood of bad adjectives our Poona friends attempt to drown
me in every week ! I thought they knew that such things

23

have ceased to hurt. But what will others think of the *Mahratta's* capacity for public discussion and his claims to political advancement? Does this sort of writing reflect credit upon the college which has educated these critics, or will it do good to the students of whom the *Mahratta* is said to be a favourite organ? Have the writers in that journal no regard for their preceptors and no pity for the rising generation?

"AT THE PRESENT MOMENT."

H. E. the Governor of Bombay made an interesting announcement last week at the Poona English School for Native Girls upon the subject of Infant Marriages. Here are His Excellency's remarks in full :—

" I am not prepared, forcibly by law, to interfere with the internal economy, I repeat, of Indian society. Now I know that if that question was put before the English people, who look upon their homes as their castle, they would not allow interference on that account. And speaking here as I do on a question of policy, which concerns not the local but the imperial Government, I should not have ventured to express any personal opinion on this subject, if I had not—not as you may think quite lately—in a personal interview with the Viceroy, discussed this all important subject and had been led to that conclusion, which fell in with the opinions I had formed at the time, by the opinion of a much more experienced statesman than myself—I mean His Excellency the Viceroy. It may, therefore, be held as a fact that no legislation is contemplated at the present moment on that subject. In speaking of a matter of this grave importance, we must always take care not to be misunderstood; and if we do not interfere by law in your internal economy, we also do not interfere by law in any discussion, or any opinion which may be held by any section of the community on that subject. I know that it is a subject on which people's opinions vary, and those who hold opinions differing from those held by the majority of the Hindu community, are perfectly not only able to ventilate their views, but are perfectly welcome to do so. And if ultimately, in the struggle of opinions, they succeed in altering the public opinion of the country, Government will then, for the same reason that they do not now choose to interfere, think it proper to alter the marriage law, because then it will be altered in accordance with the changed customs of the country. (Applause.) This is a subject, of course, in which Englishmen speak with great caution, because their sympathies are on the side of those who desire to make a change in this law, although for one I am not prepared to say that the attempts of Englishmen to make marriage laws have been very happy, because of all confused documents nothing is more confusing than the English marriage laws, except perhaps the Civil Allowance Code and the Bombay Army Regulations. (Laughter.)"

Now I do not wish to deal with this passage as an advocate, and must allow that the case has been very fairly put on the whole. "At the present moment" Government need not interfere. And for my part I wish Government had no occasion to interfere at any other moment. But that is mere sentiment which the practical inaction of the majority of Hindu leaders, *since the days of Ram Mohan Roy*, scarcely warrants one to cherish much longer. The subject of infant marriages has been discussed incidentally with that of widow marriages *for the last forty or fifty years*. If representative Hindu gentlemen would or could have helped themselves in the matter in the long interval, we might have been spared the spectacle of the Madhav Bag meeting last Sunday. Has there been anything like the same activity in moral and social as in political matters ? But let us hope an effort may yet be made in each important centre independently of abstract theories of Education (for Education alone is far too slow a process for our purpose, and as between the sexes it is so unequal that it has generally been found to aggravate the evil than otherwise). Every Indian's home is doubtless his castle, as every Englishman's home is. But

these evils are more of a national character than purely
domestic, and want of action, or action such as that taken at
the Madhav Bag meeting, is not to be counted upon as a
cure. At the same time such a great authority as H. E.
the Governor of Bombay may be allowed to know more
about the *pros* and *cons* of the question than one who is
neither a Governor nor a Hindu. And this I allow readily,
since His Excellency has publicly recognized the right
of the minority to deal with the questions as they like
and to do all they can to win over others before asking for a
law. That is fair enough, though I wish it were clearly
apprehended by the powers that be that what is wanted is
not a new law, but a little moral pressure to help the Hindus
go back to their old law, a departure from which has entailed
all this misery on the people and the country. The situation
is full of promise for Hindu reformers, if a few of them are
prepared for a life struggle.

PHILOSOPHICAL HODGE-PODGE.

The prevalence of infant marriages amongst Hindus in
these days—for in spite of the bombast about the custom
being an immemorial one it is a fact that it did not exist in
ancient times—has been ascribed variously to causes political,
social, moral and religious. But it was reserved for the
Pioneer to trace it to the *economic* condition of the people
as followed by parents from motives of self-interest, and insur-
ance against famine and distress.

Ordinarily indebtedness, poverty and distress are aggravated by universal marriage, but in India the *Pioneer* thinks
they are relieved by it, and this is the reasoning by which he
seeks to establish the paradox. The natives of this country,
we are told, are induced to marry their children in infancy,
because, first and foremost, they thereby enlarge the family
circle; and secondly, the married couple is placed beyond
the temptation of going astray. The *Pioneer* is sceptical

as to the second ground influencing many parents, but being sure of the first, he thus enlarges on it:—

" The parents marry their children because they wish to increase the family circle, and this they desire to do because they think it will be of direct benefit to themselves. We must, therefore, ascertain why it is to the interest of Indian parents in general that their circle of relatives be extended. Rightly or wrongly—presumably rightly if the experience of ages is to go for anything—they are of opinion that relatives are a good thing, and the more they have of them the better. In what way then are relatives of use to a man? What do they do for him that he should so earnestly desire to increase their number? In India for nine-tenths of the population famine looms upon every man's horizon of life, and his relatives are his great safeguard against the phantom. Like cattle who stand shoulder to shoulder and defy the wild beast against which individually they could offer but a feeble resistance, the Natives crowd together, father and son, uncle and cousin of every degree of kinship, the weak and the strong, the hale and the halt, and only by the strength of their cohesion can they ward off the dread spectre. The people are frightfully poor, and this everlasting poverty is the cause of all their manifold ills. If from any reason—the scarcity of rain, a drought, or flood—their daily supply fail, then they must fall back upon one of two resources, either on their credit at the village money-lender's, or on their relatives. If the former looks hardly on them and the latter do not exist, or existing, are in the same evil case as themselves, they must starve. "

The *Pioneer's* theory is original, but it does not, square with social facts as known to history and actual experience. As a rule parents do not marry their children in infancy because they expect from the connection *direct benefit to themselves*, except the few classes that sometimes sell their daughters in marriage. Such expectation is directly opposed to the first feeling of honour which the relationship by marriage engenders, viz., not to be beholden for any direct benefit to the opposite party. The *Pioneer* here betrays ignorance of Native customs and feelings. Help is no doubt expected from well-to-do people by their distressed relations; but it is the maternal and paternal relations that are expected to support destitute individuals, and not those by marriage. But to proceed, the *Pioneer* observes that in England there are certain safeguards against starvation which are not possessed by the people of India. There few live from hand to mouth, and the majority have either savings or luxuries to draw upon in times of emergency:—

"Very few comparatively of the British race are on the lowest rung of the social ladder, having no earthly possessions save the rags on their backs, for whom it is impossible to sink lower; and even these need not starve. They present themselves at the workhouse and they are fed, and, if able, made to labour for their food. When we hear of distress in England, we do not picture to ourselves scenes such as take place in India in times of famine. Distress with us means generally an unusual run upon the workhouse or a deprivation of luxuries that have come to be considered as necessities, and a forced consumption of humbler articles of diet. In Great Britain at least let a man, woman, or child be found dead of starvation in the streets, and a cry for vengeance upon the parish officials goes reverberating through the length and breadth of an indignant country. The noise that would be made over that poor outcast is as great as the official lament over a couple of hundred in India, not from any hard-heartedness, but from the frequency of the event."

Nor are men there, as they are here, required to help their relations who may be in difficulties:—

"We do not hold each particular family responsible for its outcasts and beggars, but we saddle the whole nation with the responsibility, and in this way distribute the burden of their support most evenly, each bearing part of the weight in proportion to his means. Our failures are individual; but our

charity is national. In India the condition of things is precisely the opposite. The Native stands perpetually on the
verge of destitution. He has nothing except his crops or
what he earns from day to day to keep him from beggary.
Unlike the Englishman he has no personal luxuries to sacrifice. His clothes are of the fewest and scantiest. He has no
furniture save that which is absolutely necessary to cook
his food and dig his fields. His house is a mud hut thatched
with tiles and leaves, on which it would be impossible to put
a marketable value. He has no money put by."

Now, as we have already hinted above, these admissions
of the absolute poverty of the Indian subjects of H. M. the
Queen-Empress, and of the freedom from it of their English
brethren, are valuable so far as they support the cry of the
Native Press that the Government of such a poor country
should be economical and not extravagant in its expenditure.
They must further silence Anglo-Indians like Mr. J. M.
Maclean, Sir Richard Temple, Mr. Ashburner and Sir
James Fergusson, who have been telling us now and again
that while the Indian peasantry is getting rich and comfortable, poverty and famine are getting chronic in England.
And lastly, they show that the custom of the Natives of
supporting their starving relations saves the Government
the trouble and the cost of keeping up workhouses and affording relief to the needy, and that the Natives, therefore, have
other claims on their purses than those of the comforts and
luxuries of themselves and their wives and children, and that
consequently it is unwise and unjust to clip and cut down
the salaries drawn by Native servants of the State alone, when
those of the Europeans are allowed to remain intact. For
these admissions, as definite as they are just, we are profoundly
thankful to the *Pioneer*.

These are important conclusions, but they do not cover the
point at issue: they have no bearing on the question of infant
marriages. It is needless here to refer to the arguments in
favour of the abolition of that custom. We have already

pointed out how sadly the *Pioneer* errs in ascribing its prevalence mainly to the prudential motives of the parents following it. But even granting for a moment the entire contention that the custom in question "originates naturally from conditions of existence that have obtained for centuries," viz., the poverty of the people (the existence of which *for centuries* is, by the bye, another gratuitous assumption)—taking all this for granted, we ask, we challenge anybody to tell us, what all this has to do with the custom of marrying in infancy. The economic conditions of existence and the alleged advantages derived from enlargement of the circle of relations secured by the marriage connection would not be affected by a hair's breadth by the postponement for a few years of the formal ceremony which makes the tie irrevocable, leads to premature consummation, enfeebles the constitution of the parties, and gives rise to virgin widowhood which involves so much misery and ends only with the life of its victim! And this postponement is all that is advocated by the 'tweed-suited' reformer who can now, therefore, much more reasonably transfer the compliments of thoughtlessness and ignorance to the doctrinaire publicist in broadcloth flourishing at holy Prayag.

HISTORY OF A REMARRIAGE.

About a year ago I referred to the persecution to which a remarried pair were submitted at Dhoraji in Kathiawar, and which persecution might have ended fatally for its innocent victims but for the timely intervention of a number of Hindu officials in favour of widow marriage headed by an English Political officer who showed unusual firmness on the occasion. To-day I have been enabled to place some interesting particulars of the case before the reader from a book published by Kavi Jeshangdas Trikamdas Patel. The facts and circumstances mentioned are of a recent date, drawn mainly from records of the Courts. The personal details, too, though they have no direct bearing on the remarriage, are full of general interest.

THE HERO.

The hero of the episode which I. have purposely dignified by the name of History is one Mr. Damodardas, a Bania Vakil. He is evidently a man of character—bold, liberal, self-reliant. Like men of that stamp Mr. Damodardas has risen from a humble origin, after many vicissitudes, to a position of credit throughout Kathiawar. Though destitute of English education he is, or was, Public Prosecutor at Gondul. In 1870, we find him a successful and rising Vakil. He was rich enough at the time to buy a wife or more than one. But girls were very scarce in his caste, and, besides, Damodardas was so convinced of the legality of widow marriage that he was determined, if possible, to rescue a respectable widow and make her his partner in life. (On the evils of Compulsory Widowhood our chronicler discourses here on this wise:—" Not only are there many advantages in encouraging widow marriage, but there are many positive disadvantages to society in suppressing widow marriages. In the first place castes are becoming extinct ; if a caste is a large one this result is not soon perceived ; in a small caste going out of existence the effect can be easily traced to the cause. Widow marriage is disallowed, and eligible virgins are not to be had for 6,000 to 7,000 Rs. each. Sometimes a girl is not to be had for any amount. On the other hand, young widows go wrong, run away with men belonging to other castes," &c., &c.) These and similar considerations must doubtless have induced Vakil Domodardas, as much in public interests as in his own, to contract an honourable widow marriage.

THE HEROINE.

Our heroine is named Manckbai. Her pet name *kidi*, which means a little emmet. Judging from her photograph Bai Manek must have been quite the reverse of a *kidi*. But she got the name, I suppose, to mark her social, not physical, insignificance. For she was a posthumous child, born a few months after the death of her father. She was brought up in the house of her maternal uncle, under whose roof her mother had sought shelter. At 5 or 7, it is hard to say which, little Manek was betrothed to a boy for Rs. 700 pocketed by her loving uncle. Some time after the boy died, and as the fact of the betrothal was not generally known, Manek's uncle thought of a proper marriage for his niece. After protracted search a match was at last found available at Jamnagar. Manek was at the time about 11 and her intended husband was about 54 (the old sinner made himself out as only 50). This was scarcely a suitable match, and there were certain other inconveniences besides. For instance, Manek's intending husband had already a " wife" at home, and apart from domestic squabbles there was the dead certainty of Manek becoming a widow not long after the marriage. At 54 a Bania is more than what European nations call *old*. But these considerations never troubled Manek's uncle. He made Rs. 2,000 on the bargain, and that is all he cared for. The marriage took place, Manek enjoying the fun as heartily as the other children of her age did during the ceremony and the feasting, little knowing what it all meant. Soon after she went to her husband's house, and had a miserable time of it for three years between a decrepit old husband and a termagant of a rival whose peace she had unconsciously disturbed. Then the old man added to his past unkindness by dying. Manek now found herself helpless and at the mercy of others. She had some joy jewels, but of this she was robbed by a brother of the deceased husband, who took her and her co-wife out for a pilgrimage and turned them adrift on their return. Manek was now without home, and beset with trials and temptations. But she soon made up her mind to go to her uncle. On the way she had an encounter with thieves whom she faced like a young tigress. Overcoming other accidents and reaching her village, Manek found her wretched uncle reduced to destitution. Her mother had been dead some time. She knew not which way to turn. At last she thought of an old aunt in another village. She went there and found rest for a while. Mr. Jeshang describes perhaps too vividly Manek's struggles during her widowhood —her struggles with temptations which scarcely one out of a hundred of her constitution and temperament could resist in a state of society by no means unfavourable to moral lapse. These realistic details we shall pass by in silence, thankful to know that our heroine came scathless out of her fiery ordeal.

THE MARRIAGE.

Soon after Manek appeals in person to Vakil Damodar to recover the joy jewels entrusted to her brother-in-law. This is their first acquaintance. By the more than sisterly interest of a friend Manek's acquaintance with Damodar ripens. One day she discusses with him the *pros* and *cons* of widow marriage ; and more patriotic than those who quote Buckle and Bentham and love to be called leaders of society, she is ready in a few days to risk a remarriage with her legal adviser. To ward off suspicion our practical reformer retires to another village for a time. Damodardas and his friends now make suitable arrangements. Before the day comes he requests his wife that is to be, to fully consider the consequences of the step she is going to take. She turns the tables upon him by saying—" take care *you* do not repent the step." " As for me," she continues, " I know that remarriage is right and proper." The happy day opens with music at Damodar Vakil's house. What can be the matter ? people ask. The Vakil is a bachelor, there are no marriageable girls for him. It may be his birthday. The secret is very well kept for a few hours, but as the day advances, they let the fact ooze out. The first intimation that Damodar, the leading Vakil, is about to remarry a widow, falls like a thunderbolt upon the town. His panic-stricken castemen do not believe it at first. But when satisfied as to the truth of the report, those of them, who have widowed sisters or daughters, rush home to see if the widows are all in ! After yielding so far to the instinct of self-preservation, they meet in a body, as Mahajan, and issue orders that everything should be done to confound the reform party that day, and that no Brahman should be allowed to perform the ceremony. On it becoming known that a young Brahman has already been secured, the Mahajan sends for his father and tells him that if the ceremony is performed by his son they will never have anything to do with him and his family. This means ruin to the Brahman; so he rushes frantically into Damodar's house, rates the company soundly, and insists upon his son walking out. The son hesitates. The reform party offer him fresh inducements, and say it would be a shame if he left them in the lurch at such a moment. But the old Brahman curses and swears furiously, and tells his son of the Mahajan's resolution. The boy leaves with his father. Damodar and his party are in a cruel fix. It is evening now. After much anxious discussion one of the friends volunteers to go through the ritual. Damodar and Manek assent to that. But before the ceremony begins, in comes an old Brahman friend of Damodar's on a visit to him. He can hardly realize the situation on entering. When the matter is put before him, he undertakes to perform the ceremony formally in spite of all the Mahajans in the world. In an hour more Damodar and Manek became one, after a *pucka* marriage ceremony, and all night, let us hope, there is singing and dancing at Damodar's house. It is certain, at any rate, that in the enemy's camp there is weeping and wailing and gnashing of teeth.

THE PERSECUTION.

The very next day another Mahajan meeting was convened at Dhoraji, at which a formal excommunication was proclaimed against Vakil Damodardas and his wife, and the following resolutions were passed :—(1) No Bania Mahajan should from this date dine with Vakil Damodar or should invite him to dinner. (2) No Bania Mahajan should engage Vakil Damodardas as his pleader. (3) No Bania Mahajan should be on speaking terms with Vakil Damodardas. (4) No Bania Mahajan should have *len den vehvar* (buying selling, lending, borrowing, &c.) with Vakil Damodar.

It may not be difficult now, even for an outsider, to understand why widow marriages are so rare in India. Mr. Damodardas was a man of character and position: if his caste, a non-Brahman caste be it remembered, dealt with him so severely, what would they not do with a less important man? And what was the Vakil's punishment? Nothing less than *civil death*. Thanks to Colonel Scott (then Major Scott) the conspiracy was soon broken. Had there been a less resolute officer on the spot, the Mahajan would not have scrupled to go further. In fact, they *did* go further. When Damodardas did not mind the excommunication, they hired others to trump up a number of charges against him. The first of these charges, preferred by a servant of the Vakil's, was that he had received stolen goods. This case was dismissed after formal inquiry and trial. The second was got up by another Vakil, named Jaganath, who deposed that Vakil Damodardas had designs on his life! This horrible charge, too, was dismissed after a protracted trial. When foiled in these and similar intrigues, the enemies tried to alienate his affection from his wife. They sent a false Hundi to Mr. Madhavdas Roognathdas at Bombay in Mrs. Damodar's name, and then brought the matter indirectly to Damodar's notice, so as to rouse his suspicions. Here, too, the wretches failed. I need not give more particulars. Those that have been given above may point to the existence of a deep-laid and wide-spread conspiracy. Who can stand such combined opposition of the caste?—which forbids not only soical intercourse with the obnoxious party, but even professional and other business. And yet, if a remarried couple pray to Government to save them from such organized persecution, or to remove the shameful anomaly it has created regarding the status of the chaste widow, actually patronizing the unchaste, Government goes into ague fits. It is humiliating, indeed, to see a body of men calling themselves Government passing an Act and suffering it to be trampled by the ignorant and the interested. When they ask for a majority in favour of a cause to which they have been committed, our present rulers forget that

Pandit Vidiasagar's Widow Marriage Act was passed on the representations of a *minority of one to five*, and that the Honourable Member in charge of the Bill declared in the Viceregal Council that if the passing of that Bill brought relief to one single widow the Government was bound to pass it. But why should I trouble myself about this part of the business? I can only show *what* has to be done; the *how* and the *when* must be left to representatives of Society and the State.

TO THE SHASTRIS OF POONA.

LEARNED SIRS,

In one or two places during your interview * you spoke of "religion." If by that word you mean the Hindu Shastras, I submit that religion not only does *not* sanction *infant* and *unequal* marriages, but it absolutely forbids them. You know this infinitely better than I do. Go to the noble *Griha-sutras*, to the admirable *Smritis*, to the moral code of Manu and the medical code of Dhanvantar—throughout the entire range of the Hindu Shastras there is not a line to be found in favour of infant marriages. There is only one miserable *shloka* giving colour to the theory. But it is so utterly at variance with the spirit of the Shastras that any one could point at it as a latter day invention, at the clumsiness of which the commonsense of even an ignorant man like myself is apt to revolt. I can well imagine your loathing for such an interpolation.

In another place, you spoke of the evils having been "most grossly exaggerated," of "unfounded and slanderous statements" having been made, and of other "monstrous charges." Well, gentlemen, if these are not exact quotations from some of the Poona papers, they are certainly a most transparent paraphrase of them. Knowing, as I do, that you are not the conductors of those Poona papers, I am sorry these words have been put into your mouths. They do not suit you, sons of Saraswati. And Sanskrit is far too dignified a speech to

---

* With H. E. Lord Reay.

descend to such expressions. Besides, will you kindly say *whom* you charge with all these sins, and *wherein*? If I am the sinner and have really sinned, please state in what particulars you hold me guilty. I am ready to abide by your judgment if you afford me an opportunity of explaining myself. I repeat that, as a rule, I have understated, not overstated, a hard case. This matter could be soon cleared up publicly or by private correspondence.

You fixed 12 years as the maximum age for girls. This is all that we want. Will you declare officially that a girl need not be married much under that age? Will you rule that it is a sin to marry away girls at 3 and 5 and 7, especially with lifelong widowhood staring them in the face?

As to the remarriage of widows you declared it to be "contrary to Shastras." Pardon me, but you seem to have forgotten that 30 years ago Pandit Vidiasagar proved remarriage to be consistent with Shastras, and that the Government of India endorsed that view by passing their Act XV. of 1856. Even now, will you argue out the point with Ragoonath Row? Don't you remember that the Shastris of Poona were willing, some years ago, to effect a compromise with Vishnu Shastri, namely, that they would not object to the remarriage of virgin widows? Is it not currently believed that even so far back as a century ago, in the reign of the Peshwa, the most learned Shastri living was inclined to favour this view? Shastrijis, do not think for a moment that I am pushing you into a corner. Why should I? I have no personal interest in the matter. What little I had has nearly died out under hard usage. But the question is one of supreme importance to you. And just as you settle it, according to truth or error, right or wrong, *Shastra* or *a-Shastra*, so will you earn the blessing or the curse of the nation.

It has grieved me to read your appeal to the Governor, " earnestly begging H. E." to take your " helpless condition into his favourable consideration " as regards grant of money in aid of Sanskrit Pathshalas. Sad, indeed, is the fate of people whose religious leaders have to seek aid from "foreigners"! What does this appeal show, together with the other appeal for the suppression of " the increasing evil of drunkenness " amongst your people? Shastrijis, you may understand me perhaps better one day when you allow me to sit at your feet for a few hours. Meanwhile I beg to be excused for thus addressing you directly.

THE MARRIAGE QUESTION TREATED HISTORICALLY.

Whatever our opponents may say as to this or that particular method, they cannot deny that the question of marriage reform in India has been thoroughly threshed out during the last two years. Besides numerous and varied contributions from representative Hindus themselves, which are of prime importance, the cause has been actively supported by the best of our English friends, official and non-official, from the Marquis of Ripon and Professor Max Müller downwards. The latest amongst these expressions of disinterested public opinion are those from the Hon. Mr. Melvill as legislator, from the Hon. Mr. West as jurist, and from the Hon. Mr. Scott as administrator of law and justice. And now comes the most welcome contribution of a historian. The Hon. Mr. Hunter's article in the *Asiatic Quarterly* deals with the question historically. The writer approaches his subject tenderly, almost reverently, but with rigid impartiality. Dr. Hunter's is out and out the best contribution that has enriched the literature of the subject. And though the " orthodox reformer" may not relish the verdict in the present temper of his mind, the day must come when he will thankfully admit that the friendly co-operation of Englishmen was indispensable in working out the reform.

The article opens with a comprehensive retrospect, in course of which our historian glances at the noble service rendered, from time to time, by a late Maharaja of Burdwan,

Pandit Ishwarchandra Vidiasagar, Dewan Bahadur Ragoonath Row, the Hon. Mr. Rauade and others. To this list,
all too short, must be added the names of the late Pandit
Vishnu Shastri, the late Mr. Karsandas Mulji, Raja Pro-
mothnath of Jessore, Raja Sir Madava Row, the late Mr.
Ramkistiah of Rajamundry, and others. Dr. Hunter also
refers with just appreciation to the labours of the Hon. Mr.
Mutu Sami Iyer and the Hon. Mr. Sankriah. Of myself
he writes far too kindly, perhaps to make up for the unkindness of some of my own countrymen and fellow-workers.
As the *Indu Prakash* shrewdly suspects, his generous
treatment may once more open the floodgates of abuse and
vituperation in some quarters. But this I do not mind.
Generosity is scarcely to be expected from the product
and victim of Infant Marriage. He is so absorbed in himself
and his progeny, that he has no kindness to throw away upon
others. To him the distance of a hundred miles from home
means Exile ; everyone outside his street is a stranger, a
Foreigner, an Alien ; such an one attempting to sympathize
with or help him must doubtless have some object of his
own to serve, and so on. I have become thoroughly accus-
tomed to this usage, so much so that unkindness has ceased
to trouble but it is kindness that somehow unnerves me now.
Dr. Hunter's kindness is very disquieting ; I hope a few
attacks from those " orthodox reformers," who are for building up a National Party in India and securing representative
government for the good of the people by showering abuse
on those they differ from, may restore me soon to my usual
equanimity.

The article in the *Asiatic Quarterly* is too rich to be
quoted piecemeal. But before the whole of it is republished
as a tract,* it may be as well as to quote one or two remarks
from the accomplished author as the extent of the evils and
the nature of the remedies that seem feasible to him at the
present moment. Dr. Hunter believes there are " one million
young widows " in India. Further that " Practically all

---

* It was so republished by Malabari and circulated *gratis.*

25

Hindu girls of good caste are either wives or widows before they reach 15." Here, I think, the evils have been somewhat understated. But that is good.

As to remedies they can be best estimated from the summing up of the learned historian:—

"*First.*—There is an almost universal concensus of opinion, both among the English administrators and the educated Native, that child-marriage and enforced widowhood inflict a grievous wrong upon the women of India.

Second.—The appeal back to the sacred texts against these unrighteous customs has been made, and is successfully upheld.

Third.—While there is a general agreement that any large measure of legislation would at present be opposed to the sense of the Hindu community, and would therefore be as inoperative as the Widow Re-marriage Act of 1856, there is also a well-founded opinion that in specified minor matters the time has come to grant partial legislative relief. Such relief would include a specific recognition of Hindu marriages contracted by a high-caste girl after her maturity: the non-for-feiture by a re-marrying widow of any property granted to her unconditionally by her husband's Will, and the non-forfeiture of movable property inherited from her husband, in parts of India where the Hindu law gives to her absolute control over such property.

Fourth.—That, while Government may aid the cause of reform by publishing the results of the inquiry which it has lately made throughout India, the reformers can much more powerfully help themselves by means of a central organization and of local bodies.

Fifth.—That, apart from the forfeiture-of-property clause, the great obstacle in the way of reform is Hindu public opinion. That the punitive enforcement of this opinion, by means of excommunication, can be fought in the Courts, and may be still more surely overcome by patient and passive resistance.

In conclusion, it must be remembered that the opposition is headed by a class of men who have a hereditary instinct of self-preservation. The Brahman caste has, with the exception of the Buddhist episode, always supplied the intellectual leaders of the Indian people. Already a section, and the most active section, of that caste is in favour of reform. Their numbers are powerfully reinforced by the educated castes just below them in the technical Indian scale. The more conservative section of the Brahmans will give way as soon as they feel that they have to choose between yielding to educated Hindu opinion, or losing their influence over the Hindu community. Their surrender will be no base striking of their colours, for they have only to turn to their sacred texts to find authority for the concessions required of them."

I shall be quite content for the present with such legislative relief as the Hon. Mr. Hunter in his article, and the Government of India in their Resolution, are good enough to hold out. It is for Hindu gentlemen now to avail themselves of this generous offer. As to coercive legislation I have never so much as dreamt of it. As explained before, I actually deprecated such legislation in my very first Note and have disclaimed and repudiated the idea repeatedly since. I have never asked for more than " State co-operation." Whatever else I have advanced has been advanced, not from myself, but from practical Hindu reformers. If in doing this I have made mistakes in language, so as to be misunderstood as asking for coercive legislation, I am more sorry for it than the opponents can well be indignant. God knows who has had real cause for indignation. But it is useless repining. It was unfortunate I could not write like a lawyer—that accounts largely for the misunderstanding. But next time I issue a Note I hope to show it to a Hindu lawyer before submitting it for consideration to the community at large.

FASHIONABLE MARRIAGES.

A Madras Native paper reports a marriage in which the bride is as old as from 7 to 8 years and the bridegroom only

60 years old. Well may the reporter ask if such a marriage is not worse than slavery for the child-wife. But who cares? After all it is only a woman.

A Madras friend told me last year of a marriage in which the bride was 18 *months* and the bridegroom about 22 years. Are such marriages heard or dreamt of in any other part of the world? So much for our progress.

"THE LIBERTY OF INDIVIDUALS."

Those of my countrymen, who oppose action on the plea that it infringes the liberty of individuals, forget that they thereby furnish me with one of my strongest arguments. This has been made clear time after time. But the following letter addressed to the *Pioneer* puts the point more clearly than before. The writer is against us in some respects, as he is for us in other respects. But the point at issue, namely that the practice of infant marriages leads directly to the infringement of the liberty of the least protected of our fellow subjects, he establishes satisfactorily. I remove the last paragraph, as it might stink in the nostrils of our lavender scented reformers :—

" SIR,—Will you allow me a few words on the subject of infant marriage? Between mere sentimentality on the one hand and conservative dogmatism on the other, the real point at issue for us, as the governing race, is not, I think, clearly recognised. Briefly, is the binding of a minor by his parents and guardians to a personal contract, the nature of which he cannot understand, the consequences of which he cannot appreciate, an infringement of his liberty, and therefore illegal ? If it is so in the mass of cases in what way does the marriage contract differ from other personal contracts so as to justify us in recognising its validity in our Courts ? Though our policy in such matters moves, like Providence, in a mysterious way, it may be broadly laid down that our theory is to administer the laws of the people we govern so far only as they do not run counter to certain principles of justice which history teaches us are necessary to the growth of a nation. Now, the inability of a minor to be bound by contracts made for him by others is universally recognised as one of these principles ; because it is distinctly inexpedient to give the present generation the power of mortgaging the possibilities of the future. The gradual recognition of the rights of infants has gone hand in hand with civilisation and is a good test of progress. The point at issue then is : Shall we continue to legalise a distinct infringement of the liberty of the individual ? No arguments of expediency, no hysterical appeals to mere feeling can touch this simple question of right or wrong, which is equally beyond the realm of tradition or sentiment. There is no need for legislation on the subject, for the custom is not criminal like *sati* and female infanticide, but simply illegal, and therefore unrecognisable *in our law* : that is to say, no suits arising out of non-fulfilment of contract would lie in our Courts."*

MR. ILBERT ON HINDU SOCIAL REFORM.

Mr. Ilbert deprecates "undue official interference." So do I. But when it is due, pray let us have such interference, or rather co-operation, as it will then be. We only want co-operation. In Mr. Ilbert's own words we want little more than the "ready and sympathetic recognition" by Government of any practical conclusion arrived at by a number of representative Hindus. But Government must meet them half way, and must *show* that they are willing to do so.

That Indian customs and usages are not unchangeable may be admitted, as a general rule. But when these customs are based on "vested interests," and when the interested classes are guided by the "instinct of self-preservation," as Dr. Hunter shrewdly observes, a modification of the customs is scarcely ever to be expected without some sort of pressure from without. Follow the current of progress in India, and

---

* Sir William Muir has expressed the same opinion.

you will find this experience verified at almost every turn. The classes enjoying social distinction in India probably have an interest in keeping up widowhood. Infant marriages lead to widowhood. Why should we be surprised, then, if they stand up for the perpetuation of these un-Aryan customs? The consciousness of the fact that they have lost or are losing their monopoly of political power and that the tendency of the British Government is to level all invidious distinctions of birth and rank and to depend more or less on personal fitness, might make the " higher" classes cling to their social advantage all the more tenaciously. It would be so all over the world ; in this country it should be more so than elsewhere. Therefore, to wait for custom of infant marriages to go out of itself, or through the unaided efforts of the people (who are ignorant) or of their representatives (who are believed to be more or less interested) would be a piece of folly and a crime. No real and lasting progress can be predicated in the matter except from the co-operation of the State with what is wisest and best in society. An improvement may be visible now and then in some of the advanced sections. But on the other hand we hear of large sections of the community, once free from the fashion, taking kindly to it from force of example. Even supposing, for the sake of argument, that the fashion may disappear two centuries hence without any assistance from Government, who is to be responsible for the havoc caused in the meantime? It is apprehended by many a thoughtful Hindu that if the present state of things continues for another half century, the community will be hopelessly handicapped in the race of life and that there will be much less chance of improvement then than at present. There are some who say it will be too late to mend matters a few generations hence.

In effecting a reform of this character it will scarcely do, I think, to trust to learned men. What does learning avail which brings no wisdom with it? Some of the bitterest opponents of progress are these learned men who do nothing themselves and leave nothing undone to thwart the attempts of others to do something in a humble way. This attitude is quite intelligible in men who, though they may have had any amount of one-sided learning, have never received a liberal scientific training. There are aspects of public questions which they can never be made to see. We hear of such men in England making respectable deacons and arch-deacons who have a morbid horror of innovations and whom we find arrayed in a solid mass against the Deceased Wife's Sister Bill. They are worthy persons, so far as that goes, and prodigies of book learning. But they cannot read even the Book of books in the spirit of its original intention. They are always for the letter, not the spirit. Can such men, often with heavy interests at stake, vote for the abolition of infant marriages in India?

Talking of the Deceased Wife's Sister Bill I must admit that it is a fair parallel. But those of my Indian friends, who fling it in my face, must not forget that the passing of that Bill (which may become law any day) will not do a millionth part of the good in England that the passing of a Bill fixing the Shastric limit of marriageable age will *do in India*. Also that the latter measure is a thousand times more urgent than the former.

A WORD WITH THE RIGHT HONOURABLES AND THE HONOURABLES—AND WITH RESPECTABLE REFORMERS.

No man living is so universally respected in India as Professor Max Müller. The Hindus cherish his name with all the fervour of hero-worship. Hindu scholars look upon him as the chief pillar of Sanskrit literature. Hindu politicians regard Max Müller as one of their wisest and safest guides. Hindu reformers consider him their final court of appeal. From the days of Suttee to those of the Ilbert Bill, we have invariably found him a true friend of India, glorifying her ancient civilization and inspiring her children with hope as to the future that awaits her under the auspices of an enlightened rule. Max Müller fought the battles of Ram Mohan Roy ; and when, many years later, his successor, Keshub Chunder Sen, was set upon by an unmanly and unmannerly faction, Max Müller was the first to join the present writer in denouncing that unholy fight of the many with the one. His advocacy of the Ilbert Bill and of Lord Ripon's administration of India generally is a matter of recent experience, but few students of current politics know how much this open advocacy of national progress has cost him. In his own branch Max Müller stands unrivalled. He has devoted his life to a loving and luminous interpretation of Aryan philosophy and religion, building up a stately Science with fragments of knowledge which, lying scattered, appeared as so many holes in the shield of early civilization. Such is the Anglo-German Rishi `whose greatest pride is that he is an Arya, claiming kinship with our degenerate race.

His opinion on the Resolution of the Government of India on Social Reform will be accepted as that of a thoroughly competent authority. Professor Max Müller glances at the Resolution from the moral, the legal, and the practical points. On one hand, he addresses himself, in vigorous Anglo-Saxon, to a Government of highly respectable and moral old gentlemen who are anxious to please everybody. On the other hand, he expostulates with those effeminate fanatics who conjure up imaginary difficulties because a real difficulty has to be overcome, and who strive their utmost to save appearances at any cost. I have no wish to add to the humiliation of either party. But it is becoming apparent to others less interested than I that the recent action of Government may prove the grave of more reputations than one. As to the orthodox Hindu reformers their attitude is very nearly discrediting a whole community. Professor Max Müller is not the first to advise an appeal to the Women of England. To one in my position such an experiment has hitherto seemed to be fraught with serious risk. But I am beginning to fear that there is scarcely another way open. It must be remembered that almost all measures of emancipation that we are aware of owe their success more or less to the influence of English public opinion ; and public opinion in this country being what it is, I do not see why the question of the emancipation of women in India may not be taken to the women of England, the land of freedom and fairplay.

And be it noted here that Prof. Max Müller is not one of your ardent reformers, who would have anything and everything reformed out of existence. His theory about the decaying tooth is too well known. As a reformer he is slow and cautious, with his sympathy leaning more towards the past than the future. In this matter it is not much that he wants the Government to do. But is not the little he requires essential to success? Let his letter speak for itself :—

"Oxford, 26th October 1886.

" I hope you do not consider the battle lost. Now seems to me the time to resume your work with double vigour. For every fight against old established prejudices defeat is at first inevitable, but it is invariably the precursor of victory. I do not see that you could have expected more from Government. Government in India is no longer what it was fifty years ago. The motive power and therefore the responsibility is at home, and ' at home,' you know, means ' in a house divided against itself.' I begin to believe that Mill, who was so much abused for his defence of the old East India Company, was right after all, and that it was an evil hour for India when it was drawn into the vortex of party government. But, as I say, Government in India being what it is, you could not expect more than that advice would be asked all round and responsibility eschewed.

" Now, mind, I am not in favour of paternal government, not even in India. But I hold that Government loses its *raison d'être,* if it does not prevent and punish what is morally wrong, even though the moral wrong has the sanction of religion and tradition. I do not say that Infant Betrothal, and even

26

enforced Widowhood, are morally wrong, but the consequences flowing from them lead to civil torts which any Government deserving that name ought to prevent. I was amused with the case that happened in Madras. By all means let the castes excommunicate, but if the excommunicated man is injured by having an open Post Card sent to him, announcing his excommunication, let that tort be redressed by Government.

That Infant Marriage has no sanction whatever from either Sruti or Smriti I told you from the very first, and I see that no Pandit now ventures to gainsay that. Manu wishes a young man to marry when he may become a Grihastha, *i.e.*, when he is about 24 years of age. As to the girl, she is to marry when she is fit for it, and that may vary in different climates. But an engagement between infants is never contemplated by any legal authority, much less are the sufferings of widowhood inflicted by Sruti or Smriti on a girl whose polygamous husband dies before she has even seen him. That argument has been treated with so much learning by your own scholars and lawyers that nothing more need be said on it. The study of Sanskrit, even by so-called *Mlekkhas* like myself, begins to bear fruit. You remember how in the case of Suttees, the Shastris quoted passages from a lost Sákhâ of the Veda, intended to show that widows should be burnt with their husbands. They actually tampered with a passage from their own sacred Veda, and not till I published the passage from the Asvaláyana, Grihya Sutras, forbidding widow-burning, would they become silent. With regard to the proper age for marriage, I published the important passages in my Hibbert Lectures in 1878, p. 352-3, and as these lectures are being translated under your auspices into most of the modern languages of India, I doubt whether any Shastri *now* will dare to invoke either Sruti or Smriti in support of Infant Marriage. But, of course, they will invoke the authority of Akara or Desadharma, unless they remember that custom and local law have no authority whenever they conflict with Sruti or Smriti.

However, the argument derived from Sruti and Smriti may

by this time be supposed to be surrendered, and the case stands simply thus :—' Infant marriage is a native custom, and we do not want the Government to interfere.' I have not a word to say against this argument, provided always that no tort is inflicted on individuals. Government does not deserve the name of Government, if it declares itself unable to protect each individual subject against personal torts, whether sanctioned by custom or not. Now, infant betrothal is a tort—it is a contract made without consent of one of the parties. If, therefore, that party suffers and wishes to be released from an unjust contract, the Government ought so far to protect him or her. Whether the Government is foreign or native, does not matter. It is *your* Government, as long as you accept it, and enjoy all the advantages of it ; and to turn round and say that your Government should not prevent and punish iniquity is self-contradictory. Do you not invoke the aid of the Government to stop drunkenness or Thuggee ? The Thugs appealed to custom and to their protected goddess, but the Government did not listen, but did its duty. Now, ask any high-minded woman, what is preferable—to be killed in the most expeditious way once for all, or to be married to a man whom you loathe— and I believe the answer cannot be doubtful. The custom of infant betrothal is unjust ; the custom of infant marriage is criminal. In the former case Government should give every relief that is demanded by the injured party ; in the latter Government should punish the criminal. But for the unfortunate feeling against Government interference—in many cases a mere excuse of interested parties,—no man worthy of the name of Arya would tolerate or try to explain away such iniquities. I wish the Government, while declaring its impotence, had at least given expression to the righteous indignation which every Englishman must feel when reading the accounts you have published of infant-brides and infant-widows. That would have been no great risk, and would at least have given some encouragement to you and those who work with you in continuing your crusade.

"However, depend on it, justice will be done. Write a short pamphlet, containing nothing but well known and well authenticated facts, and send it to the Women of England. They begin to be a power, and they have one splendid quality—they are never beaten. If they once know what is going on in India, tolerated by an English Government, they will tell every candidate for Parliament, 'Unless this blot is removed from the escutcheon of England, you shall not be re-elected.' Women at all events have courage, and when they see what is hideous, they do not wait for orders from home, before they say what they think. Secondly, educate your own women, and depend on it, this matter will soon be set right in spite of temporising Governors of half-hearted reformers among your own countrymen. I know many of my native friends will be very angry with me for writing this. I only wish I could speak to them face to face, and I should soon convince them that I care more for the good name of the true Aryas than they themselves. You know I abstained for a long time from writing on this subject. I felt it was in good hands, and I do not like, nor have I time, to give my opinion on everything. But now that apparently you are beaten, I cannot remain silent, and the more my friends in India abuse me, the more proud I shall feel. If they call you ignorant, because you are a Parsi, what will they call me, a mere Mlekkha!

"Yours very truly'

F. MAX MÜLLER."

WHAT IS A WIDOW?

The Shastris of Poona consider the prohibition of the marriage of widows not open to question; but there is a point prior to that even, *viz.*, as to who is a widow; and on this point Dewan Bahadur R. Ragoonath Row challenges contradiction. In a pamphlet recently published, he says:—
"The most important point of difference between me and my would-be-orthodox brethren in the matter of Hindu marriage is, that they believe that as soon as the Saptapadi ceremony is gone through, the bride becomes one with her husband in

Pinda, Gotra, and Sutaka, while I hold that this unity of Pinda, Gotra, and Sutaka comes into force after the fourth night of the marriage, *i.e.*, after its consummation." " The Sutras are admitted by the Honourable T. Muttuswami Aiyar to be ' collections of important Vedic texts constituting the foundation for rules of conduct.' As such they are of the highest authority. They are called Aswalayan, Apastamba, and Gobhila Sutras. They are unanimous in holding that this unity is arrived at on or after the fourth night and *not before*." The texts referred to are these :—

Aswalayan Sutra ....1—8—12
Apastamba ,, ...2—6—15—10
Gobhila ,, ...2—13—15—2,—5—1.

Other and minor authorities in support of the same view are also given, but we need not quote them here. Their purport is as given above and in the following extract from the Honourable Mr. Ranade's Introduction to the collection of papers which led to the passing of Act XV. of 1856, with which Mr. Ragoonath Row concludes his own tract:—" Marriage, unless consummated by actual cohabitation, should not be recognised as a perfect union before the limits laid down above are reached. Before such consummation the girl should not be recognised as having become one with the husband in Gotra, Pinda, and Sutaka. This is the ancient law, and our reversion to it will do away with the superstition which paralyses the action of parents in dealing with the misery of child-widows." Have the worthy Poona Shastris to say anything to this part of the question they think as settled? What have they to say to Prof. Max Müller?

"OUR WIDOWS NEVER CARE TO REMARRY, AND THEY ARE NEVER ILL-TREATED."

Parvatibai, daughter of —— a medical man at ——, aged 21, by caste Konkanastha or Chitpavan Brahman (same caste as of the promoter of the Madhavbag meeting), was left a widow about fifteen months ago. Sister Paravati's life has been worthy of a high caste Hinduani before as well as after the death of her husband. Her father has never had cause of complaint against her. But now having disgraced him and his race (!) by becoming a widow, she ought to be ready to have her beautiful head of hair shaved off by the city barber in the presence of pious Brahmans. Parvatibai cannot see the point of this argument, but unwilling to offend her father, she asks for time. Taking advantage of this reprieve, she appeals to a friend of the family. This latter speaks to her father and advises him to forego the barbarous ceremony ordained for his daughter. The father does not like the interference of even an intimate friend and forbids his ever setting foot on his threshold again. This only makes the friend more resolute and Parvatibai more desperate. While matters stand thus, the friend loses his wife. Now comes the supreme moment. Will this professing friend of Parvati and of widow marriage stand the test of personal sacrifice ? Will he act in his own person as he has been preaching to Parvati and others ? Yes, he actually does so. Not being a B.A., nourished on misquoted passages from Mill and Malthus, Parvati's friend offers her marriage in accordance with orthodox Hindu rites. The little widow sees that the life before her is a dreary wilderness infested by more wild beasts and poisonous serpents than ever a temporizing Government attempted to destroy. So she accepts the offer.

On the other side her father is preparing for the great head-shaving ceremony. The widow tells him naught of the new joy that has sprung in her heart. Who knows what may happen ? There is many a slip between the cup and the lip. To-morrow is fixed for the ceremony (not the remarriage, please, but the head-shaving), and priests and Pandits are to officiate at it, for suitable presents, of course. Parvatibai sees that the hour for action has come. So after a restless night she gets up and quietly makes for the Police Inspector's before any of her family knows of it. She tells the officer of what is going to happen and seeks his protection. He asks what she proposes to do. She offers to go to

Bombay if he gives her a safe conduct pass. This is given with alacrity. The Railway Police are instructed to protect the widow and to see that the ornaments she has on are not removed or that she is not molested personally. On Friday she comes to Bombay and is received by Mr. Madavdas Rugnathdas, protector-general of forlorn widows. In this case, Mr. Madhavdas will be soon relieved of his charge—for in less than a week Parvatibai expects to be remarried to the man who has risked so much for her. But for the head-shaving business she might probably have gone through life contentedly as a widow. But the "orthodox reformer" cannot see that head-shaving, instead of reconciling the widow to her cruel lot, only makes her more desperate.

THIS IS HOW THEY DO IT.

"We do not want Government interference," say the opponents of social reform; "we shall do everything ourselves." And how do they do it ? Let us take a recent case—that of Parvatibai, the Ahmednagar widow. This spirited young Brahmini, roused into something like public spirit by constant oppression at home, and into diplomatic foresight from the same cause, went to the Police authorities for protection on leaving her father's house. Why did she do this ? Because she knew that if she left without informing the Police, she would be hunted down, at her father's instance, *on a charge of theft*. This happens frequently. When a young widow insists upon entering into an honourable alliance again and leaves home with that object, she is immediately made over to the Police as a thief. The ornaments and clothes belonging to her are represented as having been stolen by her, or she is represented to have stolen this or that trinket which she did *not* take with her. In trumping up such a charge the Hindu policeman may sometimes be found actively assisting the orthodox party. Parvatibai knew this and baulked her father of revenge by anticipation. She made a *bandobast* with the Police authorities and came down to Bombay under a safe conduct pass from them.

So her father and his instigators had to adopt a new device. They filed a suit against those whom they suspected as having helped the girl, for recovery of Rs. 505 *to make up for the loss sustained by Parvati's father in the shape of domestic drudgery.* That is, the poor girl is looked upon as a SLAVE by whose escaping from servitude her master, the owner of her body and soul, loses his interest in this live chattel, represented by Rs. 505 ! An attempt is also made to show that the girl is a minor, athough she is really past 22. Nay, according to information already before the public, the persecutors go so far as to make an affidavit, swearing that the girl is a minor and that she is going immediately to be married again ; and praying that the marriage be stopped and the girl be ordered to return home from Bombay. Luckily, the Magistrate, a European, refuses to issue an injunction on such a transparently foolish declaration, and the party return from Court crestfallen. For this, we cannot be too thankful to the Magistrate, and to the valiant Nagar reformer, Mr. Lalshankar.

The account given above is discouraging enough. But I have learnt something much more discouraging in this connection. Parvatibai's father is an extremely poor man, poor in spirit and poor in worldly means. Why, then, has he become so implacable, and whence does he bring the money for the prosecution ? Incredible as it may appear, he is said to be supported by the so-called educated classes of Ahmednagar. Most of the Pleaders there have volunteered to help him in his unparental task. The people, it is said, are being worked upon by secret wirepullers, and the Pleaders and other men of position are trying to make capital out of their ignorant fanaticism. Have not the Government of India declined to help the widow ? That means that widow-marriage is illegal. The priests also declare themselves against widow marriage, and last of all comes the Pleader class. What a prospect for social reform in India. But for a resolute executive this conspiracy of terrorism would have fully succeeded in its aim. Cases like that have happened, ending in permanent injury to the victims, even in murder. Have the British Government any idea of how they confirm fools in their folly and bigots in their bigotry? But what is to be expected from a Government of politicians and diplomats, covetous of what the vulgar call success, who spend their energy in importing delusive reform from the West, leaving the real improvement of the nation to take care of itself? The Government of the day are worthy of Hindu lip-reformers, and the latter are worthy of this chivalrous Christian Government. Each is doubtless willing to do something towards social reform when the other has made a beginning unaided—which may be made 3,600 years hence. In the meantime the one is dallying with diplomacy, and the other is trying to transplant parliamentary government into the land of baby-brides and girl-widows. God knows how long His own law is to be thus defied and His most holy ordinance desecrated in the name of expediency.

A CHILD-WIDOW.

Suraj is a little girl hardly twelve. An old widower, losing his wife, thought of marrying this little girl about 6 months ago. There was a maternal relation of Suraj who was a friend of the widower, and our widower sent for him and paid him about Rs. 400 to negotiate the marriage. Whether the money went to the girl's mother or not, we do not know. But Suraj was married to the 50 years old widower. Six months after the marriage, Suraj became a widow.

Her husband, 2 days before his death, made a will, devising his property, a house worth about Rs. 700 and ornaments worth about Rs. 1,100, to his "little wife," as he called her—and he appointed 4 executors to take charge of this property during the minority of his "little wife." He, however, had a son by his first wife. That son had separated from him, not in estate but in messing and residence, on the old man marrying a second time. The deceased had some ancestral property which he had sold. His son, of course, had a birthright in this property, and he therefore claims that his father had no right to make any will in favour of the "little wife." What is to become of the " little wife " or rather the " little widow " ?

Suraj and her husband both belonged to a section of the Nagar Brahmins. Therefore, according to custom, Suraj's head was to be shaved on the 10th day after her husband's death. On that day also a caste dinner was to be given. One day before this date, Suraj's mother took away her daughter to her own home, and refused to allow her to be shaved unless the ornaments bequeathed by the deceased were placed in her own safe keeping on behalf of Suraj. No caste dinner can come off unless the widow is shaved among these Brahmins; Suraj's mother therefore believed that the whole caste rather than lose the dinner would exert themselves to secure her the ornaments. But the caste did nothing of the kind. They had their dinner, though Suraj was not shaved. A caste dinner is very dear to the Brahmin. Suraj was a minor and might be shaved when she was a major. The conscience of the caste was satisfied, and there was a grand dinner according to the directions of the deceased.

Suraj's mother was foiled. The caste had their dinner, and the caste, when at their dinner, didn't care if Suraj was shaved or not. But when not at dinner, the caste had something to say on the point. It placed its caste-stigma on poor Suraj and her mother, and Suraj was shaved.

Will any one tell me how long this is to last? My blood burns when I hear of such outrages on humanity. I have no doubt many of my Hindu brethren feel as poignantly as I do. Why, then, do they make no sign? Why do they not found associations and missions and organize an opposition to such custom? I honour the brave men who want no legislative or executive interference with their customs, but their bravery is not honourable if it means brave words only and no brave deeds. Is there none, I ask again, who will come forward and lead this movement ? Is there none who feels for the wrongs inflicted on child-widows, who detests the brutality of the strong towards the weak, who has a horror of such insufferable un-Aryan customs as widow-shaving and infant wedlock? If there are any, let them step forward and be missionaries of a noble cause. If there are none, then India is poor indeed!

WHAT MORE CAN WIDOWS SAY AND DO?

It is a very convenient cry with a certain class of reformers that "our widows do not wish to remarry." Here is another case which illustrates the hollowness of the cry generally. That there are Hindu widows willing and anxious to lead the life of saints is not to be denied. Such widows are an honour to humanity. But considering the circumstances under which Hindu girls become widows, their position at home, if they can at all be said to have a home; and their surroundings, it is equally impossible to deny that the majority of young widows would prefer remarriage to the living death to which they are condemned by custom and the want of courage of their natural protectors. It is to be hoped that such instances as are brought to public notice from time to time may yet open the eyes of the community, especially of the English-educated classes.

Mr. Madhavdas Rugnathdas received a letter some time ago from a widow in Gujarat, a brief substance of which, in her own words, is given below:—

" My name is Krishna, and I am daughter of Vyas Bhula Kuber, inhabitant of Thamna, near Dakore. By caste I am Audich Shahastra Brahman. I am about 20 now, and became a widow some four years ago. I do not feel I shall be able to pass my life in honest widowhood, the trials and temptations of which are too many and too well known to you. . . . Besides my great misfortune, I had to put up with such words from my mother and others that I once resolved to put an end to my miserable existence. But death does not come when summoned by a wretched sufferer, and I did not wish to incur the sin of suicide. Therefore, I made up my mind to leave my parents by fair means or foul. At this time I was advised, that instead of living a life of shame and sin, it would be much better to enter upon the married state again. * * * But I must find a man who would be able to maintain me in decency, and not make me repent the step in future. I have found no one up to this time to help and encourage me. * * * I am now asked to appeal to you to find a suitable person for me of the Brahman caste * * *. I would have come to you personally, but am not in a position to do so, nor have I the means. * * *"

Mr. Madhavdas has taken up the case and has already given shelter to poor Krishnabai, and may very shortly give her in marriage to a desirable man. Mr. Madhavdas Rugnathdas is not a graduate of the University who argues away the necessity of remarriage in India, in the case of women, by an appeal to the wise men of Spain and Turkey in Europe; nor is he a learned Pandit quoting passages to strangers in power, which he can never verify; nor an enlightened citizen who marries a second wife of ten, while preaching to his widowed daughter the blessings of Brahmacharism; nor is he that happy mortal who can approve remarriage in theory, but condemns it in practice or puts it off to the end of time. Mr. Madhavdas is a poor unlettered reformer who guides himself by principle and others by example.

ANOTHER EVIL OF INFANT MARRIAGES.

It has been observed that not a few of our educated countrymen seek happiness outside their homes, and that they justify this course by saying that, having been mated in infancy, they find no attraction within the domestic circle. This is not to be wondered at. For where there is no sympathy between wife and husband and no common taste, it is impossible to make a home. This is more especially so in the case of a husband reading Shakespeare and Byron and a wife who has to be content with being a kitchen drudge and a child-bearing machine than between a pair more or less upon the same intellectual level, however low this common level may be. And considering the difference between the education of the sexes in India, it is marvellous that we hear so little about domestic unhappiness. This is partly to be explained by the uncomplaining nature of woman and the small esteem in which she is held in this country by the " lords of Creation." But that the extent of this particular evil is more serious here than elsewhere, and that infant marriages are a fruitful source of it, cannot be denied.

Recently, I have been acquainted with another phase of the evil. I have received a requisition signed by five members of the Anavala Desai community of Gujarat, urging me to prevent what they think is likely to prove an outrage on the marriage law. The writers begin by saying that Government has established schools and colleges in order to " purify the intelligence " of their subjects. But, they add, the practical results of this education among them is that it makes some of the recipients of it worse than before, " doing worse things than done by uneducated men, even than savages." They give five or six instances in which educated young Anavalas are said to have married early and then discarded their wives on some flimsy pretext or other, in favour of better endowed brides. My correspondents are very indignant at this, and they rightly suggest that the practice is demoralizing their community. Two of them, who called the other day, gave me particulars which are scarcely fit for publication. If girls are to be married in infancy and then put aside, because they are found " ugly," or " senseless," or " sterile," or whatever else the "reformed" young husbands are pleased to call them, then 75 *per cent.* of marriages will end in the ruin of the girls. So argue my correspondents. What adds to the infamy of the thing is, that it is always the wife who is discarded, that it is the " educated " Anavalas who seem to have set the fashion, that the caste can do nothing to discourage it. I have heard it stated that even mothers of children have been thus set aside in favour of new wives, and that the bare maintenance of life has been at times denied to the discarded family, though in such an extreme case it may be said to the credit of the caste that they have upheld the claim of the family to maintenance, a miserable pittance.

The case in hand about which I have been written to is this :—An Anavala Desai, a gentleman holding high position under Government, and otherwise a very estimable citizen so far as I have heard of him, married his nephew and adopted son some fifteen years ago. The wedding took place with great *èclat*, processions, caste dinners, &c. This shows that the bride was most acceptable at the time. In the course of this interval of fifteen years, however, the bridegroom has become sufficiently " educated " to dislike his poor illiterate bride whom he and his uncle *now* find to be " senseless." So they are negotiating another "marriage." The first wife must therefore go find what consolation she can with her parents. The boy is said to be a graduate of the University, or about to be so. His guardian is a highly respectable person, who is reported to me as having married four times (not all at once, I am glad), the latest matrimonial investment taking place when he was a little under 50 and his fourth dear not a little under 10. I suppress names. It is no part of my business to give the slightest pain to individuals. It may be that the boy has conceived an honest aversion to his wife. But for that he must thank the custom of infant marriages, and not punish a girl who has already been too much victimized.

As to preventing either the repudiation of the first marriage or the perpetration of the second, I must say it is altogether a mistake to expect me to do that. The utmost I could do is to make a plain statement of facts as supplied to me. And even for doing that I have to look out for another Shastris' Conference at Poona, another Bhattia meeting at Bombay, another batch of anonymous letters and personal vilification at private meetings—with my educated co-workers running hither and thither, promising mighty deeds of reform, three hundred and sixty years hence, and the chivalrous British Government holding back or limping forward in a half-dazed manner, wistfully looking round for escape. Government shift their moral responsibility on Hindu leaders, and these gentlemen pass it on to the people and the women. " What can we do?" they ask. "Our people are not prepared for reform, and our women won't have it." We are, therefore, asked to wait till every mother in India comes forward to be enfranchised and every mother's son is prepared to help her out of her civil disabilities. We must wait till that day which will never come so far as even the eye of faith can see. Those responsible find it is so convenient to mix up the *civil* with the religious aspect of the question. In the meantime non-Brahman sects, like the Anavalas, may go on imitating the foolish vices of Brahmans and adding to them criminal vices of their own.

A BLIND SEER OF GUJARAT.

Shivadas is a *Shighra kavi*, an impromptu versifier, and a mathematician, with a memory wonderfully quick and retentive. He explains that he picked up all his Gujrati and English knowledge by hearing his lessons read out to him only once. What is more wonderful is his knowledge of life. His verified Essay on the evils of Infant Marriage, of which I have been favoured with a copy, shows marvellous insight and accuracy of description. He prefaces the Essay with the shrewd remark—" I know that infant marriages are the root of all our evils, and our social condition will improve only then when infant marriages are put down." Then follows an earnest exhortation to leaders of society, with an indignant protest —" though drowning, they open not their eyes—they wish to plunge into the well with large stones tied to their feet."

What are the causes of Infant Marriage? (1) The pleasure and privilege of bringing about a union with the attendant ceremonies and displays. (2) The lust of control over other lives. (3) The desire to have a rich man's son (or the rich man himself) for son-in-law. Shivadas goes over well-known arguments against the custom—physical, economical, educational, moral, and political. To those who give their infant daughters in marriage to elderly husbands our poet addresses the words of an ancient *Shloka*, which means :—" Sins as large as the Mount Meru may dissolve by the fervency of *Rudra-japa* (a penitential peace-offering extremely difficult to make), but the god Shiva himself is unable to obtain forgiveness of the sins of those who sell their daughters in marriage." In another place he quotes another text, which says " that he who sells his daughter will have to pass 90,000,000 births in hell." And yet the avaricious father has only to pay a few rupees to the priest who will explain away each one of these 90,000,000 living hells ! But to return to our bard : he likens this horrible practice of parents living upon their daughters as *the cow sucking the heifer*, the reversing of Nature's law. Here is a vehement fulmination against the father who sells his girl into inevitable widowhood :—" thou wilt have as many vermin eating thee up as there is hair on thy body, the messengers of Death will dance on thy breast, thy flesh will be consumed by leprosy."

Then comes a description of the trials of the repudiated wife, the victim of infant marriage, who is put aside later on for a second "wife:" of the horrors of ill-sorted marriage, wherein the wife is older than the boy-husband or the husband is old enough to be the wife's father, even her grandfather. The lines are scarcely fit to be translated. This is followed by an account of the daughter-in-law's life at her husband's—a life of unceasing drudgery, often worse than slavery, where her very girlhood is crushed out of her nature. There is a good deal more in Mr. Shivadas's Essay. But it is not pleasant to dwell upon. I must therefore wind up with a telling argument—Infant marriages lead to a general break down of the system, especially in the case of the wife. . . . "The Shastras lay down that a girl is fit to be wife after puberty, but we seem to be departing even from this rule. Poor helpless little girl, the duration of her life is forcibly shortened; she has to face the performance of social duties while yet her constitution is far from developed, while yet she has to cut her milk teeth." · · · · · ·

A word now to the Hindu reformers who excuse themselves by deploring the ignorance of their womankind— "What can we do? Our women are ignorant; they are not ripe for reform." Of such faint-hearted reformers Kavi Shivadas asks——, whose fault is it that our women are ignorant? What do we do to remove their ignorance? *How long do we keep them at school?* What with the cares of too early married life and of domestic drudgery, where are the chances of improvement?" Let our orthodox reformers meet these questions. What opportunities do we, the men of India, offer to our women to improve themselves? We are talking of their education as the best means to social reform. But is it not a mockery. to speak of *female education* when every girl has to be withdrawn from school about 10 or 11? It is idle to talk of Infant Marriage and Female Education in the same breath.

And now I must leave Kavi Shivadas Naranji for the day, commending him heartily to the public, to friends of progress and reform in particular. He is physically blind, but he sees better than most of us blessed with eyesight. Would to God that men with their vision unobscured could see half as clearly as does the blind bard of Gondal, or that they could feel half so keenly. Let our public men with eyes to see, and with the additional advantage of position and influence, remember that of those whom much has been given, much shall be expected on the day of reckoning.

CHARITY BEGINS AT HOME.

One of the most effective hits that we have noticed of recent years was that given by the *Kaiser-i-Hind*, last week, to charitable Hindu citizens. Some of these gentlemen, having raised a cry for mercy to criminals and to the sacred cow during the Jubilee holidays, were requested by the *Kaiser* in all charity to have mercy on their *gherni gáe*, that is "the cows at home," (widowed sisters and daughters,) before invoking mercy on others. The rebuke was well meant, and, though administered in the quietest manner, must have made the object of it wince under it. The Hindus ought to be the most charitable race on earth, and their charity extends to the lowest creature crawling thereon. But custom has sadly perverted their instincts. In the most cherished relations of life they stick only to the form, regardless of the spirit. They are tenderly mindful of disabled horses, bullocks, dogs, monkeys, &c., and have regular institutions for their relief and maintenance. They will pay any reasonable price for captive birds or vermin which the *Vagri* * may take to them to excite their feeling. But for the captives at home, disabled for life, they have little mercy. In his heart of hearts the ignorant Hindu believes a widow to be a criminal whom it is a sin to succour or to countenance. And hence it is that though we have a *pinjrapole* in town for beasts and birds, there is no asylum for destitute Hindu widows. For months has a sympathetic European lady striven to establish only a school for widows, to give them occupation and self-respect, lifting them from the debasing level to which Hindu usage has consigned the unhappy creatures. She promised that it would be a purely Hindu institution, without any designs on the orthodox faith. She offered to find money for it. She put aside her own scruples and convictions, and made every allowance she could for bigotry and selfishness. Like a true Sister of Charity, she went from door to door, seeking the co-operation of Hindu gentlemen. Her enthusiasm was something incredible. And it was refreshing to see her disposing of excuses and explanations as they poured in from lip-reformers. This time I thought the widow had a fair chance. But it was not to be. A hundred men had a hundred different plans which scarcely ten of them were earnest about, and which not

---

* Game-catcher.

one of them was willing to modify. So they went on attenu-
ating the original plan till they reduced it to nothing. In
fact, they discussed it out of existence, and came to the
valorous resolution TO WAIT. I should not be surprised
if the lady has washed her hands of the whole affair and
laughs at the talk which the newspapers so often report of
the political progress of the natives of India. There can be
no progress side by side with this paralysis of action where
the slightest sacrifice, or even inconvenience, is to be encountered. Surely, there ought to be enough of public spirit in
the "first city in India" to work a European lady in found-
ing a school for Hindu widows to be managed by a Hindu
committee on strict Hindu principles? But not half-a-dozen
Hindus are forthcoming to do this, while thousands will be
ready at an hour's notice to harangue Government as to the
cruelty of allowing cows to be slaughtered by the Musulmans
and rabid dogs and monkeys to be destroyed by the police.
And it is to this class of men that Government looks up for
the emancipation of women in India. God help our baby-
brides and girl-widows ! Even a rare occasion like the
Queen-Empress's Jubilee has gone by without one anxious
thought given to the most neglected of Her Majesty's subjects and sisters in India. Government might, to some
extent, have lightened the widow's burden of grief by making
a grant towards the establishment of asylums and orphanages.
But where is the pinch ? Women in India do not hold indignation meetings and pious conferences of protest to frighten
Government. And with their natural guardians and representatives so indifferent, what need has Government to go
to the rescue of the uninfluential sex? Statesmanship and
chivalry may be all very well for sentimentalists : they have no
place in the code of honour of your practical politicians.
If the alleged decline of English supremacy is to be traced
in anything, it is in this attitude of the Government towards
the most helpless of their wards.

THE QUEEN'S OWN WARDS.

" Deborah," an Englishwoman, sends a stirring appeal to the *Statesman* on behalf of Hindu widows, asking if the Jubilee of the Queen-Empress's reign could not be appropriately celebrated by the concession of some relief to the least cared for of Her Majesty's subjects. She proves the appropriateness of the suggestion by showing that Queen Victoria is herself " the offspring of a widow marriage."

Referring to the prohibition of Suttee she says " that awful fate was less painful, and far less shameful and degrading (not at all shameful or degrading I should say) than the widows' present condition." She agrees with influential Hindus in blaming the British Government, more than anybody else, for the enforced celibacy of Hindu widows, widows only in name. " Deborah " calls Government very hard names, and reproduces the observation, quoted from Mrs. Etherington :—

" An intelligent, well-educated, and influential Hindu gentleman once told my husband, that at least nine-tenths of the children who are left widows go astray, and from my own experience among Hindoo women, I fear this may be no exaggeration."

God forbid there should be anything even like an approach to this estimate in all parts of the country. But it takes very little knowledge of human nature to see that there is a vast amount of needless misery crying to Heaven for redress. And where our own flesh and blood are callous to this result of an iniquitous social law, it will take the beelike patience and industry of many a " Deborah " to obtain redress of her sisters' wrongs.

VACCINATION AND INFANT MARRIAGES.

The *Vaccination Inquirer* for February comes out with a supplement headed " Death the Vaccinator." This represents a mother sitting with the child on her knee, a policeman in uniform standing on her left with a copy of the Vaccination Act in hand, " for the Jenneration of disease," and "Death the Vaccinator," a ghastly spectre, on the right, in the act of vaccinating the baby. The look of agonized despair, mingled with reproach, which the mother gives the policeman, ought to petrify him ; but she is evidently powerless to do more. It is impossible to look at the sketch without the fear of being haunted by the mother's look for the rest of one's life. We give here an extract from the supplement :—

" What have we here? Death the Vaccinator with the policeman to assist him. Are children killed by vaccination ? Who can doubt it ? Sir Joseph Pease, speaking in Parliament, said, "The President of the Local Government Board cannot deny that children die under the Vaccination Act in a wholesale way." It cannot be denied. And when children do not die, they are often injured for life. Every mother knows of infants, who were well and hearty up to the time of their vaccination, who were never the same afterwards. Nor is this to be wondered at. The matter used for vaccination started from a diseased beast, and has passed through innumerable children, taking up in its course no one knows what defilement, possibly the worst defilement, that will blast the existence of those who receive it.

And what are children vaccinated for ? To keep off small-pox. But vaccination does not keep off small-pox. Every small-pox hospital contains vaccinated patients, who suffer and die like the unvaccinated.

Be not deceived. Vaccination will not save you from small-pox, whilst it may communicate disease much worse than small-pox. If we would avoid small-pox, we could only do so, as we avoid other fevers, by cleanliness of person and cleanliness of surroundings."

Our own views upon the subject are well known. We do not hold that vaccination is an unmitigated evil, nor have we been able to see, in spite of the advocacy of our venerated friend Dr. Benjamin Carpenter and others, that it is an un-mixed good. That a vast amount of disease, often incurable, is transmitted in the process of vaccination, cannot be denied. We have more than once cited cases in support of this assertion, from actual experience.

And yet we have had compulsory vaccination in India for years. Hindu parents allow matter taken from the sacred cow to be injected into the blood of their children. Is not this a double crime, a crime worse than that of murder? Is not the Hindu "religion" defiled by vaccination? There was of course a talk of "revolution" and "bloodshed," of "mutinies" and "massacres," when vaccination was about to be forced upon the people. But it *was* forced, and that put an end to all agitation in the course of time. And to-day ignorant parents flock to the Vaccinator with their children, some to be benefited or injured, others to be poisoned outright. Similarly, though some brave sons of India threaten Govern-ment with "mutinies" and "massacres" in the event of their dealing with infant marriages, they will be the first to acquiesce in any mild well-directed action. Such has been the experience of all who have watched the progress of affairs in India, from the suppression of Suttee and infanticide to the encouragement of vaccination and female education.

DADAJI versus RUKHMABAI.

THE ATTITUDE OF THE PRESS.

It is discouraging to see the way in which newspaper opinion is vacillating in regard to this case. There is much honest zeal shown in the matter. But of conviction one finds very faint traces, save the preconceived idea of woman's inferiority, her duty to be everything to everybody—to father, brother and husband. And the purpose underlying the dis-cussion seems to be even less distinct, unless it be that of up-holding the old order of things. Instead of the open-mindedness, the judicial weighing of evidence and the righteous conclusion arrived at on the merits of the question itself—that one should expect from so intelligent a constituency as the public press, we have here the usual talk about "revolutions" in society, the "sanctity" attaching to "time-honoured" customs, the "religious" necessity of letting these alone, varied with attempts to burke the points at issue and a gentle hint here and there as to those who think otherwise being rabid partisans.

THE MERITS OF THE CASE.

Let us once more glance at the merits of the case: Rukhmabai, a girl of 11, was "married" to Dadaji. After the ceremony Rukhmabai's father offered a home to Dadaji who was practically homeless, and he further undertook to pay for his education. For some time Dadaji remained under his father-in-law's roof, and then he began to discover an evil disposition. He returned home to his uncle's. He declined to go to school or to set himself to any honest business, and wasted his time and strength in very questionable pursuits. He ultimately broke down in health. All this while he never troubled himself about his "wife," nor did his guardian send for her, because the latter was too poor to maintain her, and the former did not wish his freedom to be curtailed by the presence of a social encumbrance. But probably when Dadaji wanted money, he sent an invitation to Rukhmabai. Her father, Dr. Sakaram Arjun, knew that he had no visible means of livelihood, and that if the girl was sent, she might be starved and ill-treated and forced to part with what-little property she had in her own right, and then turned out. These things are not of rare occurrence. Rukhmabai says she had another reason to avoid going to Dadaji—he was living in the company and under the patronage of men from whom she shrank with instinctive horror. The result was a suit for restitution, or rather for institution of conjugal rights. Dadaji has won the suit legally, and his friends are no doubt very glad of it. They will now send Rukhmabai to jail. What then? What will Dadaji gain by sending the girl to jail? According to Hindu notions he is more a brother to her than a husband, having lived under her father's roof and partaken of his fatherly care as much as did Rukhmabai. But if he and his friends thirst for revenge, let them have it. The law is for them.

OUR BENEVOLENT BRITISH GOVERNMENT.

Yes, the English law of marriage, which is of imperfect obligation in England itself, and which has nothing to do with infant marriage, undertakes to enforce "restitution of conjugal rights" where a real marriage has not taken place nor certainly been consummated! The High Court of Bombay professes to administer the Hindu law, and yet it imports into the Hindu law a point of the English Church law which has nothing to do with the marriage law of the Hindus. Henceforth we are to understand that Hindu parents may go on perpetrating infant marriages, and that in cases of dispute the benevolent British Government will aid and abet them, in the triple capacity of marriage-broker, policeman and jailor.

STEREOTYPED ERRORS.

I have been reminded for the hundredth time that marriage is a *sanskár** and that the ceremony of seven steps (*saptapadi*) completes it. This is perfectly true. But how can we postulate a *sanskár* without clear proof of the parties upon whom the *sanskár* is placed having come to years of discretion, so as to be able to give an intelligent assent to the *sanskár*? The very fact of the *saptapadi* (walking seven steps round the altar), the very text of the *Mantras* recited, the very nature of the questions asked——all this presupposes *adult age.* How can a girl of 2, 3, or even 8 understand the *Mantras* invoking the good-will of the gods, promising a full measure of wifely duty to the husband and exacting the same measure

---

* Sacrament.

of kindly devotion from the husband? How can such a child answer the priest's question whether she accepts the husband proposed? In many cases she cannot even perform the *saptapadi*. With what face can an educated Hindu call such a ceremony a *sanskár*? It was undoubtedly a *sanskár* in the old days when parties to a marriage knew what they were about, as they do among all civilized nations to-day. Our Hindu friends have gradually departed from that ideal, till they have entirely lost the spirit of it and are clinging to the dead form. There may be some excuse for the illiterate insisting upon this formality of this Hindu marriage being a "binding sacrament"; for the educated man there is no excuse. He does not believe the ceremony to be a *sanskár*. I appeal to him, in the sacred name of Education, to bear me out.

Supposing, for argument's sake, that even the present system of Hindu marriages is a *sanskár*, why should the girl alone be victimized to it? Why is it that the *sanskár* does not stand in the way of the boy marrying again, even during the life time of his wife by *sanskár*? My educated Hindu brother, who is fond of quoting Buckle and Mill, and who insists upon political equality with Englishmen, perpetuates a cruel inequality at home in the case of his women, the mothers of future generations! Not only is he content to put up with a most un-Aryan system, but he invents excuses and explanations for his conduct, and in many cases actually defends it! I do not mind his ridicule and revilement. What I do feel is that with such education as he has had, and which he knows how to utilize in other walks of life, he should prefer a dark and crooked path to the short and straight one. Why don't he make the ceremony a real *sanskár*? Let him arrange for his children's betrothal at any time, but let the marriage ceremony be deferred to the period laid down by the Shastras, just a little before puberty. Under certain conditions he is at liberty to marry his girl even *after* she has attained the period. Why not be honest, my misguided brother, when there is so much credit and benefit in it? I do not ask you to sacrifice yourself upon the altar of national regeneration. Be true to yourself, and you are everything to your nation.

But if there are some who, from sheer wantonness, look upon infant marriage as a *sanskár*, even then, why should they ask the English law to enforce such an arrangement? They do not want outside interference. And yet they ask the active interference of a foreign law to enforce their own one-sided custom! What are we to think of that? And what are we to think of the Courts of law in India which respond to a call so unrighteous? The British Indian Government do not recognize, and do not wish to recognize, infant marriages, and yet they lend their all-powerful aid in enforcing such marriages! Why not leave the matter to the community? Hindu Shastras do not seem to contemplate such a thing as the restitution of conjugal rights. But if caste has become sufficiently "educated" to import that unmanly idea without importing the system of adult marriages, it may do so. Caste is at liberty to deal with a recalcitrant member, short of resorting to personal violence.

CAUSE AND EFFECT—A CONFUSION OF IDEAS.

Many men many minds. Seldom was the truth of this trite old saying better illustrated than in the case of Infant Marriage. I have myself suggested a score of remedies against the evils of that un-Aryan custom, good, bad and indifferent, and hope to bring the figure up to the proverbial 100 before I have done with the question. More numerous are the suggestions made by others, of which the two most considerable, offered by European friends, are Intellectual Emancipation and Physical Development. Here is a sample, taken from a letter received last mail from one of our best friends in England, one who has attained to high eminence both as an administrator and an original thinker:—

" The great thing is to promote manliness. Get that and all else will be added thereto. To get manliness, study personal purity, not on account of absurd theological superstitions, but as a physiological necessity. Remember that with Nature there is no forgiveness of sins, that is any abuse of Nature. 'The—is the life' and 'give not your strength to——,' these are the two Bible texts which will regenerate India whenever they are taken to heart. They cut directly at the root of early marriage, and all marriage is too early until the joints have ceased to be mere cartilage and have become those of men and women, that is duly ossified " ......

Sounder advice was never given. And the people of India need not go to the Bible for authority (though the Bible is more our book than of the Western nations) having equally strong texts in their own scriptures. Personal purity is one of the best remedies against the evils of Infant Marriage, and so is intellectul emancipation. But what passes my rude comprehension is that these remedies are suggested WHILE INFANT MARRIAGE IS STILL IN OPERATION. How, on earth, are we to have personal purity and intellectual emancipation among a people addicted to child marriage and all the social absurdities and abominations consequent thereon ? A nation of married boys and girls can hardly be expected to be pure and strong and free. The system of infant marriages forbids all hope of national regeneration. At any rate, I hope that it would be infinitely more easy to obtain physical and moral strength after giving up child marriage than to be able to give up child marriage after obtaining such strength, even if it *can* be obtained under existing conditions. I may be wrong, but I am not a philosopher and fail to see the beauty of mistaking cause for effect.

OUR DEVIS.*

I am very glad to see it stated that " the Roman law as regards *impuberes*, if followed in this country, might do a

* Literally ' goddesses.'

great deal of good without doing any harm." But before my brother at Calcutta concedes this, he makes some general observations which seem to have been called forth by an article in the Lahore journal. In this little critique, I am afraid, the *Mirror* reflects only one side of the picture. Here, for instance, is a contrast. " In the old Testament women are classed with cattle," but in India, we are told, woman is sought to be looked upon as "worthy of the highest respect and reverence—as the Devi." This would be a striking contrast, if it could hold. But as every schoolboy knows, woman in modern India is looked upon as quite the reverse of " the Devi." Are infant marriages, enforced widowhood, and other disabilities of the sex in this country, consistent with the' rudest ideas of " respect and reverence" ? For my part, the contrast suggested is not one to be proud of. The followers of the Old Testament have raised woman from her cattle-like position to one which is the highest yet attained by her. The followers of the Vedas have degraded the ideal Devi into— what ? If all this means anything, it means shame to us Indians and credit to the Europeans.

We are then asked—" *has the Englishwoman a vote ?*" No, but is she not, on the whole, incomparably better situated than her Indian sister in matters social and civil ? It is again urged that "some mining women (in England) who wanted to dress like men" were not allowed by the men to do so. Is this intended as a parallel to the tyranny of infant marriages and so on ? Surely, there may be honest good-will in refusing to unsex the female labourers of England ? In India we do the same. Further, we are reminded that the English marriage service is objectionable, and that the English law of divorce is somewhat one-sided. What, then, about *our* marriage songs and the songs sung at the time of *shrimant* ? What about polygamy, the iron rule of the mother-in-law the shaving and starving of girl-widows ? Can there be any comparison between the two sets of evils ? The list of social imperfections in England is closed with the remark that " the coster-monger's donkey is better off than his wife."

But is the English nation made up only of coster-mongers, there wives and their donkeys ? And on the other hand, is not the evil of infant marriage all but universal among us ? It will never do to compare the evils incidental to individuals or classes with national evils. We have to deal only with systems. The *Indian Mirror* seldom minces matters, and I hope my brother will see that there is another view of the question, which has been persistently ignored, but which utters a formidable indictment against some of the most cherished of our modern institutions. The crime of infant marriage in India cannot be justified by an appeal to the minor evils which afflict other societies, but in spite of which those societies are to-day immeasurably superior to the eldest branch of the human family, both in physical and in moral development.

SOME COCKNEY CROAKERS.

More amusing than the attitude of the Hindu journalist, but much less excusable, is the croaking of some of the Cockney penny-a-liners of England. The latest prophesy in this line is, that if the British Government in India attempted to secure to them the personal liberty of women, there would be a rebellion in the country. Are the prophets of evil so utterly ignorant, or do they conjure up these harrowing pictures in order to leave the " niggers " to be " stewed in their own juice"? " Mutiny " and " rebellion " *now*, when there was no such thing in the days of ignorance and fantacism—at the time that Government put down Suttee ! Surely Suttee was more " sacred " to the Hindu than is Infant Marriage, and surely, again, the Hindu is less ignorant to-day than in the days of Bentinck. A revolt against the British Government means madness; and the " orthodox reformer " is an eminently sane person, always taking care of number one. The highest pitch of patriotism to which he could nerve himself might be perhaps to murder me in cold blood. And this I should rather be glad of, for it would pave the way for practical reform, even though it gladdened the heart of the

Amrita Bazar Patrika and kept the prophets of evil in countenance.

ON THE HORNS OF A DILEMMA.

The *Hindoo Patriot* has been so glorifying himself about the humanity of the Hindu law, and holding up the barbarity of the English law in regard to woman, that it is difficult to see why it should get into such a violent fit of anger with Mr. Justice Pinhey for his decision in the Conjugal Rights case, or not welcome the effort of Professor Wordsworth's Committee to keep away English barbarity from Hindu households; for to our recent remarks in this sense that paper replies :—

" We still adhere to the opinion that *our law looks upon the use of force on woman with the greatest abhorrence.* We may add in perfect sincerity that had it not done so, we would have denounced it. So particular is the Hindu law on the subject that it makes exceptions of female offenders in regard to severe or degrading punishments. For instance, for some heinous offences the law ordains shaving of the head and deportation: but for a woman guilty of the offence, says *Parasara,* the shaving should be emblematical, and the cropping of three inches of the ends of the tresses should be accepted as equivalent to shaving. We like much this decorum and sense of propriety; but we cannot on that account forbear denouncing Mr. Justice Pinhey of sickly sentimentalism, unworthy of his judicial character. His office required him to administer law faithfully and fearlessly, and not to enact his part for the entertainment of the gallery, and he failed in this duty. Let us for a moment suppose that, instead of Dadaji, a Hindu carpenter, the plaintiff in the case had been a Christian Jones, Smith, or Robinson, and the marriage had been contracted with the consent of the bride then in her thirteenth year,—when she was qualified to give her consent under the English law,—would the judge have been justified in indulging in dithyrambics about " barbarous," " cruel," and "revolting" compulsion of a "young lady" like a "horse or

a bullock" ?   He would have passed his sentence, following a
long line of precedents laid down by the Ecclesiastical and the
Divorce Courts, and never dreamt of sentimentalism.   If he
failed, the Appellate Courts would have soon taught him his
duty.   In the case under notice, he failed in his duty by playing to the gallery, and we were in duty bound to denounce him,
and we did.   That we were right in our remarks is obvious
from the fact of the Appellate Court having set aside his
judgment.   Our contemporary tries to drive us to a corner by
giving us the choice of either co-operating with Professor
Wordsworth's Committee to set aside the Hindu law, or,
" despite the glorious humanity of the old (Hindu) law," good
enough for wordy boast, accept the condition of " adult consent—which is the essence of English law."   We reject the
dilemma in toto.   We deny too that " adult consent," " is the
essence of English law."   That law recognises the validity of
infant consent, i.e., " consent given at the thirteenth year of
a girl."

This is smart writing, no doubt; but it is full of inconsis-
tencies and misconceptions.   For, on the writer's own showing, either Parasar is as guilty of sickly sentimentalism and
of playing to the gallery or Mr. Justice Pinhey upheld
" decorum and a sense of propriety " in looking "upon the
use of force on woman with the abhorrence."   It was precisely
because the latter was dealing with a Hindu and not a Christian
case that he disregarded the precedents laid down by the
English Ecclesiastical and Divorce Courts, as he fully explained ; and if the Appellate Court of two Judges against
one has reversed his decision, it is not, therefore, shown to
be infallible in the first place, and in the next, it has distinctly held that the British Courts have assumed the jurisdiction of the Hindu castes in such matters, and it has applied
to the case a foreign procedure to carry out its decree.   If
this result is welcome to Hindu patriots of all grades and
shades, who on other occasions protest against State interference with their social institutions, all that one can say is

that Heaven may save India and her womankind from such patriotism ! Those members of the genus, who see the spirit of the Hindu law duly embodied in Gaikawadi and Holkarshahi rules, under which a recalcitrant wife is delivered over bound hand and foot by the police to the husband, and hold consequently that this mode of enforcing marital obligations has been of long standing in this country and 'it is incorrect to speak of it as a creation of the British legislature,' are at least partially free from inconsistency in decrying Mr. Pinhey's judgment and deprecating Prof. Wordsworth's efforts ; but then they sadly mar the glory - of their Calcutta congener's boast about the decorum, the propriety and the humanity of the Hindu law. For according to them force is properly used on woman and she is justly treated as a horse or a bullock. These latter no doubt divest themselves of their long borrowed peacock's feathers in the eye of some of their admirers, but they are consistent. There are, then, two species of Hindu law, and this duality so far from proving inconvenient is eminently favourable for patriotic tactics in all polemics on the subjects. One species of the law—the humane and the decorus—serves within the limits of the Maratha Ditch the purposes of glorification and boast of superiority over barbarian nations ; while the other—little differing from barbarity—exists for use in Maratha States and available to disarm criticism in the opposite direction. There is still another service which the *Hindoo Patriot* can extract from this felicitous situation. In the second sentence of the extract made above, the *Patriot* states in all sincerity that it would have denounced the Hindu law if it had not looked upon the use of force on woman with abhorrence, and yet lower down it declines to co-operate with Prof. Wordsworth's Committee, because it seeks to set aside the Hindu law. Now this last assertion is not true in the sense of the *Patriot's* Hindu law, but it is true as regards the Gaikawadi or Holkarshahi version of it, though, as a matter of fact, it is the application of a barbarous provision of English law—which has itself been discarded in England—that the Committee is seeking to set aside. The *Hindoo Patriot* is, therefore, grossly misinformed as regards this Committee's aim, or wishes the barbarous law of the rod and the string—or force, in other word—to be applied to the Hindu woman; but of course our contemporary rejects the dilemma *in toto*. Who, under the circumstances, can deny him the right to reject reason and consistency alike? Its last argument, that the English law recognises the validity of infant consent, *i.e.*, consent given at the thirteenth year of a girl, can deceive no one; for even granting that girls in England are married at that age, Hindu girls are married much earlier and their consent to the match is never obtained. They are simply treated like dumb animals in the bargain, and no expenditure of " perverse erudition" can serve to hide the ugly fact.*

THE HINDU AND THE RED INDIAN.

We were told the other day by an eminent Hindu that though infant marriages were bad in theory, in actual life they did not imply the sort of misery which outsiders might expect. In short, that bearing in mind the respective conditions of the two, the Hindu household was no less happy than the English. Now, accepting this for argument's sake I contend that it is no justification for *infant marriages.* If the Hindus are happy at home, and brave, patriotic,

* The *Hindu Patriot* replied as follow :—" Our friend of the *Indian Spectator* is determined to pin us down, but we are on the alert, and agile enough to slip between the two mighty horns he presents to us. We are ready to meet him on fair field to discuss the merits of our ancient law, but cannot *allow* him to import, as he has done in his last issue, Gackawadi or Holkarshahi or any Halalkhori practice as a part of Hindu law. The attempt is disingenuous and unworthy of him. Even as regards Hindu law, we must stick to one point at a time, and that too with every regard to the demands on the space of a small weekly newspaper like ours for other and more pressing subjects than consummation of marriage among carpenters."

Malabari's comment was extremely brief :—"Who can fail to perceive the ingenuousness of this defence ? We may now leave the matter to be settled amongst the patriots of Poona and Bombay who welcome the ' Halalkhori practice as a part of Hindu law,' and their brother within the ditch who conveniently ignores in the above his latest discovered of hoary Mann's injunctions regarding the treatment of a wife who walks away in wrath, &c."

30

enterprising abroad, in spite of the custom of baby marriages, how much happier, braver, more partriotic, more
enterprising they would be, if they eschewed the unnatural
custom ? But in the second place, I say that is impossible
for any nation to be happy or prosperous with the social
habits and usages which the Hindus have unfortunately contracted during the last few hundred years. However, a good
deal depends on how we define happiness. If it means a state
of brute contentment at home, we Natives are doubtless a
happy race. But in that case the happiest of mortals are our
cousins, the red Indians. Are we prepared to go by this
standard in determining happiness ?

PROF. MONIER WILLIAMS ON THE MARRIAGE CUSTOMS OF INDIA, ANCIENT AND MODERN.

After the verdict pronounced upon this subject and those
interested in its discussion, by an authority like Max Müller,
there was scarcely any need for further pronouncement. For,
though college boys may find it convenient for a time to
scout the venerable *guru* of the nation, in their hearts they
feel him to be right and themselves to be wrong, and Hindus
of maturer experience still look upon him as their guide and
philosopher. But the opinion of an eminent representative
of another school is worth quoting, as it cuts the ground from
under the feet of pretended orthodoxy by asserting that
Manu, the most authoritative law-giver of the Hindus, " is
clearly not in favour of child-marriages." Nearer home we
have Professor Wordsworth uttering his conviction with a
vigour that is irresistible. He has a right to address himself
thus to the educated class. And yet we have educated Hindu
gentlemen, who say they " highly reverence" Mr. Wordsworth, laughing at him for his pains in this connection.
Thus, then, " high reverence " itself is a matter not of
conviction, but of convenience. We " highly reverence "
all the gods and goddesses in the pantheon, so long only as

they echo our wishes or answer our prayers. With such principles of action, how could this class of reformers do good to the country? They do not work for reform themselves nor assist others who slave at it; their efforts are confined to opposing reform in every shape and direction. In the guise of patriots they seem determined to perpetuate inequalities as between the sexes and between classes. They have had sufficient acquaintance with the tactics of European agitation to make them a force, and Government are only too eager to recognize it as a force and to exaggerate its importance. But how long will enlightened Christian rulers continue wringing their hands helplessly and going into hysterics at sight of this loquacious Frankenstein of their own raising? The course is clear enough for them, as indicated by Sir Monier Williams. Let the betrothal be distinguished from the marriage; let not the name be mistaken for the thing. At any rate, let not Government legalize such a mistake. This is what Professor Williams says about it :—

" It may not be known to every one here that the really crucial part of a Hindu marriage ceremony which may be protracted for several days, consists in the child-bride walking round the sacred fire hand in hand with the child-bridegroom in seven steps. Not till the seventh step is taken is the marriage held to be irreversible. It seems extraordinary to our ideas that a girl, even if betrothed, should not be allowed to put off the irrevocable seventh step till she is old enough to plant her foot down firmly and willingly. In the opinion of many, to compel her to take this irrevocable walk round the fire, without exercising any will of her own, is nearly as bad as forcing her, should she become a widow, to enter the fire as a Sati. Happily our Government, though it made the mistake of allowing Sati, never permitted compulsion. Though in one particular year no fewer than eight hundred widows were burnt, our officials were required in every case to see that no force was used. Why, then, permit any woman in the present day to be forced to do what many women would regard as little better than entering the fire, had they sense and education enough to know the real meaning of marriage? Of course, our Government is very properly reluctant to meddle with customs believed to be deeply rooted in ancient Hindu law. But is this compulsory system in the matter of marriage more deeply rooted than the Sati system was? What more authoritative lawgiver has ever existed in India than Manu? All the latter codes are supposed to be based on his code; yet in the ninth book of Manu, verse 90, we find the following:—"A girl, having reached the age of puberty, should wait three years, but at the end of that time she should herself choose a suitable husband." It is true that modern commentators maintain that this self-choice is only legal when there are no parents to give a daughter away. But it must, at any rate, be admitted that Manu concedes the principle of self-choice in certain cases, and, what is more, he is clearly not in favour of child-marriage. We know, too, that in ancient times girls of the military caste were often allowed by their fathers to choose husbands for themselves, and the highest poetical talent of India has been consecrated to description of bridals where the bride selected for herself from a crowd of assembled suitors."

'SECRET' AND 'SILENT' REFORM.

One of the most convenient excuses put forward by "orthodox reformers," who are for introducing reform "secretly" and "silently," is that in their locality there is no such thing known as infant marriage, the average* marrying age for girls being about 12. This is a curious assertion, to say the least of it. The average age for girls is generally admitted to be about 7, and a large number of children are married every year under that age, in some parts of the country as early as at 2 and 3. But supposing for a moment that marriages are delayed in some castes till 12, what prevents those castes from welcoming the suggestion that that minimum

---

* This is not correct.

limit should be fixed by the State for all India, especially as such limit has been laid down by the highest of their sacred authorities ? They lose nothing by such a regulation, while the rest of the country gains considerably by it. A regulation like that applies to all castes, and few parents will be forced under it to give their daughters to old, diseased or disreputable husbands. What prevents the local representatives from fixing this limit themselves, by means of corporate action, or getting the Legislature to fix it ? It is, after all, only going back to the best traditions of our race. What prevents our reformers from starting Associations for practical social reform, each member pledging himself to carry out the programme ? Why don't they force Government to amend the abominable law which makes over a girl-wife of 10 to her husband or the law which hounds such a girl to the jail if she refuses to yield herself up ? Why don't they arrange among themselves to see that girls of three and upwards are not made the victims of a formal and perpetual widowhood ? How is it that not a single effort has been made in the course of these three years towards these beginnings of practical reform ? On the contrary, we are noticing a distinct tendency towards retrogression in social matters, while the clamour for what is supposed to be political progress is becoming louder and louder. Surely, all this cannot be said to indicate the growth of a healthy public opinion.

A CHILD-WIFE OF SIX BRANDED ON THE SOLES OF HER FEET.

Some of our contemporaries are indignant that Mr. Hamilton, the Third Presidency Magistrate, considers justice fully vindicated by a fine of Rs. 8 levied from a man found guilty of having branded his wife of 6 " on the soles of her feet." "The pain caused by the burns was so great," says the *Mahratta*, " that the girl could not walk." And the writer continues:—

"We fail to understand, then, how the Magistrate awarded such a very light punishment. The offence was most brutal and should have been dealt with accordingly. The *Advocate* quotes Section 326 of the Indian Penal Code, wherein it is laid down that "whoever. . . voluntarily causes grievous hurt by means of . . . fire or any heated substance . . . shall be punished with transportation for life, or with imprisonment of either description for a term which may extend to ten years, and shall also be liable to fine." The case noticed above falls under this section and we are surprised to see the Magistrate punishing the accused so lightly. We pity the poor girl. Her brutal husband will be at large to revengefully inflict further injuries upon her."

The case has a lesson of its own for others besides Mr. Hamilton. Here is a wife of 6 branded by her husband of, say, between 20 and 40 (it is a pity some of the important particulars were not elicited during the trial). And yet we have been assured by our educated wiseacres that there is no such thing as infant marriage in India! We have also been assured by the head of the Government in India that he views infant marriages "with horror." And yet he can do nothing to protect this little girl of 6, a helpless minor, from further violence on the part of the man to whom she appears to have been given away to do what he likes with! The man has paid his 8 rupees, and he will not fail to make his wife of 6 smart for the loss. "What have I married her for?" he probably asks himself, as many of his betters ask.

NEW DEFENCE OF AN OLD EVIL.

A shrewd Hindu gentleman, neither a graduate nor a reformer of the mystic firm of " Malabari & Co.," told me about two years ago that the real secret of the system of infant marriages and enforced widowhood in India was the intense selfishness of the people—the selfishness of individuals and the exclusiveness of caste. It could not well be denied that infant marriages are often brought about chiefly with the view to shirk parental authority (which is one form of selfish-

ness), and that girl widows, the direct outcome of such
arrangements, are condemned to perpetual widowhood mainly,
if not solely, with the object that the property she inherits
from her husband goes not to any other member of the community, not even to the next door neighbour. This theory is
curiously confirmed so far at least as it refers to infant marriages, by no less an authority than Mr. J. N. Bhattacharji,
M.A., of Calcutta. In the course of an article contributed by this gentleman to the pages of a new monthly, he
observes :—

"Notwithstanding all that is said by our ' reformers ' against
what they call child-marriage, our belief is that the amount of
good which has been done by it is incalculable. Our Shasters
reveal the fact that in ancient times, when adult marriages
prevailed in the country, bastards and children of secret birth
like Tom Jones were so numerous that they had to be classi-
fied for legal purposes, and had recognised positions assigned
to them by law. Thanks to the legislation of the sages, we
have no longer the *Kanina* and *Sahodraja* sons amongst us."

Mr. Bhattacharji, M.A., is not going to mince matters and
so he proceeds to say :—

" We must state it as our belief that at the time when child-
marriage was first enjoined by the Shasters it was one of the best
safeguards against incestuous connections. Reason and experience alike point to the conclusion that in the primitive state
of society sexual intercourse between near relations was not
regarded with that horror which we now feel at the enormity
of sin. The feelings and associations of men are now so moulded that it is regarded by us as an offence against the law of
Nature, a violation of the essential fitness of things. But, in
all probability the case was quite different in ancient times.

And a great deal of good was done then by enjoining the
disposal of girls by their fathers before maturity. It is true
that there has been since then great improvement in the

feelings and morals of men ; but our belief is that even now adult marriage cannot be enforced with advantage. We are strongly of opinion that in matters governing the relation of sexes it is not possible to be too far on the safe side.

Where girls remain unmarried after maturity, they very often run the risk of being suspected and rejected as "rotten orange" like the lovely daughter of the good Leonato in Shakespear's *Much Ado About Nothing*. The practice of child marriage leaves no room whatever for such suspicions, and saves both parents and girls from the kind of agony and anguish which well nigh killed Hero, and made her father miserable."

Bravo, Mr. Bhattacharji, M.A., you deserve credit for plain speaking. But my difficulty with you is this. Conceding for a moment that the Shastrakars introduced infant marriage as a preventive against incest and that this preventive worked well three thousand years ago, when, according to Mr. Bhattacharji, M.A., our people went in for promiscuous intercourse, does it follow that the same preventive is called for under the vastly altered circumstances of the present day ? And if promiscuous commerce can be prevented only by the system of infant marriages, are we to condemn all those nations who do not adopt the system as guilty of the horrible sin ? Further, what are we to think of parents who dare not keep their girls unmarried *till* 12 ?—for fear the latter should go wrong. What sort of life must be theirs ?—of the parents, I mean ; and what are we to think of their ideas and associations? Again, if unmarried girls of 12 are apt to go wrong, what is to prevent their going wrong *after* marriage, when, in fact, they could do so with less risk of exposure ? Lastly, if the assumption is legitimate, that girls may go wrong if not married *before* 12, what becomes of the boast of female education in India? These are some of the questions which our educated defenders of the principle of infant marriages will have to answer before they satisfy " Malabari & Co." as to the soundness of their latest discovered theory.

THE CLIMATE ARGUMENT.

It is sometimes said that the miserable physique of some
of the Indian races is not due to infant marriage, but to the
climate of India. Our climate is so hot that we cannot but
have puny little children. How do this gentlemen account
for healthy and well-developed births among Europeans in
India? Do we not often mistake European children to be
much older than they are? The *Indian Witness* has another
way of meeting the climate argument. The Esquimaux are
bad in their marriage customs as are some of the Indians.
But though they live in a cold climate, they suffer as much
from premature marriages as do the Indians in India. What
will the climate-walas say to that? We have doubtless an
enervating climate in parts of this country. But that is all
the greater reason why we should eschew premature
marriages.

THE MAJORITY CRAZE.

In a recent issue the *Indian Mirror* had these very sensible
remarks:—

"We are having rather too much of politics to the neglect,
probably, of social, moral and religious matters, which, under
the present circumstances of India, are, in our opinion, of
far more importance than politics. Politics, unaided by an
improved tone of our society, by morality and religion, will
not be the means of regenerating India."

Now, we may be told by politicians in their teens that this
is not the opinion of the majority. But *who* are the majority,
and what if this was not *their* opinion? Are nine fools any
better than one wise man? India must have fallen upon evil
days, indeed, when her dearest interests are supposed to be in
the keeping of a gang of fools who would rather defame their
ancestors than admit their own backslidings. It is not the
fool, however, whose folly can do much harm. The real
mischief comes from the knave fooling with wisdom.

INFANT MARRIAGES—FOR AND AGAINST.

We owe an apology to Mr. Bipinchandra Pal for having unwittingly neglected his valuable leaflet examining the position of the Bengali convert, Mr. Shome, in defence of the system of early marriages, by which we mean premature marriages. For convenience sake, Mr. Pal gives his opponent's views on one side and his own remarks on the other in juxtaposition. The latter appear to us to be crushing both by reason of historical analogy and force of logic. We can glance here at a few of the issues only. For instance, the argument that marriage is a gift is met by Mr. Pal in this wise :—

" In primitive society, women and children were regarded as personal or tribal property,—were objects of barter. Marriage by gift is simply a refined form of marriage by purchase. Gift and sale are both means of conveying property from one person to another. Arguing as Mr. Shome does, may it not be said that if the American slave-dealers, instead of selling their slaves, had only made a gift of them to their friends, the relation of master and slave arising from the gift would have been a heaven-ordained relation,—an act of God, and not of man ? Negro-slavery was also supported on the authority of the Christian Scriptures. Let us not forget that."

To Mr. Shome demurring to the proposition that the conjugal relation cannot be established between two parties unless they would at once enter upon the duties of that relation, Mr. Pal opposes this verse from the Shastras:—

"No father should give a girl in marriage who does not know the respect and the service due to the husband, and who is ignorant of the injunctions of religion."

Mr. Shome wants " facts to prove the degeneracy of the race " (through infant marriages). His critic quietly cites the infant mortality of India and of the different provinces. If we had the figures before us we would show that the death rate in India up to 11, and also the rate of mortality, not to say anything of disease, among girl mothers, is fearfully heavy indeed. The very ancient argument that infant marriages are necessary to the joint-family system is thus faced by Mr. Pal:—

"The joint-family system is dying. It has lost most of its pristine glory and sanctity. Will 'it be wise, then, to perpetuate an evil custom to meet the emergencies of a dying system of domestic organisation? Besides grown-up marriages are not so inconsistent with the joint family system as Mr. Shome seems to think. There is the joint-family system in Madras, but no early-marriage among the non-Brahmin classes. In China the joint-family system is so compact that the first of the seven reasons for which a Chinaman may divorce his wife is her unfilial conduct towards her father-in-law and mother-in-law. But, says Mr. J. N. Jordon in the *Nineteenth Century* for July 1886, "A girl" in China "generally gets married about seventeen, a man about twenty." Besides, Mr. Shome himself says that in certain parts of this country premature consummations do not follow early marriages. Evidently, on his own showing in those places at least, girls, although married in infancy, continue to live with their parents till they come of age; and those places, the introduction of grown-up girls into the joint-family does not interfere with its peace."

The Rev. Mr. Shome contends that:—

"If marriage was ordained by God for the procreation of children, this object is as effectually fulfilled by early marriage as by any other system of matrimony."

And this is Mr. Pal's refutation:—

"The procreation of children is not, and cannot be an end by itself. The maintenance of the race is correctly speaking, one of the chief objects of marriage; and early marriage *does not* fulfil this object. The conditions which guide the efficient maintenance of the race are—(a) minimum of mortality between birth and reproductive age; (b) elongation of the period

244

that precedes reproduction; (*c*) decrease in the number of children borne and reared; (*d*) lengthening of the period that follows cessation of reproduction. (*a*) Instead of a minimum of mortality, we have in India a mortality of more than 72 per cent. among the population between the ages 0—19. (*b*) The average marriageable age for Hindù girls in India is 10—12, according to the last census; and not even Mr. Shome will hold that 10 or 12 is the proper age of reproduction of even the precocious Hindu girls. (*c*) There is a higher birth-rate in India than in any other civilized country. (*d*) The largest number by far of Indian women die during the reproducing period of their life, *i.e.*, between the ages 4—21."

UNANSWERABLE ARGUMENTS.

Babu J. N. Bhattacharjee, M.A., D.L., has another article of the marriage question, this time with the case of Dadaji *versus* Rukhmabai for his text. To show that I have no grudge against the learned Doctor, I hasten to transcribe the following passage from his article :—

" Where the wife not only refuses to perform conjugal duties, but would not live under the protection and control of her husband, there the latter is entitled to relief, for the purpose of enabling him to discharge his duty as guardian. But the very object of giving such relief is defeated, if, under the circumstances, the wife be sentenced to suffer imprisonment, in a public jail, for refusing to comply with the order of the Court. The Hindu Codes are altogether silent as to the procedure by which the husband's right of guardianship should be enforced. It seems to be meant that the procedure should be similar to that laid down for securing the custody of minors. The sanctions prescribed, by the Code of Civil Procedure, for compelling recusant wives to submit to the control of their husbands, are not only objectionable from a sentimental point of view, but they are inconsistent with the substantive law which our Courts are called upon to administer where the parties are Hindus. It must therefore be highly gratifying, both to orthodox Hindus and to the philanthropic friends of Rukhma Bai, that the Supreme Legislature has been sent in motion for the amendment of the obnoxious section of the Code of Civil Procedure. Imprisonment in a public jail is a kind of punishment which is altogether unsuited for female offenders especially to those in the prime of youth. Whatever be the nature of their offence, it does not seem proper to punish them in a manner which ruins them for ever and involves indelible disgrace on their families. By imprisonment in public jail female offenders are exposed to the worst risks, and are so lowered in their own estimation and that of the public, as to be in danger of becoming confirmed sinners. If it be possible to punish them adequately, in some other manner, as we think it is, then there can be no justification whatever for dealing with them as at present. It seems, therefore, that Hindus and non-Hindus will all agree in hailing with delight an amendment in the criminal law of the country that would exempt female offenders from imprisonment. At any rate, there can be no objection to the amendment of Sec. 259 of the Code of Civil Procedure, for the purpose of exempting recusant wives from incarceration in criminal jail. According to the principles of Hindu law, we can even go further, and recommend their total exemption from all punishment. In fact, considering the substantive law of our Shasters as to matrimonial rights and duties, they ought to be so exempted."

This is highly creditable to an upholder of the system of infant marriages. Dr. Bhattacharjee will see that I am anxious to give credit wherever it is due—even to an M.A., D.L.

The learned gentleman then goes off again at a tangent, and sets up a defence of infant marriages. But his data, his arguments and his deductions appear to be based upon one lofty " national" sentiment:—

" The Parsi gentleman, who has acquired a cheap renown by his continual vaticinations against our most cherished social institutions, can have no concern whatever with the laws and customs of our society."

This is, indeed, the underlying idea of the whole reactionary agitation in Bengal. But that is a trifle. Look at the sub-limity of sentiment, ye mortals, embedded in these choice extracts quoted by Dr. Bhattacharjee in support of infant marriages—look at it and tremble at the fate waiting you in the "abyss of hell":—

" So many seasons of menstruation as overtake a maiden feeling the passion of love and sought in marriage by persons of suitable rank, even so many are the beings destroyed by both her father and mother: this is a maxim of law."—*See Dayabhaga, Chapter XI., Sec. II.*

Paitinashi says :—"A damsel should be given in marriage before her breasts swell. But if she have menstruated before marriage both the giver and the taker fall into the abyss of hell: and her father, grandfather, and great grandfather are born insects in ordure."—*Ibid.*

Babu J. N. Bhattacharjee, be it noted again, is a Master of Arts and a Doctor of Law. Such arguments from such an authority are unanswerable.

ADVANTAGES OF INFANT MARRIAGE—A PRESENT TO ADVOCATES OF THE SYSTEM.

A little girl of nine was married some eight years ago to a boy of eleven. Both were Brahmans. Soon after his marriage the boy took to mendicity as a profession. He used to stay away from home, eleven months out of the twelve. Probably he was a Bhikhshuka Brahman. The girl in the meantime remained with her mother. She was an only child— the only one left to the mother out of nine children. The poor Brahmani (a widow) kept cows, and her daughter, wife of the wandering beggar, assisted her in the household duties and in disposing of the milk. Some time ago the husband reappeared, and suspecting the girl-wife (because she had to sell milk for a living, as he could not or did not maintain her) tied her down one night and branded her in 38 places, hips, thighs, and so on. Who could help feeling for the delicate young creature treated to such cold-blooded brutality at the dead of night? And the perpetrator of this act of worse than butchery was a Brahman. The girl was married to a miserable young beggar, probably because her parents were not rich enough to expect a better alliance, and at 9 she was considered fit to be married. She must of course marry in her own little groove, be the husband young or old, well-conditioned or ill-conditioned, healthy or diseased. And this is the result. Branding at midnight in 38 different parts of the body.

ANOTHER INFANT MARRIAGE CASE—
WORSE THAN RUKHMABAI'S.

The parents of a little girl died during the famine of 1876-77. The child, having none to protect her, was admitted to the Pandharpur Orphanage. It was since discovered that she had been married to her maternal uncle by her parents before they died. But the uncle-husband did not come forward for several years to claim his niece-wife. At the Orphanage, the latter was allowed to learn up to the 4th Vernacular standard. She was then sent to the Poona Training College. But here it was urged that the consent of the husband was necessary to train her as a school mistress. The girl knew not about the marriage except that her parents were sometimes speaking to her about it—that is, I presume, that she was too young even to know that she was being married to her uncle. The uncle was now called upon to explain. He asserted his right of a husband over the girl, but at the request of some public-spirited gentlemen allowed her to prosecute her studies. Perhaps the worthy man did this more as a matter of business than of charity. At any rate he knew he was killing two birds with one stone—he was obliging the bigwigs of the town and at the same time allowing his niece-wife to qualify herself the better to earn *him* a decent little income as school mistress. Not a bad investment, this, for the shrewd Kunbi. But the real difficulty is this—he has already married another woman and has children by her. The girl holds a scholarship at College, but as soon as the course is over and she secures an appointment she may be pounced upon by an illiterate cultivator who has already a wife and children. And the Mabap Sirkar, through their court of justice (?), may make her over to the uncle-husband, perhaps to be suspected and branded and required to slave at home after earning her wages at school for him. There can be no sympathy between such a pair—the union is unholy on the face of it. But what matters it to a "practical" Government taking "commonsense" views of life, and treating justice, public morality and such other trifling inconveniences as beneath notice? Government will eat, drink, and make themselves happy even if this niece-wife of an already married uncle-husband is dragged to jail, or worse still, to his house. And what is this girl to "educated" reformers that they should appeal to the man's manhood for very shame to let her alone? What is she to the virtuous priest that he should call upon the married uncle not to ruin her and disgrace their holy Shastras? No, things must take their course till "education" makes indubitable angels of what are doubtful men. And then—a matter of a few centuries at the earliest—the mighty Government of India *may* step in and our "educated" reformers *may* consider if the marriageable age of girls is to be 7 or 9. Meanwhile, I should be glad to pay a few hundred rupees to the uncle if he gave a *fargati* to his unhappy sister's daughter.

He is a poor illiterate man, and unlike some of our educated gentlemen, may listen to reason. It will be worse than useless for him to enforce his so-called right. I trust he will be prevailed upon by friends. But even if he releases the poor girl, that cannot absolve Government from their duty which is to make such arrangements impossible to be enforced by law.

SPEECHES.

SPEECH AT LAHORE.

A grand meeting, composed mostly of representatives of several local public bodies, including the Anjuman-i-Punjab, the Widow-Marriage Association, the Hindu Sabha, the Arya Samaj, the Brahmo Samaj, the Guru Singh Sabha, the Aror Bans Sabha, the Kayasth Sabha, and others, was convened at the Siksha Sabha Hall on the 7th October 1885, at 6 p.m., for the purpose of offering a welcome to Mr. Behramji M. Malabari and to consider his revised statements on the subject of "Infant Marriage and Enforced Widowhood." There were upwards of 500 gentlemen present, among whom were observed Raja Harbans Singh, Sirdar Dyal Singh Majithia, Mr. Justice Ram Narain, Doctor Brij Lal Ghose, Rai Bahadur, Bhai Mian Singh, Hony. Magistrate, Babu Navina Chundra Rai, Assistant Registrar, Punjab University, Sheik Nanak Buksh, Pleader, Lala Gunga Ram, Executive Engineer, Doctor Ram Kishen, L.M.S., Lala Jai Kishen, Accountant, Pundit Manohar Nath, Accountant, Lala Das Ram Mullik, Accountant, Doctor Guran Ditta Mall, Assistant Surgeon, Lala Sain Das, President, Arya Samaj, Lala Madan Singh, B.A., Pundit Jawala Pershad, Lala Lal Chand, M.A., Pleader, Lala Gobind Ram, Pleader, Lala Gunda Mul, Secretary, Brahmo Samaj, Lala Luchman Pershad, Missionary, Brahmo Samaj, Pundit Guru Dutt, B.A., Bhai Lal Singh, Editor, *Ikhbar Anjuman-i-Punjab*, Bhai Jawahir Singh, Secretary, Guru Singh Sabha, Bhai Ditt Singh, Secretary, Sut Sabha, Lala Amolak Ram, Munsiff, Diwan Narindro Nath, B.A., Mr. Moharim Ali Chisti, Mr. Rama Krishna, Secretary, Hindu Sabha, and many others. On the motion of Babu N. C. Rai, Raja Harbans Singh was unanimously voted to the chair. The Chairman, in introducing Mr. Malabari, said :—

"GENTLEMEN,—I have the greatest pleasure in introducing to you my friend, Mr. Behramji M. Malabari of Bombay. As a matter of fact he is too well known for any introduction. All of us here are, I believe, fully acquainted with his philanthropic efforts for female emancipation. You will, I am sure, be gratified to know that our respected guest has secured the active sympathy of almost all the highest members of Government, down from our illustrious ex-Viceroy, Lord Ripon. I may also quote here a few words from the letter of a distinguished English friend to me :—' Mr. Malabari has spent in this work his time, money, and health, and is entitled to the warm sympathy of all generous and thoughtful men.'—Such is the friend of our country who will address you this evening."

Mr. Malabari, who was greeted with cheers, made this elaborate statement of his views:—

Raja Harbans Singh, Raises, and gentlemen of the Punjab,—This meeting is somewhat of an accident and a surprise to me. For my object in coming here was only to meet a few friends privately and to compare notes with them, so as to be able one day to take combined action against the social evils

32

which have now arrested the attention of every sensible man in the country. And I assure you, gentlemen, I was not at all prepared for such a splendid gathering of my brave Punjabi and of some of my clever Bengali friends this evening. I thank you for your sympathy; and as one good turn deserves another, I promise not to detain you long. At the outset I must ask you, my friends, to look upon me not as a stranger, as one outside the Hindu circle, but as one of yourselves. Some of you may be aware that I have often been described by prominent Hindu journals as ' a Hindu,' ' more than a Hindu,' and so on; my respected friend of the *Indian Mirror* so described me once more only the other day. My work has been mostly for and amongst Hindus; so much so that Parsi friends at times taunt me with being always for the Hindus. I cannot say whether my Parsi countrymen are right, but it is necessary to ask my Hindu countrymen to note the impeachment, such as it is. (Cheers.) Gentlemen, my connection with this movement is not a matter of yesterday; it is now nearly fifteen years since I took to studying the social problem in India. (Hear, hear.) And my experience is that social progress is retarded in this country mainly through ignorance, by ignorance of two kinds, popular ignorance and official ignorance. With the former kind we are unhappily but too well acquainted. But of the latter kind of ignorance I may venture to give you an instance. I must here remind you, gentlemen, that I am not a radical or a revolutionary worker. You, no doubt, remember that I at once withdrew some of my proposals last year as soon as they were generally disapproved. Throughout the struggle I have remained open to correction. So am I now, and so will I ever be, provided some sort of action is guaranteed. (Applause.) It was in May or June last year, gentlemen, that I appealed to Lord Ripon personally to consider the position of women in India. (Hear, hear.) His Lordship was then at the height of his popularity with us, and might have earned an additional laurel by taking up my appeal. But like a thoroughly honourable and conscientious statesman, that he was, he confessed his want of acquaintance with the subject, and doubted if the Government of India could do anything in the direction of reform. I put the whole question fairly before him, and urged him with all the earnestness I could command to look into it. Never before had I appealed to man so fervently, for, gentlemen, it was to me a matter of life and death. (Loud cheers.) When hard pressed in this manner, his Lordship remarked laughingly—" My friend, you are leading me into a jungle where the lions may devour me." This was cold comfort, but I took heart of grace and replied somewhat to this effect:—" My Lord, there are no lions in the path so far as I have been able to see. If there is any obstruction, it comes from a very poor class of animals. But even if there *are* lions in the way, I am prepared to go *before* your Lordship. Let them eat me up, and while they are eating me your Lordship may discreetly retire." (Laughter and cheers.) The good Marquis laughed at my offer heartily, but, as might be expected, the implied taunt was too much for a brave-hearted and generous Englishman. Lord Ripon sat up straight in his chair, and said he would take time to consider my request. This was all that I wanted at the time, and imploring him, by the memory of all that he had done, and all that he had suffered in doing, for the people of India, not to lose sight of the matter, I retired. Four days after, I again waited upon his Lordship and was greeted with the cheering words—" Come, Mr. Malabari, we can now discuss your subject somewhat profitably." During the interval he seems to have consulted his friends and colleagues and to have thought over the matter with care. In the course of this second interview Lord Ripon rebutted some of my views and made me see the extreme difficulty of taking action on some of my proposals. And thus, in the presence of this most virtuous ruler, I had the opportunity of modifying my views and curtailing the scope of the proposed action. His Lord-ship then promised to give his best consideration to my Notes; and content with this, I left Simla. In August 1884 Lord Ripon wrote a most encouraging letter to me. Soon after, he referred my Notes to the local Governments for an expression of opinion from representative Hindus. On his return to England, in his address at the annual meeting of the National Indian Association, our noble ex-Viceroy again referred to the subject at length, and though he still felt that Government could not do much in the matter, he had no hesitation in saying that Government might well guide and direct public opinion. And this is about all that we want.

So much, gentlemen, for official sympathy. This sympathy would be much more useful practically, if it were combined with a knowledge of the social life of the people generally. For, though most of the members of Government were deeply interested in the movement when it was started, not a few of them surprised me by saying that they could not take part in discussing the *religious* customs of the people. The theory that these customs have anything to do with Hindu religion, has been successively disproved by Ram Mohan Roy, Vidyasagar Vishnu Shastri, Raghunath Row, Ranade, and a host of others, most enlightened Hindu gentlemen, Brahmins by birth and training, whose names will ever adorn the pages of Indian history. Far from being religious, infant marriage and enforced widowhood are probably the most *irreligious* practices, according to Hindu religion. (Loud applause.) Let me call your attention, gentlemen, to the Hon'ble Mr. Hunter's " Imperial Gazetteer," Vol. 4; pp. 284-85. In this invaluable work Dr. Hunter shows that the domestic law, especially the marriage law of the Hindus, in the post-Puranic period (after 800 to 1000 A.D.) is different in essential points from the domestic and especially the marriage law in the Vedas and the Grihya-Suttras. That the degradation of women during these 1,500 years proceeded not from any legitimate development of Aryan institutions, but from the commixture of these institutions with baser ones introduced by successive hordes of Sythic invaders and the Naga or aboriginal tribes. Dr. Hunter was good enough to give me some useful information on this point, which fits in wonderfully with the opinions of the highest Hindu authorities. And I am glad to be able to tell you that in the forthcoming edition of the "Imperial Gazetteer," Dr. Hunter intends to pursue the line of research to its final result.

You see, then, my good friends, that the evils are admitted on all hands, and all are anxious to remove them, the difference of opinion being confined to as to how to remove the evils. Well, gentlemen, popular ignorance is fast giving way to the light of reason. And official ignorance is yielding to the same beneficent influence. We have now arrived at a stage when Government seems to say—Come to us in reasonably large numbers, and we are ready to work with and for you. What more can we expect from Government? Far be it from me to suggest even the suspicion of Government interference of any kind or degree. No, gentlemen, such a suggestion would be inconsistent with my position as one of the staunchest upholders of individual liberty. But at the same time we know by bitter experience of nearly fifty years that individual reformers and even corporate bodies have failed to achieve practical good. Are we in a position to spurn friendly aid from outside? Have we been able to do anything, even in social matters, during this hundred years and more without the co-operation or the countenance of friends in authority, who alone have the power of regulating the affairs of the subjects? Why should we suspect that such aid will degenerate into interference? Are we not strong enough to oppose interference? My friends, it is a slave or a coward who begins by suspecting the motives of his neighbour. It is a sin to do so. I should like my own countrymen to be more confident. And confidence, you know, gentlemen, is a consciousness of our own strength. Let us avoid suspicion and jealousy, and welcome all offers of aid in a frank, manly spirit. But, remember, brethren, this is my personal feeling. If the sense of the meeting is against it—[cries of No, No] I will bow my head to you.

In this spirit I now beg to submit to you a few definite proposals formulated in consultation with Hindu friends, especially my friend the Hon'ble Mr. Madhava Govind Ranade, whom we look upon as one of the wisest among our wise men.

Here Mr. Malabari suggested the fixing of the marriageable age of girls at 12, and showed at considerable length that the oldest and the best Shastras favoured the postponement of the marriage of girls to at least 16. He repeatedly asked if any one at the meeting objected to this limit. There was no objection. The other proposals had reference to the remarriage of virgin-widows, widows only in name, having never been wives. Mr. Malabari gave an affecting picture of widowhood, and the meeting went with him enthusiastically in denouncing the evil. The third proposal was as to discouraging the marriage of a young girl with an elderly man. The audience accepted Mr. Malabari's suggestion heartily in this matter, as well as on another important point, that there ought to be intermarriages between closely allied castes. All this, Mr. Malabari thought, was for the people to do. But he added that the State, too, could do something towards discouraging those ruinous non-Aryan practices and encouraging those individuals who attempted to break away from their trammels. Among other things he suggested that special facilities might be offered by the State to widows intending to remarry, that Government might register all the Reform Associations and Societies in India, and thus enable these bodies to enforce their rules practically. He looked upon this suggestion, which had come from his valued friend, Mr. Dayaram Gidumal of Kurrachee, as unexceptionable. And the meeting viewed it with great favour. Another suggestion in regard to infant marriage was that originally made to the Government of Bombay by Mr. Mahipatram Rupram, C.I.E., as to enabling Municipal and Local Boards to fix a limit of age and familiarize the masses with the idea of gradually raising the limit. The last proposal was that Government should be asked to remove the glaring contrast existing between the position of an unchaste and a chaste Hindu widow. All these suggestions were favourably received by the meeting, and some of them were promised to be taken in hand as soon as a working committee was formed.

Mr. Malabari took his seat amid enthusiastic cheers. Bhai Mian Singh proposed that "We, the members of the public meeting assembled at the Siksha Sabha Hall, consisting of representatives of the *Anjuman-i-Punjab* and its affiliated societies, the Hindu Sabha, the Widow Remarriage Association, the Arya Samaj, the Brahmo Samaj, the Aror Bans Sabha, Sri Guru Singh Sabha, the Kayasth Sabha, &c., &c., all combined, offer our hearty welcome to Mr. Behramji M. Malabari." The above proposal was seconded by Pundit Jwala Dutt Pershad, and was unanimously passed.

Lala Amolak Ram proposed :—"We are of opinion that Mr. Malabari has earned the lasting gratitude of India by his efforts to improve the position of women." He added that though he differed a little here and there from Mr.

Malabari in matters of detail, he nevertheless admired his disinterested motives, by which he was led to sacrifice his time, money and health, in order to ameliorate the condition of women in this country.

Lala Surdha Ram seconded this proposal, and Lala Bhagut Ram warmly supported it.

Lala Rama Krishna moved the following resolution : " His (Mr. Malabari's) present proposals are moderate and reasonable, and we are prepared to give them effect by all means in our power." He said that those who thought that Mr. Malabari advocated Government interference were labouring under a great mistake. What Mr. Malabari meant was Government support, and not Government interference. There was a wide difference between the two. He could not agree with those who justify Government interference in the case of Satti, but condemn it in the case of child-marriage. According to his way of thinking, the pernicious custom of child marriage offers much more justification for State interference than the voluntary act of ascending the husband's funeral pile.

Dr. Brij Lall Ghose seconded the proposal, and observed that the statements of Mr. Malabari required slight modifications in matters of detail, according to the difference in circumstances in this province. Dewan Narindro Nath and Lala Kirpa Ram supported the proposal.

Babu Navina Chandra Rai moved:—"We have every confidence in Mr. Malabari's intentions and acts, and whilst he is here, we propose that a standing committee be formed in connection with the Widow Marriage Society, on the spot, in support of his great national movement." Bhai Jowahir Singh seconded the motion, and a committee was accordingly formed, consisting of the representatives of the various societies on the spot.

Munshi Mahomed Hussain observed that the two evil customs complained of, though opposed to the injunctions of the Quran Sharif, were unfortunately as much prevalent among the Mahomedans as they were among the Hindus. Sheik Nanak Buksh supported Munshi Mahomed Hussain's observations, and added that enforced widowhood led to adultery and infanticide. The former Mahomedan gentleman suggested that a few Mahomedans might be put upon the Committee. His suggestion was adopted with great alacrity. Sodhi Pertab Singh said that the pernicious custom of infant marriage did not obtain in the territories of the Amir of Kabul. One Atma was fined Rs. 2,000 by Amir Shere Ali for having given his daughter in marriage before she attained the age of puberty. Babu Navina Chandra Rai then gave a very brief account of the widow marriage movement in the Punjab. Mr. Moharam Ali Chisthi and Lala Mungo Mall made speeches condemning Government interference in matters purely social. Mr. Malabari corrected them, repeating that he did not pray for Government interference of any kind, but for support. The meeting dispersed with a vote of thanks to the Chairman.

SPEECH AT AGRA.

A largely attended and influential meeting of the Native community of Agra, probably the very largest held in this town for a public purpose, was held in the Victoria College on Thursday, the 10th February 1886, to take active measures to put a stop to the practice of infant marriages. The *elite* of all sections of the Native community, Hindus and Mahomedans, were seen at this meeting. There were Native officials of all grades, from the highest to the lowest, almost all the Municipal Commissioners and Honorary Magistrates, the principal Native representatives of all the different castes, and a very large number of College students. In addition to this a number of European gentlemen and a lady were also present. Letters of sympathy were received from Mr. R. E. Hamblin, Joint Magistrate of Agra, and Thakur Umrao Singh, Rais of Agra district. Amongst others present were : Mr. W. Young, C. S., Judge of Agra, Mr. Thomason, Principal, Agra College, Mr. Pargiter, Principal, St. John's College, Rev. Mr. and Mrs. Wilson, Messrs. Pogose and Martin, Messrs. Parter, Mackintosh, and Smith, Moulvi Fariduddin, Sub-Judge, Babu Promodha Charan, Judge, Small Cause Court, Choube Ram Das, Honorary Magistrate, Munshi Nand Kishore, Honorary Magistrate, Hakim Aulad Ali, Honorary Magistrate, Moulvi Fariduddin, Rais of Agra, Hakim Walait Husain, Municipal Commissioner, Master Amiruddin, Municipal Commissioner, Moulvi Hashmat Ullah, Pleader of the High Court, Munshi Tsaduq Husain, Rais of Ghatia, Sheikh Bisarat Ali, Seth Pitam Chand, Lala Harnaráin, Rais, Lala Dwarka Das, Vakil, Lala Girdhar Lal, Vakil, Munshi Jagan Parshad, Vakil, Pandit Jagan Nath, Babu Perbhu Dial, Mir Qazim Husain, Mirza Mehomed Ali, Pundit Girraj Kishore, Babu Jamna Das Biswas, Babu Shankar Dial, B. A., Mir Mehomed Ali, Mr. Murli Dhar, Head Master, Victoria College, Pundit Thakur Pershad, Lala Kanhai Lal, Lala Nihal Chand, Assistant Manager, U. C. S. Bank, Babu Uma Charan Banerjee, M.A., Secretary to His Highness the Mahraja of Dholpore, and others. Mr. W. Young, Judge of Agra, was voted to the chair. The Chairman, in introducing the guest of the evening, Mr. Behramji M. Malabari, expressed his very great pleasure at having this opportunity of publicly evincing his sympathy with a movement calculated to do immense good to India. Mr. Malabari was animated by a noble spirit, and he was possessed by a great idea which, when carried into practical effect, would result in not only social, but also political regeneration. The natives of this country, as was remarked by Sir Alfred Lyall the other day at the Agra College, though possessing much intelligence, were wanting in thoroughness and accuracy, and Mr. Young hoped that movements like this would supply that defect. He, the Chairman, had always taken great interest in these matters, and he felt certain that the seed sown to-day would result in a rich harvest of moral unity and social and political activity hitherto lying dormant. Mr. Behramji M. Malabari then made a few touching remarks :—

I am glad to have this opportunity at last of redeeming a promise I made to Lala Baij Nath, Munsiff of Agra, some time ago. That gentleman will be able to tell you what was done at the National Congress at Bombay for the attainment of that unity of purpose to which the worthy Chairman has just referred. When two years ago, I appealed for co-operation in putting a stop to the evils of Infant Marriage and Enforced Widowhood, I was advised to collect the opinions of representative men in the country. The result of this inquiry was more encouraging than I had hoped for, and now comes the time for action to be taken by my Hindu brethren. Here I will confine my remarks to Infant Marriage, because the other topic is likely to cause unnecessary irritation. I ask the gentlemen present if Infant Marriage is not productive of infinitely more harm than good? What is the cause of the wholesale degeneracy that has come over modern India? Some say it is owing to material impoverishment; others ascribe it to neglect of religion, and others still to want of scientific knowledge. All these gentlemen are perhaps equally right. But I think that probably the most patent cause of this national decay has been lost sight of. I refer to want of moral perception. Now I must not be misunderstood to mean, as some of my over-educated young friends have misunderstood me, that my countrymen are an immoral race. Very far from it. The Indians are as moral a people as any on God's earth. For instance, as public men, our judges and doctors, and journalists and school-masters are as morally disposed as Europeans in the same lines of work. But let us accompany them home. What a deplorable difference between the two races! In domestic matters we natives have a very faint perception of the moral law. I contend that infant marriages are inconsistent with a sense of nationality, with true patriotism. What public spirit is visible amongst us is, no doubt, as indicative of the marvellous vitality of the nation as of the beneficent influence of the British rule. But on the whole the season of youth, the most glorious period in the life of the individual, as of the nation, is denied to the Indian under this custom of infant marriages. Consequently there is so little

33

of enterprise in India as compared with other countries. I appeal to my hearers most earnestly to discontinue the practice, which has nothing to be said for it and everything to be said against it.

The Resolutions passed were :—(1) " That this meeting is of opinion that the practice of Infant Marriage amongst all classes of the Native community, being prejudicial to our best interests, ought to be put a stop to by every available means."

(2) " That a committee consisting of the following gentlemen, with power to add to their number, be appointed to devise measures for carrying out the first Resolution:—Mr. W. Young, President; Mr. H. B. Finlay, Vice-President; Babu Promada Charan Banerjee ; Moulvi Fariduddin ; Lala Baij Nath ; Moulvi Mahomed Mohsan Khan Bahadur; Munshis Raja Lal; Sheo Narrain; Nand Kishore ; Jagan Pershad ; Girdhar Lal ; Dwarka Das ; Choube Ram Das, Moulvi Fariduddin, Rais, Agra ; Hakim Aulad Ali ; Munshi Amir Uddin."

(3) " That the most cordial and sincere thanks of this meeting and of the Native community of Agra be accorded to Mr. Malabari for his initiative, zeal, and sacrifice in the matter of social reform."

SPEECH AT ALIGARH.

A public meeting of the Hindu inhabitants of Aligarh, of all sections of the community, was held at the Society's Rooms on the 14th February 1886, to hear Mr. Malabari upon the question of Infant Marriage in India and to devise practical methods of co-operation with him. Raja Jaikisen Dass Bahadur, C.S.I., was voted to the Chair. Amongst those present at the meeting were Raja Jaikisen Dass Bahadur, C.S.I., Raja Har Narayan Singh, Raja Ram Pal Singh, Kumar Benarsi Dass, Kumar Luchmi Narayan, Kumar Parmanand, Thakore Luchmun Singh, Thakur Hanuman Singh, Thakur Ram Shankur, Thakur Gauri Shankar, and many others, Pandits, Reises, Pleaders, &c., Raja Ghan Sham Singh, Rao Karan Singh, Thakur Gurudut Singh and Thakur Govind Singh Sahib, having also expressed themselves as active sympathizers. The Raja Bahadur opened proceedings by introducing Mr. Malabari in a brief but appreciative speech. He observed that there was no need of introducing to the public of Aligarh or of any part of India a gentleman who had been travelling all over the continent, like a messenger from God, intent upon redeeming the whole nation. Mr. Malabari, added the Raja, had been spending his strength and his substance on freeing the Hindu race from the tyranny of an evil custom, and the least that the suffering community should do was to aid his noble efforts practically. Mr. Malabari had been flying across thousands of miles for earnest and intelligent co-operation. The Raja felt sure that the Hindus of

Aligarh would give him such support, together with their most grateful thanks. With these remarks Raja Jaikisen Dass left his honoured friend to explain himself. Mr. Malabari then addressed the meeting in the following manner :—

" Mr. Chairman, Pandits, Reises, and gentlemen of Aligarh, —As I told you, last night, I have come here, not to speak but to listen, not to dictate my own terms to you, but to submit to your dictation. I have given you such time as I could spare to consider the matter. Is Infant Marriage an evil? You have assured me unanimously, and unanimously you are assuring me even now, that it *is* an evil, that it is at the root of many evils, and that it should be put a stop to. Now, gentlemen, this admission is a great gain to the cause. I will, therefore, dismiss this point after telling you what you scarcely need being told—that premature marriages have been the ruin of the race, physically, intellectually, and spiritually—that they are making us less and less fit every day for the duties of modern life. As individuals and as a nation we have lost almost everything worth having under the operation of this custom. We have suffered in public spirit under a series of domestic afflictions entailed by the practice; we have become strangers to pluck and enterprise of most kinds; in a word, we have very nearly lost the power of action, certainly of self-action. How, otherwise, could we account for our present position? We have had to make room for stronger and more united nations from abroad. Thus, masters have become servants and great thinkers have become small, very small speculators. Look at our Mahomedan brethren. There was a time, and not so long ago, when I thought that the Hindus were far ahead of the Mahomedans. I have had to change my opinion since. And never before was I so confirmed in my opinion as yesterday when I sat for one hour by the side of that veteran educationalist and intrepid reformer, Sayad Ahmed Khan, listening to the speeches of some of the young Mahomedans returned from England, in whose honour was organized that enthusiastic demonstration. When will you Hindus go in numbers to Europe and America, to bring over to the old world the sciences and arts of modern civilization? When will you go to China, to Australia, to the trade coasts of Africa and elsewhere, for purposes of colonization or commerce? I repeat the Mahomedans are leaving you behind on the highways of life, so to say. Why?—because they are generally free from those social trammels under which you have been groaning for centuries. Far be it from me to exalt one nation at the expense of another. I am bound to the Hindus by ties of lifelong gratitude. To the Mahomedans I am bound by equally strong ties—those of close personal association. But after all, India belongs to the Hindus. The Hindu community is the mother of all the Indian communities. And it has often occurred to me, gentlemen, that if the different nationalities are to rise, they can do so best with the rise of the mother nation. You may call this a theory, a mere whim—with me it has been a deep-rooted principle. Rightly or wrongly I have always worked, and worked all along the line, upon this principle.

But I must not prolong this digression. You say you are prepared to discourage the practice of infant marriages, but are powerless to do so. I fully appreciate what our friend, Dr. Mulraj, said last night in the bitterness of despair— "we profess to do everything, but can do nothing." The same evening a venerable Pandit assured me in the presence of Raja Jaikisen Dass and others that practical reform in the matter is impossible without *rajaya sahela* in some form—that is, without the moral support of the State. This has been the experience of the strongest and most earnest Hindu workers. But on that point, which has now become the *crux* of the whole question, I can offer no opinion of my own beyond this—that there is urgent and vital necessity for action. That infant marriages are not only *not* sanctioned by our *shastras*, but are actually interdicted by them, and that all that we have to do, now that we recognize the evil, is to follow the teaching of our *shastras* more faithfully. Let me appeal to you, my brethren of Aligarh, to be true to yourselves, to your instincts, to your best reason. I ask you to be true Aryas. As such, last night many of you told me that the minimum marriageable age for our girls should be fixed at 14. There were some amongst you, including two learned Pandits, who were for 16. There were four or five of you, however, who thought 12 might do to begin with. Well, my friends, I am content with the lowest minimum. Give it me unanimously, and I'll be well content. I have not come here to appeal to your feelings. All that I ask you is to exercise your judgment. Exercise your judgment, dear friends, and may Heaven guide it to a righteous conclusion!" (Loud and prolonged cheers.)

After a translation of Mr. Malabari's speech by Kumar Parmanand, and after a few questions from some of the gentlemen present, it was proposed by Pandit Meherchand and seconded by Pandit Bhairava Dutt—that " The custom of infant marriage is contrary to reason and to the present circumstances of the country, and must be stopped by the different castes by every means possible, if need be, with the support of the Government." The proposition was formally submitted to the meeting in English and in Hindi, and was carried unanimously.

The second proposition ran thus:—"That the marriage of young girls with old men be strictly prohibited." This was proposed by Pandit Nathuram, who addressed the meeting in Hindi, quoting *shloka* after *shloka* in support of his views. Pandit Nathuram's eloquent address, full of learned citations, produced a great effect on the meeting. And he was loudly and repeatedly cheered as he spoke about the value of self-sacrifice with special reference to Mr. Malabari, whom he likened to one of the Rishis of old, and so he exhorted his audience to follow the example. The proposition was seconded by Babu Gour Ballabsahe and was carried unanimously.

The third proposition, moved by Kumar Luchmi Narayan and seconded by Pandit Kaniah Lal, was carried by acclamation. It ran thus :—"That a working committee of different castes be formed on the spot to co-operate with Mr. Behramji M. Malabari ...... to whom the Hindu community owes an immense debt of gratitude."

SPEECH AT LUCKNOW.

The following notice was issued on the 10th February 1886, by Raza Husain Khan, President of the Rifa-i-Aum Association, Pandit Pran Nath, Secretary, Jelsa Tehzib, and Babu Bhoban Mohan Roy, Secretary, Ajudhia Brahmo Samaj:—

" A public meeting of the inhabitants and residents of the City of Lucknow will be held at the Kaisar Bagh, Baradari, on Wednesday, the 17th instant, at 5 P.M., to welcome Mr. B. M. Malabari of Bombay, the illustrious promoter of social reforms in India, and to devise means for an organization here, having for its objects the abolition of infant marriages and the promotion of other important reforms urgently needed in the country."

A similar notice was also issued by Pandit Sri Kishen and Munshi Naval. Kishor, two of the foremost citizens of Lucknow. As advertised, the meeting took place on the 17th instant. Dr. W. Duthoit, D.C.L., Judicial Commissioner, Oudh, was good enough to take the chair, and amongst those present were observed the following:—Rai Narayan Dass, the Rev. Mr. R. C. Bose, Sheik Raza Hussain, Sheik Anayat Ullah, Babu Rampal Chakarbatty, Munshi Naval Kishor, Pandit Shyam Narayan, Pandit Pran Nath, Mr. Ganga Prasad Varma, Mr. Avinash Chunder Ghose, Mr. Bepin Behari Bose, M.A., Pandit Sri Kissen, and many others, Honorary Magistrates, Municipal Commissioners, Reises, Pleaders, graduates, and College students.

Dr. Duthoit being indisposed, Rai Narayan Dass was called upon to commence the proceedings. He did so in a brief speech, referring to Mr. Malabari's work in the highest terms and requesting the audience to give him every possible attention. The Rai at the same time hoped that Government interference might be averted in such a matter, and trusted to the good sense and public spirit of the inhabitants of Lucknow. As to the urgent necessity of reform in our marriage practices the speaker thought there could be no two opinions.

Mr. Malabari then spoke as follows :—

" Mr. Chairman and gentlemen of Lucknow,—I have come to you for a little business, as you are aware. And as I come for it all the way from Bombay, I think you will give me credit for expecting that the business will be done. It is more your own business, gentlemen, than mine. I look upon myself only as a humble instrument in the hands of Providence for a cause the success of which is, in my judgment, an absolute and a vital necessity. I stand before you as a mere interpreter of the wisdom of ancient India as appreciated by the most thoughtful of our countrymen in the present day. The object of my mission is nothing new, nothing strange. Infant Marriage has been generally recognized as an unmitigated evil. It weakens our physical capacity and interferes sadly with our intellectual and spiritual development. It has almost destroyed our powers of cohesion and organization. You also know, gentlemen, that Infant Marriage is nowhere sanctioned in our *shastras*, nor can it be approved by common sense amongst any community of men. Infant Marriage is more of a fashion than anything else. How is it, then, that knowing it to be an unmixed evil, at any rate as vastly more harmful than beneficial to the race, we have not yet been able to shake it off? Surely, we are not such a nation of suicides. We have tried, we are still trying, to get rid of the evil. Efforts have been made since the time of Akbar to put down Infant Marriage and its attendant evils. Those early efforts, more or less spasmodic, had not the slightest effect on society. Under the present rule, with its marvellous capacity to evolve order and system, more serious and more strenuous efforts have been put forth now nearly for a century. But the custom is just where it was before the British came to India, in some parts of the country more aggravated and intensified. The thing has grown up a fashion, as I told you. Individuals have failed to cope with it; it has defied corporate action itself. What appeared to be success at times has been swamped by the tide of reaction. There can be no stability in spasmodic efforts; they often end in discredit to the cause and disaster to its advocates. The fact is we have never been able to help ourselves effectively in the matter. The wisest and the strongest amongst us, Brahmins like Ragoonath Row and Ranade, for instance, Brahmins like Vidiasagar and Madava Rao, have had, after prolonged struggles, to appeal for extraneous aid —to be saved from themselves. But not a few of the present generation seem to be disinclined to profit by the experience of their predecessors. They think, and rightly, that they are not bound to abide by the decision of others in such a matter. They will try the thing for themselves. Now, I cannot help admiring this spirit. So long as this self-respecting zeal remains among our youth, so long may we hope for better things.

But let us see, gentlemen, what are the weapons with which we propose fighting the custom which has laughed at the efforts of intellectual giants? Remember, my friends, that men who could build up a new Church for India have practically failed to demolish this custom. Well, education, you say, should be our main support. Nothing could be stronger or a more legitimate support to lean upon. But what is the state of education in the country? Is there anything like a reasonable, an appreciable similarity between the educational acquirements of our boys and girls ? See how unequal is the standard. That standard will never be the same, I believe; nor is such equality or identity at all desirable. But surely we must have *some* intellectual sympathy between the sexes for the reconstruction of the domestic fabric in the manner proposed by advocates of education as the only remedy for the evil. Speaking as a practical man I find male education itself more as retarding than facilitating social contentment. For whereas, if both sexes were to remain in ignorance, there would be some chance of their pulling together happily in life, the chances become smaller as one of the sexes keeps advancing rapidly and the other generally lagging behind. I do not, of course, imply that the education of our young men should be suspended till female education has been brought up to something like the same level. No ; that would be foolish and mischievous. My only object in putting the matter thus before you is to demonstrate what is to my mind a serious difficulty in the way of timely reform. For this purpose it will never do, I contend, to trust entirely or even mainly to a spread of education in the country.

We are then asked to look upon Female Education as a specific. Female Education is undoubtedly one of the best remedies at hand. But, as I will presently show, it is by no means a panacea. For instance, what is the state of Female Education, so called, in your own provinces ? I am not quite sure, but scarcely 1 girl out of 200 girls of school-going age actually goes to school. What do you think of that, my friends? And listen—if we take the total female population of the North-Western Provinces into account, scarcely one female out of 500 knows reading and writing. Further, if we confine ourselves to the total Hindu population only (there are the Europeans, Eurasians, Mahomedans, Brahmos, &c.,) the proportion could not possibly be better than 1 to 800. Gentlemen of Lucknow, do you intend trusting for ever to this wonderfully well-spread Female Education as your only hope? (No, No.) And let me ask you again, is it not idle to talk of 'Female Education' when girls have to be withdrawn from school before 10-11? (A long pause.) My friends, Female Education is at best an idea; Infant Marriage is a hard cruel fact. (Applause.) The idea of Female Education is radically inconsistent with the practice of Infant Marriage. (Loud applause.) It is all very well for European friends to lay so much stress on Female Education. *You* know better, you are *bound* to act more sensibly. (Cheers.) Do not, I beg, mistake the end for the means. (Loud cheers.) '

I hope, gentlemen, I have succeeded to some extent in laying bare the idols of clay that have been perhaps too long worshipped by some of our sentimental reformers. Let me warn you against this amiable creed, which teaches you to trust to some dimly discernible force that has to be generated by some other more dimly discernible self-created cause, in the remote future, when you and I and the sentimental philanthropists will have gone to our rest and to our account, shirking what appears to me to be an obvious duty for each one of us individually. Go into committee this very evening and try to find out practical remedies. Make some *bandobast* amongst yourselves to work out the problem honestly. Otherwise you have a poor look-out, my friends. I cannot venture to say exactly what your future will be under this grievous system of baby marriages. I am speaking to you under great restraint, imposed by my unfortunate position and by friends for whom I cannot but feel a real respect. I wish I were a Hindu—then I could have spoken to you more freely. But this at least I must say in conclusion, that if you continue much longer to be the slaves of Infant Marriage, you will cease to be men, you will cease to be a nation, you will cease to be Aryas worthy the name. (Cheers.)

It was proposed by Rai Narayan Dass Bahadur and seconded by Pandit Sri Kishen that. "this meeting accords a cordial welcome to Mr. B. M. Malabari to Lucknow and records its sense of high appreciation of his noble, disinterested, and patriotic exertions in the cause of social reform in India." Both proposer and seconder spoke warmly to the Resolution, which was carried by acclamation.

34

The second Resolution was proposed by Pandit Pran Nath, seconded by Munshi Naval Kishor, and supported by Sheik Raiza Hussain. It ran thus: "That this meeting is strongly of opinion that the custom of Infant Marriage is a curse to India and is·productive of manifold evils to society, and that immediate steps should be taken by all right-thinking men in Oudh for its abolition with such moral support of the State as they deem necessary, and the meeting is further of opinion that unequal marriages in point of age should be equally discouraged." Pandit Pran Nath and Munshi Naval Kishor spoke at some length in favour of this Resolution, which was carried unanimously.

The third Resolution, for the formation of a strong committee from amongst the different Associations in Oudh, was proposed by Babu Bepin Behari Bose, M.A., and seconded by Pandit Shyam Narayan. The veteran Pandit addressed himself to the Resolution in a vehement speech, denouncing infant marriages from several points of view. No one cared for Government interference, he said ; but there were many ways in which the Government could help the suffering community in its own interest as also in the interest of the Government itself. The Pandit spoke from personal experience, which was that young men of the age were in a miserable way physically and otherwise. Was not such a Government as ours, which did so much for us in every direction, bound in honour to come to our rescue ? Mr. Shyam Narayan was loudly and repeatedly cheered in the course of his address in Hindustani.

SPEECH AT ALLAHABAD.

A Conference of many of the leading Hindu representatives of Allahabad was held at the Kayastha Shala Hall on the 19th February 1886 to hear Mr. Malabari upon the subject of Infant Marriages and to devise practical measures for the suppression of the custom. Amongst those present were Shastris, Pandits, Municipal Commissioners, Professors, Pleaders, &c. The following names may be noted down :—Pandit Adityaram Bhattacharyaji, M.A., Professor of Sanskrit, Muir Central College, Babu Charn Chunder Mittor, Sr. Vice-Chairman, Municipal Board, Pandit Govind Rao Goray, Munshi Jwala Prasad, Senior Government Pleader, High Court, North-West Provinces, Pandit Nanda Lal, Vakil, High Court, Munshi Kashi Prasad, Vakil and Municipal Commissioner, Pandit Lukshmi Narayan Vyas, President, Hindu Samaj, Mr. R. N. Banerji, Municipal Commissioner, Dr. A. C. Banerji, Municipal Commissioner, Dr. M. N. Odhedar, Kumar Shiva Nath Sinha, Barrister-at-Law, Thakur Mahabir Prasad, Honorary Magistrate, Babu Sital Prasad Chatterji, Vakil, Honorary Magistrate and Vice-Chairman, District Board, Babu Soshi Bhushan Chatterji, B.A., Babu Taraprasad, M.A., Babu Ratan Chand, B.A., Vakil, High Court, Lala Girdhari Lal, B.A., Pandit Karta Kishen, B.A., Pandit Budri Dutt Joshi, Pandit Hari Ram Pande, B.A., Pandit Balam Bhutta Shastri, Pandit Ramprasana Acharya, Moulvi Habibulla, Barrister-at-Law, Mr. R. C. Saunders, Solicitor, Lala Hardew

Prasad, Vice-Chairman, Theosophical Society, Babu Bhola Nath Chatterji, Secretary, Theosophical Society, Babu Ram Das Chakrabatty, Vakil, Pandit Madan Mohan, B.A., Pandit Jai Gobind, Head Pandit, Government High School, Pandit Suraja Prasad, Babu Nand Lal Ghose, of the *Indian Union*, and others. Kumar Shiva Nath Sinha proposed that Professor Adityaram Bhattacharyaji do take the Chair. On Dr. Banerji seconding the proposal Pandit Adityaram took the Chair, and began by saying that the Kumar's kind proposal was a surprise to him. That he was not only unfit to introduce a gentleman like Mr. Malabari to such an audience, but that he thought himself unfit even to be introduced by Mr. Malabari. However, the subject was of such pressing importance, and there was so much work to do that evening, that he would not stand upon ceremony, but at once request Mr. Malabari to enlighten the meeting upon the great problem to the solution of which his gifted friend was contributing so materially.

Mr. Malabari thereupon addressed the meeting thus :—

" We have not met here, gentlemen of Allahabad, to talk about this question, but, as our learned Chairman suggests, to do some practical work with regard to it. And yet it has once more fallen to my lot to begin with talk and with talk only. I am, however, assured that this Conference will not rise before doing some solid work. And work being our principal object, I'll be as brief as possible this evening. To say, gentlemen, the infant marriages are a curse to India, as our hard-headed friends at Lucknow declared the other day, would be a mere truism. This scourge of child marriages has afflicted our race for centuries and in a variety of ways. Not the least amongst its baneful consequences the custom gives rise to virgin widowhood. Infant marriage is admittedly a great evil. No one in his senses pretends to dispute the proposition. The only difference of opinion that can exist as regards this wretched fashion is how to put a stop to it. How indeed ? Well, many men many minds. But let us here consult only those minds that are worth consulting. There are three favourite methods suggested by a not inconsiderable body of our educated men—I. Education; II. Female Education ; III. the setting of examples. The former two remedies I had an opportunity of examining day before yesterday at Lucknow. To you to-day I will only say that education is too unequal between the sexes to be of much avail in the near future. Female education is an excellent means. But, really, is it *the* means, is it the best means to the end in view? How can we talk of female education when our girls are, as a rule, married off too early to obtain any real education at all? Are we honest in talking of Female Education and Infant Marriages in the same breath? To my mind, gentlemen, the coupling of the two phrases is like mocking all hopes of practical reform, every possibility of progress. (Cheers.)

Along with education we are advised to have tracts and pamphlets and lectures and missionary tours. Excellent suggestions. Let us have all these good things; the more the merrier. But, my friends, *whom* are you going to lecture and write tracts and pamphlets for?—not to ask you about organization and the sinews of war. And how much do you expect from prematurely married missionaries?—granting, for argument's sake, that you will have volunteers for the asking, and that caste and locality and language will not stand in the way of success. God forbid that I should make light of your remedies. They have their value, and I think I have contributed my mite to each one of these methods of work. But at the same time, I must beg of you, gentlemen, not to make too much of these auxiliary, these subsidiary methods. Do not mistake ends for means, my friends. Tracts and pamphlets and lectures and missionary tours— organized efforts, in short,—will be best available then and then only, when women in India are able to co-operate with men in this cause. (Cheers.) And this co-operation is impossible (and with it every form of national progress) so long as we stick to this suicidal practice of infant marriages. (Loud cheers.) Yes, gentlemen, is there much to choose between suicide and infant marriage? If there is, I think the balance inclines in favour of the former crime. (Hear, hear.) And supposing for a moment that education and the other means suggested may prove efficacious in the distant future, are we to do nothing else in the meantime? Have we any right to prolong the misery of the nation? The heart of the nation has been grievously oppressed for centuries. How long is this oppression to last? Have we not suffered enough—have we not fallen sufficiently low? Do not wrong me, my friends, by mistaking this persistence for a species of selfish impatience. I am ever ready to work and content to wait. But we have waited too long already, and I hold it a sin to wait longer, under the altered circumstances of the country. Under a settled Government like this it is more than ever necessary to discard a custom which handicaps the people and keeps them down in almost every concern of life. (Hear, hear.)

Now come we to the setting of practical examples. This is a remedy worth trying. Let leaders of the community set concrete examples, and the people are sure to follow. The progress will, no doubt, be slow, in India much slower than in any other country; but it will be sure nevertheless. (Hear.) Let every Hindu father say he will not marry his daughter under 12, and the thing is done so far as he is concerned. He has done his duty manfully. If a few fathers set this example in every town, the future of the people may be taken as assured. Caste may oppose the movement and ex-communicate its promoters. But if these latter stand firm, caste may find herself an outcast in the long run. But let the practical reformer ask himself—"is this possible for me to do?—is it desirable in my own interest and of society at large?" I am very doubtful about it, gentlemen. Individuals have made the attempt and have been crushed under it. They have failed invariably, within my experience; and what is worse, they have discredited the cause and thrown it back for long. Why? Because they attempted more than human beings could do under the circumstances. (Hear, hear.) Those who have the slightest acquaintance with the inner life of the Hindu—of his joint family system, his reverence for elders, and his regard for relations and connections of all degrees—will understand me without any further explanation. They will agree with me in thinking that so long as society in India remains what it is, it will be all but impossible for an individual reformer to set the example. I say it is unjust to him and inexpedient on public grounds to insist upon this course as the only feasible one.

What, then, are we to do? Well, gentlemen, I will not keep you waiting long, especially as most of you seem to have anticipated me. Let us make persistent and organized efforts. Let us have committees on which every considerable section of the community is represented by its leaders. Let these representatives be honest, earnest workers. Let these men devise practical methods—lectures, pamphlets, missionary tours, with all my heart ; let them fix a minimum limit of age for the girl; let them take a pledge to this effect, and let them ask the Government to enable them to enforce the pledge upon themselves, so as to be above the control of foolish women and selfish priests. (Hear.) Let them arrange among themselves that an infant marriage, which is neither a *sanskar* (sacrament) nor a *karar* (legal contract) shall not be recognized as such by the Court of law in case of dispute. Let them make adequate provision for the victims of infant marriages, especially for the girl whom they are so anxious to condemn to perpetual widowhood. This may put a check upon extravagance in many ways. If parents insist upon marrying infants, are they not bound legally as well as morally to take the consequences? (Hear, hear.) Let the committees ask Government to raise the age for consummation. In short, it is open to these representative Committees to try the educational test, the municipal test, the service test, and a number of social tests which will suggest themselves to practical men the minute they sit down with a will to work. (Hear, hear.) The Committees will be the Punchayets of old, capable of uniform action without which you must expect no results to speak of. Thus, you see, gentlemen, I am asking you to do nineteen-twentieths of the work yourselves. But there is the remaining one-twentieth, essential to the success of the cause, which must come from elsewhere. Gentlemen, I do not wish to thrust this view upon you. I myself resisted it for four years. For four long years I set my face against extraneous aid.

But the more I studied the problem, the nearer was I driven to the conclusion arrived at by Ragoonath Row and Ranade. Two years ago, after more than ten years of study and after four years of struggle to escape this conviction, I found myself at last convinced of the soundness of that view. The position is this. Every nation has its marriage law. So have you— or rather you had your marriage law when you were a nation— the wisest law yet devised by human intellect. I am referring, of course, to the law of Manu. (Cheers.) Well, gentlemen, in an evil hour you departed from that law—perhaps you were forced by the then existing circumstances to depart from the law. Those adverse circumstances ceased to operate long since, but the departure has grown wider with the lapse of time, with results which no Arya can contemplate without anguish. Well, gentlemen, the conscience of the nation, such as it is, has awakened to the necessity of immediately going back to the old law. But it cannot go back in a body without some aid from the Government which can best guide and direct its steps, which alone can regulate its action.

Why hesitate to utilize this beneficent agency? Because, we are reminded, it is a foreign agency. In that case, gentlemen, is not the agency of God a foreign agency? Here we have a number of educated men telling us that if the Government were their own, they would gladly avail them-selves of its regulating authority. (I trust some of our enlightened Native Princes will take the hint.) So it is because we are under a foreign rule that we decline to reform ourselves. Good. And what do those mad men, Ranade and Ragoonath Row, wish this alien Government to do? To help you, at *your* instance and with *your* consent, to go back to your own. (Loud cheers.) This is the head and front of their offence. You would gladly have this form of co-operation from your own Government. But because the country happens to be entrusted to an alien power—which is likely to remain here as long as, say, infant marriages are perpetrated in India—because of this circumstance alone, you refuse to have that which you cannot do without. You are anxious to improve ; some friendly impulse from outside is indispensable to your improvement ; and still you go on arguing in a circle and putting off the realization of your cherished hope. My friends, this is sheer wantonness. As I said before, you are flying in the face of Providence. (Hear.) As well may you say to God Almighty, " Go away, we don't want providential interference ; we are B. A.'s and M. A.'s. (Laughter.) We have read Bentham and Buckle, have you read Mill and Spencer ? Go away, we *will* commit suicide, and you *shall* not save us. Who are you ?—You are not we !" (Cheers and applause.) Gentlemen, one of you was telling me last night that this attitude of mind might imply " intellectual emancipation." And he quoted high authority for the purpose. I cannot say if this opinion is largely shared in the North-West Provinces. But one thing I may venture to assert—that in fathering such an opinion upon the gentleman whose respected name was mentioned last night, our friend did injustice to that gentleman, to myself, to the idea conveyed by the words " intellectual emancipation" and to the cause which is equally dear to us all. (Cheers.) Such an attitude does not betoken intellectual emancipation, but perhaps intellectual emasculation. It implies want of that robust masculine sense of confidence which I long to see revived in our countrymen. (Hear, hear.) It will be better for you and for others, my friends, if you begin with confidence, instead of distrust. Suspect no one till you have cause to do so. Fear nothing if you have truth on your side. Work on with truth as your guide, and you will succeed in spite of the whole world. (Loud cheers.) Gentlemen of Allahabad, I will not detain you any longer."

Munshi Kashi Prasad, before proposing the first Resolution, briefly translated Mr. Malabari's speech, after which he addressed the meeting on his own account. The Munshi Saheb spoke with great energy, denouncing infant marriages from every conceivable point of view, and tracing to them the present degradation of a noble race. He passed some scathing criticism on the apathy of his countrymen, and held them responsible for the ruin of the country. Mr. Kashi Prasad's humorous remarks made the audience laugh heartily, as he described the ludicrous ceremony of baby-marriages, and then he turned upon them fiercely saying, " Why do you laugh?—there is good reason to shed tears of blood over these misfortunes." In this strain he spoke for a few minutes, holding the audience spell-bound. The speaker's reference to the condition of Hindu widows was most painful, and he himself fairly broke down as he referred to the condition of girl-widows. The cares and anxieties, as well as other evils attending premature marriages, forbade all hope of social amenity in India, and in this state of society to expect political unity or material prosperity was out of the question. Mr. Kashi Prasad gave practical illustration of this view, and concluded with an impressive appeal to leaders of the community to devise practical measures of relief. We regret we have not been supplied with notes of this and other speeches, which were mostly in Hindustani. Munshi Kashi Prasad proposed that :—

" This meeting is of opinion that too early marriages of boys and girls, so widely prevalent in the Hindu community, are productive of the physical, intellectual, and moral deterioration of the race, and that they lead, in a large measure, to increased percentage of child-widows—a great social evil in itself; and that it should be the duty of every thoughtful, patriotic Hindu to discourage this evil practice by all private efforts and with such moral support of Government as may be conducive to a speedy removal of this baneful custom, without creating popular alarm by its action."

This Resolution was seconded by Thakur Mahabir Prasad Singh in a neat little speech.

The second Resolution about forming a Committee was proposed by Pandit Lukshmi Narayan Vyas, the famous Vaid, who made an important speech, examining the physical and the spiritual results of early marriages. About the former he spoke from professional experience, and his remarks made a very painful sensation. He described several instances of premature consummation in which the girls had been ruined for life. The Pandit spoke freely, as he observed the audience did not contain school-boys. For the crime above referred to, Pandit Lukshmi Narayan invoked the aid of a penal law, as nothing less could cope with this terrible evil. On the spiritual side of the question also the Vyasji dwelt at some length. He ridiculed the idea of a certain priest advocating marriages at 8 and 9, and quoted an array of unimpeachable authorities, shastric, medical, and legal, against that solitary modern instance. The old Vyas was loudly applauded in the course of his speech. His Resolution was seconded by the venerable Pandit Balam Bhatta Shastri. It was supported by Pandit Rama Prasana Acharya, who referred to the evil effects of child-marriages and widowhood on the morals of society. The Acharya observed that the Government was bound, in the interests of society, to have criminal rulings on the subject, based upon shastric rules like the civil law of the Hindus based on the same ground. Such a course would divest the action of every appearance of interference.

The third Resolution, "that this meeting expresses its sense of gratitude to Mr. Malabari for his disinterested labours towards this great cause for the welfare of the Hindu people," was proposed by Pandit Madan Mohan, B.A.,

35

who said that infant marriage was like a cancer, and that instead of allowing it to fester and mortify, it would be the part of wisdom to use the lancet on it. To this extent, the Pandit said, he had been converted to the view that some aid from the Government might be invoked for the timely suppression of the practice. The Resolution was seconded by Pandit Govind Rao Goray. The three Resolutions were then one by one put before the meeting and were carried unanimously.

Before dissolving the Conference the President, Professor Bhattacharya, said he had to make a "confession of faith." He observed that he had been up to yesterday strongly opposed, on principle, to Government help of any kind. But that the previous night he had a long and animated discussion with Mr. Malabari, and in the course of that discussion he had to yield to the voice of reason. On parting Mr. Malabari gave him some papers by the Hon'ble Mr. Ranade and Dewan Bahadur Ragoonath Row, a perusal of which overnight confirmed him in the new faith. The Chairman concluded by saying that though it might be possible for society to reform itself by its own unaided efforts, no one could say *when* such a time would come and that, therefore, for speedy relief it was wise to accept some sort of support from the Government. Pandit Bhattacharya's explanation was listened to with great attention, as he has the confidence of all sections of the community of Allahabad. Towards the formation of the Working Committee only one gentleman hesitated to give his name, as he was not sure as to the desirability of Government action. But at Mr. Malabari's suggestion, that he might co-operate so far as his principle allowed him to do, the gentleman was good enough to agree.

SPEECH AT MATHURA.

On the 25th of February 1886, Mr. Malabari, . . . accompanied by Munshi Baijnath, B.A., of Agra, arrived at Mathura at 7-45 p.m. He was received at the station by Pandit Alopi Prasad, the Munsif, and Babu Dwarka Prasad, Secretary, Mathura Institute and Indian Temperance League, and Vice-President of the Arya Samaj, Mathura.

The party then drove to the house of Munsif Alopi Prasad, where Mr. Malabari stayed over night. Immediately the guests got down the carriage they requested Pandit Alopi Prasad to circulate a notice, which was done accordingly.

Next morning a special meeting of the principal residents of the City and Sudder Bazaar was held at the house of Pandit Alopi Prasad, and it was resolved that a public meeting should be held in the Government High School building at 6-30 in the evening the same day.

In the evening, at the hour fixed, the most enthusiastic and one of the largest meetings ever held was witnessed, consisting of all the Raises and other inhabitants of Mathura, Brindaban, and Mahaban. The hall was full and the verandas and the roads were crowded. Most of the eminent Pandits of the town were present, and among others were seen the following :—

Seth Mangilal, Rais ; Munshi Ram Chandra, Rais ; Pandit Alopi Prasad, Munsif ; Munshi Jaggan Nath, Pleader ; Babu Tarin Charan Sanyal, B.A. ;

Munshi Ganga Prasad; Chobey Gendalal, Pleader; Pandit Sant Lal; Munshi Narayan Das; Pandit Kesho Das; Kuir Hidayaṭ Alikhan, Tehsildar; Babu Vazir Singh, Pleader; Babu Kuir Sein, Postmaster; Babu Rama Nath, Rais; Babu Kali Chand Banerjee; Pandit Baldeo Narain Singh, Rais; Pandit Shamlal; Babu Ram Dial; Raja Udit Narayan Singh, Rais; Pandit Baddri Datta Joshi, Deputy Collector; Pandit Radha Charan Goswami; Babu Atma Ram, B.A., Head Master; Moulvi Abdool Hadi, Pleader; Munshi Ram Narain; Chobey Gordhan Das; Munshi Dwarka Prasad; Munshi Har Prasad; Pandit Radha Keshan, Deputy Collector; Munshi Radhey Prasad, Pleader; Munshi Gulab Chand, Pleader; Babu Narayan Das, Rais; Rao Balwant Singh of Awah; Babu Ram Narain Singh Verma; Moulvi Riazuddin Amjad; Babu Shamlal Chowdhri; Babu Jaggan Nath Khattri; Pandit T. Nath Munshi; Pandit Daya Shankar; Pandit Ambika Prasad; Pandit Radheyal; Swami Swatma Nand Saraswati; Babu Gopal Singh, &c., &c.

Seth Lachhman Dass, the famous Seth of Mathura, was to preside on the occasion, but having been prevented by an engagement in the Temple, and having sent a message of sympathy, Pandit Baddri Datta Joshi, Rais of Kumaun, and Honorary Deputy Collector, Mathura, was voted to the chair.

Munshi Dwarka Prasad acted as Secretary to the meeting.

The worthy Chairman, remarking on the custom of infant marriage, said that it was a matter to be deeply regretted that while a stranger tried so hard to help us, we, interested most in the matter, should sit silent. He then referred to Sati and other practices already put down, and said there was no necessity of putting a check on infant marriage then (even if the custom was prevalent in the days of yore), but the want of suppression is extremely felt now. If the Indians expect any help from the State in this regard the State cannot help us without our doing something and going before the Government. Pandit Baddri Datta dwelt at great length on the various evils arising from infant marriage and then spoke of Mr. Malabari's work in terms of the highest praise.

Mr. Malabari then spoke as follows:—

"Gentlemen of Mathura,—The worthy president has spoken so much and so ably on the subject of infant marriages that there remains very little for me to add. But let me ask you, gentlemen—what do you mean by *Infant Marriage?* I asked the same question to our learned friends at Benares, and the only answer I got was—hanging down of their heads and clapping (which appeared like wringing) of the hands. What meaning do you attach to this impossible combination of words, infant marriage? Is it human language or what? I can understand what is meant by *infant,* which means a human being too young to speak its mind. I can also understand the word *marriage*, being a married man. But I really cannot make out what *infant marriage* means. No other nation on earth uses this expression. Your own sacred books give not a trace of either the idea or the practice of infant marriage. If you were to speak to anyone outside of India about *infant marriage* he would not be able to understand you. Our English friends in India do not realize the full significance of the words. What is marriage? It is either a civil contract, or a sacrament. I prefer the latter interpretation. Well, if marriage is a *sanskar*, how can you put *sanskar*, the most important, the most sacred, the most binding ceremony, on an *infant?* (Cheers.) How dare you put *sanskar* upon a piece of clay? (Renewed cheers.) There is no sense, no religion in such a ceremony. It is the most nonsensical, the most irreligious thing we could do, according to Shastras. If you think about it for a moment you will agree that there can be no such thing in nature as *Infant Marriage*.

And what, again, is a *Virgin Widow?* My venerable friend Ragoonath Row started me the other day with the question——pray what is a Virgin Widow? I repeat the question before you. What is a Virgin Widow? Do you apply the expression to a human being? A *virgin* who is at the same time a *widow !* A *widow* who is also a *virgin* at one and the same time ! What a contradiction in terms ! (Loud cheers.) And what is a *girl-wife,* what is a *boy-husband?* (Cheers.) What, I ask you, gentlemen, is a *girl-mother* and what is a *boy-father?* (Cheers.) What are all these extraordinary beings we have been speaking about? Are they a playing with words or the creations of some deranged intellect, or are they realities? Refer me to a single nation, modern or ancient, who uses or has used such phrases as I have quoted above. (Applause.) Really, there can be no such phenomenon in nature as a *girl-wife* or a *girl-mother,* a *virgin-widow* or an *infant marriage.* And yet, you know that both the ideas and the practices implied by these phrases are by no means uncommon in India. (Cheers.) Just think of the enormity of your unnaturalness—your sin against yourselves, against your country, against Nature and Nature's God. (Loud cheers.) My friends, make up your minds not to live under such conditions any longer. Try to follow the law of Manu ; you have fallen so low by neglecting that law. (Applause.) Don't wait till things mend themselves. (No, no.) Don't wait till somebody else comes to your rescue unasked. Don't wait till all the women of India become educated and independent of you. That time, you take precious care, is never likely to come. If you care to rise as a nation, politically and materially, if you care to be public-spirited citizens, patriots, merchants, masters ; if you care to keep pace with your fortunate Mahomedan and Parsi brethren, give up these evil things in life, to begin with. (Prolonged cheers.) I have nothing more to say to you, gentlemen of Mathura."

The following Resolutions were then passed :—

I.—Proposed by Pandit Radha Charan Goswami, seconded by Pandit B. D. Joshi, and supported by Munshi Jaggan Nath Prasad, and carried unanimously, that "this meeting of the principal inhabitants of Mathura and others, after hearing Mr. Malabari, is decidedly of opinion that Infant Marriage and its attendant evils are a very great obstacle in the way of the general progress of the country, and that concerted action should be taken by the heads of the different sections of the community, in conjunction with Government, to put down this ruinous custom."

II.—Proposed by Pandit Alopi Prasad, seconded by Babu T. C. Sanyal, and supported by Moulvi A. Hadi, and carried unanimously, that "a working Committee, with power to add to their numbers, be formed to take active practical steps in co-operation with Mr. Malabari to carry out the first Resolution, and a working Committee of the representative men of Mathura, with Seth Lachhman Dass as President and Munshi Dwarka Prasad as Secretary, be accordingly formed."

III.—Proposed by Babu Atma Ram, B.A., seconded by Babu Kali Chand Banerji, and supported by Munshi Ram Narain, and carried by all the members with loud cheers, that "this Meeting, whilst expressing their utmost confidence in Mr. Malabari's mission, desire to place on record their sense of deep gratitude to that gentleman, and also to Munshi Baij Nath, B A., for his patriotic interest in awakening public interest in the matter."

36

RAMBLES.

RAMBLES OF A PILGRIM REFORMER.

Travelling has been to me at once a luxury and a torment. Motion was, I believe, the first conscious enjoyment of my infancy. And the love of it has grown with my growth. I love motion above every other amusement, think it a panacea against most evils of mind and body, the very elixir of life. I sometimes get rid of fever and divers other physical ailments, of anxiety and other mental troubles, by putting myself in motion and on short commons. " Starve out thy fever, my son, and make *her* sick of *thee* by constantly moving about." So said my friend Abdul Kadir. Fashionable ladies and gentlemen might follow this golden rule with advantage. Three-fourths of them are always ailing and useless, because they have never studied the philosophy of motion. People must not, of course, over-do the thing, as I do—loving nothing so well as what I hate, and being never so happy as when unhappy. How, otherwise, could rough travelling be a luxury ? Now, as to it being a torment : I have had sixteen different tours, by land and by sea, in the course of the last twelve years, each of them as arduous as man could stand, and not a few of them really perilous. And each one of these campaigns I have had to open in the worst part of the year. The last one was one of the worst. It was ill begun, with the pilgrim himself out of sorts, with his little ones ill, with a most important religious ceremony impending, and with business considerably in arrears. It takes a desperate worker to start on a long tour under such circumstances, and with the sultry October ahead. But now or never—that was the position. The one friend to whom I could leave the work was only then able to relieve the weary, anxious pilgrim. So scattering rupees all round to avert the gathering squall at home, our pilgrim left one evening amidst black looks, disguised for the moment, with a dark cheerless sky overhead. It was with a heavy heart and a faltering tread that the platform was reached ; no man becomes homesick so soon after leaving home.

GAY AHMEDABAD.

Slept off the miseries of parting during night and reached Ahmedabad Station at the usual hour, to find it aglow with life and animation. The platform was decorated with flags and buntings and other idle little vanities, amongst them municipal commissioners, professors, lawyers, police, military and medical officers, merchants and civilians, most of them shaved and scented for the occasion. When an Aryan gets shaved, you see he means to make a day of it. I was rather puzzled by this odd mixture of men, things and nothings. Could they have come all the way from town to see *me*? No, it was only a Mr. Grant Duff, somebody coming from Madras. Pooh! What extravagance for a mere Governor! If it had been for me—but people will never perceive the fitness of things. However, there was some consolation, a balm for my wounded and outraged feelings. Had I not anticipated His Excellency—in fact, taken the wind out of his sail? So the honours of the forenoon were first paid to me, and the poor man from Madras had to make shift with the after-taste of everything. I was received heartily by a medico, a don, a budding bureaucrat, and several of the burghers. I was pressed to make a halt at Ahmedabad for a few days; then asked to stay for a few hours; finally, for half an hour, to see "the Governor and Governess" of Madras. I had met the former some years ago at Dr. Wilson's, I explained, and as for the generous and accomplished "Governess," that was not the time to make her acquaintance. An Aryan then advised me only to "have a look at her," which I most distinctly declined to be guilty of. And before the Special whistled her arrival, I felt an irresistible desire to—run away. This I did without further ceremony, and was soon ensconced in a corner of the Rajputana train.

MR. GRANT DUFF.

Poor Mr. Grant Duff! How they have been worrying him! I know he has not the patience of an angel. I do feel, also, that he thinks himself too knowing to care to know more.

Fatal mistake for a Hakim ! This is partly the cause of his failure. The other cause is the bureaucratic influences in which he has been enveloped. But who was it that threw him into the arms of bureaucracy ? I am afraid it was partly the Press of Madras. Your publicists are at times so exacting, so unreasonable. They began by condemning him for doing what almost all his predecessors had done before him. If they wanted a change, they ought to have suggested it before the new Governor took action. They did not do so ; the Secretaries showed to His Excellency how hollow was the cry of the Press, and H. E. naturally resented what he thought to be injustice. As time went, the ruler and the representatives of the ruled became more and more estranged. The Press attacked the ruler, and the ruler cut the Press. This was exactly what the Secretariat wanted. Then came the Salem and other cases. Here, too, Mr. Grant Duff went wrong from ignorance. But I hold that it was in the power of the Native Press and public to set him right in time. Instead of that, they drove him into a corner by a lavish use of language that could not but be galling to an able but over-sensitive ruler whose first impulse is always to do good in a lordly way. The Press wanted Mr. Grant Duff to release the Salem prisoners at once. He could no more do that than ride the back of the Moon. No constitutional ruler could defy his responsible advisers. He might differ from them now and then, but even that he could not do in every case, notwithstanding that he had right and justice on his side. This is the curse of constitutional government, especially in a country like ours. He is a wise ruler who yields to his colleagues in small matters, so as to prevail upon them on questions of principles. Now, in my opinion, Governors and Viceroys have to concern themselves more with leading principles than with the details of administration. It is best that, speaking broadly, they should do so. They cannot meddle with every paltry matter, nor can they always side with the people, as against the officials—that would make good government altogether impossible. The Press must be sensible enough to put up with human imperfections. It must not take it for granted, that every high official who comes out from England is the natural enemy of this country, and will always band himself with our enemies. The rather, our public writers and leaders of public opinion should welcome the new comer as a friend, give him a fair trial, forbear with him for small errors and eccentricities, taking care to save him from ugly mistakes in policy. In short, they must try to keep him a friend of the people, till they actually find him out to be otherwise. And in most cases, they may be assured, his own impulse will be to side with the people. Our friends seem to have no idea of the mischief caused by ungenerous suspicion and wanton opposition. Because the Governor is an Englishman, therefore he is bound to side with the English Collector or Judge—this is a foolish and a very injurious theory. Why, the two men belong to different castes, and it is only when you withhold your sympathy from the new friend that he is driven to make common cause with the old enemy. Besides, a little civility does not come amiss in dealing with men in authority. It is not the man we respect, but the office. Your mother is, I suppose, your father's wife. But I leave it to you, dear Aryan brother, to realize the enormous difference between calling a woman " my mother" and " my father's wife"!

Poor Mr. Grant Duff!—so poor in his impatience, his infallible wisdom, and utter want of adaptability! I expected him to return home one of the most honoured Englishmen who ever came to India. The man who knows Europe, and perhaps other parts of the civilised world, more intimately than any other English politician of the day, who can boast a rich and mellow scholarship, who is generally actuated by high aims, who is the son and disciple of an impartial historian and the god-son of one of the best English rulers India has been blessed with, has confessedly failed to manage the affairs of a presidency which any Collector of average ability could handle with credit to himself and lasting advan-

tage to the subjects ! O it is grievous. But the fault seems
to be threefold, and the blame must be equally divided thus—
one-third to the credit (or discredit) of the Right Honourable Mr. Elphinstone Grant Duff, one-third to the credit of
the "baneful bureaucracy," and one-third to the credit of
Gentoo journalism.

RECRUITING IN INDIA.

Had a hearty breakfast in the train—a Parsi breakfast—before leaving Ahmedabad, as between there and Umbala, I
would have to be content with biscuit, fruit, tea, and lemon.
I do not remember having entered a refreshment-room save
under the protecting shadow of a Parsi. Thus protected I
must have more than once sneaked in and out after fortifying
the inner man or making a few purchases. But as a general
rule, it appears to be more agreeable to go on light-stomached.

Among my fellow-passengers I had the pleasure of meeting
a Subedar-major, or some such thing, who was on a recruiting
trip. He was a fine soldier, a Mahomedan, who had long been
stationed at Surat. We became friends very soon, and the
Subedar treated me to a long narrative of his services. His
English was tediously slow, so I broke in Hindustani, which
encouraged him to spin the yarn to the full length. The
account was by no means uninteresting, in some parts it had a
thrilling interest, even for a lover of peace-at-any-price; only
the dates of the famous battles he had fought did not tally
with dates given in history books. But the Subedar was not
a B.A., as he confessed, and my own chronological lore being
extremely limited and uncertain, he had it pretty much his
own way in fixing dates. After a very long talk about the
pay of Natives and Europeans respectively, the relations
subsisting between the two, &c., I broached the subject of
recruiting, and asked how he managed the business. He spoke
of it in a roundabout way, which showed that he was not at
all proud of the work he had to do. I am afraid recruiting is
still a very unsatisfactory business in India, so I philosophised,

and gave him to understand that no patriotic recruiting-
sergeant should enlist a married man, the only son of a family,
or a young man engaged in agriculture or other useful work.
" We would have none to enlist in that case, save widows,"
put in the Subedar sharply. "I do not care," I replied, and
then launched out, like a rabid reformer, upon the injustice
of wholesale enlistment, telling him that even the Prophet and
the Khalifs were against such conscription, and otherwise
working upon his patriotic and superstitious feelings. The
Subedar admitted that he did not like the work, but was an
unwilling agent.

At Abu he sent for his little son, from the mother, who was
in the women's carriage. It was an uncommonly pretty little
fellow, with a delicately chiselled mouth and lovely eyes. He
was suffering from fever and was restless. I gave him a dose
of aconite, put him to bed on my own *asbab*,* and hoped I
would relieve him of his little trouble before parting at
Ajmere. The boy soon went to sleep; the father was very
grateful. "He is my only child, all the rest died young, they
did not grow to be five years old," so saying the soldier
passed the back of his hand across his eyes, thinking, may be,
about the fate of the only hope left to him. Seizing this
opportunity, I returned to the subject of recruiting, though
it was rather mean to do so. But the fakir-reformer must
do his duty. "How many parents have to grieve even more
than you, when they are deprived of their grown-up sons, the
mainstay of the house? My friend, let us think of others, just
as we think of ourselves." The Subedar appeared to be
very shaky. His son and heir woke up soon after, perspiring
like a little whale, and looking decidedly less seedy than he
did an hour ago. I dosed him again, and set him free to play
about in the carriage. The father's gratitude knew no bounds.
And that brings us to

HOMŒOPATHY.

It was about seven years ago that I was first drawn to this
truly scientific system. I was put in the way by the wife of

---
* Kit.

an English officer. At first I was a sceptic, and when the lady spoke very earnestly, I replied, "How can these infinitesimal globules and pilules, attenuated out of all strength, work upon a young elephant like myself?" She was very angry, and sent me a batch of papers and things to study. These set me thinking about the matter seriously. A few months later I was snatched from the jaws of Death by a homœopath at Wadwan. What wonder that I became a convert, and a thorough-going homœopath? To-day I would prefer to be killed under homœopathic treatment, than be cured by the allopath. The new system, which is really the old and the true one, has a brilliant future in the East, and I would advise European or American homœopaths in want of practice to rough it for a few years in India. I am glad homœopathy is already becoming popular in Bengal and Bombay. The advantages it offers are manifold, though in rapidly destructive diseases and in surgery I am not quite sure about its superiority. The cures it effects in nervous and similar diseases are marvellous. The system has its enemies, but these are soon apt to turn into its best friends—all save those who are guilty of what Akhlak-i-Jalali calls *Compound Ignorance*.

IGNORANCE.

There are two kinds of Ignorance that the reformer has to encounter—Simple Ignorance and Compound Ignorance. Simple Ignorance is not a sin, and every man born of woman is subject to it. It can be remedied; in fact, it is an evil carrying its own remedy. The man who suffers from Simple Ignorance knows that he is ignorant; that is, he knows that he does not know a certain thing. And this fact of his knowing that he does not know such and such a thing, will stimulate curiosity and ultimately bring him acquainted with the object of his inquiry. But Compound Ignorance is a sin and a vile disease. I believe it is mostly incurable. Compound Ignorance differs from Simple Ignorance in that whereas the latter knows what it does not know, the former knows not what it knows not. It is, indeed, a hopeless case when a man says he does not like such and such a thing, without assigning an intelligent reason for his dislike, that is, a reason based on actual, personal, or at any rate, credible human experience. We must give up such a man for a mule. I mean no disrespect towards a most deserving class of men ; but those of our "educated" young Hindu friends who say they dislike social agitation because they dislike it, will have to be classed amongst those bit by the intellectual or rather spiritual disease, Compound Ignorance. The man who rejects everything new, simply because it is new, is scarcely fit himself to eat rejected straw. For even a mule will prefer an allowance of new mown hay to his stale old provender. He will smell both, and prefer that which smells sweet. The mule is, therefore, a more promising pupil than the man who foolishly turns away from a new thing on the score of its being new.

Our recruiting Subedar went out at Ajmere about midnight, with his sprightly little hopeful by his side, after elaborate leave-taking, *Khuda hafiz*, and hand-shaking, followed by the wife who returned her thanks from behind the veil.

A MISSIONARY AND HIS WORK.

Reached Delhi Station next evening, quite fagged. Porter-boy introduced himself as old acquaintance and asked if he should fetch the usual seer of boiling milk. He brought it later on in an earthen pot. Milk turned out stale and sour. It was our New Year's Day. I was anxious to drink to the health of the year that had just set in, and finding nothing else handy, took a bottle of iced ginger ale. From hot milk to cold ginger ale is an abrupt transition ; but neither comes amiss to a wanderer who can face the extremes of cold and heat with equal composure. Met my old friend, the Jeypur Missionary, and had a bellyful of talk with him. One day, I hope to give an account of Jeypur after Maharaja Ramsing's death. My friend the Missionary was going up to one of the hill stations to recruit his health. He had a companion with him, also on the sick list. They looked very poorly, but hoped to be all right in about a month's time, what with complete rest, enlivened by a Hindustani translation of the Revised Bible. I do not quite like the Revised Bible. It may be more correct, and so on, but the antique grace and beauty of expression which lent such an impressiveness to the Book of books, seems to have become lost in modern phraseology. This pious vandalism at least might have been avoided. But the " zealous" Christian is perhaps the most destructive among reformers-militant. My Jeypur friend is not a zealous official reformer. Does he indulge in the nasal twang ? " Perhaps he do, perhaps he don't." But I like him much. He is working hard for his flock, and besides his sacred mission, he attends to what I may describe as the mediæval literature of the province under his charge. About five years ago he showed me part of his literary work. I urged him to carry it through. But alas ! he seems to have had scanty encouragement. You see he is not a Political Agent, nor is he a somebody of somebody whom everybody finds it useful to oblige. The Government of India might well support such a worker. The Jeypur Durbar, too, is bound to co-operate with him ; if it don't do its duty I trust some Kattywar prince on our side will send him help. It is likely to prove a good investment. Further particulars on application. While engaged in these labours, I wish my Missionary friend wrote of a life of Dadu. It would be a valuable contribution to a literature very faintly representing the realities of a great national upheaval. Why will not some of our graduates describe the struggles and triumphs of Nanak, Dadu, Kabir, Chaytanya, Tukaram, Sahajanand and others ? Our Hindu reformers do not seem to be aware that Dadu scouted the idea of marrying his daughter even at 16. She must become fully developed physically, morally and spiritually, before she undertook the serious responsibilities appertaining to a wife and mother. Happy daughter ! Thrice blessed in the three relations of life !

38

THE PULL-UP.

Got out at Umbala early in the morning. Made friends with Parsi manager of the Refreshment Room, and had breakfast, hot, savoury and homelike. Arranged for a rush to the hill the same evening, though feeling very queer all over the body. But what use halting? I would rather die at a stretch than by slow torture. Could not afford special phaeton. Started about 10 P.M. for Kalka, reaching there about 4 A.M. greeted by a brisk shower. Left Kalka in about an hour, after tea and toast, and with a touch of fever and headache. Tumbled out at the foot of Simla Bazar about 5 P.M. with a feeling of all-goneness in back and limbs and of dislocation of neck and knee joints. Marched up to Parsi friend's with a cheerful, nothing-has-happened exterior, and thence taken to the Hotel. No room there; must make the best of the reading-room on the ground-floor. Took out medicine chest and threatened to be very ill if not at once given a better room. Translated to the top-floor directly; clean and cozy. Had light supper, pleasant enough, only every dish smelt suspiciously of lard. Turned in at 10, not, however, before despatching a couple of notes to announce arrival. Slept like an honest man, a very hopeful sign. But on getting up in the morning felt a freezing sensation in the stomach. Oh demoralized beast of a stomach! Hast thou no gratitude? The more I respect thy infirmities, the more peevish and unreasonable thou growest. Must walk thee into good humour. Had a long tramp beyond Chota Simla. Felt uneasy all day. Hotel fare very trying—roast and grill and boil, and boil and grill and roast—every dish so heavy! And that inevitable lard—in pudding, in custard, in pie—I almost felt it in tea or coffee itself. Stomach quite in a revolt. Hard work all next day. Invitation to dinner. "I am quite alone," wrote mine host temptingly. Thankfully accepted a cup of tea and asked for a long talk. Kept the appointment, had tea and canned fruit and biscuit. We mingled tears over the widow and the infant wife till 10 P.M. Returned to Hotel and had a good tramp in the room before going to bed. Next morning the first thing was a visit from the steward-ess—"Please don't tramp so, the Giniral under yer room is roarin' like a lion and swarin' that the food is all stale and cold, and he is quarrelin' with me and the sarvants. Please don't tramp with yer boots. I know I should not spake to a gintleman. But he is an old lodger. And you can order kaunji, if you don't like our things; shall I send you some tapioca?", &c., &c. From that day had to walk in the room in socks—but the kanji was good, and our pilgrim was thank-ful. The feverishness, however, went on increasing; the cramp in the stomach and the nausea became troublesome. Had to work very hard three or four days. Rest of the two weeks taken up in calls and sight-seeing. Could not walk much and had to use jinrikhsha. So thoroughly ashamed of it! Why don't they allow regular gharis now? The roads are broad enough. The horses are said to be restive, and it is so cruel to force a man to use jamphan or jinrikhsha.

DINING OUT.

More invitations to breakfasts and dinners. Declined all with thanks. Haven't dined at an English friend's these seven or eight years. You must be a free man to do so, that is free in spirit. And you must be up to all conventionalities, the bowing and the smiling to order, and the laughing over stale jokes. And you must always say " Yes, thank you " to the ladies, and " no " to nobody. And worse still, you must seem to enjoy every dish and every glass, must never mind the time that is consumed in tittle-tattle with strangers, whom you must treat as dear old friends. All this is too much for a heathen like myself, short-tempered, plain in dress and address, and miserably lacking in " small morals."

Went to tea with a particular friend, who had asked me to breakfast. " How are you, how do you do Mr.——, keep your turban on, it is rather chill this morning."

"Thank you, I am quite well," I replied, as I entered the room, smothering a cry of anguish on finding strangers at table. "Yes, really, you are looking remarkably well," replied mine host. Wretched hypocrite to "look remarkably well" with the fever burning itself into your very bones! But what could a fellow say in reply to a friendly greeting? He can't reply—" Hang you, I am unwell." As a gentleman, he is expected to tell a fib—that homage of hypocrisy is due to Mrs. Grundy. No man has a right to be a marjoy at table, or in the drawing-room, no matter what his sufferings. And that is why I do not join dinner parties, or any other parties, for that matter, where social amenities have to be cultivated at any risk. The only meal I enjoyed at Simla was a picnic at Mashowbra in Mr. Paliti's bungalow. It was a genuine picnic, squatting like Turks, picking, tearing, biting like savages, and drinking like—well not exactly like whales. We ate everything, down to raw onion, and then made a descent to the hollow of Seepi. It was a good day's work.

THAT WRETCHED NIGHT.

Walk, walk, walk! work, work, work! how could the fever abate? Fairly upset one evening by a paragraph in the *Indian Spectator* condemning Mr. Justice Pinhey's decision in the matter of restitution of conjugal rights sought by poor Dadaji. Good gracious!—that my own paper, of all others, should oppose the judgment! Read the paragraph again and again, and again and again did a cold shiver pass through the heart. Could it be done by an enemy? No, that was impossible. True, the para. was from a correspondent, but still, what a sell! No sleep till 11 that night. The brain on fire all the while. How shall I meet the eye of the world? But let me sleep over it—now lying on the left side, now on the right, now on the back; now with the pillow in, now with the pillow out, now with the head tied with a wet handkerchief, the eyes firmly closed and the ears stuffed with the finger ends to keep out the sight and sound of public ridicule. But no sleep till one. I must prepare a telegram discarding the correspondent. It took more than an hour, but brought sensible relief. Took a draught of cold water and turned in once more to enjoy a few blessed winks.

A WORD ABOUT SIMLA.

Simla is beautiful to walk about in, especially mornings and evenings; you see innocent health all around, bent upon enjoying the hour. The faces are so lively, and with such a glow of keen relish! Oh the lovely faces, still lovelier dimples, and loveliest smiles of all, offering welcome to the weary stranger! Their happiness is reflected in their eyes, and they spread sunshine up hill and down dell, wherever they are. Dear little rosebuds in the garden of life! May heaven shield them from the breath of the wily serpent!

The *genus* male among the European population of Simla did not strike me as particularly attractive. That may be because I am not a woman. As to the indigenous population, the Punjaubis are a fine race, tall and shapely, so are most of the hill tribes. But the people coming from the interior are generally broad, loose and baggy, with a flat smutty face, relieved by a dash of the Mongolian cheekbone. Their vocabulary seems to be fully of ag-ag-mag-ag-mag-mag-gag-ag-gag-gag-gag. Hang their everlasting gutturals and gunpowder looks! The women folk are a trifle more look-at-able, especially as they march past, carrying planks of wood across shoulders in a right martial style. I have not been able to hear one of these pahari women sing. But they seem to smoke liberally instead. No Professor of Chemistry smokes with such energy.

Amongst several other attractions of Simla may be mentioned its numerous smells. I was not long enough at the station to be able to count the number, or to distinguish one from another. But to the best of my knowledge and belief the smells of Simla are very near reaching the number fixed by Coleridge. This is mainly due to over-population, want of water, bad habits of the bazar people and the proverbial wickedness of the official classes. The first three are, I believe, preventable causes. I have nothing to say against the Municipal Secretary, except that he met me very often during my rambles, so often indeed that I sometimes felt he was dogging my steps, although I tried hard to keep out of his way. He has greyish eyes, sometimes laughing, sometimes scolding; and the tip of his nose is always rosy. I wish every Municipality had such an energetic Secretary.

Left Simla half a week later than the time fixed, hoping by that time the official swells on visit would have gone home. But Mr. Grant Duff and party seem to have left on the same day. They overtook us beyond Kalka, driving past in rickety old carriages, some of them dragged by broken-winded beasts, leaving behind nothing more substantial than clouds of dust. We counted 11 carriages as we stood by, making way for the gubernatorial procession. It took nearly three-quarters of an hour for the 11 carriages to drive past. Some of the animals seemed to be so homesick that vigorous stimulants were necessary to make them move. Or perhaps they did not feel honourably employed. What a difference between this procession and the other that passed by our house at Bombay last year, headed by the carriage containing Lord Ripon! The horses in the latter case behaved like gentlemen born and bred. Horses are sometimes better gentlemen than human beings, and have a more correct judgment either than journalists or bureaucrats.

DINNER AND DEATH.

Reached Umbala Station about 8 P.M., after a rough, hot fatiguing journey, shifting positions in the mail van every five minutes. Staggered up to the Manager's private kholi * at the Refreshment room, faint with hunger and thirst. "The more you nourish an unsound body, the more it increaseth in ailment"—so says Akhlak-i-Jalali. I have found this true to the letter, especially while travelling. My friend the Manager came up and whispered—" Will you pardon my absence for half an hour? The Governor of Madras is at dinner. In

---

* Room.

the meantime please make yourself comfortable in this chair and order whatever you want." "Oh well," replied the foolish pilgrim in a huff, if it is to be the Governor first, I have no orders to give; I only want rest till the Lahore train comes in." Manager did not wait to hear. As I sat in the easy chair, half dozing under the influence of fever, I could not but reflect upon the vanity of human wishes. My rich Parsi dinner, of which I had conjured up so many and such bright visions, all vanished in an instant! When will the Governor and his colony of followers have dined? Ah! Mr. Grant Duff, you have been fully avenged. Bitterly do I repent me of my triumph at Ahmedabad. In the room, partially darkened to give relief to the eyes, I saw the servants moving stealthily about with dishes and things. They were, of course, dressed in white. But the clothes seemed to have been borrowed from the dhobi, some of them being too short for the wearers, others too long. The sight of the latter curdled my blood for a moment, they appeared so very like Parsi corpse-bearers. The darkened kholi, the subdued bustle in the refreshment room, broken by whispers, the hush and *chip chip* * over the Station platform, and the white, loose, unironed dress of some of the waiters—all these had a very disquieting effect on my nerves, already unstrung. I could not help transforming the whole scene to a Parsi house in which a patient was dying! It is a mistake dressing these men all in white. Where the dress is too short, it makes the figure ludicrous. If too long, it positively makes one look like the ghastly nasa-salar.† White is the emblem of purity and solemn grace. Such a dress for table servants seems to be so out of place, wanting in taste as well as natural fitness. At any rate, I think it ought to be relieved by streaks of red.

LAHORE.

Left for Lahore by the up train and reached there in the morning. A number of friends on the station. Found on inquiry that Naidu's Hotel, which had been specially recom-

---

* "Be quiet, be quiet."
† A Parsi corpse-bearer.

mended to me at Simla, would not be so quiet a place as I should wish. And there being no Dak bungalow near about the town, was prevailed upon to go to a Mahomedan hotel, which proved quite a failure. But the four days' stay was very successful from a business point of view, though unfortunately the fever became developed, and the hands began to be blistered by painful eruptions. Saw several leading Punjaubis, and requested my friend, Babu Navin Chandra Rai, to arrange for a quiet meeting with these gentlemen. Now Mr. Rai is a whole-hearted, thorough-going man, and before I was aware of it, he and his friends convened a public meeting under the auspices of half-a-dozen different Societies and Associations. This was cruel kindness in my present state of health. But there was no backing out after the invitations had been issued. Everything, happily, went off well that evening, and the two or three hours of talk did me good for the time, no matter how serious the reaction. The Punjaubi Hindus are a race of men to be proud of—free, open and manly. They do not begin with a stranger in suspicion, as most Hindus and not a few Englishmen do. This characteristic is due, I believe, to Mahomedan associations. The Hindus look and talk like Mahomedans, and are socially very agreeable, though by no means wanting in dignity. Judging from several circumstances, the Hindus of the Punjaub seem to me to be the true Aryas, descendants of the first emigrants from Central Asia. Many of their notabilities whom I saw looked like Parsi priests. Not only was their appearance so prepossessing, especially of the Sikhs, but even in their tones and general address, habits, modes of wearing the hair, &c., they reminded me of the better class of Parsi Mubeds. I was really sorry to leave the capital of the Punjaub so soon. This was the second time I had to hurry back without a careful study of men and things.

AMRITSAR.

Left one morning for Meerut and halted for a few hours at Amritsar. Visited the Sikh temple in the evening. Less attractive than when I saw it about six years ago. There is no life in Sikhism as it is practised inside. It is all dead formality. The essence of the new faith seems to be vitiated, and the unity of the central idea is being broken up into castes. It is a grievous misfortune. But wherever I go I find that a reformed Hindu creed does not last long. There is a hidden craving for the idolatrous which the Hindus—I mean the masses—can never be made to shake off. They relapse so readily after purification. Will the Brahma Samaj and the Arya Samaj be ever able to wean the heart of the people from traditional object-worship? Will Christianity have any influence on this immense mass of superstition? God alone knows—to me the outlook is not very hopeful. All the greater reason for united action on the part of the spiritual leaders of the people. On my way to the temple, I saw the Ramleela or some other ceremony of the Hindus— a very saddening sight! Old and young seemed to take delight in hideous disguises and other tomfooleries. Even in its artistic effect the thing was an utter failure. It was the grand annual fair, I suppose. To a friend of the people no sight could be so sickening. Happily, women did not seem to take part in the affair. But the men, some of them presumably very respectable, made asses of themselves in a most liberal manner, and the narrow streets, crowded to suffocation, emitted an odour which would baffle any Chemical Analyser to describe.

MEERUT.

Telegraphed to Meerut friend, and started that same evening. Reached there about noon next day, the eruptions in the meantime spreading themselves on the face and neck. No one to receive me at the station. Felt very faint. A Hindu gentleman offered the shelter of his house, without knowing me—Mr. Ganga Saran, Sub-Judge at Saharanpur. I had the pleasure of his acquaintance during my stay at Meerut, and now count him amongst my worthiest co-adjutors. I requested him to take me to Babu S. K. Chatterji's. Took time to

39

trace him, as he had left the old house. Found the new one at last, but mine host was not in. Left the kit at his house, and went in search of the owner. Fever very distressing, and heat of the. noon-day sun no less so. Spotted Mr. Chatterji after all. He had received neither the telegram nor the letter; was so sorry. Sent for the station doctor, first thing. Doctor himself laid up with fever. Sent for a private practitioner. After half an hour's examination, doctor looked very grave. It was malarial fever, and would take time to be coped with. The spleen also seemed to be affected. Absolute rest essential. Quinine must be taken anyhow, and some mixture also. Sent six pills of quinine, each large enough to serve an elephant. Swallowed the vile stuff regularly. Fever appeared to be checked, but in the morning I found the eyes almost blind with heat and the ears deaf and covered over with red spots. Had many calls from Bengali and Meerut friends. A most encouraging meeting at the house of Mr. Prahlad Sing; long discussion with two venerable Pandits. The meeting dealt with our pilgrim very generously. This proved an effective febrifuge so far. Started next morning for Delhi in company of Messrs. Raghobir Sarma and Prahlad Sing, the two leading pleaders. Had an excellent breakfast at Mr. Raghobir Sarma's before we left Meerut. Wish I had strength enough to do justice to it. Mr. Chatterji, too, was ever kind and attentive. It is curious, but I always like the Bengali better out of Bengal than in. One day I may explain the why and wherefore of it. I hope also to introduce to the Bombay public the notables of Lahore, Meerut, and elsewhere, whom I had the pleasure of meeting. They are gentlemen worth knowing.

DELHI.

Reached Delhi about 2 P.M. and was taken in hand by my friend Mr. Madan Gopal, the only M.A. in the province and leader of the Native Bar. Quite stricken down by fever. Doctor examined the patient carefully; he was luckily a homœopath. He thought it was eruptive fever, somewhat of the nature of scarlet fever; that there were some symptoms

of gastric derangement, that the blood had become poisoned.
Rhus tox. was the only remedy, and I was trying it. He gave
it in tincture and for application. Night restless. Had a
preliminary meeting next morning, which did not end very
satisfactorily, though the amount of sympathy from local
reformers was large enough to drown myself in. Will have
to take Delhi by storm one day. Doctor called again—no
relief. He could not make out what it was really. But it
was a malignant form of fever, and the best remedy was to
return home immediately. Offered to pay him his own price
if he set me up in a couple of days, only so far as to enable me
to carry out my programme—Cawnpore, Lucknow, Allahabad,
Bareilly, Benares and Agra. "I value your life more.
Please go away early to-morrow." That was the final verdict.
Mr. Madan Gopal exceedingly kind, and as he did not know
my state exactly, took me about for long drives both days
I was with him. In ordinary health I would have immensely
enjoyed his hospitality. As it was, I think I made him and
friends miserable—the only consideration which made me
oh ! so wretched. That I should not be able to break bread
with Hindu friends ! But little did they know what an effort
it was to move the limbs or even the tongue. Witnessed the
Ramleela procession that evening. Much better every way
than the discreditable *fiasco* at Amritsar. The Delhi procession was somewhat imposing. But there was not much in
it that could be called really artistic. In a word, the thing was
wanting in good management. We Indians are very poor
organizers. This is largely due to mutual jealousy. The
Hindus of Delhi are a fairly united body, but I suspect they
do not like any one of them in particular to take the shine out
of them. Foolish creatures ! Then, again, the Hindus and
the Mahomedans seldom pull on well, though nowhere in
India do the two races appear so like each other. This is
owing to the Cow Question. I am tempted here to give the
oracular opinion that he who solves this vexed Cow Question
will be known to generations as "a bull amongst men "
(Sanskrit phrase). I sometimes feel I could settle the question

with a jury of Hindu and Mahomedan friends, and thus establish my claim to the bovine distinction. Will some honest Hindu reformers relieve me of the present engagement?

DELHI—ITS DARK SIDE.

I have seen Delhi thrice in all. The first visit was uneventful. But the second, in 1880, has left some very vivid impressions on my mind. I found Delhi more extensive and populous than Agra, also more comfortable on the whole as regards climate. The sights, too, were very attractive to me, though scarcely to be compared with the best sights of the old capital of the Moghuls. I remember having sent for a barber on arriving at the hotel, with whose help, and of the khansama, I drew up a programme. The programme was found by no means to be dull in carrying out. On the contrary, in some parts it was very exciting—my visit to a Turkish Bath, or *hamam*, for instance. I remember a wiry old man accosting me one evening, and expatiating on the luxuries of a Delhi bath. He did not care for money. He belonged to a noble race, was the grandson of a celebrated physician. Times had changed with him. But still he was not so anxious to be paid for the bath as other fellows were. " Give me a trial, and you will know for the first time what a luxury this *gosal** is." After further conversation I said I would call in the morning. He thought it would be better if I went that evening; it would be a moonlit night and his best hands would be in attendance. But I preferred the morning. So he went away salaaming elaborately, and promising to call in the morning. This he did. We went to the *hamam* about 9 A.M. I was very pleased with the construction, and the uses of the different receptacles, as he explained them. The pavement was beautiful marble. After inspecting the room, I asked to be left to myself for bath. " That is not the way, janab," he explained, " your honour will be bathed by others. Shall it be men or women, one or more than one?" I now began to understand this *hamam-gosal* business and was very

* Persian word for ' bath.'

glad it was morning instead of the night. So I replied
cheerily to the handsome little tempter—" I am rather a
grown-up child, as you observe, and it will be hard for a man,
much more for a woman, to wash me, put me to bed, and rock
me to sleep, as you most generously propose. Don't you know
that we Parsees do not observe your zenana system?" "I am
lachar,"* he replied, smiling, "but there can be no bath without shampooing, *aur jatjatka hunar*; besides I have already
hired a Kashmiri woman for the purpose." It was no use
quarrelling, because I felt sure the man was in league with our
hotel servant, and I also knew the case was not fit for a policeman. Nor would it do to show the least confusion. So I
proposed that the syren he had engaged should sing outside
the room, while I took my bath. " In that case have her
brother to bathe and shampoo you," he suggested. I agreed,
to cut the matter short. The bath was really worth the money,
the shampooing was also good. The pressure on, and stretching of, limbs, was sometimes violent. But what would I not
suffer in the cause of science? The passes the man made
across my eyes and forehead were, however, mere tricks. The
singing in the room outside was also getting on, and so far as I
could catch the refrain, it appealed to the lover whose *love*
had been *fasting*, &c., &c. After the bath I came out and
was shown a book in which visitors had recorded their
experiences of the bath—what the old man, no doubt,
regarded as certificates of character. Some of these certificates were ticklish to a degree. But the hot bath had
made me quite a proof against all such devilries. (My son,
never despise a bath. When your flesh is in revolt, have
a good hot bath. Water is the best purifier of body and soul
diseased.) I paid the Mussulman tempter handsomely,
though he deserved something other than kindness. But
it was a narrow escape, and I wished to mark my sense
of thankfulness. Visitors to Delhi would do well to avoid
the *hamams*, because I was told that the one I had been to,
was the most respectable and that its owner was really a man

---
* Helpless.

of much social consideration. What a life for such a man! They say there are many such in Delhi, scions of a noble race, reduced to hopeless destitution—some of them recipients of Government pensions. The pensions range from Rs. 5 to Rs. 20 or so a month; and for the survivors of noble families they have to be somehow supplemented. Surely, Government might open some other career to the unhappy men and women. It is true that they have no claim upon the generosity of the British, the latter having suffered not a little at the hands of their forefathers. Nor can Government justly divert the general revenues of the country to the relief of special classes. But still it is not possible to save a few families from gradual extinction. The poverty of some of the old Mahomedan houses of Delhi is indeed something phenomenal. And what is worse is, they seem to be too proud to work. Mahomedan gentlemen, heirs of a race renowned in their day, are found attired in rags, and Mahomedan *ladies* may be seen even to-day passing through the streets and lanes, shrouded in the thickest and dirtiest of cloth, too proud to beg openly, and yet too poor to keep body and soul together. This state of things is a reproach to the Mahomedan princes and chiefs in India; their co-religionists have many qualities to commend them to the sympathy even of strangers. They are patient, devout, self-sacrificing, and not a few of them possess a sense of honour very rare even amongst their betters. And in ready ingenuity, be it in art or literature, they are probably unsurpassed, in India at any rate.

Amongst the people at large the begging nuisance is very common; and there is probably more of incurable disease here than I have seen elsewhere. With this evil of mendicity there is the other evil; which shall be nameless. Houses of ill-fame face several of the mosques; and you can any day see the pious Mohla, * on one side, reciting prayers with his flock, and on the other side, those Peris of Peristan luring spellbound country swains with the help of rouge and borrowed tresses. I have myself been at times furiously oggled by some

* Priest.

of these artful ones, as I stood to witness the devotions on the top of a musjid. And every time I received their horrid attentions, I felt sure I was mistaken for an Inspector of Police, or a Constable, or a medical man under the C. D. Act.

Left Delhi in the morning with quite a dispensary of drugs in the carriage. Passed the whole time almost on the back, as it was impossible to sit up much or to lie on either side. Had to keep hands, face, neck and ears constantly under cold bandages. It was a gloomy return home, and the pilgrim sometimes felt very like going off. But he has been pulled through—which means that a good deal of work is still reserved for him. Lucky mortal!

NEGLECTING A MILCH COW.

This time I left Bombay in search of fresh information for my "Gujarat and the Gujaratis." The third edition was promised to subscribers in the beginning of 1884, but I have had no breathing time all these months. What with feeble health, anxieties, and work hard and incessant enough to tax the strength of twenty men, the wonder is I have survived to spin this traveller's tale. But I fancy I have had no leisure to die; for lying ill, making a will and doing the rest of it, is, after all, a question of leisure. Well, after several ineffectual efforts, I did go out to Gujarat last month in order to collect materials from the Native States, as suggested by a friend in England. "Gujarat and the Gujaratis" has proved a good investment. For nearly four years I have found it more remunerative than the Kaiser-i-Hind or the Ripon or any other gold mine which was to have enriched all Bombay. My books have been to me a mine of gold. I do not care how they read, but they *sell*, which is the main thing. And they seldom need advertising. So off I start one day for Gujarat. Scarcely, however, do I reach the first Native State when I am asked to go off to Agra on public duty.

It was a struggle, short but very sharp. I pushed on to Ahmedabad with closed eyes, and once beyond Palanpur, forgot everything in the contemplation of the beauties of——Infant Marriage and Enforced Widowhood.

AGRA—ITS SOCIAL POLITICS.

Reached Agra full speed and put up at the Kala-Mahal with friend Baij Nath Munsiff. Council of War met the same evening. "Please say nothing about widow marriage in the North-West Provinces," said one of the warriors. "That would be awkward," I complained, "am I not pledged to both questions?" "Yes," replied warrior No. 2, "but your object is to do good; we know what good you could safely attempt to do at Agra and what harm you would do by attempting further. You want us all to be practical. Kindly be practical yourself. Do not talk of widow marriage." "I may not mention it prominently," I replied, "but talking of infant marriage I cannot absolutely ignore the allied subject." Then said warrior No. 3, "*janab*, the world is governed by words. There is something in the word *beva* (widow marriage) which our people don't like. The minute you utter the word, they will take you for a maniac and run away. You may speak about widow marriage elsewhere. But so far as Agra is concerned, let me warn you, Sir." The choice lay evidently between doing *something* and doing *nothing*. I never take long to decide. After a minute's consultation with Mr. Baij Nath I surrendered at discretion. And this I did without much self-reproach, as I knew that compulsory widowhood is not so fashionable in Northern India as in the priest-ridden parts, nor the condition of the girl widow so utterly desolate. But is not the number of Hindu widows in the N.-W. Provinces larger to-day than it was, say, 15 years ago?

"Now about the public meeting," began Mr. Baij Nath. "Surely, you have not called me all the way from Bombay to make a speech?" I asked, half frightened at the idea.

"Yes, of course," he replied with the assurance of a friend. " You will have to kick up a row at Agra; that is the only way." " But I am going to do nothing more than submit my proposals, you had better do the speechifying yourselves." " Oh, Sir, you will address the meeting, and excite the people and carry the resolutions," he retorted with a glitter in his eyes. The other Councillors sided with Mr. Baij Nath. I then spoke to them seriously, and when I speak seriously I generally carry the point. But this time there was a packed opposition. I submitted that speech-making was not in my line, but was assured that nothing was impossible to me, &c. At last I said, " No, anything but that." " Now look here, Sir," rejoined Mr. Baij Nath; "let us be plain and practical. Have you not come here to make some capital out of us?" " Yes," I admitted readily. " Then are we not justified in making some capital out of your visit?" he asked. " You are, my friend." I allowed, feeling anything but friendly towards mine host. Public meeting settled upon. Council broke up about 10 P.M.

A WHOLE MAN *and* A FRACTION OF A MAN.

Drove out to the Taj in the morning with Mr. Baij Nath. Met Mr. Smith, the Gardener. Could not help admiring at a glance his appearance and intelligence. Tall, well-built, handsome, in green old age, keen in appreciation,—not only a gardener, but also a student, and a politician, with an eye for almost everything that is beautiful in nature and in art, and familiar with the outlines of modern science. This is Mr. Smith, the Taj Gardener. He discussed the social topic with us for a few minutes, then drew us into his favourite subjects, arboriculture and landscape, then told us something about the books he had been recently reading and finally passed on to politics. He spoke about the situation in Ireland, about Mr. Parnell, and Mr. Gladstone, showing how he feared the Premier was halting between principle and expediency. Then he spoke of the politics of Queen Anne's

40

times and of the glorious days of Cromwell winding up with —— "upon my word I cannot see what is going to happen this time." As I strolled about with Mr. Smith, listening to his shrewd intelligent remarks on things generally, I confess I felt humbled to the dust. What was I, a "leading journalist," a "thinker," a "patriot," and a heap of other things, as the newspapers describe me, before this simple English gardener? I have been sometimes addressed with two, and sometimes, with three letters after my name, also as Town Councillor, and so on. An eminent Civilian the other day pointed me out as a likely Member for the Secretary of State's Council. About four years ago I narrowly escaped quarrelling with my old friend Colonel Waller by telling him I was nothing at all. Happening to be under his roof for a night I asked Colonel Waller how he had obtained his V.C. He spoke to me about his Central Indian campaigns, and then asked how I had smuggled myself into the cerements of a C.I.E., (in poor Ali Baba's style) at so early an age. I told Colonel Waller there was some mistake. But he laughed knowingly. He then asked if the Town Council gave me about a couple of hundred for pocket money. I again pleaded " not guilty," at which the gallant Colonel was fairly roused. " What,— you are not going to tell me you ain't a Member of the Town Council, the Corporation, and all that? I have read your name in the reports." I assured him I was an honest man, at which he laughed again and said he would have satisfaction out of me in the morning. At breakfast the Colonel was restored to equanimity. " I think it is a Parsi gentleman from Bengal who is a C.I.E.," he explained. " Ah," I asked, as the light dawned upon me, " don't you think Bengal and Malabar are wide apart?" " By Jove, they are"; " but you deserve to be a   ", added my warm-hearted friend. I said I preferred another cup of tea from him, and as I took it I explained how it was that I wished and prayed to be nobody in particular. But the superstition is widespread. Outsiders often mistake me for a somebody, at times for a big swell. All that is nonsense. But though I am nobody in particular, I will not affect to be so modest as to deny that I am as decent and intelligent a person as any of my years and position. That is my opinion about myself. And yet I, a public journalist, could but feel my worthlessness in the presence of Mr. Smith, only a gardener, whom I looked upon as almost every way my superior. What makes him so? Because I tell myself, Mr. Smith is a whole man, whereas I am less than 3/5ths of a man, with all my pretensions. And what made Mr. Smith, the gardener, a whole man? He is not an M.A. of Bombay University, nor a B.L. of Bengal, nor a D.O.L. of Lahore. Where on the earth, did he get all his knowledge and culture from? How did he learn to find true happiness in his knowledge and to diffuse that happiness? I say he got it mainly at home, from his mother. It was maternal influence particularly, and domestic associations generally, that made Mr. Smith the whole man he is, a force in politics as in social matters—— one likely to make an excellent householder, patriot or public man. Thus, at the very outset Mr. Smith had an immense advantage over me, which he takes care to maintain. He was born under natural conditions, and is free from most of the ailments to which I am a prey. He did not marry early, as most of us Indians do, ruining body and mind, and marring most prospects of public usefulness. The difference between the English patriot and the Indian is little more than the difference between the mother in England and the mother in India. What grievously unfavourable conditions we have been working under! Are we not, many of us, abortive births physically? Born in misery, we grow up in ignorance at home——what can *our* mothers teach us? Then we go to school and are taught grammar and geography. Some of us pass on to college and stuff our puzzled heads at the expense of the decrepit body. Soon after, in many cases even *before*, this, we have to find food for hungry stomachs at home, and at the same time we are expected to be thinkers, philosophers and patriots. All this, of course, we *cannot* do. What little we *can* do under the circumstances indicates the marvellous vitality of the race. · But in attempting to do that little, we generally break down in mid career. We are old before forty, our women old about thirty. General culture, the power of being happy and making others happy, is out of the question. It is hard to say, but say it I must, that I know few Native gentlemen who equal Mr. Smith in the qualities briefly referred to above, however high their other attainments. I am talking of Native *gentlemen*, the best educated, the most advanced of my acquaintance.

Mr. Smith sent me a lovely bouquet before I left, not so delicious, however, as the one with which I was favoured by my good friend Mr. Willis, the Solicitor, whom I was glad to meet before leaving Agra.

THE MEETING.

So they whipped up a public meeting. It was "the largest ever held at Agra," though that is scarcely saying much about its largeness. As usual, the Chairman exhibited me to the company of strangers, and then left me to my fate. Soon after I began making mouths at the gentlemen present. No, I did not feel nervous, because if I have to address an audience I merely speak out what I think, and speak just as I speak at home or at office. But I cannot make a speech on set purpose, not happening to be an orator. It is little likely for the average man to *become* an orator, less so for a student, least of all for a recluse. As I stood making mouths at the audience, I could not help being reminded of my extremely awkward position. After raving so often at the professional speech-maker, whom I have not scrupled to liken to the dancing girl, here I was overtaken by the *rôle* of a professional speech-maker myself! For a moment I felt staggered, but recovered breath at the thought that this was only an additional sacrifice. What, after all, if I have to imitate even the public dancer for such a cause? The meeting was voted a " great success."

The rest of my stay at Agra (this was my sixth visit) was spent in talks and walks, alternated and often combined. I did a fair amount of political work, too, as I always try to do, by way of bringing people together, now stimulating, then moderating their zeal. The people, as a rule, are frank and unsophisticated. Everything is comparatively cheap and dull in the North-West Provinces ; in other words, there is chronic poverty to be met with in many places. The people do not seem to have much faith in the judicial service ; against the revenue department they have an active prejudice. The tours of the Viceroy, the Lieutenant-Governor, and others, are dreaded by the ryots as calamities, as, in the name of the Sirkar, the underlings make something out of almost every official tour. That is the impression left upon my mind. But I believe this particular evil is less rampant now than it was ten years ago.

The Income Tax seemed to be bitterly resented wherever I asked about it, not so much perhaps on its own account as for the opening it will offer to dishonest subordinates. I urged here and there that cases of dishonesty or oppression should be exposed. But the explanation was that when a poor wight appealed against assessment, the revising officer would almost invariably send the appeal to the assessor himself, who would remark :—" this man is a budmash"—or something like it, whereupon the Collector would dismiss the appeal. People did not like to spend time and money to be in the Collector's bad book and at the mercy of the vindictive Tehsildar. There is much force in this. Like the people, the upper classes, land and property holders, too, appeared to be very raw. The Zemindars all over India feel that next turn will be theirs. Do what they might, they are not likely to escape the Income Tax. The mercy of the *mabap* Sirkar may be extended to them any day, probably sooner than they expect. I have often wondered if a capitation tax would not suit India better?

THE PURDAH AND HIS PREYS.

The Purdah system is almost universal in the provinces. I daresay it is a cruel bad system, injurious to both sexes. But you cannot tear off the Purdah at once. Besides, the light of the day has begun to penetrate the Purdah itself.

Infant marriages are said to be common; unequal marriages in point of age are by no means uncommon. A recent case was cited to me, in which the wife appeared before the court as guardian to her little lord and master. Even where husband and wife are of the same age, the wife is apt to out-grow the husband. The result is comical, occasionally with a strong dash of the tragic element in it. In such a case the wife ages much faster than the husband. This is bad for her and at times for her children. On the other hand boys suffer no less. They break down prematurely and give up study. Those who can afford to persevere at school or college at times conceive a dislike for their wives. The results may be ima-gined. Altogether, the effects of infant marriages in the North-West Provinces are sad to contemplate. They may be traced on many a face in the street, though a large number of faces are hidden from your view. These effects are more marked upon the prosperity of the nation than of the indi-vidual.

MINE HOST.

Left Agra for Aligarh on the 12th, after a pleasant stay of nearly half a week at Kalá Mahal. This palace is about eleven times as commodious as our little house at Bombay, for which we pay a monthly rent of Rs. 120. And what rent does Munsif Baij Nath pay for his *palace?* Rs. 10 a month ! The name is not Kálá Mahal, (Black Palace) as vulgarly understood, but Kalá Mahal (the palace of art). It may have been a museum under the Moghul empire, or was looked upon as an artistic structure and named Kalá Mahal. It is admirably well built, the zenana even being roomy and well-ventilated. But in the midst of rich masonry and carved stone work the wooden doors and windows are a positive eyesore. The surroundings, too, of the palace are anything but look-at-able. It was built by a poet about a hundred years ago, when the site was probably much more eligible than it now is.

Munsif Baij Nath is a Bania——not a "mild Bania," please—and one of the shrewdest Aryans going, though softened by liberal culture and contact with refined influences. He is a self-made man, and like myself, has gone through sore trials. He is not so much of a thinker as an organizer—with a cool head and a firm grip. His chief aim seems to be to make the rulers and the ruled understand each other and to promote their common interests. In this, as in other matters, he is a man entirely after my heart. In public affairs Mr. Baij Nath is already a force. In personal matters he is generally wide awake, believing honestly that his scope of public usefulness will widen with his own advancement in life. In matters professional he stands without a rival, enjoying the confidence of suitors, the bar as well as the Government. His superiors have a very high opinion of him, and in spite of his small eccentricities I believe his heart is in the right place. Mr. Baij Nath may live to be a Sayed Ahmed among Hindus. In time, I think, he will be within measurable distance of a seat on the High Court Bench. During my stay with him up and down Agra we prayed together, ate together and drank together, so far as such things could be done together between us. His vegetable dishes were simple and wholesome, if not nourishing, and as he often served the food himself it tasted sweeter than ever. There was perhaps too much of ghee and sugar in spite of my protests. But a Hindu seldom feels happy unless he smothers his guest in ghee and sugar. On the whole, however, the meals were light, frugal, and savoury, and only once did a dish smell of *hinga*. I corrected the mistake by explaining that I would prefer an ounce of prussic acid to a drop of asafœtida. When at

Bombay Mr. Baij Nath, like other Hindu visitors, is my guest. And yet the *Pioneer* laments our exclusiveness, and worse still, my friends Bindobin Bosh and S. L. Sandaskar say I am "only a Parsi!"

A COMBUSTIBLE PATRIOT.

I made a number of friends at Agra this time, some of whom are not likely to be soon forgotten. Pandit Jagan Nath, Pleader, is an amiable eccentric, never agreeing with anybody except when he is differing, and yet working heartily with everybody. He works and grumbles, and grumbles and works, by turn. He is what I may call a combustible patriot. He is his brother Pandit Ajodhia Prasad's own brother, and seems to be of opinion that public men are either self-seeking hypocrites or raving monomaniacs. As a friend I hope he does not think worse of me than as being a mixture of the two. For my part I like him the better for his sturdy, pugnacious, ever-contradicting attitude. I hope Jagan Nath Bahadur will live to be a rabid anti-infant-marriageist.

AN ARABESQUE PATRIOT.

Moulvi Farid-ud-din I had the happiness to see for the first time at our public meeting. He talked aloud to me in Arabesque Hindustani. My first impulse was to tell him that I could not follow such erudite Urdu. But I refrained. The Moulvi Saheb thereupon took me regularly in hand, and as he warmed up to his work, I sent him out my heart in sympathy, as poets have it. To his smile of satisfaction I gave a double smile spreading over the whole face. When he sighed over the fallen condition of the country, I emitted something like a sob to convince him of my deep interest. And when the Moulvi Saheb made the tear of pity glisten in his eye, I passed the back of my hand across my eye in the approved fashion. The result was that Moulvi Farid-ud-din mistook me for a profound scholar and an eminent patriot, without an equal in the land except one of us two. And accordingly, though he had come to oppose me, he spoke me up at the meeting in the loudest and most adjectival of Arabic Hindustani, eliciting thunders of applause. Next morning I got a common friend to explain to Moulvi Saheb that I knew not a word of Arabic. Two days hence we met on our way to Aligarh. Moulvi Farid-ud-din looked reserved and unhappy. Evidently there was something weighing upon his mind. I felt guilty. But, then, why will people insist upon over-rating a fellow ?

AND OTHERS.

Pandit Thakur Prasad is another man whom I have good reason to remember. He said I was possessed by the——, for, otherwise I could not have moved the people of Agra. He assured me that one so thoroughly maddened by an idea was bound to succeed, only he must impart his madness to half-a-dozen others.

In Mirza Mahomed Ali I found another excellent friend, cool and self-possessed, but with the courage of a lion. Another stout-hearted reformer is Pandit Girdhar Lal whose creed is that it is a greater sin to put up with an evil once known than to be in ignorance of it. Meer Kassim Hussain, Pandit Giri Raj Kishore, Mr. Pirbhu Dial and his worthy brother —— these and others deserve more than passing mention.

LIGHT READING.

Left for Aligarh on 12th February. At Tundla Station I came across a very exciting little book by a member of the Calcutta detective police. It made very pleasant reading for about an hour. Another interesting book I read at Agra was *Round the World in Eighty Days*. Fine little story, though the picture of English character is somewhat exaggerated, and that of Indian life and manners very inaccurate in parts. This book was carried away by a monkey, and was recovered after much trouble by Mr. Baij Nath's man. Ran through it on the day of the Agra lecture, and enjoyed it. A third railway companion I got was *The Two Madcaps*, a characteristic story of the modern London life. Too *fast*

41

to be held up as a model, but none less enjoyable. I am very fond of such literary chow-chow; in my reading days used to devour the smaller tales in *Family Herald*, especially during examination days. Never cared for the longer stories.

TEA AND TEA.

Had a cup of tea at Tundla, real tea. Found it extra agreeable, not having had it for some time, and in fact being forbidden its use. Have you read about the French lady who, being asked how she liked a certain bevevage, replied—— " it would be heavenly if there were a dash of sin in it"! Just so. No use pretending to be better than your neighbours —only don't do it secretly. That is a coward's part. How is it some of our Hindu friends are so voracious about meat and brandy? I have at times seen them tearing away at chops and steaks like tiger cubs, and imbibing liquor like young whales. Whence this avidity? Because they eat and drink in secret, poor fools. Let them do it like honest men, and in a week's time they will begin to feel disgusted both with flesh and brandy. These things are not meant for us Indians. I am a great believer in the power of publicity. Give me the most confirmed sinner—for instance, a Collector in the district or a Brahman defender of enforced widowhood—if I could only expose the creature to the light of public criticism, he would be sure to mend his ways. It is the secrecy in which he works that makes him so powerful for mischief. Of course, it is his cue to tell me that he cares not a straw for criticism; but I know better than that.

Is it not curious?——but I have seldom had a cup of genuine tea from a Hindu. In fact the orthodox Hindu does not seem to be up to it. Munsif Baij Nath's cook tried it the other day——half a pound of milk, quarter pound of sugar and a handful of the leaves. The mixture smelt horrible, let alone tasting. I said so to Mr. Baij Nath. Next morning he prepared the decoction himself. It was no better, I explained with a most ungrateful shake of the head, adding that the Hindu genius appeared to be too elephantine to distinguish between the lights and shades of colour or to appreciate the niceties of flavour. But stúng by this remark, the Munsif Sahib replied—"Aji Janab, return from your tour and I will give you real tea and force you to remove this reproach from our house." Well, after I left Agra, Mr. Baij Nath seems to have gone to the Bazar himself in search of good tea. He must have got samples from several shops and experimented upon them during my absence. On my return he insisted that I should taste his tea. He ordered the grate, the kettle, the water, sugar, milk and tea, into the drawing room. I fixed the proportions—but again the draw was as disappointing as before. It then occurred to me to examine the leaves. It was *cast off* tea, the leaves breaking into powder on being rubbed, without yielding the slightest moisture. I fear a large quantity of such tea, which the butlers and cooks supply to small shop-keepers, goes up-country every year, to be used by orthodox Hindus and Mahomedans. The making of Mr. Baij Nath's tea was good, but the tea itself had probably been used by some European family at Bombay.

About eight years ago I tasted Brahman tea. My friends at Junaghar gave me a tea party on the top of the Girnar Hill. About eight o'clock in the evening we squatted on the floor in the right Oriental fashion—and were soon confronted with three large silver plates containing mango slices, sweet-meat, dry fruit and pan supari——queer accompaniments for tea. Soon after came tea—a pot of liquid smelling furiously of pepper, cloves, cardamom, cinnamon and some bitter herbs. Altogether, it was a noxious draught. Mine host served it to me in a silver cup, and having served the others and him-self, placed the pot in front of my happy self. Then they began sipping the mixture, and I had to keep them company. I touched the cup with my lips and passed my left hand over the chest, as they did, showing how keenly we enjoyed the tea and what a world of good we expected from it. In the intervals we attacked the plates. I dare say there was much sense in this decoction of herbs and spices, to be taken with such a heavy meal. But it wasn't *tea* ; was it? I avoided swallowing my dose so long as I could. But when asked obligingly if I would have more, I unconsciously betrayed the secret. There was no escape now. I drank it off at a pull, and all the night felt my inside to be on the fire of——.

A DAY AT ALIGARH.

Reached Aligarh about 11 ; and was received at the Station by Raja Jai Kisen Das. A kindly affable gentleman of the old school, modest but exceedingly well-informed ; of active habits, in fact a man of action. He seems to have rendered signal service to the Government. Though still in official employment, the Raja Bahadur is now resting more or less on his laurels and educating a family of intelligent sons. He does not know English, but keenly appreciates the advantages of liberal education. He has much influence in Native circles, is esteemed by Hindus and Mahomedans alike, and has very friendly relations with Europeans. He deeply laments the present condition of Hindus and traces much of it to moral backsliding. Raja Jai Kisen Das is an Arya Samajist. He spends not a little of his time and money on the cause he has so much at heart.

There was a public meeting at Aligarh the same forenoon that I arrived. It was held to welcome a few Mahomedan students who had returned from England after a successful course. I was invited to the meeting, but though pressed hard, begged to be excused. At last my friends urged that absence from such a gathering would be misunderstood. So I had to go, and was glad I did go, for, besides listening to some very interesting speeches by the ex-pupils (Mahomedan) and Professors (English) of the Aligarh Institute, I had the pleasure of meeting its renowned founder, Sayed Ahmed Khan. The Sayed turned out exactly as I had pictured him to myself——a stout, burly figure, with large, rugged, bull-dog features, betokening courage, fortitude, determination, a will to do the needful at any risk and cost. The Sayed

Saheb gave me a hearty welcome, and after a little talk urged that I should address the meeting. I explained that I was not speech-maker, and that having come to speak to our Hindu brethren on a matter of painful interest to them, no way in harmony with the object of the present meeting, it would be spoiling my own cause, without advancing the cause of Mahomedan education in the least, to speak on such an occasion. I left Sayed Ahmed Khan and other friends to consider with what grace we could discuss Hindu social reform at a Mahomedan meeting. They appeared convinced, but were by no means satisfied. I witnessed the proceedings for about an hour, and was much impressed by the progress already effected by our Mahomedan friends. The enthusiasm that marked the speeches appeared to be quite genuine. One Mahomedan speaker, especially a student at the College, seemed to me to be a born orator. If he cultivates his gifts and has opportunities, that boy will live to be a power in Islam. About 3 P.M. I took leave of Sayed Ahmed Khan, promising to see him again next day. I kept my word and went to his house with Raja Jai Kisen Das. We explained again why we had avoided inviting Mahomedan friends to our Hindu meeting. He said he approved the omission, but rewarded what he mistook to be our exclusiveness with a very sly remark addressed to me——" all this that you have been doing is good and noble work—the people cannot rise before shaking off these customs. But it sometimes seems to me as if *your* asking our Hindu brethren to give up their customs were like *my* asking them to become Mahomedans or a *padre* asking them to become Christians ! " We laughed at this clever hit and I saw at a glance that Sayed Sahib was an expert in the game of diplomacy. In an instant I bethought me of how best to ward off any untoward effect of his insinuation on Raja Jai Kisen Das. So I turned to the latter and asked innocently——" Can our Mahomedan brethren be particularly anxious to see the Hindus give up the evil customs which stand so much in the way of fair competition between the two ?" We laughed again. This time I laughed well, killing two birds with one stone, settling the Sayed Sahib and reassuring the Raja. And with that I left the eminent Mahomedan reformer, hoping to understand him better on another occasion.

RACE AMENITIES.

The feeling between Hindus and Mahomedans is none of the best at Aligarh, though I had expected pleasanter relations owing to Sayed Ahmed's presence there. All over the North-West Provinces I have heard the complaint that Government is not strictly impartial in dealing with the two classes. But the reasons for this alleged partiality, as given by the aggrieved, are rather far-fetched. The facts seem to me to be these :—Mahomedans are not so numerously and hopelessly divided as are Hindus ; even the two large sects, Shiahs and Sunnis, are not at all so exclusive as any two near sects of Hindus. Consequently, Musulmans combine more easily ; they organize public movements with greater success ; they go about the country and out of it much more freely, being comparatively free from the curse of infant marriage. Thus, with great moral and physical advantages, it is no wonder the Mahomedans are pushing the Hindus aside in some walks of life. Our Hindu friends must remember that the genius of the British race is identified with progress and reform; pluck and enterprise are the salt of life to the muscular Briton; he loves pushing. This appears to me to be the secret of the supposed partiality, though from some quarters I have been assured that the Anglo-Indian official is partial to the Mahomedan because he is afraid of him. I think this is a mistake. But even if otherwise, it only adds to the force of the contention—that Hindus must learn to unite socially, to break through domestic and priestly thraldom and to assert their position as the mother community. To me personally Hindu and Mahomedan are the same. To one I owe the gratitude of a lifetime ; to the other I am bound by ties of affection and brotherly regard.

BANS BAREILLY.

Left Aligarh about 8 P.M., after a prolonged discussion of things generally with Raja Jai Kisen Das at the station, reaching Bareilly after midnight, and driving up to Rai Peary Lal's, chattering like a monkey in the chill raw northerly wind. Went to bed for a couple of hours, as a sort of make-believe to soothe mine host's anxiety. I picked up Mr. Peary Lal's acquaintance at Delhi last year, and though it was rather impudent to invite myself to his house so suddenly and on such a slender excuse, I am glad I went to him. Instinct is an unfailing guide. Mr. Peary Lal has worked himself into a philanthropist, perhaps unconsciously. He lives for others more than for himself. His benevolence is quiet and unobtrusive. He was very kind and attentive for the few hours I remained with him. Early in the morning he went about seeing friends for a preliminary meeting. On his return he bustled up to me and asked after my personal wants. With his permission I put myself under a barber and then indulged in the luxury of an orthodox Hindu bath, in a dhoti. Mr. Peary Lal and his servants were astonished at the masterly manner in which I used the dhoti. I could bathe in a dhoti just as a fish bathes in his skin. But the master of the house could not help exclaiming —— "I say! who could have thought you had gone so far?" The servants, too, who were making preparations for bath, breakfast, &c., in the European style, appeared considerably relieved. This was my reward. They gave me a cup of excellent tea, with biscuit, dry fruit, &c. Then, after prayers, came the preliminary meeting. We had some earnest workers there, men of faith as well as action, who said "yes" and meant it, who said "no" but would still listen to reason. I wish I could give here a sketch of some of these Bareilly notabilities. But the fact is I have got hopelessly mixed. And not until the faces are before me shall I be able to say which is which. In the evening we had as good a meeting as was ever held—all intelligent, representative Hindu gentlemen. In about two hours we went through the formal business. Then we had a special meeting of a special set of friends. We carried it rather late into the night. But I felt as if we could not prolong it too much, everything said by the friends was so interesting and to the point. What splendid material there is at Bans Barielly, as in other parts of the Provinces, to build up public opinion with! Rushed off to the Station about 2 A.M. to catch the train for Lucknow, finding there that it would not be in before 4. Made the best of the interval, holding a levee of coolies, gariwallas, porters and other dignitaries of the station and the street. Not much of infant marriage among them, honest fellows; but *wages were very poor*, they whined. I asked if they had any other grievance. The *police had no mercy*, some of them replied, the others assenting readily.

THE DANCING GIRL.

On my way to Lucknow I had some curious company, a number of smartly dressed young men, with a dancing girl. One of the former was evidently the great man of the company, and the dancing girl appeared to be his property. The rest were some of them *his* men, others *her* men. As they neared the carriage I gave them a look which scared them away, but finding no accommodation elsewhere they hastened back and one of the fops explained they had not far to go and would not disturb the *janab*, &c., &c. The guard also put in a word for his acquaintances, and so they came in quietly. The great man then observed that they were returning home from a spree and were so pleased to have my company! His dancing girl smiled cheerily and asked if she could " sit at *janab's* feet?" She seemed to be the only sober one of the party. I made no reply to her, but put the whole of my bedding kit between her and me and ensconced myself in my corner, making room for her at the other end of the bench. The poor thing appeared to be older than she could really have been. She was a handsome little body, with a heart somewhere, though perhaps not in the right place. Her eyes proclaimed the professional flirt, and I pitied that hulking fool of a fellow who thought himself her lover. I cannot say why—but I see very little difference between one dancing girl and another, they are all so alike, of one class, one trade, one everything. The last nautch performance I witnessed by a dancing girl was at Surat, three and twenty years ago, as a boy, when, after the usual antics she was thrown bodily into the arms of a specially invited guest. The fellow was as ugly as sin, and notorious for being as miserly as a German Jew; but the dancing girl made a beau of him, appealing to the love of her beloved Majnum, caressing him under the chin, &c., he protesting all the while —— "I say don't, don't, I say" —— with choice epithets that a Parsi *can* use when he is in trouble. The spectators heartily enjoyed this by-play, and when, at last, the dancing girl took her Majnum fairly in her arms and smothered him with mock kisses, the room was convulsed with laughter. She was under a pledge to have some *bukshis* out of the curmudgeon. He held out as long as he could under her ardent overtures; but when his fair tormentor threatened to go beyond the kissing stage, he surrendered with ill grace, forking out a rupee to appease her violent love-making.

A FASHION.

There was no such exciting scene in the railway carriage, but on alighting at Lucknow Station, where Munshi Naval Kishor and another friend were good enough to be present, what do I see? I see the dancing girl nowhere—literally vanished—and her swain standing before me with hand extended, and our friend introducing him to me as "————, son of ———— Bahadur, leading Rais, who will be very useful to you." I pretended not to see the young man's hand, but expressed a hope to see him some other time and have a talk. On our way to the Hotel, where Mr. Naval Kishor had kindly made arrangements at his expense, I spoke of the young Rais and the dancing girl. My companion laughed at it and explained it was a fashion. People did not think much of

42

going about with a dancing girl, especially when, owing to the practice of infant marriage, hundreds of unions turned out unsatisfactory. Good God! While there was some excuse or another urged invariably in favour of the husband, who ever thought of the wife, the wronged and neglected, pining away in her Zenana?

LUCKNOW.

Met some very strong men at Lucknow, and had a good deal of discussion with them. The remarkable thing about it all was that none of them argued in a circle. They were sturdy, honest, self-respecting men, with the courage of their convictions. If infant marriage is not soon knocked on the head it will not be for any fault of the principal Hindus of Lucknow.

This was the second time I missed *doing* Lucknow. There was little time on hand, so little indeed that I could not return the visit of some Parsi friends. Started from Lucknow about 11 P.M., Munshi Naval Kishor kindly seeing me off.

ALLAHABAD.

Reached Allahabad early in the morning and drove off to Munshi Kashi Prasad's. Mr. Kashi Prasad was not quite prepared, and felt rather puzzled as to how to dispose of the guest he knew nothing about. But I at once set him at his ease. A *kholi* was soon got ready, and water, fruit, and sweetmeat were offered to the itinerant Aryan brother.

First thing I did was to sit down on the floor and despatch a few letters and a "copy" to Bombay. Worked myself into a fit of rheumatism. Then rushed off to see a couple of friends. Met Kumar Shiva Nath Sinha for the first time. He was good enough to offer me the shelter of his roof. There was no occasion for it, however. Took a cup of tea with him. Went off in search of Sir Dinkar Rao. He was out of town. Then looked up Pandit Adityaram Bhattacharya, the Ranade of the North-West Provinces, as a friend aptly describes him. Had a long talk. Returned to Mr. Kashi Prasad's, had a pleasant breakfast about 12, at which his little daughter presided with a priest, then went off to the High Court to see the Pleaders. As I entered the common room I could not help feeling like a lamb going into a den of wolves. Fancy a layman, ignorant of the ways of the world, and "only a Parsi," attempting to convert a number of veteran Hindu Pleaders, the leaders of Allahabad society! But nothing like impudence, my gentlemen of the long robe. If you are pleaders, I am a special pleader. So in I· rush, take the bull by the horns and run him into a corner. There was something like a flutter in the beginning, a good deal of scepticism, and some legal fencing. But I overbore all resistance by a tremendous stretch of loquacity. Now or never —— that was the principle on which I attacked the invincibles. And one by one I got most of them round. A public meeting was arranged for on the spot, a meeting to consist of the most intelligent Hindu representatives. With three exceptions all the luminaries of the law agreed to attend and take part. Pandit Ajodhia Prasad begged off, saying he liked the institution of infant marriage. Judging from his fine Aryan face, I suspect the Pandit spoke only as a Pleader. He is his brother Pandit Jagan Nath of Agra's own brother. Sorry I had no time to cultivate his acquaintance. The other defaulter was Munshi Hanuman Prasad, a dear old gentleman, full of intelligence. He really could not attend, as he was making preparations for the marriage of his *young* son. The third gentleman's name I forget. He agreed with me as to the necessity of some action being taken to put down infant marriages, but could not make up his mind as to the exact nature of the remedies. Another friend was also of this opinion, but he was good enough to attend and join our Committee. Mr. Saunders was the only European present, coming, like myself, self-invited. I am glad he came—as a witness on the day of judgment. At the meeting Mr. Kashi Prasad made a fierce onslaught on the custom and cried shame upon those who followed it after being convinced of its mischievous effects. I have seldom heard a speech of so much power.

We returned home about 7 P.M. and had a conference at Munshi Kashi Prasad's on one or two other questions in which I am deeply interested. Conference broke up rather late. Mr. Kashi Prasad appeared to be touched by the self-denying zeal of his guest, and begged hard that I should allow him to keep me in money, as I was spending so freely. "You may return it if you like," he added gently. I had some cash still left, so thanked him for his generous offer and promised to avail myself of it should I ever need it. Had a hasty supper after 11 P.M. At 1 A.M. the servants came to awake me, saying it was train time. What a hardship! Reached the station before 2, to be told that the train would leave after 4 ! Most aggravating. We Natives have no idea of time and space. A few hours or a few miles this way or that matters nothing. The station was dead asleep—and I felt very annoyed at having been dragged out of bed so early. I turned fiercely upon the disturber with the question—— "why are we here so much before the hour?" "Because," explained the cold-blooded monster, "if I once go to bed, I won't get up till morning." That was a straight answer, at any rate ; so I could not withhold his bakhshis.

A SAD REMINISCENCE.

On alighting at Benares Station I found Babu Ram Kali Chaudhary's carriage waiting. I also met there an old friend, the Musulman "boy" in charge of the Waiting Room. It is perhaps as well that the station has to go without a pucka Khansamaji, it having no Refreshment Room. This is because Benares, though important enough, is but a branch Station, and because there are hotels within hail. Whatever the cause, I do not regret the absence of a full-blown Khansama, which means escape from stale meat, poisonous liquor and the picking of your pockets in a fashionable sort of way. I was glad to see my friend the chota Khansama whom I gave a little custom before stepping into the carriage outside. Some years ago I had to stay at the Waiting Room for two days and nights, in high fever and with only a few rupees left after an arduous campaign across Bengal and the North-West Provinces. I wanted to see the Maharaja, about the Max Müller translations. He was not in town. But I met Raja Shiva Prasad and caught fever. This enlightened educationist promised to speak to the Maharaja and let me know at Bombay. But Maharajas and Rajas are busy mortals, and not until I meet them again will they be reminded of the little mission. Returning from Raja Shiva Prasad's I took to the bed. It would not do to tell anybody of my condition. So confiding the secret to the boy, and wiring to Bombay for remittance, I laid myself down patiently to starve out the fever. The boy kept watch for two weary days and nights, scaring away all intruders from the Waiting Room. On the third morning the Station Master, who had come to know something about the state of affairs, requested me to shift, as the room was to be taken up by the family of an official. Unwilling to go to friends, and unable to find any other refuge, I had a charpai drawn up under a tree close to the railway store-house. And there, in the sultry hot winds of May, I passed another day and night. That was one of the bitterest of my travelling experiences. Next day came pecuniary re-inforcement from Bombay. I repaid the boy's kindness well enough to enable him to set up a small business if he were so inclined, pinching myself so far as to take the Intermediate class on my way to Rajputana. The value of the boy's services lay in the fact that they were given to a poor man, perhaps he might have thought to a dying man.

BENARES—MEN AND THINGS.

Drove up to Mr. Ram Kali's and was warmly welcomed. I met him first at the National Congress at Bombay (you see these Congresses are national in more than one sense). He is retired Sub-Judge and Small Cause Court Judge, highly respected by all sections of Benares society, old and young, European and Native. Taken all in all,

I found him the most sagacious guide in the provinces, with a love of useful knowledge and a wide range of practical experience. Like other thoughtful men Mr. Ram Kali seemed to be deeply impressed with the moral and material poverty of India, and thus he was prepared to meet me more than half way. The success of the Benares meeting is much more due to him than to me. The Pandits, Raises and other principal citizens were willing to be led by him. We had a few visitors in the afternoon, and in the evening we went out for a stroll, after arranging preliminaries. Early in the morning Mr. Ram Kali took me out for a walk in the course of which I had to pay my respects to several leading citizens. The meeting in the afternoon was very creditable, considering the short notice. I attended it with all my luggage in the ghari, so as to be able to rush off to the Station from the Town Hall. Finding half an hour on hand after the meeting I walked hurriedly through some of the streets of Benares, with three or four excellent guides. Benares may be a holy city, but it is by no means a healthy one. The streets we went through were dark, dank, extremely narrow, built as if it were with the special object of generating and propagating cholera. In about ten minutes I counted more stenches in native Benares than somebody did at Cologne. The streets appear to have been built without the slightest idea of sanitation, ventilation, &c., though the material used in house-building is said to be fire proof. On the way we visited a Maratha Sannyasi, reputed to be 150 years old. I entered his *kholi*, looked him over carefully, and thought he could not be even 100. But the friends who were with me, gentlemen not likely to be taken in, assured me that the Sannyasi was considered old as many as 80 years ago. Mr. Biswas, the Small Cause Court Judge, explained that the Sannyasi had managed to preserve himself mainly by *mauna*, that is by holding his tongue. He does not seem to have been heard to speak for years. One may be justified in saying, therefore, that this Benares ascetic is a living protest against the vanity and waste of energy of professional speech-makers. To this extent my opinion about speech-making as a trade has been wonderfully well confirmed.

During my stay at Benares I made some valuable friends, Bengali and Hindustani, who vied with one another in liberality of sentiment and a desire to be practical. I have been told by friends that much of what I heard in the provinces was mere talk. That remains to be seen. Meantime I cannot help observing that I am not a very bad judge of character nor a very sanguine dreamer after the heavy knocks received in the battle of life. Oh that I had leisure for three years and three lakhs of rupees to spend! With these two weapons I would undertake to make Widow Marriage itself popular.

BACK TO ALLAHABAD.

Leaving Benares about 5 P.M. I reached Allahabad Station after midnight and was received by a messenger from Messrs. J. Shapoorji and Co. That was the second time I enjoyed the hospitality of this well-known Parsi firm, and yet up to this day I am unacquainted with Mr. J. Shapoorji, the Proprietor, though both of us live at Bombay! But what of that? Did I not know his brother Mr. Dinsha once upon a time? And, after all, even if I know not him or his still as a matter of history, I can prove that Mr. J. Shapoorji is my cousin. Why, then, should I scruple to accept of his hospitality, especially as members of his firm are always so kind. This time I had to do more with European than with Hindu friends, and found Mr. Shapoorji's house very convenient. I spent a day and a half there and was much refreshed by savoury Parsi dishes and genial Parsi company. Had to do a good deal of writing work, a good deal of grinding; but found time enough to pay and receive visits. Wound up the visiting business by a call on Mrs. and Mr. Knox (High Court Judge or Legal Remembrancer). I believe I have visited all the sacred shrines of Hinduism except Hardwar, and if *swarga* is to be attained by this means, I may fairly

look forward to a more exalted heaven than most even of Brahman pilgrims. Still, having traced so much of silent good
to work Mrs. Knox, and being so near, I could not resist undertaking a pilgrimage to the Shrine of Unselfish Usefulness.
Had a long and most interesting conversation with our Lady
of Allahabad, as the Roman Catholic would call her, about
her work of love and charity, and left her well impressed, I
hope, with its approaching success. In appearance and
otherwise Mrs. Knox reminded me of my excellent school
mistress, Mrs. Dixon of Surat, now at Belfast. What glorious work these Englishwomen have in India !

Finding the cash box nearing depletion I sent for Rs, 10
from Munshi Kashi Prasad, and started for Agra about
9 P.M., arriving there in the morning, and putting myself
at once under the protection of my guide, philosopher and
friend, Lala Baij Nath Bahadur, Mukam Agra.

MUTHRA AND ITS CHOWBES.

Next day we left for Muthra, feeling very doubtful as to
our success at this " citadel of Hindu orthodoxy." We had
been dissuaded from making the attempt by several friends
who knew the people of Muthra. This dissuasion, however,
induced me more than ever to risk a trial, and in the evening
we found ourselves at Muthra. We put up with Mr. Alopi
Prasad, the Munsif, a smart young official, but new to the
place. Notices were circulated the same night. Early in the
morning we had a select conference, and in the evening as
enthusiastic a public meeting as one could have wished for
even in an advanced centre, presided over by an able and
persuasive chairman, who was followed by indigenous thinkers
knowing the subject intimately and addressing themselves to
it in a masterly manner.

At Muthra I saw for the first time a number of Chowbes,
the Chatur Vedi clan of old. They are Brahmans out and
out, with all the vices of that exclusive caste, but very few of
their virtues. Splendid in physique—tall, sleek, muscular,

do-nothing, care-nothing devils, the Chowbe priests are a study both for the physiologist and the social reformer. They pretend to be conversant with all the Vedas, and as a matter of fact know little beyond vulgar traditions. But for their general ignorance they make up by a transcendental knowledge of gymnastics and gastronomy. You may find one Chowbe eating and drinking what is enough to surfeit three wild bulls. As to domestic customs early marriage is common among them, as also is the exchange of girls. Marriage with some of them seems to have a very limited significance—thus, for instance, the wife goes to her husband's in the evening, and returns home to her parents' early in the morning, declining to attend to household duties as a wife. How she manages it when she is encumbered with children, I could not find out—probably the little ones are left to the care of the paternal grandmother or aunt.

Before the meeting I had a pleasant drive to Brindabin, and was shown many a sacred spot associated with the memory of the lover-saviour of the Hindus, whose mission has been so grossly caricatured by some of his own worshippers. The lives of the Vallabhkul Maharajas at Muthra seem to be about the same as at Bombay, and, curious to say, the most ardent amongst their votaries also belong to the same community—the Bhattias of Bombay. This is a ticklish topic to pursue.

www.ingramcontent.com/pod-product-compliance
Lightning Source LLC
Chambersburg PA
CBHW022008110726
47901CB00006B/1443